About the author

Katie had a ten-year NHS career before leaving to write full-time. She lives in the countryside with her family and her novels include the 2018 World Book Night pick *My Everything* and the eBook bestseller *A Life Without You*. She loves strong coffee, the promise of a blank page and stealing her husband's toast. *Unbreak Your Heart* is her fifth novel.

Say hello on Facebook @katiemarshauthor or chat to her on Twitter or Instagram @marshisms.

Also by Katie Marsh:

My Everything
A Life Without You
This Beautiful Life
The Rest of Me

Unbreak Your Heart

Katie Marsh

HODDER

A CIP catalogue record for this title is available from the British Library

Paperback ISBN 978 1 473 68574 1
eBook ISBN 978 1 473 68571 0

Typeset in Plantin Light by Palimpsest Book Production Limited,
Falkirk, Stirlingshire

Printed and bound in Great Britain by Clays Ltd, Elcograf S.p.A.

Hodder & Stoughton policy is to use papers that are natural,
renewable and recyclable products and made from wood grown in
sustainable forests. The logging and manufacturing processes are expected
to conform to the environmental regulations of the country of origin.

Hodder & Stoughton Ltd
Carmelite House
50 Victoria Embankment
London EC4Y 0DZ

www.hodder.co.uk

For Richard, with love

'Hope' is the thing with feathers –
That perches in the soul –
And sings the tune without the words –
and never stops – at all

Emily Dickinson

Spring

1

Beth

Beth's sole aim in coming to the Lakes was to disappear, but it seemed that her car had other ideas. Heads turned wherever she went, following the grind and bump of the engine as she rattled past. Black smoke puffed from the exhaust as if trying to skywrite her arrival and it was becoming clear that, during her ten years living in the States, she had totally forgotten how to drive a manual car.

She jerked down a winding lane into another village, muttering 'Fresh start' at scattered white houses through increasingly gritted teeth. Pale pink clematis climbed up walls, fells rose majestically around her, but she was too busy trying to control her vehicle to drink them in. A clutch of walkers in sturdy boots and bright kagoules looked up from their maps to stare, and a woman in thick-rimmed glasses stopped watering the hanging baskets outside the village shop to peer in her direction.

Beth flushed. In the four hours since handing over the last of her savings she had discovered that the only part of her used car that was ever silent was the horn. Trying to wind the window down unleashed a squeal not unlike her own when she had accidentally sat on an ant's nest last summer and she was becoming increasingly concerned that the driver's door was about to fall off. If evidence were needed that she hadn't thought any of this through, this car was it.

She put her foot on the brake and was pleasantly surprised when the wheels slowed in time to avoid flattening a sheep that was ambling across the low stone bridge in front of her. It moved on sturdy legs, waggling its black ears, a ragged purple patch sprayed onto its shaggy left shoulder. Its nose sniffed one way, then the other, before it decided to settle itself down in the middle of the road, about five metres from her rusty bumper.

Beth checked her watch, stress beginning to prickle. Her new start would become a dead end if she didn't get a move on. She had been travelling against time ever since leaving Brooklyn and her knuckles were so white they could give the smattering of late snowdrops swaying by her front wheel a run for their money. She pressed the horn again, but there was no sound. She tried to wind the window down, winced, and pushed the door instead. Unfurling herself from the seat, spine cracking after nearly four thousand miles of constant travel, she awkwardly climbed out.

Beth breathed in the sweet air as she looked around. Daffodils bobbed and waved in the chilly April breeze and she could hear birdsong and the bubble of the stream as it foamed over mossy stones beneath the grey arch of the bridge. To either side green hedges edged the lane, and purple crocuses were bursting through the grass as if arriving for a party that was just about to start. Gnarled trees arched above her, their twisted branches thinning out as they reached for the breathtaking blue of the sky. All around her the world was waking up from the grip of winter. Maybe she could come back to life too.

'Fresh start.' She swallowed. 'Fresh start.'

As long as she could get to her interview on time.

She walked towards the sheep.

'Excuse me? Could you move, do you think? I need a job, and you're kind of in the way.'

The sheep glanced idly at her, before settling its head back down on its forelegs and closing its eyes. Beth looked around for back-up but the lane was deserted. The sheep twitched. Beth's watch ticked on.

She decided to drive straight at it to scare it into moving, and got back into the car. She turned the key.

Nothing.

'Noooo.' Beth turned it again. A cough, and then silence. She stroked the steering wheel, trying to coax it, as if it were the hand of a patient coming round from an anaesthetic, eyelids flickering, the pain yet to hit. 'Come on, car. We're a team now. We can do this.'

One more try.

Not even a cough this time.

Frustration brought tears to her eyes. She hit the wheel, biting back a sob, and turned the key one final time as her mobile began to ring. It was probably Jas, wondering where the hell she was. As she reached for the phone the engine sputtered into life and Beth was so shocked she released the hand brake and rolled forwards before she could check what was coming.

Crunch.

'No!' She braked sharply, her fingers fumbling with the seatbelt, eyes scanning the road. Two bikes had appeared from nowhere and she could see a figure on the ground. A child. His arm was thrown back above his head and he was still. Too still. Then, as her mouth was opening to scream, his hand moved and he pushed himself up, blue cycling helmet askew.

'Thank God.' Her only thought was to get to him. She was opening the door when the airbag belatedly realised that there had been a collision and inflated with surprising speed. Now she was pinioned against her seat, a man's face blocking her window. It was seventy percent beard, but the remainder was pure rage. His brown eyes flashed and a deep line bit into his forehead. He yelled at her to wind the window down, not that she needed to. She could hear him quite well enough as it was.

'You didn't even look!' He climbed off his bike, and lowered it to the verge. 'Didn't anyone ever teach you to drive?' He turned around and dropped to his knees in front of the boy, eyes searching, hands checking for injury.

'I'm so sorry.' Beth started fighting the airbag, struggling to get out. She managed to extract her left arm, and then her leg, holding her breath in case it made it any easier to escape. With her mind playing relentless disaster scenarios – haematomas, brain injuries – she finally managed to slide across into the passenger seat and stumbled on unsteady legs around to the man and child.

'It's OK, Dad. She didn't hit me. Just the bike. The bumper's a bit scratched.' The boy was pale, with tousled red hair and skin splattered with freckles, as if a paintbrush had been flicked at his face. He was wearing a bright green sweatshirt dominated by The Grinch's grin and long denim shorts that flapped around his knees.

Beth looked at the bike. A scratch split the red paint in two.

'I'm so sorry.'

The boy glanced at her, then away, addressing the man still bent over him. 'I'm alright, Dad. Can I get back on my bike now? I'm not tired at all.' He stood up straight. His huge white trainers were almost cartoonish below his slender ankles. He only looked about five. God, the damage she could have caused.

His dad didn't move. 'I need to make sure you didn't get hurt before we go anywhere.' His fingers tracked a huge black bruise on the boy's calf and Beth caught her breath.

The boy followed her eyes. 'It's OK, I had that anyway. I get lots of bruises.'

His dad frowned as he finished checking every inch of every limb. From the severity of his expression Beth suspected she had a lawsuit coming her way.

'Dad.' The boy put his hand on the man's shoulder. 'I'm fine. Let's go.'

The man lifted the boy's leg, still searching, clearly certain that damage had been done.

'Did you hear me? Dad? I'm OK.'

'Are you sure?' His dad looked up, shielding his eyes from the sun.

'Yes. Come on.' The boy's voice had a note of impatience now.

'You should have looked.' The man turned towards Beth.

'I'm so s-sorry.' She couldn't stop shaking. No matter where she went she was a liability.

The man looked like he had plenty more to say, but the boy tugged him away.

'Come on, Dad!'

The man pointed his finger. 'Make sure you drive more carefully next time.' He picked up the boy's bike and wheeled it across to him.

'I can give you money?' The second it came out she knew it was the wrong thing to say.

His eyes narrowed. 'No thanks.'

'To repaint the bike, I meant?' Beth ran a mental list of things she could go without in order to pay for her latest mistake.

'We don't need your money.' This man did a great line in looming. He was part human, part grizzly.

She held her hands out wide, palms upwards. 'I just wanted to try to make up for what I did. I wasn't . . .' His expression was incredibly forbidding. 'I'm sorry.'

'Aye, well, that doesn't really help, does it?'

'I can take you anywhere you need to go?'

He took a good look at the car, which was wheezing beside her. He shook his head.

'No.'

'Are you sure? I feel so bad, and I—'

'One hundred percent sure, thanks.'

She took a breath, trying to get her trembling under control. Fresh starts weren't all they were cracked up to be. 'Well, let me know your address. I'll bring you some paint, at least?'

'I told you, we're alright.' The man checked the boy was safely on his saddle, then mounted his own bike.

'Come on, lad.' He tucked a lock of long brown hair behind his ear.

She stepped towards him but they were already moving off. 'Are you sure I can't . . .?'

'Yes. I'm sure.' He waved a hand dismissively as they rode slowly along the lane that had borne her here, back towards the cluster of slate-roofed houses nestling at the foot of the hills.

She called after them. 'Please?'

The boy looked round. 'We're the first cottage on the left as you come down the lane into Thistlethwaite. Number 1, The Rise. You can't miss it.' He wobbled dangerously.

She heard his dad's reply as they rounded the bend. 'You shouldn't have told her.'

'Why? She did say she'd like to . . .' Their voices faded into the distance.

Beth turned, leaning on the car, pressing her hands against her forehead, as if she could somehow expel the memories that had followed her across the Atlantic. She took a deep breath, forcing herself to focus. The car creaked gently as if in sympathy. She opened the door and hit button after button until she managed to get the airbag to deflate, catching a glimpse of herself in the rear-view mirror. It was still a shock. She had cut her long brown hair short a few weeks ago before the final hearing, craving agency, needing control over something. Now she stroked her cropped fringe self-consciously, wishing that she hadn't made her face feel so exposed. She had nothing to hide behind now.

It was time to go. She turned the key, checked her mirror and blind spot at least ten times and drove off, stopping for every twig, every squirrel, every bird hovering on the breeze. Half an hour later, after several detours down tiny lanes leading to farm gates or ramshackle huts, she arrived at a health centre with a predictably rammed car park. She squeezed into a corner space and walked to the parking meter, noticing as she queued that the contrast with her last workplace could not have been greater. The Mercy View Hospital in New York had been all gleaming windows, steel and light – this place was grey concrete, brown brick and NHS blue.

The entrance door slid open to reveal her old friend Jas, in blue scrubs, her hands thrust deep in her pockets. Beth waved and Jas strode towards her, dark curly hair still fighting to escape from her ponytail as it always had. Seeing her took Beth back twenty years and she was eighteen again, reaching for a croissant in the uni cafe. 'I'll fight you for it,' Jas had said. In the end they had both eaten half, and by the final bite they were already looking for flats to rent together.

Jas threw her arms around Beth.

'All these years of friendship, and interview day is when you choose to start being late?'

'I'm sorry. I got lost. A lot. And I hit a child too.' Beth's voice cracked.

'You what?'

'I hit a child. With my car.' She felt sick thinking about it. 'I mean, I hit his bike.'

Jas's eyebrows disappeared into her hair. 'Is he OK?'

'Yeah. Thank God. But I might not be if I ever see his dad again. Man, he was angry.' Beth got to the front of the queue for the meter and started feeding change into the slot with shaking fingers.

Jas watched, arms folded. 'Well, of course he is. Someone accidentally bumped Saffy with a Tesco trolley the other week and I wanted to kill them.'

Beth pushed her final coin in. 'Oh God. I feel so bad about it.' The machine whirred and clanked before begrudgingly issuing Beth with a ticket. She turned and Jas walked with her back towards the car. 'Was Saffy OK?'

'Yeah. She was teaching the checkout guy how to do the Floss five minutes later. Nothing keeps my daughter down.' Jas put her arm around Beth's waist. 'It's so good to see you.'

'You too.' Beth stopped in front of her car. Jas gave a low whistle. 'This is yours? No wonder you were late. It's a miracle you made it at all.'

'Hey.' Beth patted the bonnet, only to receive a loud groan in return. 'She may not look like much, but . . .'

'What a colour.' Jas grimaced. 'Reminds me of A&E shifts at drunk o'clock.'

'Have you quite finished?' Beth put the ticket on the dashboard and shut the door. She locked it, even though she was certain no thief would be stupid enough to take it. 'She's vintage.'

'Scrapheap material, more like.' Jas stared at Beth. 'Wow, you look so US of A. Love the hair. It really suits you. And your teeth are so white they're blinding!'

'Sorry.' Beth covered her teeth with her hand. 'Is that better?'

'No.' Jas walked as fast as ever and Beth trotted to keep up. 'Now you just look knackered, even with all that make-up on.'

Beth swallowed. 'Oh God. Is it too much? I did it on the plane. I haven't slept in weeks so I was trowelling it on. Should I take it off?'

Jas arched an eyebrow. 'I was joking – you look great. Where's your sense of humour gone?'

'Missing in Action.'

'Not surprising. And believe me, once we're done here we'll head straight to the pub and you can tell me all about it.'

'I'd rather just get drunk.' Maybe with enough wine inside her, she might sleep.

'We can do that too.' Jas came to a halt in front of the entrance, leaning over and adjusting the collar of Beth's green blouse. 'I'm so sorry about everything that's happened.'

'Me too.' Beth stared at a patch of chewing gum stuck to the pavement, tears prickling her eyes. 'I'm so stupid, Jas.'

Her friend's voice went up a note. 'You are not stupid. You're going to ace this interview, you'll see. I'm not on the panel, for obvious reasons, but you'll be great.' She leant closer. 'Don't let Tyler ruin things for you, OK?'

'I'm perfectly capable of ruining things all by myself.' Beth barely felt capable of doing her teeth, let alone convincing strangers to employ her. 'But thanks for telling me about the job – whatever happens.'

'Don't thank me. Really. We're crying out for people like you to be school nurses.'

'Are you sure?'

'Yes.' Jas exuded a certainty Beth couldn't even begin to feel. 'Of course you're madly overqualified. And it's not like we can offer you any perks, either, unless Digestives and cups of tea count. Though . . .' She grinned. 'The boss is pretty great, so I hear.'

'Is that so?' Beth was relieved to find she was still capable of smiling. 'I won't have to call you boss though, will I? If I get it?'

'Not every day. Just on Fridays, when you buy me lunch at the pub and give me a head massage.'

'Hey.' Beth punched her lightly on the arm.

'Stop that!' Jas shook her head as they walked through the sliding door into the small grey foyer of the health centre. 'You're meant to be looking professional!'

Beth shook her head, clouds looming again. 'I don't feel it. Not after . . .'

Jas held up a hand. 'Beth, stop. You're a bloody great nurse. OK?'

'How can you say that?' Beth's voice was tiny.

'Because I know you.' Her friend pulled away, hands on Beth's shoulders. 'Top of the class at uni, and Ward Sister at a leading hospital in NYC? Trust me. You've got game.'

'But . . .' The lump was rising in her throat again.

'Now is not the time for this.' The kindness in Jas's eyes only made Beth feel worse.

'I . . .'

'No, Beth.' Jas shook her head decisively. 'Not now.'

She had a point. Beth dug her nails into her palms to stop the tears.

'Come on, then.' Jas held out a tissue. 'Wipe that snot off your face and let's get this show on the road.'

Beth turned to follow her.

One step at a time.

Stop crying. Get a job.

Don't look back.

EMILY!!!!

I hope you enjoyed your party last week. I did. I ate so many iced buns that my tummy stuck out like Dad's does. He didn't look very happy when I told him we matched. Grown-ups are weird, aren't they?

It's time to start our plan. The one we talked about at Christmas? You were right – Dad needs a girlfriend. I don't want him to be alone. I've been watching Jean's soppy films after school and falling in love doesn't look too hard. I know Dad's a bit hairy, but he's really good at hugs. He can burp the whole alphabet too. I'll get him a girlfriend, easy.

See you soon.

Love,

Jake xxx

2

Simon

Tamsin wasn't coming. However much Simon stared across the road towards the revolving hospital door, hoping for a glimpse of her long red hair, it was time to accept that he was on his own again for this one. Every six months, as Jake's clinic approached, he sent the date and the time to the only number he still had for her. Not once had he received a reply.

Yet still he hoped.

Stupid.

He put the rest of his Mars Bar into his mouth, swigged it down with Fanta and stood up. 'Come on, lad.' He held out his hand. 'Time to go.'

'Not yet.' Jake was hunched over his game, brow furrowed. 'I've nearly got him now. I just need one more minute.' His thumbs moved so fast Simon could barely see them.

Simon sighed. That bloody console was starting to feel like a more important member of the household than he was. Soon it would be pushing ahead of him into the bathroom and complaining when there weren't enough chips for tea. Half of him wished he hadn't done overtime to buy it for Jake's Christmas present, but the other half liked seeing his son doing something everybody else could do: not huffing and puffing his way round the playground far behind his peers; not needing a rest on the fifteen-minute walk to school. In the land of Nintendo, Jake could hold his own.

And at least it was distracting Jake from what awaited him inside the vast grey building in front of them. Sometimes Simon dreamt of its concrete walls and narrow windows, and woke up covered in sweat. And he wasn't even the one at the centre of things – the one having electrodes attached and needles inserted and phial after phial of blood sent to the hospital labs for testing.

'It's time to go in, Jake.'

'In a minute, Dad, I told you.' Jake's voice rose to a whine. 'They're always running late anyway.'

'I know, but—'

'So I can finish this game, can't I?'

Simon sighed. Jake didn't want to go inside. Fair enough.

He didn't want to either.

He sat on his haunches, face level with his son, feeling his belt buckle biting into his belly. He must start running again. Or swimming. Or doing anything to counteract the hours he spent hunched miserably over his desk at work, keeping himself awake with fizzy drinks and chocolate.

'Jake. Come on. You know the drill. Let's get this over with.'

It wasn't the most inspirational speech the world had ever heard. Unsurprisingly, it didn't win Jake over.

'I don't want to.'

'I know. But this is your team, remember? They've known you since you were born.'

No answer.

'They're always so excited about seeing you. Miss Maya? Phil the physio? Nurse Shanice?' He thought of her gentle brown eyes as she had brought him and Tamsin toast in the middle of the night after Jake's first operation. His boy had just had open heart surgery. He was six days old.

'Come on, kiddo.' He checked his watch for the twentieth time. 'Let's not keep them waiting.' He got his son's favourite cuddly toy out of his bag. 'Superchick's ready.'

Jake's face became stone. 'Stop it, Dad. I'm too old for that.'

He hadn't been too old when he was cuddling him last night.

Simon tucked the duck away again. 'But . . .'

'Just chill, Dad. I'll be ready in a minute.' Jake's leg kicked against the bench as he kept killing baddies. Simon could see the dark purple bruise on his arm from when that terrible driver had hit him a fortnight ago. He knew he had been rough with her – he had seen the tears glistening in her eyes – but he had no time for people who took risks like that with other people's lives. Jake had enough to deal with already. Now Simon examined the bruise every day, to see if it might be growing into a blood clot beneath the skin – one of the many daily checks that were as much a part of his life as brushing his teeth or wishing Sunderland would win a game of football for once.

'I'm chilled.' Simon paced the length of the concrete garden, just to prove his point. 'Look at how chilled I am.' He did a dance, waving his arms in the air and wiggling his bum. Once it would have made Jake laugh, but now it only produced a roll of the eyes. A man with thick black hair cast Simon a pitying look as he strutted past in a cloud of aftershave.

Simon dropped his eyes and picked up their lunchtime debris, including the banana skin on which he had written *You Rock* in Sharpie next to a wonky electric guitar in an unsuccessful bid to cheer Jake up. He put everything into the overflowing bin by the edge of the green metal bench. Once, when he was four, Jake had clung to its leg with such determination that Simon had been totally unable to move him. He could still hear his son's screams as one of the nurses had helped Simon to detach his fingers one by one and carry him inside.

He looked at his boy, head down, still. This was preferable, he supposed. At least people weren't looking; at least judgements weren't being made.

He was considering tactics when a familiar voice rang out behind them.

'What are two nice lads like you doing in a place like this?'

'Barney!' Jake was off the bench in a nanosecond, game forgotten, smile a mile wide.

'Mate.' Simon was embarrassed to hear his voice cracking. He was turning into a right wuss. 'What are you doing here?'

'I dunno.' His best friend shrugged, running a hand through his short blond crop. 'Didn't have anything else to do, so . . .'

'You thought you'd come and annoy us?' Simon felt a rush of gratitude.

'Something like that.' Barney leant down to greet Jake.

Simon was more touched than he wanted to admit. He and Barney didn't talk about feelings – they talked football results and pints – but they were always there for each other when they were needed. Barney knew that Simon dreaded taking Jake to these clinics alone – particularly this time, when Simon thought he knew what the doctors were going to say. The hardest thing was trying to keep his game face on – making Jake think everything was fine when inside the fear was galloping. When he was smaller Jake had been easily distracted with a sweet or a magazine, but now he was increasingly able to see the cracks beneath Simon's smile.

'Jakey boy.' Barney ruffled his hair, the only person on earth who was allowed this privilege. 'How are you, mate?' His voice was light, but his hand on Simon's shoulder was warm and strong. 'God, I can't believe you let your dad out wearing *that*.'

Simon looked down at his black sweatshirt. A dolphin curled across his chest above battered white letters spelling the name of the Koh Tao dive school where he and Tamsin had met. 'What's wrong with it?'

'Where do I start?'

'I like it.' Simon flushed. 'It's an old favourite.' Tamsin had got it for him. He could still see the gleam of her smile as she had slipped it over his head on the way to a Full Moon party, before kissing him, her mouth sweet with papaya and strawberry. He wore the sweatshirt to every clinic. He told himself it brought them luck – he had put it on the night Jake was born, when he was facing only a twenty percent chance of survival. Nearly eight years later, his son was still here.

Simon would keep wearing the sweatshirt, whatever anyone said.

'Alright, don't get your knickers in a knot.' Barney rolled his eyes at Jake, who responded in kind. 'Now, Jake, I thought you might want a personal piggy back service to this clinic of yours?'

'Yes please!'

Simon smiled to himself. Only yesterday Jake had claimed to be too big for piggy backs. Now, he climbed up on the bench and wrapped his arms around Barney's neck, giggling as his godfather stood up and started progressing towards the doors at a light jog.

'Are you coming or what?' Barney turned at the level crossing, not even breaking a sweat.

'Yeah.' Simon heaved his rucksack onto his shoulder and followed them. He had been dreading this appointment for weeks, ever since the letter had arrived announcing the date and time. In the months between clinics Simon could just about convince himself things were OK. He could pretend that there was nothing much wrong with his boy – that the ups and downs of their life together were almost normal.

But when he was here it all came back. His head was starting to buzz as it ran its familiar showreel: frowning doctors, alarms, a Perspex box containing the tiny figure of his baby son. Wires, so many wires.

He stopped, closing his eyes, forcing the images back.

It was time to get his game face on.

Barney leant towards him, holding Jake's legs with his hands. 'Are you sure you're OK? You look like you're about to murder someone.'

'I'm fine.' Simon's jaw was tight. Once, back when he had been a physiotherapist, he had loved hospitals. Every day he had walked in, uniform on, feet springy in his trainers, feeling that he could help people, that he could play a small part in healing the sick. But since Jake had arrived, everything had changed. Now hospitals were an obligation, places where nights were spent sitting at bedsides, holding lifeless fingers. Places of pain and fear and hoping against hope.

His stomach churned as they passed the cafe where he and Tamsin had stared silently into coffee cups after Jake was diagnosed during their twenty-week anomaly scan. He looked resolutely ahead as they passed the toilets in which Jake had collapsed four years ago, and then the door to A&E, which was as familiar to him as his own back step. This hospital, with its crowds and its corridors, was a map of his son's pain – every department a reminder that his heart could never be made whole. Simon clenched his jaw. He had to power through – if he let one thread of emotion loose he would unravel. His son needed him to be strong, so strong he would be.

If only he had Tamsin's hand to hold.

They joined the throng waiting for the lift.

'Hello.' Jake beamed down at a young girl in skinny jeans and a red top. Her hoop earrings glinted as she looked up. 'I'm Jake.'

He held out a hand and, clearly surprised, she took it.

Simon wondered what his son was up to. The doors opened and they pushed their way inside, the girl beside them. Jake continued his conversation as they juddered upwards.

'Are you single?'

The girl twirled her ponytail between her fingers and didn't answer. She was leaning into someone who must be her boyfriend. Simon cringed as Jake leant closer. 'My dad's single. And he's really nice. Maybe you could have a coffee or something?'

Simon did his best to blend into the wall, praying that Jake wouldn't point him out.

Jake pointed him out. Simon tried to smile, but the girl cast him the kind of look she might bestow on a pile of vomit and he felt his ego dwindle yet further. Barney's grin could have lit up the Blackpool Tower. He whispered behind his hand. 'Wow, mate. Didn't know your own son was pimping for you nowadays.'

'That's enough, Jake.' Simon spoke out of the corner of his mouth. The lift halted for a second and he suddenly had visions of them all being trapped inside.

'What, Dad? You are single.' Jake shrugged. 'I'm just trying to help.'

Barney snickered and the lift juddered on. Simon held his breath as they reached the fifth floor. Mouthing apologies he ran past the girl, head down, face burning.

'Jake! What were you thinking?'

His son gazed at him from above Barney's laughing face, head on one side. 'She had a nice smile. Nothing wrong in asking, is there?'

'I like being single.' Simon's voice was sharper than he had intended. 'And she was at least fifteen years younger than me!'

'So?' Jake was undeterred. 'Age isn't everything. I read it in one of Jean's magazines.'

Simon swallowed a snort. Later. He would sort this out later. He exhaled as they passed pale yellow walls, decorated at intervals with giraffes and smiling lions. When he saw the familiar brown doors he felt nausea start to rise. Their feet halted on a huge sun mosaicked on the floor next to the wall covered in hundreds of childish handprints arranged in a giant heart around the words: *Maybell Suite: paediatric cardiac services*.

Here they were again.

Barney lowered Jake to the floor and Simon felt his son's hand slide into his. He held his head high. He could do this. For Jake.

He pressed the small blue intercom, said Jake's name, and squeezed antibacterial gel from the wall dispenser onto his hands. When the door buzzed, he put his shoulder to it and led them in.

'Jake! Hello. Good to see you, pet. Hello, Simon.' The receptionist, Chloe, had first met them when Jake was only a baby. She had brown hair piled up in a bun so big that Simon sometimes wondered if that was where she hid the stickers that she handed out to the children as they were leaving, a reward for what they had undergone. 'High five, Jake.' Her rings gleamed as she reached around the reception desk.

'Down low. Too slow!' Jake whipped his hand away.

She shook her head, her glasses slipping down her nose. 'You get me every time, pet. You're too quick for me!'

Jake made straight for the Hot Wheels cars that were in a box in the carpeted play area by the window. A curly-headed toddler was busy cooking a bit of plastic lettuce in a toy oven, while a girl with blonde hair was trying to squeeze long legs into a green toy bus designed for someone half her size.

Simon found seats for him and Barney in the corner, and tried to avoid staring at the door in case Tamsin suddenly walked in. Along the far wall a mum hugged her little girl, who was reading a brightly coloured book and chewing a thumbnail. By another, a pale boy with bright red glasses held tight to his parents' hands. Simon couldn't help assessing all the children he could see. Some were pink-cheeked, loud, energetic. Did they only have half a working heart, like Jake? Or were they siblings with hearts that were whole and healthy, dragged along for a day out in the big hospital? As always he looked for older children – living proof that Jake had more time ahead of him.

'Great toys here.' Barney stretched out on his blue plastic chair, leaning his head on the wall behind him. He had a gift for looking comfortable wherever he went.

'Yeah.' Simon crossed his legs, feeling stiff and awkward. He uncrossed them and leant forwards, hands clasped together. 'The kids spend a lot of time here, so parents donate stuff, and there's fundraising too.'

'Jake Withers.' A blonde nurse in a crisp navy uniform beckoned to his son. Jake looked up from arranging the cars in neat rows inside the garage. Simon braced himself for resistance but Jake smiled, stood up and walked over to her.

'It's OK, Dad. You stay there.'

Barney nudged Simon. 'He goes on his own?'

'Just for this bit, yeah. They're just doing his height and weight.'

'What else do they do here, then?'

Simon stared at his fingers, checking things off. 'Quite a bit. An ECG to see if his heart is working normally, an echo test to see how the valves and chambers are functioning, blood tests to detect if there's any infection. They'll check his oxygen saturation too. He's been a bit grey and tired recently, so hopefully we'll find out why.'

'And you said he might have another operation?'

'He definitely will, yes. The Fontan Completion. It's the third open heart surgery for any kid born with Hypoplastic Left Heart Syndrome, like Jake. If you have HLHS the left side of your heart is underdeveloped and can't pump blood. Jake had the first two operations when he was a baby – back before Tamsin left.'

'Yeah. I remember.'

Simon swallowed. He still couldn't speak about what had happened back then.

He forced himself onwards. 'Anyway, most kids have the third operation by age five or so, but Jake hasn't needed it yet. But . . .'

'But you think it might be time?'

'Yeah. He's grown a bit, and he's been struggling more to keep up with his mates, hasn't he? You've seen it. That PE class still gives me nightmares.'

'That was a rough one, yeah.' Barney taught in Jake's primary school so he had seen it all. It was the only thing that made Simon able to leave the village and get to work every day – knowing that Barney was right there with his son when a crisis arose.

That PE class had ended in an ambulance and five nights in hospital. One game of dodgeball in which Jake had tried too hard. That was all it had taken.

Barney rubbed his stubble with his fingertips. 'It's a lot, isn't it? More than I've ever had to deal with.'

'More than most of us have.' Simon folded his arms. 'Thanks for coming. Even though you hate needles.'

Barney shook his head. 'It's the holidays. I've nowhere to be. And I don't hate needles!'

'Really? Remember your flu jab last year? You ended up with your head between your legs for half an hour.'

'Shut up.' Barney looked nervously around the room. 'You said you'd take that to your grave.'

'I will.' Simon wished the heaving in his stomach would stop. 'I'm just saying though – there's no need to stay if you've got better things to do.'

'I'm not going anywhere.' Barney got out a packet of Smarties, threw one up in the air and caught it in his mouth. He offered the tube to Simon.

'Want some?'

'No thanks.'

Barney poured some into his own hand instead. 'Doesn't seem fair, does it? All this.'

Simon didn't say anything. He didn't need to.

He forced a smile as Jake came back. His boy sat down

27

beside him this time. As the afternoon wore on he would get closer still, leaning into him or climbing onto his knee, and tonight Simon would go to bed when he did and hold him until he slept.

Jake was grinning up at the nurse who had weighed him. 'Dad, this is Sarah. She's single, you know. Pretty, isn't she?'

God, not again. 'Um . . .?'

'Maybe you could get her number? Take her out?'

Sarah looked around, as if desperately trying to locate a trapdoor.

Simon squirmed. His voice was a squeak. 'I think Sarah's got more patients to see, Jake.'

'Yeah.' Sarah fiddled with her hair. 'But thanks for the offer. Your dad's great – I'm sure he'll find – erm, someone.' Her words held an absolute lack of conviction. Barney mouthed 'MATE' as Simon put his head in his hands. He could practically hear her squealing with laughter as she told her colleagues about that desperate dad who got his son to ask people out for him. Whatever had got into Jake, it needed to get the hell out right now.

'What are you doing, Jake? That poor woman.' Simon glanced around to see several amused smiles being aimed in his direction.

Jake didn't answer. He pulled his Nintendo out and restarted play. 'Don't worry, Dad. There are plenty more fish in the sea. I'll keep trying. And guess what?' Despite his embarrassment, Jake's smile gladdened Simon's heart. 'I've put on half a kilogram since last time.' He flexed a non-existent bicep.

'Hey. Strong Man.' Barney raised his hand, waggling his fingers. 'How about an arm wrestle? I want to see if I can get revenge for last time.'

'No chance!' Jake grinned.

They were just getting down to it when Jake was called through for his ECG. Then the other tests began, one after another, and with each one Simon was more proud of his son for patiently submitting; for getting in the right position, for not complaining when they stuck things on his chest as he ran on a treadmill, or asked him to breathe out for the twentieth time.

And then finally, there Simon was, alone in the room he dreaded most, as Barney led Jake back out to the play area. It was best his boy didn't hear this. Miss Maya, Jake's surgeon, sat in front of him. She looked at her screen, presumably scrolling through Jake's results, frowning and tapping her finger against her chin. Simon watched her hands, long fingers ending in pale pink nails. His son's life lay in the palms of these hands. His son's future was hers to give.

She looked up, her brown eyes bright as they met his. Simon fleetingly wondered who she was when she wasn't here. Whether she liked gardening or swimming or going nuts on a dancefloor on a Saturday night.

Miss Maya spoke just as fast as he remembered. 'OK, Simon. As you know with HLHS, Jake's heart is running on one pump rather than two, so no matter what he's doing, his heart is racing at a permanent sprint. It's full tilt, all day, every day. It's why he gets so tired and breathless, yes?'

Simon nodded.

'Tests today show that his oxygen levels are looking lower than we'd like – and with the recent increase in his size as he approaches his eighth birthday it's time to do his next operation. As we've talked about before, it's the third stage of our palliative treatment for him. There's no cure for HLHS, as you know, but the Fontan Completion should increase his oxygen levels, his energy levels, and give him the greatest chance at a less limited life.'

'I see.' *No cure.* Those words got him every time.

She held up the model of the heart that he had got to know rather too well over the years. He looked at the chambers, wishing his son had got all four – that he hadn't been the one baby in five thousand born with HLHS. Miss Maya continued. 'As you know, we'll be changing the plumbing of Jake's heart.' She indicated a large vein at the bottom of the model, coloured a reddish brown. 'The inferior vena cava will be disconnected from the heart and connected to the pulmonary artery instead. This will redirect blood flow so that oxygenated blood can be pumped around his body.' She made it sound as simple as writing a shopping list or starting a car.

'We're keen to proceed soon. Waiting times are significant at the moment, but we hope to get the procedure done this year if at all possible. December looks the most likely, but we'll send a letter through as soon as we can.'

She steepled her fingers, leaning forward in her chair. 'If you don't have any questions we need you to sign the consent form now, so we're ready to go when the time comes.'

Oh God. This was the worst moment. Consenting to a procedure that could prolong Jake's life, but one that would put him in danger too. Across the table it came, the thick blue form that he knew so well, full of terrifying what-ifs.

Miss Maya didn't beat around the bush. 'Now, it's important that you know that, as with his previous operations, this is complex surgery and this always comes with risks.' She crossed her legs, leaning forward, her gold necklace catching the light.

'Yes.' The shakes were here, right on time.

'Jake might have a cardiac arrest on the operating table, or a stroke. Either could lead to brain damage or death. His blood might clot or he might have lung or kidney failure, or get a wound infection after surgery.'

Simon could only think about the small boy busy playing with cars outside. His shoulders were too small to bear this. Simon's would have to be broad enough for both of them.

'Any questions, Simon?'

'No.'

He forced himself to click the biro in his hand, fingers trembling.

Miss Maya gave a rare smile. 'Having said all that, this operation is what Jake needs. And without the Fontan his heart function will gradually deteriorate, as our tests showed today.'

'I know.' He felt the weight descend upon him, the

pressure of the build-up to another operation. More months spent waiting for Jake's pain. Days anticipating the walk to the anaesthetic room, the blood and stress of the recovery room. And underlying it all the memory of that first surgery, the Norwood, where they had left Jake's chest open to reduce pressure on his tiny heart, and Simon had seen it beating through a clear plastic film.

He shivered.

Miss Maya held his eyes. He saw a gleam of compassion. 'He'll probably be here for a couple of weeks, minimum. He'll be in ICU, and then stepped down from there as he progresses.'

'OK.' He bit down hard on his cheek. He mustn't cry. Jake must never see him cry.

'As ever, if he has a cold or anything then we can't go ahead, so best to keep him off school for a week or two beforehand, and for his caregivers to be extra careful too. Many people quarantine, just to make sure they're ready.'

'Got it.'

'Good. Could you sign here, please?'

Simon pressed the pen to the paper, wishing he didn't have to put his son through this. Wishing he had a choice. Then he signed, pushing the form back across the desk as rapidly as if it was radioactive.

This was his job: signing forms; staying vigilant; holding Jake down when doctors needed to hurt him to save him.

Blocking out the screams.

Blocking out the fear.

Remembering how lucky Jake was to be alive.

3

Beth

She still woke up thinking she was living her old life in New York: Tyler's face on the pillow next to hers; a busy day on the ward ahead; evening plans to meet friends in her favourite cocktail bar near Washington Square Park. Instead she found an orange teddy with a bedraggled right arm eyeing her from only millimetres away.

'Um. Hello?'

Beth rubbed gritty eyes. She wasn't in Brooklyn. She was on a sofa bed in the open-plan kitchen-living room in Jas's flat in Keswick. No arms around her; no coffee brewing; no distant gleam of the river Hudson when she drew back the shades.

Just a little girl and her teddy bear.

'What time is it?' She stretched, yawning. She couldn't have got to sleep before 4 a.m, maybe 5. Another night spent staring at the ceiling. She felt like a demolished wall.

'It can't be time to get up, can it?'

'It's time for you to help Milo.' Four-year-old Saffy's concerned expression told Beth that there was an urgent problem to be solved. 'He needs help.' The little voice was determined, and its owner scrambled up and sat on

Beth's legs before she could reach out for her phone and see quite how early it was. She had been staying at Jas's place for three weeks and her daughter consistently appeared at 6 a.m. Beth was so tired she regularly forgot her own name.

'His arm hurts.' Saffy's black ponytail was sticking out at right angles as she helpfully held out a packet of Peppa Pig plasters. 'Operation please.'

Beth rubbed a hand over her face.

'Now.' It was an order.

Beth's back clicked as she sat up and took Milo gingerly by the paw. From what she could see a washing machine would be more use than an operating table, but she laid him out on her knees and began to check him over as seriously as she had once examined patients in the spotless hospital in New York.

Jas swept into the room, red dressing gown flying behind her. 'Saffy. I told you about this. No waking Beth up in the mornings!' The sternness of her words was belied by the smile she gave her daughter as she kissed her and swooped her up high in her arms.

'It's OK.' Beth swung her legs to the floor. It wasn't far. The sofa bed's springs had given up the struggle long ago. 'I couldn't sleep anyway.'

'Still jet-lagged?' Jas put her daughter down.

'Yeah.'

'Is that all?'

'Yeah. That's all.'

'You are such a bad liar.' Jas arched an eyebrow. 'You know you were whimpering in your sleep again?'

'Was I?' When Beth did finally fall asleep it was only for her nightmare to repeat. The same one, every time. She woke sweaty and tangled, a scream on her lips. 'Sorry.'

'It's OK.' Jas shrugged. 'I was wondering though – if maybe you want to talk to someone? About what happened?'

'No.' Beth felt adrenaline spike through her. The whole point of coming here was to leave the past behind. She didn't want to sit in a nondescript room, telling a stranger all about it. 'I'm fine.'

'If you say so.' Jas walked behind the breakfast bar and flicked on the kettle. 'I just hope you can get some sleep before you start work with us next week. School nurses are meant to be cuddly. Sympathetic. At this rate the primary school cuties will have nightmares whenever you turn up to do their flu immunisations or whatever. You look like something off the chain gang in *Les Mis*.'

'Gee, thanks.'

'Well, I can't have complaints about the newest member of my team.' Jas opened a cupboard and surveyed the contents. 'Which cereal would you like this morning, Saf?'

'All of them!' Saffy bounded across to the table, Milo's perilous medical condition forgotten.

'Any for you, Beth?' Jas rustled a packet of Rice Krispies.

'Thanks. I'll pass.'

'What are you up to today?'

'Looking for somewhere to live. Again. I know you need your sofa back, for . . .'

'Watching TV?' Jas winked over her daughter's head.

She had filled Beth in on all the details of Sam, the dark-haired paramedic she had met last month. Beth knew that she was getting in the way of their budding romance and was keen to move, however much Jas assured her there was no need.

Beth nodded. 'Exactly.' Saffy didn't know about Sam yet and Beth didn't want to be the one to let it slip.

'What are you looking at today?' Jas added Cheerios to Saffy's bowl.

'Anything I can.' Beth felt her spirits plunge. 'There's not a lot out there.'

'Bloody holiday homes. It's no wonder you can't find anywhere decent.' Jas poured milk into the bowl and Saffy eagerly tucked in.

'I just need to keep trying.'

Jas held out a mug of coffee. 'Take your medicine first.'

'Thank you.' Beth wrapped her hands around the mug, leaning against the counter. 'You're a lifesaver.'

Jas took a sip, wincing. 'Ugh. Not enough sugar.' She plopped another heaped teaspoon into her mug. 'I wish I could come with you.'

Beth shook her head. 'It's fine. Honestly. I'm so grateful for everything you've done.'

She put her arm around her friend. Jas held on tight and for a precious moment Beth felt understood.

Jas shifted. 'You know, you have the worst morning breath.'

Moment over.

'You should clean your teeth.' Saffy put her spoon down and merrily shovelled a fistful of cereal into her mouth. Milk dribbled down her stripy red nightshirt. 'That's what Mum does before her boyfriend Sam wakes up when he comes for sleepovers.'

Jas's mouth fell open.

'From the mouths of babes.' Beth grinned and headed for the shower.

Three hours later she was seriously contemplating buying a tent. Even in this sleeting May rain she felt life under canvas would be preferable to the stifling bunk-bedded cupboard in flat one, to the army camp bed with added hamster cage in house two and to sharing a cottage with a man whose T-shirt announced that he was a member of the National Front on her third stop of the day.

Beth frowned. This was the problem with leaping into the unknown – there was no safety net to catch you if you fell. She parked up for her final task of the morning – dropping off a present for the boy she had collided with on her first morning here. Whatever his dad said, however much he had protested, she had to do this.

She parked by the bridge, which was mercifully clear of sheep today, and meandered up the twisting lane, past hedgerows frothing white with Old Man's Beard. The only sounds were birds and bleats as she reached a bend and turned off, following the boy's directions. She leant down and wrestled with the rusty latch on a low white gate, admiring the yellow roses that were climbing determinedly up the cream pebbledash wall towards the grey slate roof. Above the door an oval sign proclaimed in a twirling scrawl that this was Number 1, The Rise.

She ran a hand over her hair, looked left and right, and leant down to put the present on the doorstep. She would just leave it and run. The thought of having to talk to the dad again was . . .

'Hello.' A white-haired lady in a plaid skirt and cream blouse pulled the door open so fast that Beth practically fell inside.

'Hi.' Beth was so relieved it wasn't the human grizzly that she smiled.

'Can you stay a minute?'

'Um. I . . .'

'Thanks. I wouldn't normally do this, but you have a kind face.'

'I do?'

The lady grabbed a large black handbag and disappeared out of the door. 'Boiler emergency. I'll be back in two shakes of a lamb's tail.'

'Wha . . .?'

'Jake's out the back.'

'But . . .'

The lady had already gone.

OK. It didn't look like Beth had much choice. She couldn't leave the kid here on his own.

'Hello there,' she called out, taking a tentative step into the narrow hallway. A scooter and a bike were fighting for space by the bottom of the stairs and shoes were piled haphazardly on the doormat.

'Oh. It's you.' There was the boy, standing at the other end of the hall, baggy grey jumper flapping at the wrists. He walked towards her.

She smiled. 'Hi. I'm Beth.'

He blinked wide brown eyes. 'I'm Jake. And it's OK. Dad's not here. No need to be scared.'

'I'm not scared.'

The corner of his mouth lifted. 'That's what Dad says when I climb a tree. And he always is scared, really.'

'Why? Do you go really high?'

He shrugged and didn't answer.

She took another step forward. 'I brought you a little something. To say sorry for hitting your bike.'

'Thank you!' His face lit up, making this journey very much worth it.

Then he frowned.

'It's not bike paint, is it?'

'No. I realised I didn't know which was the right red.' She held out the package. 'And I thought paint might be a bit boring. So – I got you something else.'

He fell on the present, ripping the paper off and throwing it to the floor. Beth prayed that she had chosen right. 'Oh wow, the Lego Minecraft Zombie cave!' He beamed. 'This is amazing. I've been trying to make one for months out of my other Lego sets, but it just doesn't look right.'

She felt a wave of relief. 'I'm glad you like it.'

'Can I start it? Now?'

'I . . .'

'Dad won't mind. I've done my homework with Jean.

It was just boring ten times tables again.' His slender fingers ran over the box, clearly itching to begin.

'OK. If you're sure.'

'Will you help me?'

Beth considered. There was no sign of Jean yet, so she might as well.

'Sure.'

'Great.'

She closed the front door and followed him down the corridor, past a spindly staircase and a cluster of coats. The cottage was dark and smelt of biscuits and wellies. She glanced into an open door as she passed, seeing T-shirts drying over a flaking radiator and a pair of jeans lying on a black and white checked bedspread. She hastily looked away, feeling like she was intruding.

'In here.' Jake pushed open a door to what must be the living room, which had a galley kitchen with bright yellow tiles carved out of the far corner behind a high counter with two mismatching stools. Beth bit back a swear word as her foot crunched onto what proved to be part of a train track. Models were everywhere, half-built or fully completed: trains, houses, helicopters, hotels and even what looked like a submarine. The mustard-yellow carpet was covered almost entirely in an explosion of bricks, and a black and green space rocket was propped up against peeling cream wallpaper in the corner.

'Let's do it over here.' Jake sank down to the floor, by a radiator covered in men's underpants smelling strongly of Persil. Beth looked the other way, before realising that there were more hanging over the dining room chairs.

She thought of their owner and swallowed nervously.

Then she looked at Jake, who had already opened the box, and was happily unpacking the little plastic bags of bricks. She sat down next to him. This, she could handle. Her dad had spent years lying beside her on various carpets, creating castles or buses or hospitals or boarding schools – whatever she had been into at the time. When he died she had found the tiny Lego heart she had made him for his fortieth birthday tucked away in his bedside drawer. It was still in her suitcase now, one of the few things she hadn't wanted to leave in the States. How she wished she had her dad here instead. His wisdom, his understanding – the way he always made her feel bigger, better, bolder.

Her spirits were falling, and she was grateful when Jake started to speak.

'I bet this cost a lot.' His freckled nose crinkled thoughtfully. 'I can give you some of my pocket money if you need it.'

'It's OK.' She helped him to open the first bag, pouring the bricks into a bowl he had ready. He was obviously a pro. 'No need.'

Beth knelt forwards, chin in hands. 'Shall we get started?'

'Yeeeeeahhh.' Jake was already turning the instructions to the correct page.

'Did you say your name is Beth?'

'Yes.'

'You know, our dinner lady at school's called Beth.'

'She is?'

'She smells of onions.'

'Does she?'

'You don't smell of onions.'

'I'm happy to hear that.'

He started snapping grey bricks together. 'You smell of coffee.'

'I guess that's better than onions.' Beth saw that she was surplus to Lego requirements and sat back on her heels. She glanced around, taking in the cans piled up next to the sink in the kitchen, the brown bread half open on the side, the crisps spilling out of a packet next to the small white radio belting out pop tunes. Above it, in a nook in the wall, was a picture of a man with butterscotch skin and a smile that stretched to the stars and back. He was cuddling a toddler with red hair and a blue T-shirt.

She stood up and went to take a closer look.

Jake glanced up. 'That's my dad and me.'

'Really?'

'Yeah.' He snapped brown bricks into place.

'Your dad looks . . .'

'Thin? Yeah. Everyone says that.'

'No.' She shook her head. 'I wasn't thinking that.'

'Yes you were.' He clipped more bricks together.

He was spot on. Beth took a step closer to the picture, trying to work out how the man in that photo had become the wild-haired fury who had shouted at her. She wondered if she had changed as much as him. When she went to the USA with Tyler she had been long-haired, ambitious, confident that the world was at her feet. And now look at her. Anxious, fearful, sleepless.

Guilty.

Another photo caught her eye. A woman with cascading red hair, gazing over one shoulder, her stomach swelling gloriously beneath a long green sundress.

Jake glanced up. 'That's my mum, Tamsin.'

'She's beautiful.'

'Yeah. Dad says I have her eyes.' He batted his eyelids at her.

Beth giggled. 'I can see you do.'

Jake looked down again. 'That's me in her tummy.'

'I thought so. She looks really young.'

'She was nineteen when she had me.'

'Wow.'

Jake crossed his legs, head bent over his evolving zombie cave. 'She had to go away when I was little.'

Beth looked at the girl's dancing eyes. 'Do you miss her?'

Jake started jiggling his knee. 'No. I've got Dad. He's the best.'

Beth stayed silent, sensing there was more to come.

'And she loves me very much, Dad says. He's told me loads about her.' His words bubbled like froth on a cappuccino. 'And she left me Superchick to cuddle whenever I think about her.' He turned and grabbed a yellow toy duck from the sofa. Its fuzzy white hair stuck straight up and its black eyes stared beadily above its soft orange beak.

Jake cuddled it tight.

Beth stared at the picture, trying to equate the delight on Tamsin's face with the subsequent years of separation from her child. But every photo is just the beginning of a story – Beth of all people knew that. She thought of the wedding portrait that had hung in the living room of their Brooklyn apartment – her and Tyler leaning into each other, her hair dark against his white blond crop, their hands entwined.

'Are you OK?'

She remembered Jake, remembered where she was. She was clutching the empty spot on her ring finger so hard it hurt.

'I'm fine.'

'Good. There's tea, if you're not. Dad drinks lots of tea.'

'Does he?'

'Yeah.' Jake flicked a strand of fringe out of the way. 'You know, Dad says Tamsin was really good at Lego, just like me. And probably football too.'

'Is that so?' Beth knelt back down next to him, gazing out at the hazy outline of the fells that seemed to rise straight up from the window. Way above she could see a jogger moving steadily up the incline, mist clouding around him as he neared the top. She itched to get her running shoes and disappear up there herself. What a view – one worth getting up for every morning. It was the greatest possible change from yellow cabs, busy pavements and subway signs. She loved those too, loved the fizz and pulse of New York, but right now she needed this – earth and silence, air and sky.

Maybe here she could sleep.

Jake stopped, his head on one side. 'Do you think this bit goes here?'

She checked over his work so far. 'It could do. Or maybe – here? If you move this blue bit across?'

'Yes.' Jake nodded. 'You know, you're a rubbish driver but you're pretty great at Lego.'

'Thanks.' Her mind returned to her fruitless morning. 'Maybe I can build myself a Lego house to live in.'

'That sounds awesome.' He snapped more bricks together. 'Or maybe a treehouse. I've always wanted to live in a treehouse.'

'Me too.' Beth stretched her tired legs out in front of her and leant against the sofa. 'Or a boat.'

'Yeah. Swimming every day! Amazing.' He flipped over the page. 'But why don't you have a house?'

'I just moved here. I've been looking but haven't found one yet.'

Jake shrugged. 'You should move in next door then.' Snap. Snap. Snap.

'Really?' Her own cottage, right here next to the fells. Deep down, excitement sparked.

Then she thought of Jake's dad and it died out. 'No. I don't think . . .'

'Jean owns these two cottages. She needs someone to move in soon, or she won't have enough money for her next trip ballroom dancing in Blackpool. She told me.'

'Really?' Beth looked again at the view. It was tempting. Very tempting indeed.

'She wants someone nice to live there. And you seem nice.' He smiled at her and she felt a glimmer of something like contentment.

Then the front door banged and loud steps clumped down the hall. Jake's dad was back.

Beth sprang up, instantly feeling somehow in the wrong.

'Er. Hi.' She raised a hand in an awkward wave.

He didn't return it. He stood, glowering, his shoulders so wide that he blocked the doorway. 'How did you get in here?'

She folded her arms defensively. He was so damn tall. 'Did your friend not tell you?'

'Tell me what? And where's Jean?' He flung his rucksack roughly down on the floor, but she noticed how gently he rested his hand on his son's head as he kissed him hello.

Then he turned back to Beth and the frost returned. Her words started falling over themselves to get out. 'She had to leave. Jean. She asked me to stay and watch Jake.'

'She what?' He ran a hand through his long hair, which hadn't got any less wild since she had last seen him. It skimmed his shoulder blades and she doubted it had ever seen a brush. He clearly didn't believe her. 'Jean?' He went back out into the hall. 'Jeeeeaaaaaan?'

Jake tutted quietly. 'Dad? Jean had to go. Beth's doing us a favour. And she came here to give me *this*!' He eagerly pointed to the box. 'Isn't she the best?'

'To say sorry for hitting his bike.' Beth took a breath. On this, at least, she couldn't be perceived to have screwed up.

Simon's expression told her otherwise.

'What the hell . . .?' His mouth a line, his eyes flashed fire.

'It's just a present. To say sorry.'

'I told you we didn't need anything.' His voice was absolute. Shocked, she took a step backwards.

'Didn't you hear me? Or are you as bad at listening as you are at driving?'

'It's just a Lego set.'

'Do you think we're charity cases or something?' His anger filled the room.

'What? No. I—'

'Because we're not. We're doing just fine. Aren't we, Jake? We don't need this.'

Jake's face fell. 'But Dad . . .'

'Do we, Jake?'

The boy hung his head, defeated. 'No, Dad.'

'Right.' His dad had won, but he didn't look happy about it. He was pacing, restless, a muscle flickering in his cheek. She had seen people like him before at the hospital: unhappy, on edge, lashing out. Part of her wanted to ask if he was OK.

Then he snapped at her. 'So you can take this – this thing – and you can go.' He tried to pick up all the pieces of the set, but they were too scattered now. She watched him, frustration rising. Yes, she had hit Jake's bike, but it wasn't about that any more. This was a present for a little boy.

'Please. Keep the set. It's for Jake – I want him to enjoy it. And it's not charity. It's me saying sorry. I screwed up the other week – I'm just trying to make it right.'

'No.'

'Please?' If only she weren't so tired she could find the

words she needed. 'You have to let me make it right!' This time, she would say sorry properly. This time, she wouldn't be denied. 'I made a mistake, OK? And I'm just trying to say sorry.' Guilt simmered within her. 'Please let me. Please? I just want to show how sorry I am.' She was speaking to another person in another place – a person who could never hear her.

She took his silence as acquiescence. 'Thank you.' Beth took the box from the man's hands and gave it back to Jake.

In a flash the boy was back down on his elbows, manoeuvring bricks into place, head down, face relaxed. He didn't care about her apology. He just wanted to build.

She turned and started to walk down the hallway, glad when the man didn't follow her. Her hand was on the front door. 'Goodbye, Jake, and . . .' She didn't even know his name. 'And Jake's dad.'

'Simon.' The voice was rough. 'My name's Simon.'

'Simon. Sure.'

She was shaking. She stumbled down the steps, sobs catching in her throat, chest tight. Then she turned around, staring up at the hills above, at the clouds scudding across the sky, casting dark shadows over the rugged slopes of the peaks surrounding her.

Her breathing slowed as the landscape steadied her. These fells had been here for centuries – they must have seen troubles like hers before. Maybe they had seen them pass too. Maybe they could heal her.

She heard a crunch behind her, as Jean came through the gate.

It was now or never.

It might be another mistake, it might become another regret, but something in Beth told her to act. She would have a look at the cottage next door. Just in case. She had moved continents to leave her past behind – Number 2, The Rise, might just be the perfect place to start again.

4

Simon

Simon looked up to see his boss, Holden, walking down the office towards him. His curly hair gleamed with wax and his tortoiseshell glasses were sliding down his narrow nose. He held his head high, arms swinging. He meant business.

Simon hastily looked down at his keyboard, hoping that he wasn't in Holden's sights today. He had barely recovered from the lecture last week on how to organise his desk space for maximum efficiency. Holden had been on a series of management seminars and the entire office was suffering as a result.

Simon adjusted his headset, trying to move it away from the sore spot behind his ear. 'One Team One Dream' was printed in navy and red above their cubicles but next to it their sales total for the month was way short of the target that Holden had ringed in red. Trying to sell garden furniture during the coldest spring in living memory was proving a challenge.

'Simon. Can you come with me, please?'

Like he had any choice.

He slid out of his chair, feeling the sympathetic glances of his teammates following him as he walked past the photocopier and the printer towards what Holden liked to call his 'Office'. In reality it was a slightly bigger cubicle rejoicing in its own bin.

'Now, Simon.' Holden sat down in his swivel chair, leaving Simon on his feet. He inhaled as if sniffing a fine Bordeaux, drumming his fingers on his shiny 'I'm a manager' trousers. 'How are you?'

'Alright.'

'Good, good.' Holden pushed his phone so that it rested at a perfect ninety degrees to the edge of the desk. His pen was next. When everything was arranged to his satisfaction he looked up again.

Simon waited to be told what he had done wrong this time. He had sold a swing seat and a rattan sofa set in the past week, so he didn't think he had too much to worry about. He stared at the pencils in Holden's pot. All perfectly sharpened, all the same length.

No one used pencils any more.

He wondered about calling school to check on Jake. His boy had been up all night with sore legs again and Simon had felt bad about taking him in that morning, however much Jake had said he wanted to go. He would call in a bit, once Holden had finished talking. Simon looked out of the window at a blackbird flying determinedly across the sky. Freedom. Simon couldn't begin to remember how it felt.

Holden was now staring at Simon inquiringly.

He must concentrate. 'Sorry, could you say that again, please?'

Holden sighed as if exhausted, even though it was a

safe bet that he had enjoyed a full eight hours of sleep, rather than a night of Calpol syringes and leg-rubbing. Lucky beggar.

'This is exactly what I mean, Simon. Poor concentration. Lack of focus. Look, I know you've got a lot going on in your personal life, but we're paying you to do a job. It's time for a change. We can't go on like this.'

Simon gritted his teeth as he awaited whatever patronising insight was coming next. They had been at school together and it seemed to Simon that, for Holden, very little had changed. He still lived with his parents. He went on pub crawls every Friday and played football religiously at weekends. He had endless disposable income and took at least two overseas holidays a year. His responsibilities appeared minimal, yet still he liked to share his wisdom with the team – opining to Mags that she could cure her arthritis by eating Manuka honey, or to Andy that his newborn baby would stop crying if he put a drop of whisky in her bottle. It hadn't done Holden any harm, apparently. Simon would beg to differ.

'This is very hard for me, Simon.' Holden's phone buzzed and he flipped it over. He grinned and punched out a reply before resuming his previous troubled expression. 'But I'm afraid that this week we've had to make the decision to let you go. And I hate being the one to tell you, what with us being school friends and all, but . . .'

Wait.

Simon leant forward. Maybe he had misheard. 'What?'

'Your sales figures are too low, Simon. We can't carry you any longer. Most of your calls seem to end up with you listening to people's problems – and while we all appreciate your very big heart . . .' He actually laid a hand on his chest as he said this. Simon clenched his fists. 'The fact is we're a business, and we need to make some money now and then, you know?' He laughed, despite having said nothing funny at all.

'But listening to customers is how I sell.' Simon spoke through clenched teeth. 'You know it is. I sold loads in my first month. Things might have slowed a bit since then, but . . .'

'And then there are the absences.' Holden didn't even have the guts to hold Simon's gaze. He leant forward and clicked his mouse, turning the screen to show Simon the red blocks in the team calendar. 'Three emergency days off the first month. Four the second. And rising to – oooh . . .' He grimaced. 'Five this month already and it's only the 20th.'

It did sound bad, said like that, just days missed, without any story behind them. But what you couldn't see were the number of times Simon had set out in the morning only to get the call from school to say that Jake was clutching his chest or was struggling to breathe. Every red square on that spreadsheet represented danger, and Simon never had any choice but to get back to Jake and face whatever was coming at his son's side.

'But I always make the time up. And Mags covers for me. I always make sure of that.'

Holden held up a finger. 'Not the point, my friend. Not the point. It's my job to organise the rotas, not yours. You just need to turn up when you're told to.'

'I try to. Things are – complicated.' Simon's mouth was dry. He needed this job. The shifts were flexible enough to fit around Jake's school day. Finding it had dragged them out of rent arrears and weeks spent eating from the supermarket bargain bins. 'But Jake gets sick and I have to be there for him. I thought you understood that.'

'I do.' Holden's voice was honeyed. It made Simon's hackles rise. 'And I think I've been very understanding. I know how hard things are for you, with the little one's mum being gone and all.' He took a pencil from his pot and rolled it between his fingers. 'And I hope you know that we've all been there to support you. As a company. I bought a charity T-shirt only last week, for my next Fells Climb.'

Simon blinked. 'Um. Thank you . . .?'

'You're welcome.' Holden nodded graciously. 'But, to return to my original topic, I'm afraid that we are going to have to let you go. You're on a week's notice, but I know how things are, so I've decided to waive you working out your notice period and we'll pay you right up to next Friday. Can't say fairer than that, can we?'

Simon thought about the phone bill. The electricity bill. That Minecraft Lego set he had bought for Jake's birthday only for that bloody woman to give it to him instead. 'But you didn't warn me. I . . .'

'Now, Simon.' Somehow even the way Holden inhaled was patronising. 'Blame is not a positive reaction to change.'

Simon raised his eyes to the ceiling. The grey panels held no answers.

'But I can do better.' He couldn't let this slip away. He couldn't face the months of trawling through adverts online, applying for jobs that he didn't really want.

'Please, Holden? Give me one more week. Two. I promise I'll chat less and sell more. Go team!' He tried punching the air, hoping he didn't look as much of a tit as he felt.

'I'm sorry, mate.' Holden shook his head. 'We can't go on like this. This decision has been very hard for me, you know.' He was still staring at his precious pencil. Simon was strongly tempted to snap it and jam it up his nose. 'Very hard indeed, given that we're friends and all. It's been a very difficult time.'

They were absolutely not friends.

Simon's head was motoring. He would be OK until the end of the month, but beyond that he had absolutely no idea. The panic made him dizzy. Jake turning on the tap only for nothing to come out; Jake eating baked beans out of the can because Simon couldn't afford to heat them.

His boy deserved better.

'Please?' God, he hated himself.

'I'm sorry, Simon. We just can't take any more of your unreliability. The business can't sustain it. And there are plus points for you, surely?'

'How do you work that out?'

'Well, you can spend more time with Jake. Go see the bluebells? That sort of thing.'

Much as Simon loved them, bluebells weren't a lot of use if you couldn't eat.

For a horrible moment, he thought he was going to cry. Yet another problem. Another tree falling, blocking his path, forcing him to pivot and redirect. He didn't know if he had the energy. He didn't know if he had the heart.

He was damn well going to hold his head high though. 'Thanks, mate.' He turned. 'Thanks a lot.'

He dragged himself back to his cubicle and picked up his hoodie and backpack. His colleagues gathered round him, patting his back and muttering commiserations, but he just wanted to get out, away from their pity, away from his own failure.

This wasn't the first time this had happened. He had lost count of the number of jobs he had started since Tamsin left. After leaving his job as a physio he had been a waiter, a cleaner, a Christmas postman and a delivery driver. He had also been a bin man, a bottle washer and a highly unsuccessful juggler. None of these jobs had lasted over four months. He was simply too unreliable.

He knew he could go on benefits but something stopped him. He wanted to earn his own keep, to look after himself and his boy, to be the man he believed himself to be. If only the P45s would stop getting in his way.

He sighed, clearing his desk of wrappers and mugs, and taking his chocolate digestives out of his drawer. Raising his hand to his colleagues, he walked to the door and pushed it open. It creaked shut behind him and he paused for a second, staring back through the glass door. His cubicle was empty and quiet. It was as if he had never been there at all.

He turned away and stood in the silent foyer, leaning against the wall, his legs threatening to give way. Every time he felt he had some solid ground beneath him another crack opened at his feet. Firings. An engagement ring lying on a breakfast table. A funny cry in the night. Blue lights in the darkness.

He never knew what was coming, he only knew what mattered. For Jake, he had to keep going. For Jake, he had to keep food on the table and a regular routine. His mum was gone – Simon had to do everything he could to fill the gap she had left and to stop his son worrying that his dad would disappear too.

There was only one person who could help, but he was the last person Simon wanted to call. He felt in his pocket and found only loose change. He had no choice.

Before he could talk himself out of it, he got out his phone and dialled his father.

5

Beth

'Wow, this takes me right back.' Beth gazed out across the sunny field behind Thistlethwaite primary school, where sports day was just getting going. White lines had been painted onto the grass to make a running track, a small podium had been erected in the middle and a red and yellow striped tea tent was at the other end. 'I can't believe there's bunting. Actual bunting.' She pointed towards the merry blue, red and white triangles dancing in the breeze. 'Look!'

'I know. You're well and truly back home now.' Jas sipped tea from her Thermos. 'What was your race when you were little, then? Sack race? Three-legged?'

'God, no.' Beth flicked a fly off her blue top and checked her *'Hello, I'm Beth'* name badge was in place. She was on duty: a school nurse, ready to help with the cuts, scrapes or falls that were inevitable when over a hundred children tried to exercise at the same time. 'I hated sports day. I liked the tea afterwards, though.'

'But you run all the time now.' Jas closed her Thermos and put it back in her bag. 'Those poor trainers of yours need their own physio.'

'Yeah.' Running was Beth's therapy. It was the one

thing that made her feel in control. 'I got into it in New York. Tyler and I used to—' She stopped.

Jas's eyebrows shot up. 'Tyler alert! You said his name out loud. Let's see if there's a lightning strike.' She peered melodramatically upwards.

'Hey!' Beth batted her on the arm. 'Not fair.'

'Sorry.' Jas put a hand on hers. 'It's just that you never talk about him.'

Beth felt her throat tighten. The truth was that if she started talking about Tyler she might never stop. Even though they had been apart for months now, she still turned sometimes, expecting to see him, wanting to share something she had read or thought. Then it would come back – the image of those two heads turning towards her as she stood in the bedroom doorway, her greeting dying on her lips.

The humiliation was acidic, vicious, endless.

Jas was watching her, brows drawn upwards in a question.

'It's just too hard.' Beth hung her head. 'I can't. I'm sorry.'

Jas squeezed her fingers. 'No need to be sorry. I'm here when you're ready.' She withdrew her hand. 'Best not have too much hand-holding on duty. All the parents will think we're having a torrid affair.'

'Torrid? Ha.' Beth shook her head. Her torrid days were far behind her. Once she and Tyler had kissed on buses, on beaches, in lifts and in libraries – their hands exploring, their breath hot, their bodies entwined. He couldn't get enough of her, reaching for her in the hospital cafeteria, fingers tracing the bare skin of her thigh over a family dinner at his parents' house in Connecticut. Her doctor, a man who could save lives and who seemed to want to be part of hers for ever.

'Earth to Beth!' Jas was tugging at her sleeve.

'What?'

'When you tune back in, there's a little girl over there who's come off her pogo stick. Are you up for it?'

'How bad is it?' Beth stiffened, eyes searching. If there was too much blood or too much danger she couldn't do it. She wasn't ready. Not yet.

'Don't panic. I'm breaking you in gently. She's still moving. Over there. Do you see?' Jas pointed.

The girl was lifting her head and frowning at her foot. Beth breathed again. 'Sure. I'll head over now.'

'Thanks. I'll take on that boy who missed the high jump mat. May the force be with you.' Jas did a mock salute and moved rapidly away.

Beth headed in the opposite direction, grinning at the kids in their yellow caps and T-shirts as they lined up to take on challenges involving scooters and balls and bean-bags. Some of them were frowning and intent, whooped on by proud parents. Others were staring the wrong way, their fingers disappearing up nostrils or into ears, with one boy even trying to sneak off to the tea tent when he thought nobody was looking.

She reached the little girl, who was clutching her ankle with her hands, long hair flowing around her heart-shaped face. No bone sticking out. No blood. Perfect.

'Hello. I'm Beth.'

The girl blinked. 'I know. It says so on your badge.'

'Good point.' Beth smiled. 'What's your name, my lovely?'

'Maisie.'

'So what happened here then, Maisie?' She felt a rare confidence as she knelt down. There was a comfort to this kind of nursing, to assessing and supporting, providing a hand to hold or an ear to listen. It took her back to the time she had first put on her uniform – the simplicity of those first nights on the ward, carrying out observations as the clock on the wall ticked its way towards dawn. A drip checked here. A pulse taken there. A sip of water. An extra blanket.

'I fell off in the pogo race and my foot hurts.' Maisie's lower lip was wobbling.

Beth squeezed her hand. 'Can I just take a little look?'

The girl proffered her foot. 'Yes.'

Beth picked it up, gently resting it on her knees as she examined it. She rotated it one way, listening for clicks and feeling for tension in the muscles. It seemed strong. She checked again, just to make sure. Maisie would be fine.

She reached into her pocket for the stickers she had tucked in there earlier. 'You're going to be fine, but I think you need to rest for a bit. I know it's boring and you want to run, but it's a bit bruised and we don't want to make it any worse.' She saw that tears were imminent. 'And I had a quick word with the tooth fairy earlier, and she says that she knows you'll be fine if you get up and go and have a cake, because you're really tough and your teeth are too.'

'Really?' Maisie's face cleared. 'Great.'

She leapt up, injury forgotten.

'Well done!' Beth applauded. 'The tooth fairy was right, wasn't she? Now, have one of these to take with you, for being so brave.'

'Thanks.' Maisie took one, beaming as she attached a galloping unicorn to her lapel. 'You're lovely.'

Beth soaked up the warmth of her smile as the girl raced off. She straightened up, hearing loud shouts from the running track, where a big crowd was gathered. She followed the noise, wondering what could have attracted so many people, only to see that an egg and spoon race was in progress. The competitors were halfway down the track and the entire crowd was yelling one name. JAKE. JAKE.

She made her way over, peering over someone's shoulder, and there he was. Red hair on end, shoulders hunched, face furrowed with concentration, Jake was making his way up through the pack. He was fourth now. Another spurt and he was second. With the tape only metres away it looked like he was going to win. He was about half the size of the other children, but his blood was up, his thin legs moving fast.

He was passing right by her now. She couldn't help herself. 'GO ON, JAKE.'

She saw him hesitate and panicked that she had over-done it. The egg wobbled and he stumbled.

No. She watched in agony as Jake struggled to regain his focus. On the other side of the running track Simon was frowning at her. She mouthed an apology but he had already turned away. Another black mark against her and she was moving in next door to them at the weekend.

Simon cupped his hands around his mouth. 'You can do it, Jake!'

At his dad's words, Jake started moving again. A boy with glasses and a huge T-shirt powered towards him, laughing, but Jake kept fighting. He was speeding up again. He was nearly there.

Jas appeared beside her. When she saw what was happening she joined in. 'COME ON, JAKE.' Beth looked around. Every hand was clapping, every mouth cheering. The crowd loved Jake and he must have known it because he made a final push for the line and crossed it first.

Everyone went wild. 'YES!' Jas danced in delight. Beth stared at her. Simon was attempting a cartwheel and the cheers all around them were deafening.

She nudged her friend.

'What's going on? I mean, it's nice he won and all, but why isn't anyone supporting their own children?'

'Oh, I forgot, you don't know! It's your first time at Thistlethwaite, isn't it?' Jas leant closer.

'Yes.'

Jake was standing still now, chest heaving, but still raising his hand to give other kids high fives.

Jas spoke rapidly. 'That boy's Jake Withers.'

'And?'

'He's got HLHS. The heart condition?'

It took a second to penetrate.

'HLHS?' Beth couldn't equate this with the boy she had played Lego with only a couple of weeks ago. She would have noticed, surely. 'Really?' She hadn't seen any medication in the cottage. No INR machines or oxygen. He had seemed fine.

'Really.' Jas nodded decisively.

'Are you sure?'

'Yes.' Jas folded her arms. 'Normally he sits on the sidelines, or doesn't make it to sports day at all, so the fact he came first in a race is amazing – that's why everyone's going nuts. He'll be dead in the water tomorrow, mind you.' She put her head on one side, eyebrows rising. 'What's eating you?'

'I . . .' When Beth was training she had done a rotation on the paediatric cardiac ward, and the memory of those little babies had stayed with her. The way they lay so quietly in their Perspex pods. The stickers on their tiny chests saying 'Chest Open', the walnut-sized hearts beating bravely beneath. And the parents. Worried, tired, despairing, hopeful, hands clutching small pipettes of breast milk, squeezing them painstakingly into tiny mouths.

Simon must have been one of those parents. And she had crashed into his beloved boy. No wonder he was angry. No wonder he couldn't stand the sight of her.

Something collided with her legs and she looked down to see Jake's enormous smile. Even his freckles seemed to be dancing. 'Did you see me, Beth?'

'I did.' Beth was still reeling. 'W–well done!'

'Thanks.' The sun shone from his smile, but she could see how tired he was. 'What I did was, I started slow . . .' He appeared determined to give her a blow-by-blow account. 'I just wanted to get my eye in, you see. Then I—' He turned his head. 'Wait. Dads' Race. Got to go.'

Beth could see Simon among the men gathering on the start line, his baseball cap flung backwards on his head and his hands in his pockets. He laughed, and above the beard she could see his whole face soften. She found she was still staring at him as the starting gun went off.

Simon took a second or two to get going, but soon he was making headway. He was so tall his long legs outstripped the competition, even in his cargo trousers and desert boots, and Beth could see the determination on his face. He was third from the front now, inching past a man in a stripy polo shirt and shorts. Only someone in spikes and high-vis running leggings to go now.

'Come on, Dad!' Jake was jumping up and down. Beth saw Simon glance across at him, before raising his arms above his head and forming a heart with his fingers. Jake did the same. Then Simon got his head down again, the tape nearly within his reach. But Mr Spikes was still ahead. Simon was one metre closer. Two.

'GO, DAD.' But Mr Spikes was holding his own and brought the tape down seconds before Simon crossed the line. Simon's head dropped and he put his hands on his knees, gulping for breath. All the other competitors came up and clapped him on the shoulder. Absolutely none of them did the same to Mr Spikes.

Jake was there, pulling his dad in for a hug.

'How do you know Jake, anyway?' Jas nudged Beth.

'He's the kid who told me about my new place. My new next-door neighbour.'

'Oh. It was *that* Jake? Shit.' Jas's eyes widened. 'Does that mean . . .'

'That he's the kid I knocked off his bike? Yep.' Beth grimaced.

'Wow.' Jas's eyes widened. 'No wonder you got a bollocking. Simon lets no one and nothing hurt that child. Takes him to school and picks him up himself, takes time off when he's ill. His mates can barely persuade him out for quiz night every now and then. It's all about Jake, for him. It would have been nice for that git to give him the win there. He'd have aced it once, but . . .'

'What do you mean?'

'Simon Withers was King of Thistlethwaite when he was younger. Captain of the soccer team, on the county athletics team – the works. He was going places.' Jas frowned. 'It's been hard for him, with Jake's heart and his mum leaving like that.'

Beth looked across at the father and son, arms tight around each other. She wanted to turn back time. She wanted to check her mirror before she pulled out that morning.

She shivered. She was right not to trust herself. She had come here to escape her mistakes. Instead she appeared to have only succeeded in making a new one.

6

Simon

'Did Grandad play football?'

Simon had been timing how long it would take for Jake to bring up football again. It had been a whole ten seconds.

'I think so.'

'You don't know?'

'Yeah. I do.' Simon turned off the road and his pickup bounced onto the lane that twisted its way through the thick woods that ran up to the farm. Bluebells carpeted the ground beneath the trees, bravely bobbing their heads in the relentless rain, and the hedgerow was creamy with blossom. 'I mean, everyone plays football, don't they?'

Jake clutched the medal he had barely taken off since his egg and spoon triumph.

'I can't wait to play on the school team.'

'I know, lad.' This had been Jake's theme since time began, and his sports day victory had only made it even more of a favourite. Simon didn't know if it was good or bad that his boy had forgotten how he had been unable to go to school the day after sports day, how he had lain on the sofa alternately watching telly and sleeping as his heart tried to recover. Jake now believed he could do anything. How Simon wished it was true. But they had been here before: swimming lessons ending in exhaustion and screams; the climbing birthday party they had left early after Jake couldn't even make it halfway up the toddler wall.

Jake bounced on his seat. 'Can I get some football boots, Dad?'

Simon felt another clench of desperation. His bank account was hanging on by a thread. 'I'll think about it.' He put the handbrake on and got out to wrestle with the gate that marked the outer edge of his dad's farm. It had been hanging off its hinges for several years. The metal nipped Simon's fingers as he dragged the frame to one side.

He got back in and closed the door, rain dripping from his hood.

'I can't wait to see Grandad.' Jake clung on to his seat as they bumped up the track.

'Hmmmm.' Simon found the waiting part much easier than the seeing part. They had so little to talk about that sometimes he wondered if they were actually related. Needs must, though. His phone conversation with his dad had been so awkward that Simon had looked for other jobs, sent CVs, sent enquiries – and established, depressingly, that this was the only option he had. He swung his pickup around a bend and the unkempt ditch loomed alarmingly. He gripped the wheel, slowing down, eyes tiny after too many sleepless nights working out quite how little money he had.

Rain pelted against the windscreen so hard that Simon

started to worry that the chip on the driver's side was going to crack. Yet another thing he couldn't afford to fix. He felt his spirits droop still further as the farmhouse came into view. Every time he came he hoped his dad would have cheered the place up a bit. Maybe the roof wouldn't still have bin bags fixed over the huge hole just above the kitchen chimney.

Simon peered through the rain. There were now planks of wood too.

He sagged.

'We haven't been here for ages.' Jake unbuckled his belt.

'No.'

'I hope Grandad will teach me really cool words.' Jake cast a sideways look at Simon, his eyes gleaming with mischief. 'Like last time.'

'He probably will, the old devil.' Simon swung the wheel round and parked up, brakes squealing in protest.

Limbs heavy, he got out, feet landing firmly in a huge puddle which splashed over his boots and onto his socks. He squelched round and took Jake's hand as they walked towards the back door. He saw damp blooming on the back wall and the down pipe was hanging detached from the gutter.

Simon sighed. He knew that his dad kept the rest of the farm immaculate – anything for his precious sheep – but since his beloved Mary had passed away the house had fallen into disrepair. It was never like this in her day. Simon's mum would have been out here organising, tidying, painting, hauling firewood, keeping things cooking and the fire lit. When she had run out of tasks she used to tour the fields on her red quad bike, dark hair tied up in a scarf, her bag full of cakes or sandwiches for her William and the farmhands.

Simon had never realised how much of a team his parents were until his mum had gone. He had rarely noticed the silence between him and his dad when she was alive. She had covered the gaps in their conversation, like pastry laid over pieces of apple in a pie.

'Evening.' The flaking green door creaked open, and a tangle of collie dogs were jumping at their feet. Jake beamed, hunkering down and submitting his face and hands to an ecstasy of licking.

'Jake.' Simon took his arm, trying to pull him up. 'Jake. You can't let them do that.'

'Why, Dad?'

'You might get an infection. You know you have to be careful.'

Simon could feel his dad's eyes on him, a knife being run over his skin. He was a boy again: too slow, too careful, too soft.

His dad opened his mouth. Simon knew what was coming. 'You can let the lad play with the pups, can't you? Just this once?'

Simon bit back his reply. 'Well, it would help if you could let us in, Dad. It's coming down in sheets out here.'

'I know that. I've been out on the top field all day. Fences needed mending.' His dad stood back to give them room. 'Come in.'

Jake didn't need telling twice. He ran in, dogs whirling at his feet.

Simon's dad leant up to adjust the cobwebbed lamp hanging over the door. Simon could see the veins crisscrossing his cheeks, the hunch of his shoulders, the way his chin jutted forwards as if he was expecting an attack.

'In you come then.' His dad jerked his head towards the hallway. Simon stepped inside, pulling the door shut as best he could despite the swollen wood bulging at the bottom.

The hall was so cold Simon drew his anorak closer around him. The house smelt of sadness. No rose water perfume, no baking smells coming from the kitchen. His mum's absence was everywhere – one of the many reasons why Simon didn't make the trip up here more often. The same pictures hung on the walls, exactly where his mum had put them, but their light had gone out. At the bottom of the stairs, in a big gold frame, he could see his parents on their wedding day, his mum in a white dress with yellow rosebuds scattered down the skirts. How he missed that smile, the love that could rewire him, that could make a bad day golden.

He rapidly moved on to the black and white pictures just by the kitchen door: his dad holding a trophy above his head at the local show; his mum gazing down at a plump mouse-haired baby that she had told Simon many times was him. Above the door was a tapestry sewed by his gran – the names William and Mary intertwined in floral script, along with the date of his parents' wedding day.

His dad had reached the kitchen, with its red tiled floor and battered wooden cupboards. It was even colder than usual. Simon noticed that a pane of glass was missing at the bottom of the big window that opened onto the yard. Cling film and tape were doing their best to keep out the elements, but they couldn't compete with the wind outside.

'Are you going to fix that, Dad?' Simon walked across and examined it. 'What happened?'

'A bit of wood went the wrong way.'

Conversation over. His dad was reaching into a cupboard. He turned back to Simon, holding up a bottle of whisky.

'Drink?'

Simon knew he was just an excuse. His dad would have one anyway.

'No thanks. Just water.'

'You and your water, lad.' His dad tipped some from the jug on the table into a murky tumbler and slid it towards Simon. He turned back to the whisky. 'One for Jake, maybe? Fancy trying whisky, lad?'

Jake looked up from playing with the dogs on the hearth, eyes alert. Simon opened his mouth to protest, only to see a rare grin split his dad's face in two. 'Only joking, lad. I thought you might like this, though.' He reached down behind Jake's ear and pulled out a Cadbury Creme Egg.

'Wow.' Jake's eyes were enormous. 'How did you do that?!'

'I learnt a bit of magic in my time.'

Simon couldn't remember him using it.

Jake took the egg wonderingly, and sat down with the

dogs again. 'Eat it later, alright?' Simon went across and cleaned his son's hands with the antibacterial wipes he always had zipped into the pocket of his fleece. 'No fingers in your mouth, OK?'

'Yeah, Dad.' Jake started tickling the collie's tummy. The dog raised all four paws in the air, tongue lolling in an ecstasy of love.

Simon's dad nursed his tumbler. The amber liquid came over halfway up and there was no ice. He lifted it, downing half his glass in one go. His cheeks were hollow as he sucked it down and lines dug even deeper into his forehead than Simon remembered. 'So. Haven't seen hide nor hair of you for weeks.'

'I've been busy.'

'Oh aye?' Simon wondered whether his dad had always sounded this disbelieving, or whether it was just with him.

'Yes.'

'You still need work I take it?'

Simon sipped his water.

'You know that. We talked on the phone.'

'Thought as much. Call centre not suiting you, then?' His dad leant his forearms on the table between them – the long oak table he had made for Simon's mum when they had got married. Simon wondered if she was up there somewhere, watching them, wishing she had taught them how to talk to each other in more than monosyllables and barbs.

'No, I . . .'

His dad sucked air through his teeth. 'Got the sack again, did you?'

'Yes.'

'Shame, that.'

Simon braced himself.

'What did you do this time?'

His dad's lack of belief hurt less every time.

'I had to miss some shifts. I made up the hours, and always got someone to cover, but they let me go anyway.' He was still smarting. 'It's hard, you know, with Jake—'

'He can't always be your excuse, can he?'

Simon was filled with a familiar urge to tell his dad how sick his grandson really was – how unpredictable a day, let alone a month, could be. But he had learnt by now that William didn't want to listen. Simon looked at his boy, at the copper hair amongst the black and white fur. Jake was his blood. His strength.

'He's not an excuse, Dad, he's my boy. And I put him first.' *Unlike you*, he wanted to say. The farm had always come before everything for his dad. The whitewashed walls, the endless sheep and the rolling fields. That was what mattered to William. Simon was just another pair of hands to look after it. The next in line. His dad had made that very clear on the day that Simon had told him he had other plans – that his dream was to be a physiotherapist, not a farmer. William's disappointment was a wall between them, thickening with every meeting and every passing year.

'Cake?' His dad got up, his jumper loose above ancient green cords held up with bailer twine. The belt Simon had given him for Christmas was probably tucked away in a drawer upstairs, label still attached. His dad got out the Union Jack tin that had been on the shelf above the hob since the dawn of time. The Queen and Prince Philip, still in the first flush of youth, were emblazoned on the front. His mum had adored Queen Elizabeth II and had curated an ever-growing collection of memorabilia until her death when Simon was fifteen. He remembered sitting on her knee, breathing in the smell of the bread she made every morning for the farmhands, lifting objects from her drawer of treasures with eager fingers as she explained all about the royal family she had revered.

Simon leant back on his chair, wincing at the noise it made as the legs scraped across the flagstones. 'Cake would be great, Dad.'

'Here you go.' His dad had already cut him a thick slice and put it on a chipped china plate with pink rose-buds blooming around the edges. Simon took it, hoping it was a bit fresher than the jam on the table in front of him, which was topped with a thin layer of mould.

'So can I come and work here for a bit, Dad?' He took a bite, relieved to find that it tasted good.

'Alright.' His dad could not have sounded less excited.

At least he hadn't made Simon beg. 'I can start next week. I need to work around Jake's school hours, though.'

'Aye.' His dad had despatched his cake in two bites. 'Nothing too early? Nothing too late?'

Simon hated the way his father made it sound like he had a choice.

'Well, I can come back with Jake in the afternoons, once I've picked him up from school. Now the evenings are getting lighter, I mean.'

'Awesome! I love it here.' Jake appeared from beneath a mass of fur. 'Are there any women working here, Grandad? Any single women?'

'Ja-ake.' Simon was getting tired of this now. Last week Jake had asked the checkout girl in Sainsbury's if she wanted to come round for dinner, just as Simon was beeping through his economy spaghetti.

'What? I'm just asking.'

William's eyes widened. 'Why? In case that father of yours might have an eye for someone?' He threw his head back and laughed. It sounded like a broken hinge. 'Not likely. He's got eyes for nobody but your mother.'

'Well, that's because she's amazing.' Jake's defiance made Simon proud. He did his best to keep Tamsin real for Jake, sharing stories and photos and the occasional white lie, but how he wished his son could feel her arms around him. He worried about Jake not having a mum – about the hole that would be there even though his son couldn't see it. He knew how much he missed his own mum – how much she had given of herself, always there for Simon until – quickly, horribly – she wasn't.

His dad was still laughing. 'She might be amazing, but she's not bloody here, is she?'

Jake's face crumpled. Simon could handle his dad insulting him, but not crushing his boy. He got up. Nothing was worth this. He would find another job. The sausage factory was always on the lookout, if only he could make the hours work around Jake. Anything was better than this.

'This was a mistake.'

His dad remained seated. 'Your temper hasn't improved then?'

Simon stayed on his feet. 'My temper has nothing to do with it. Apologise to Jake. That's his mum you were talking about.'

His dad sighed, putting his glass down on the table. 'You can start Monday, alright?'

Simon hesitated.

'It'd be a real help.' His dad almost looked as if he was trying to smile.

Simon needed to hear more. He jerked his head towards his son, eyebrows raised.

Sighing, his father turned to Jake. 'I'm sorry, lad. For saying what I did. And how are you, any road? I heard you did pretty well in a race last week.'

'You did?' Jake beamed and Simon began to thaw.

'Aye. Word around the village is that you got a silver medal in the egg and spoon.'

Jake jumped up. 'Not the silver, Grandad. The gold!'

He saw his dad's lips twitch. 'Oh.' He scratched his head. 'Are you sure it wasn't the silver?'

'Yes.' Jake lifted the medal that was now a permanent fixture around his neck. 'Look!'

'Oh my, lad.' His dad examined it carefully. 'Aye. That's gold alright.'

'Next year I'm going to win the one hundred metres!'

Simon's heart twisted. Jake would have had the Fontan Completion by then. How he hoped it could make his boy's dream come true.

Jake was still bubbling as one of the collies put its nose

on his lap in a bid for more stroking. 'I was so fast I might be able to join the football team.'

William's face lit up. 'Really, lad?'

'Yes! I want to play on the wing.' Jake's eyes were dreamy.

'You go for it, lad.'

Simon had let this go on long enough. 'Jake. You know it's a risk for you to do contact sports. You're on warfarin. You could . . .'

His dad turned on him. 'Oh, come on. Do you want him to grow up soft?'

'No, Dad, I want him to grow up safe.' Or grow up at all.

'It's just a bit of footie.'

'It's not that simple, Dad.' Simon wouldn't say any more in front of Jake. 'It's not *just* anything.' He stood up again. 'We've got to go back for tea, anyway.' Simon held out his hand to Jake. 'Thanks for the cake, Dad.'

'And the Creme Egg.' Jake threw his arms around his grandad, who surprised Simon by hugging him back. With his head bent, Simon could see the thin grey hair on the top of his head. It made his dad seem fragile – as if somewhere, deep down, he might be vulnerable too.

It only lasted a moment. Then his real dad was back, head up, lips set in a line.

'Bye, son.'

Simon nodded in return and took Jake's hand as they ran back towards the pickup, heads bent against the pouring rain. His dad had shut the door by the time Simon had put his key in the ignition.

As he dried Jake off as best he could, Simon thought about that word. *Soft*. It made him want to scream. Jake was the least soft person he knew. Jake was a lion, a gladiator, braver than the brave. And Simon was his carer and his gatekeeper. He would say no again and again in order to keep his son safe. It was all he had to do – it was all he wanted to do.

He got the antibacterial wipes out of his pocket again and started work on Jake's fingers. One job, then the next. One day, then another. One moment, one breath, one problem at a time.

7

Beth

'Here you are.' Jean unlocked the door and handed over the key. It was as shiny as the buckles on the landlady's navy-blue loafers. 'I've given the place a good once over, so hopefully you can just settle straight in, pet.'

'Thank you.' Beth tried to put the key into her pocket but it was too big. She let it dangle from her finger, the metal cold against her skin. The last time she had moved house it had been with Tyler. He had lifted her over the threshold, laughing as they kissed, his hands tugging at the buttons on her shirt. She'd had a ring on her finger and a heart full of stars.

Dropping clothes as they went they had progressed to their new bedroom, with its floor-to-ceiling windows and dimmed lighting. Champagne was waiting in a cooler, but they hadn't had time for that. His mouth was on hers as they threw themselves onto the enormous double bed, laughing, exploring, desperate to make their home their own.

'Did you hear me, pet?' Jean's brows were raised behind jaunty purple glasses. 'No sanitary products in the loo or it'll get blocked.'

Beth blinked her way back. 'Oh. Right. Sure.'

'And bin night is Tuesday.'

'Great.'

'Anything you want just ask. I'm just round the corner – the bungalow with the yellow roses and the green gate. You can't miss it. And Simon next door is a right sweetheart. He'll help you out.'

Or blow her off. She wouldn't blame him if he did.

'Thanks, Jean.'

'Oh, and I popped some tea, milk and scones on the table for you.' Jean checked her battered silver watch. 'I thought you might be hungry getting all your things in, but . . .' She glanced at Beth's suitcase and rucksack. 'You travel light, don't you?'

'Yeah.' She could feel Jean's curiosity nipping around her, searching for a chink, seeking her story.

'I suppose the rest is coming later? You're sending it on?'

'Sure.' Beth picked up her suitcase. The less she said, the better.

'Right.' Jean hovered for a moment more then turned, pulling her canvas bag up her shoulder. 'I'm off to the church. It's my turn to do the flowers today.' She smiled. 'You should come in sometime. It's a lovely service. You can hear the sheep gobbling up the grass outside. You'd be very welcome, if anything's troubling you.'

'Thanks.' Beth stared at her feet. Too much kindness undid her. 'I will.'

'In you go then.' Jean gestured her inside. 'It's all yours now, pet.'

Hers.

Just hers.

Swallowing her loneliness, Beth walked inside. The cottage was so quiet she could hear the clock ticking in the living room at the far end. The floor plan was the mirror of Simon and Jake's – a long dark hall with a bedroom and a WC opening off to the right, with the living room and galley kitchen at the end. Upstairs was another tiny bedroom under the eaves and a bathroom with yellow sunflower tiles. Her cottage was plain and peaceful, decorated in neutral greys and whites. After weeks on a sofa it should have felt like a step forward to have her own place, but through her fog of exhaustion all she could see were nights by herself, solo breakfasts and a gap where someone else's smile should be.

She wondered if Tyler was looking for her, if he even cared that she was gone.

Probably not.

'Are you alright, love?' Jean was hovering in the doorway.

Beth looked into the bright blue eyes. Suddenly she wanted to tell Jean everything – about Tyler, about New York, about the day she had come home early and the shift she should have missed.

Instead, she forced a smile. 'I'm good, thanks, Jean. Excited to get settled.'

'I'll leave you to it then. If you're sure. Bye, pet.' Jean raised her hand and got on her rusty bike, disappearing off in a flurry of gravel.

Beth shut the door and slipped off her trainers. So here it was. The beginning of whatever came next. Weariness overcame her and she sat down on the stairs, head resting against the wall, wondering how to find the energy to unpack her minimal luggage and make this place a home. Last time it had been so easy – her and Tyler finding antique pictures in thrift stores in the village, or shopping for a couch at Modani, hand in hand, sipping on their coffees from the Turkish cart on the corner. They had drifted around the city, buying curtains from The Shade Store and throws from Chelsea market, sipping champagne at their new window as the sun came down.

Now it was just her. She put her case and bag down in her new bedroom. It was furnished with a small white wardrobe, complete with the kind of gaudy knitted hangers she hadn't seen since her gran had gifted her a set on her sixteenth birthday. She dropped her key and phone on the shallow pine bedside table, and smoothed the white cotton bedspread on the double bed. On the wall was a watercolour showing a vase of flowers that must surely have looked better in real life, and another of an indigo lake, surrounded by rolling hills of russet and green.

Time to look at the view for herself. She almost ran through to the living room, leaning her elbows on the windowsill, cupping her chin in her hands. There they were – the fells that had called to her as she was sinking in New York, weighed down with pain and grief. And now here she was, back in the Lake District, the place her parents had brought her every summer when she was growing up. Such sun-filled sweetness: her dad squealing dramatically as he ran into a freezing lake; her mum raising her arms in triumph as they conquered Scafell Pike. Ice cream sandwiches, sandcastles built on Allonby sands, picnics on exposed hilltops, chasing paper plates across the bracken when the winds blew strong.

Her parents had been walkers. Hills weren't just scenery to them – they were friends: every footstep a story, every peak a treasure to be savoured for years to come. When Beth's dad had died, her mum had refused to head to the Lake District again. She had found new territory, had moved on, and now lived in the Outer Hebrides with her new partner.

But Beth was here, back with the peaks and the valleys and the endless sky. She had been lucky that Jas was here, lucky that a vacancy had come up at just the moment she needed it. Beth breathed in. Tall and timeless the hills rose before her. Maybe, in time, they would give her strength.

'Why are you crying?'

A face had appeared on the bottom back step, directly below her.

'I'm not.' She wiped the tears from her cheeks. 'Hello, Jake.'

He walked up the steps until he was standing at the back door, his breath misting the glass.

'I made you something.'

'Thank you.' She slid open the bolt. 'You didn't need to do that.'

'I know.' He came in, his long-sleeved Minecraft T-shirt half tucked into his tracksuit bottoms.

He held out his hand, palm upwards. 'Here you go.'

She caught her breath. It was a tiny bunch of pink roses in a red pot, with green leaves spreading outwards to either side.

'A Lego bouquet. Thank you.' She stroked the bricks with her fingers. 'I love it.'

'I knew you would.' He grinned from ear to ear, looking behind her as if he was searching for something. 'Did Jean make you scones?'

'Oh.' Beth put her present down on the kitchen counter. '*That's* why you're here.'

'No it's not.' The flush on his cheeks gave him away.

'But you'll have one, now you're here?'

'Yes please!' A sideways glance. 'Since you're asking.'

Beth picked up a scone. It was still warm. 'Does your dad know you're here?'

'No. He was on the phone.'

'Well, go and tell him. I don't want to get in trouble with him again, OK?'

'OK.' Jake disappeared, and she rapidly discovered that the wall between their cottages was very thin. She heard the low rumble of Simon's voice. The thought of him next door, resenting her, put a cloud over the boiling kettle and the scones and the little boy who seemed to want to be her friend.

He ran back up the steps.

'Dad says it's fine.'

'Great.' Beth handed him a scone.

'Do you have any plates?'

'I'm not sure. Jean said it was fully set up, so . . .' Beth opened one cupboard, then another. 'Oh yeah. Here they are.' She handed a white one with a rainbow rim to him, before taking a blue and white checked one herself.

'I like it here.' Jake bit into the scone, crumbs flying all over his tracksuit bottoms and T-shirt. 'I can come round every day, if you like.'

'That sounds great.'

Jake chewed and swallowed. 'Do you have a boyfriend?'

For some reason the question didn't hurt when it came from him.

'Nope.'

'Oh good. How about going out with my dad?'

Beth nearly choked on her scone. 'What?'

'He could be your boyfriend.'

'I don't think so, Jake.'

'Why not?'

Because he hates me.

No. She couldn't say that.

She hesitated for a moment, mind racing. 'Because he's too tall. My neck would hurt if I kissed him.' She wondered how she would ever find his mouth under all that beard. Just as well she was never going to try.

'Oh.' Jake considered this, scone crumbs flying.

'And I just got divorced.' The decree absolute had come through just before she left. Despite Tyler's infidelity, she hadn't contested a thing. She just wanted out. 'I need to be on my own for a while. Or for ever. I'm not sure yet.' The thought of trusting anyone again made her skin crawl.

'OK.' Jake reached for a second scone. 'Dad doesn't like you anyway, so it would have been hard.'

His honesty amused her. 'Does your dad even want a girlfriend?'

He didn't answer, instead piling so much cream on his scone that it looked like a cheese sandwich. 'He needs one.'

'Why?'

Jake whirled the plate around on the table, and then drew his knees up to his chest, hugging them. 'He's lonely.'

'He's got you. I doubt he's got time to be lonely.'

'Yeah, but . . .' He licked some cream off his finger. 'He needs someone else. For when . . .' He stopped, frowning. 'It's harder than I thought, though.' Then his face cleared. 'If you've been married, then you must have been in love.'

'Yes, I've been in love.' Tyler's hand in hers, Tyler's mouth on hers, Tyler's voice telling her this was for ever.

If only.

Jake was watching her as if she had all the answers in the world. 'How does it work? Love?'

'It doesn't.'

'What?'

Shit. She hadn't meant to say that out loud. Beth regrouped. 'Well, it's different for everyone.'

He sighed, exasperated. 'But I want to know how it *works*.'

She drew her cardigan closer around her. 'Well, you meet someone. You like the look of them. You talk. You hold hands.' *And if you're really lucky they don't bugger off and sleep with one of your colleagues.*

She wouldn't share that thought.

He frowned. 'Then what?'

'Well, it's not a formula. I can't give you exact steps.'

'What happened with you?'

'We met at university. Dancing. I was dressed like a Dalek, some theme night or other.' She could still feel the jolt in her stomach when he had approached. So tall, so blond, so sure of himself. His lips against her ear as he asked her if she wanted a drink, yelling to be heard over the Spice Girls telling them to 'Viva Forever'.

'Dad doesn't dance.' Jake shook his head regretfully.

'Well, then we – I mean, two people – they spend time together. Like, maybe, walking dogs and stuff.'

Jake nodded thoughtfully. 'I could see if Jean's daughter would lend me her pit bull.'

Beth swallowed her last piece of scone. 'Er . . . yeah. Maybe. And then they might go for coffee.'

'Dad hates coffee.'

'Well, a drink then.'

Jake's face lit up. 'Beer. He likes beer.'

'OK. They go for a beer. And they talk.' She remembered how she and Tyler had talked. About religion. About where they would go if they won the Lottery. About whether books were better than movies, about the best flavours of ice cream, about whether Michelle Obama would ever run for President. Those long nights, her head on his chest, her legs wrapped around his.

Jake was watching her and she did her best to unclench her face. 'And then they're boyfriend and girlfriend?'

She nodded. 'Yeah.'

Jake beamed. 'OK. That's easy, then.'

'What's easy, lad?'

Beth looked up. There, at the top of her back step, was Simon. He looked even more exhausted than at sports day, his eyes hollows, his mouth downturned beneath his beard. Half of Beth wanted to make him a cup of tea, while the other wanted to turn and flee.

He looked at the scones, at the chairs, anywhere but at her.

The temperature in the room dropped several degrees.

'Nothing, Dad.' Jake stood up and patted his tummy. 'I've helped Beth to eat her scones.'

'How kind of you. I bet she was struggling on her own.' His brown eyes met hers for a second, amusement glinting.

'Hi Simon.' She got to her feet and held out a hand. 'It's good to see you again.'

'Aye.' She could feel callouses against her palm as he squeezed her fingers. 'Just thought I should say hello.' He appeared to be addressing his feet. 'And also . . .'

'Yes?'

'I'm sorry. For being so rude when I last saw you. When you gave Jake the Lego.'

'Oh, no.' Contrition surged through her. 'It's fine.'

He shook his head. 'That's kind, but – it wasn't fine. I'm sorry.'

'That's OK.' The silence thickened, threatening to drown them all.

'Well, we'd best let you settle in.' Simon reached out a hand to his son. 'Come on, Jake.'

'But . . .'

'No, lad. Time to go.'

'Oh.' The word was a protest. Jake's lower lip protruded as he reluctantly followed Simon down the steps. He turned at the bottom, his grin lighting up her day. 'Thanks for having me.'

'My pleasure.' She raised her hand. 'See you soon.'

'Tomorrow?'

'If that's OK with your dad.' Simon was nearly inside his cottage already. Despite his apology, he couldn't get away from her quickly enough, that much was clear.

'Dad?' Jake disappeared up his own back steps. 'Dad?'

Beth shut her door quietly and returned to the kitchen table. It seemed bigger without Jake. Sadder, too.

Time to start unpacking. She stood up, went to the bedroom and unzipped her case. She took out her speaker, placed it on the bedside table and turned The Killers up loud, the music powering her through unpacking socks and pants and shirts until she got to an official folder of papers at the bottom. She took it out – the records of her last year in a job that she had once loved; witness statements, rotas, testimonials, emails sent but ignored, evidence of her failure and of her guilt. Even looking at its brown cardboard cover made her start to shake. She quickly shoved the folder under the bed and moved onto the small white envelope zipped into a side pocket.

She picked it up, holding her breath, and tipped its contents into the palm of her hand. A gold band and a diamond engagement ring. That was all she had left of her marriage now. She was Beth Carlyle again, back to her maiden name, her social media shut down, a new phone number and a new email address too. She had run away, a child climbing beneath a tablecloth, closing her eyes and sticking her fingers in her ears. Disappearing was easier than dealing with the pain. It was easier than facing what she had lost.

Tears stung her eyes. She walked back to the window, staring out at the darkening sky, wishing she could go back and change what she had done that night. On the plane over here she had fooled herself that she could leave her guilt behind, but it had come with her, as real as her passport or her ticket or the bag she carried in her hand.

A sob escaped her just as she heard a clang from the next-door step.

Her eyes flicked towards the sound and she saw Simon, a bin lid in his hand, his face turned up towards her. Their eyes met. He took a step forward.

She saved him the trouble of saying anything by moving away.

She hoped he hadn't seen her tears.

She didn't want anyone here to know how close she was to falling apart.

8

Simon

'How was your first week at the farm?' Barney put a pint down in front of Simon.

'It was alright.' He and his dad hadn't argued, so maybe that counted as a win. His dad's only feedback all week had been that Simon needed to dig bigger holes for the fence posts on the lower field. He had made no comment on the quality of Simon's ploughing or the fact that he had fixed the kitchen window. Working at the farm made Simon feel like a teenager again, coming home bearing football trophies or athletics medals, only for his dad to sniff dismissively and start talking about his precious sheep.

It was money, though, that was what mattered. Simon picked up his pint and sank half of it in one go, stopping only because he was running out of breath. Then he drained the rest, putting the glass down emphatically on the table. 'I'm just glad it's the weekend.'

'Me too.' Barney ripped open a packet of pork scratchings and put it in the middle of the wooden table between them. 'Bloody SATs. Our Year 6s genuinely seem to think they are life and death. They're crying on rotation.'

'Poor little beggars.' Simon rolled the empty glass around in his hands. He needed something to connect with, something to touch. 'Do you remember the time we got stuck up on the Stacks and missed our maths GCSE?'

'Yeah.' Barney scratched his head ruefully. 'It was all your fault – twisting your ankle like that.'

'Only because you pushed me!'

'Still can't face the truth, eh?' Barney sucked air through his teeth. 'How's Jake?'

'Loving seeing Dad's dogs more often. I left him telling Beth next door all about them. He goes round to hers all the time. The two of them and Jean were having a right old chat on the back steps.'

'Oh aye?' Barney put his glass down. 'Deadly driver Beth? He's mates with her now, is he?'

'Yeah.' Simon swallowed. It was harder to be angry with her now that he had seen her crying. He heard her sometimes at night – the tap running in her kitchen in the small hours, when he was trying to find the energy to stop dozing on the sofa and take himself to bed.

'And you? Are you friends with her too?'

'No.' Simon shook his head. 'Not friends.'

'But . . .?'

'Not enemies either.'

'That's good, seeing as you're neighbours and all.' Barney clapped his hands together. 'Let's get more drinks in, then. Celebrate.'

'Celebrate?' Simon eyed his friend, puzzled. 'Celebrate what?'

'All will be revealed.' Barney's eyes danced.

'In for a big night, boys?' Betty the barmaid had come to clear their glasses, her bubblegum-pink hair piled up on top of her head. She joked that she had been working here since time began and she dyed her hair a different colour to mark the dawn of each new year. When she hit her fiftieth anniversary she was going to shave it all off for charity.

'Always.' Barney raised his eyebrows suggestively.

'Don't you get cheeky with me, lad.' She pointed a finger. 'I used to babysit you. I could blackmail you from here to Christmas.'

'You wouldn't do that to me, Betty, would you?' Barney pressed his palms together as if in prayer.

'Don't test me.' Betty skilfully stacked glasses against her shoulder. 'And don't take the mick with this lovely lady of yours either.'

Barney stood up. 'Evening, gorgeous.'

Betty turned to the new arrival. 'Lina. You brave girl. You've got a lot on your hands with this one.'

'Don't I know it? Hi Simon.' Lina's cheek was cool against his as she kissed him.

'Hi Lina.'

She slid in beside Barney on the opposite side of the table, dark hair pulled straight back from her face, a chunky gold necklace around her throat. She shrugged off her leather jacket and kissed Barney hello. They looked so perfect together. She was Barney's thunderbolt, his strike of Cupid's arrow, his one and only. Simon had introduced them at his birthday drinks just over two years ago, and they were living together within six months. After a lifetime of mocking romantic comedies, Barney started living one. He bought flowers, he left notes taped to the fridge or the dashboard of her car, he missed football matches for anniversary weekends away, he put Lina first.

And she was flying. While Simon's career had languished, hers was flourishing. Once, he had been her mentor; now she was doing his old job, leading the care of the elderly physio team at the local general hospital, while he was shovelling shit on his dad's farm.

Simon wondered if he would ever feel proud of himself again. He shifted in his seat, conscious of sweat pooling beneath his arms, wishing he had worn a T-shirt that hadn't got quite so small. He moved his chair closer to the table, trying to tuck his belly underneath so it couldn't be seen.

'How are you, Lina?' Small talk. He could do that.

'Great.' She was looking at Barney, stars in her eyes. Their love encircled them; private, alive. 'Really great, actually.'

'That's good.'

She tore herself away from Barney's gaze. 'And you?'

'Alright, yeah.' She was waiting politely, but that was all he had.

Jake was happy, that was the main thing. He didn't seem to be worrying about what was coming in December – the operation, the pain – he was just hell-bent on playing football and building a Lego spaceship to complete his fleet. That, and getting Simon a girlfriend. The lollipop lady was the latest candidate – Simon liked her well enough for a greeting and a chat, but he didn't want to date someone whose main ambition was to own a boa constrictor.

'Simon, mate?' Barney was staring at him, head on one side. 'Are you alright?'

'Yeah.' Simon blinked his way back into the crowded pub. His head swam as he stood up. 'Yeah. I'm fine. More drinks all round, yeah?'

He pushed his chair back, nearly sending Betty flying as she chatted to some farmers on the next table. By the time he'd finished apologising he was the colour of a letter box, needing to move, to get away from the fears crowding into his mind.

He gripped the bar with both hands, trying to stop them shaking. He stared down at the red patterned carpet until he got served, wondering if he would ever feel as if he was getting anything right; if he would ever see himself the way that Tamsin had once seen him, on a Thai beach long ago. There had been stars in her eyes once too.

Here he was again, harking back. This was his first night out in weeks and he didn't intend to waste it. He ordered drinks and carried them back to the table, weaving carefully between wagging tails and muddy walking boots.

He put the tray down and messaged Jean to see if Jake was OK. He stared at the moving dots until he got a message back saying *Of course he is, you daft bugger.*

'Thanks, mate.' Barney passed Lina her drink. Their looks were intimate, complicit. Simon wondered if they'd rather he wasn't here. He looked away, eyes darting around the pub. In one corner a farmer shook out his paper, head bowed as his finger traced the racing results. A family tucked into fish and chips over by the bar.

He reached for his glass.

Relax, Simon.

His neck got tighter still.

'We wanted to talk to you.' Lina was at her most earnest, leaning towards him. 'About a couple of things, actually.'

'Like what?'

'Well, first up, Barney would like to ask you something.' They even smiled in unison nowadays. Simon looked at them – so bright, so gleaming, so lit up from within. How he missed there being someone on his side of the table too.

'Yes?'

Barney looked uncharacteristically nervous, his eyes landing on the table, the chair, Lina's watch.

Simon started to worry.

'What is it, mate? Are you OK?'

Barney put a hand on his arm. 'I'm good, mate. Really good. But I was just wondering . . .' His smile could fire up a barbecue in a rainstorm. 'If you'd like to be my best man?'

'Best man?' Simon paused, his glass halfway to his mouth.

'Yeah.' Barney was clutching Lina's hand.

'You want me to be your best man?' Simon put his glass down. Safer.

'Yeah.'

'You mean you . . .'

'Popped the question? Yes.' Barney beamed. 'And she said yes!'

So this was what joy felt like. Simon had forgotten the rush, the thrill.

'Oh my God, amazing! I'm so happy for you both. And of course I'd love to.' He leant over and kissed Lina, patting Barney's back at the same time. The pork scratch-ings did not come out of it well and their pints nearly went flying.

'Congratulations!' Simon put his hand to his mouth. 'Wow, I can't believe this. Best news ever.' He sat back down, raising his pint. 'Cheers. And it's all thanks to me.'

Lina nudged Barney. 'Told you he'd say that.'

'It's true, isn't it?' Simon put his glass down. 'Without me, you wouldn't be sitting here, all loved up and – bloody hell – *engaged*!'

Barney sat back against the oak settle. 'You know what, mate? I'll let you have that one. I'll even let you have a proper gloat in your speech.'

Shit. The speech.

He could worry about that later. 'When's the wedding?'

'We've booked the church for December, and guess where we're going for our honeymoon?'

'Where?'

'Mauritius!'

'No way.' Barney had been wanting to go to Mauritius since he was a teenager.

'I know, I know!' Barney drummed his hands against the table, buzzing with energy. 'We've been saving for ages, and then I found this amazing deal. Two weeks. One time only offer. A luxury resort, poolside villa, right next to the beach. And as much diving as we want. I cannot WAIT.'

'Wow.' Simon suppressed his stab of envy. His last 'holiday' had been to London, when he had run there to find Tamsin all those years ago. He had gone to every place she had mentioned, every address he could recall

98

but he hadn't even seen a glimpse of her. Not a breath of her perfume, not even one tiny fragment of hope.

Barney was waiting for his reaction. 'Mauritius!' Simon high-fived his friend. 'That is bloody great.' His mind snagged on Miss Maya telling him that Jake's operation was very likely to be in December. He told himself not to be silly. It would all work out. For sure.

Lina watched him, head on one side. 'Are you OK?'

'Yes, yes.' Another thing to worry about later. Simon pushed it to one side, swallowing more beer and raising his glass to them again. 'Here's to you.'

'I told you he'd cry.' Barney rolled his eyes, but Simon could see that he was wiping something from his cheek too.

Lina's hand lay in Barney's, reminding Simon of the way Tamsin's had once been glued to his, before the scan that changed everything. After that awful silence as the sonographer stared at the screen, searching for half a heart that wasn't there, nothing had been the same. The box room that was going to be the nursery remained half-painted. Tamsin had not wanted to buy any baby clothes, no nappies, no tiny hairbrush, no crib. There was no pram in the hallway, no car seat, no bottles. She had turned inwards, bracing herself for the worst – knowing that there was a strong chance that Jake would die in surgery before he was one week old.

Tamsin had blamed herself: the cocktails she had drunk before she realised she was pregnant; the fast food she had eaten; the time she had tripped over a kerbstone and landed on her belly – reason after unlikely reason was plucked from her memory and made fact. It didn't matter what the doctors had said. It didn't matter how much Simon told her that it might be his genes that had led to the diagnosis. The rage on her face as she screamed at him that it was *her* body, *her* fault. The fury in her was like nothing he had ever seen. From the minute the scan was over she withdrew behind an ever-thickening wall of anger and self-hatred, and there was nothing he could do to penetrate it. He would always blame himself for not finding a way to help her – he would always think that he could have done more.

Simon swallowed. He had to cheer up, for God's sake. Tonight was their night. He wasn't going to ruin it.

'So, your stag is in my hands, is it?'

'Yeah. Three nights in Amsterdam, please.'

Simon's face fell. 'Um. OK. I . . .'

Barney laughed. 'Only joking! One night in Blackpool will do me. I want to save my cash for Mauritius!'

Simon exhaled. 'Great.'

'Oh, and I've got loads of cricket matches coming up, then it's the football season again, so it'll have to be soon.' Barney shrugged. 'Not that I'm a diva, or anything.'

'No.' Simon gave an exaggerated roll of his eyes. 'Not at all.' He clapped his hands together. 'Consider yourself sorted.' He could do this. It might even be fun. He might still be really good at organising a massive night out; he had done it all the time when he was younger. He had always been the one ringing everyone up, sorting out venues, arranging group discounts. He was starting to make a list in his head when his phone buzzed and panic spiralled as he instantly imagined something was wrong with Jake.

It was just a message from his mobile phone company warning him he was nearly over his data limit.

He really needed to chill out.

'Hey. Simon. Focus.' Lina clicked her fingers in front of his face. 'There's one more thing.'

'What? More great news? Yes. Bring it on.'

'No.' She shook her head so hard her earrings danced. 'Nothing like that. I just wondered . . .' She chewed her lip. 'Whether you want to . . .'

'What?'

She smiled. 'Come back and work with us again? At the hospital?'

He thought he'd misheard.

'You what?'

'We've got a few vacancies coming up, and we all want you back. Would you – maybe . . .' Her leg was jiggling up and down, just as it had when he had interviewed her for her first job. She must be really nervous. 'Think about it? You could do supervised hours till you get your registration back, and we could be really flexible on shifts.'

Her question touched him, but he couldn't say yes. Jake came first. End of. He had tried to carry on when Tamsin had left, but Jake's health, or lack of it, meant Simon had been late or absent so frequently that he wasn't the physiotherapist his patients needed him to be. They deserved better, so he had done the right thing and resigned.

'You're very kind, Lina, but I can't.'

'Why not?' Her dark eyes clouded and he was touched

by how much she had wanted him to say yes. Barney leant forwards, clearly keen to persuade him too. It was too much, just for him. Too much kindness. He didn't deserve it.

Besides, this was their night. Simon didn't want to bring them down.

He shook his head. 'Thanks, Lina, but Jake needs me. And you need a team which is one hundred percent reliable. That's not me. Not any more. So – it's kind of you – but no thanks. Now. More drinks? Then we can chat about what happened the last time that fiancé of yours wore a tuxedo.'

Simon stood up and walked to the bar again before they could answer. He was trembling. He hated remembering what he had been, back when he was doing a fulfilling job where he had felt useful and learnt something every day. It was easier just to pretend life had always been this way – to accept reality. He had a wonderful son. That was what mattered.

He leant against the bar, aware of their concern following him, searching and nudging, trying to find a way to help. He stared at the row of optics gleaming behind Betty and wished that he had someone next to him, someone to talk to, someone who understood.

He wished he had Tamsin. Over six years gone and still he wanted her. She had sent no letters. She had written no emails. She hadn't even called.

Yet still she was the hole in his heart.

She was the one he would run to.

No wonder his dad thought he was soft.

Summer

Emily!!!

Here's a bluebell I picked for you. I know you love them. I went to the woods today with Dad and paddled in the stream. It was awesome but I missed you. You make everything more fun.

The Plan isn't working. The women I talk to don't seem keen, and Dad keeps getting all cross and weird. I think I know what the problem is, so I'm moving onto Phase 2. It'll be hard, but I'm going to wait till he's asleep and do it then. I've bought everything I need. I'll let you know how it goes.

Love,
Jake xxx

9

Beth

Beth woke to a yell. For a second she thought she was back in New York and that Tyler had passed out to one of his favourite cop dramas. She forced her gritty eyes open, mouth dry, exhaustion weighing her down. Even here, in her quiet cottage, sleep was still eluding her.

She closed her eyes again. Just five more minutes . . .

She heard a crash.

Jake. Before she was fully awake she was pushing herself off her bed, crossing the living room, opening the back door and running down the steps. She had no idea what time it was or what day it was. All she knew was that she had to see if she could help.

She sprinted up the other side, banging on the back door with her hand to announce her presence. It was open.

'Is everything OK?' Her eyes darted around the room. She saw a mess of papers piled up on the coffee table, toy cars all over the floor, and Simon hopping around the room with half his eyebrow missing and blood dripping down his T-shirt.

'What happened? Did someone break in?'

'If only.' Simon swore as his foot collided with a table leg.

His face looked different. Lopsided. It took her a moment to work out why.

Half his beard had gone. She took a step towards him, only for her bare toes to land on a long, lank ponytail that was lying on the floor. She squealed and hopped to the side, landing on Jake, who was holding a razor aloft as if it was a murder weapon.

'Jake, are you OK?' She turned to him, checking for injuries.

'He's fine!' Simon grimaced. 'It's me who's bleeding.'

'Let me have a look.' She stepped towards him, but he turned away with a moan. A battered green Heineken tray lay on the floor next to the sofa, covered with scissors, shaving foam and a mirror.

Simon turned back. 'I look even worse now, don't I?' He turned to his son. 'What were you thinking?'

'I was giving you a makeover.' Jake was close to tears. 'I just thought it was time people could see your smile, but you woke up before . . .'

'Before you could slash the other half of my face?' Simon rolled his eyes to the ceiling. 'Didn't it occur to you that I liked my beard? That I was happy it was there?'

'I wanted to . . .'

'Well, just for once, maybe life isn't about what you want, Jake.'

Beth watched him, this giant of a man, head lowered, hands on his hips and felt a sharp pang of sympathy.

'I was trying to help.' Jake's lower lip was trembling

now. 'Loads of people say you'd look better if you got rid of your beard.' He folded his arms and slid down the wall, lip jutting defiantly, a tear splashing onto his Lego pyjamas.

Simon went over to his boy, visibly controlling himself. 'You could have asked me first.'

'You'd just have said no.' The last word was a sob.

Simon threw his arms around his son, absorbing his sadness and making it his own. Beth stood by the window, staring up at the early morning mist on the peaks above. She could feel the love in this room, as radiant as any sunrise, as strong as the granite that ran beneath the fells.

When the sobs became sniffs, Simon pulled away. 'It's alright, Jake. I'm sure I can sort it out.'

This she could help with. She turned. 'Why don't you let me finish it off?'

Hope returned to Jake's face as Simon took a step back.

'No.' He held up his hands, fending her off. 'No. I couldn't ask you to do that.'

'It's no bother.' She inched forwards. It was like approaching a wounded animal – baby steps. Gentle voice. Kindness.

'No. I can do it myself.' He put a hand up to the back of his head, his expression dissolving into panic again. 'Where's all my hair gone?'

She pointed to the ponytail on the floor, trying to think of something positive to say. 'It'll grow back . . .?'

'Not for years.' Simon was tapping around the top of his head, as if still hoping to find it. 'Oh God. I've been growing that for ages.'

Beth rallied. 'Your hair looks good though.' She smiled at him. 'If you cut it a bit more you could look just like Justin Bieber? You know?'

'Are you mad? I'm a 35-year-old single dad. What would I be doing trying to look like Justin Bieber?' Simon looked like he might be about to cry.

Beth needed to take some action.

'At least let me stop the bleeding. Your poor face. I'll be back in a second.'

She ducked back to her cottage, getting plasters and antiseptic cream, plus clean cotton wool to absorb the blood.

'OK, just sit down here.' She hastily kicked the pony-tail under the sofa, where it curled up like an abandoned slug. It made her feel slightly queasy.

Simon sat down slowly on the sofa.

'Is it really only 7:30 a.m?' He looked around him, dazed. 'I must have fallen asleep on the sofa last night. Next thing I knew, Mr Makeover was looming over me.'

'Dad. I told you. I was trying to . . .'

'Help. I know, Jake.' Simon nodded wearily. 'I know.'

'Can you keep still for a sec?' Beth held out the cotton wool. 'I'm just going to apply pressure to your cheek for a bit.'

She pressed her hand to the long gash running along Simon's cheekbone, suddenly aware that she was only wearing a Disneyland nightshirt and minimal cotton shorts. Simon's skin was warm, his breath rapid. His eyes looked away from her and she could see sweat beading on his brow.

'Relax, Simon. I don't bite.'

'I know.' His brown eyes met hers for a second, and then slid away. 'I think I'm in shock.' He nearly managed a smile.

'OK.' She tapped a plaster down gently over his cut and turned her attention to the rest of him. 'Now, your face. I can get things evened out for you. If you'd like?'

Simon stood up. 'I can just do it myself.'

She grabbed his wrist and held his hand up. 'Not with shakes like that. You might lose an ear.' She pushed him gently down onto the sofa. 'Pass me the razor, Jake.'

He did so, and she dabbled it in the mug of water on the tray until it was clean. Then she squirted the shaving foam into her hand, before rubbing it all over what remained of Simon's beard.

'Wow, Jake. You trimmed first and everything! You're such a pro.' She wanted to bring his smile back. The cottage felt colder without it.

Jake hovered at her shoulder, fingers twisting in and out of each other. 'Dad does sleep for England. That helped. And I looked it all up on YouTube first. You can look anything up on there. Did you know that, Beth?' He spoke with all the earnestness of a vicar delivering a sermon.

'I did.' She held the blade just above Simon's face. She was so close to him she could see the pulse flickering in the hollow of his throat. The last time she had been this close to a man she had been married to him. She forced the thought away, bending over Simon, lowering the blade. She ran it along his skin, seeing the dark hairs coming away until there was a clear stripe of skin, feeling a surge of satisfaction as his cheekbone emerged, then the other half of his chin. She swept the blade down until she could see the whole of him. His skin was white but clear. His eyes looked deep into hers, the way Tyler's had when he placed his hand gently at the nape of her neck and drew her close.

'Please don't stop now.' Simon's voice brought her back to the present. The blade was held high, away from him. Her lips were only inches from his. 'I'll look even more crazy.'

'Sorry.' She bent to her work, tongue sticking out between her teeth, as she removed line after line of hair. 'That's you done.' She stood back to admire her work.

'Wow.' She was staring too hard, but she couldn't stop. 'You look . . .'

'What?' There was a fresh gleam of panic in Simon's eyes. 'Do I look even worse? Oh God.'

'No, no.' She put her hand on his arm. 'You look great.' He really owed Jake a favour. She could see his broad nose now, the strength of his upper lip, the hollows beneath his cheekbones.

Jake was next to her. 'She's right, Dad. You look awesome! You look like that guy off *Corrie*.'

Simon's brow furrowed. 'Which one? Not Mike Barlow?'

'No. The other one.'

At last Simon smiled. 'I look like the other one. I'll take that.' He put his hand on his son's head, pulling him close for a hug. 'Just no more surprises, alright? What's with you at the moment? Is this another "get me a girlfriend" thing?'

'No.' Jake's eyes retreated to the carpet and Beth could see that Jake had his fingers crossed behind his back.

Simon looked unconvinced but let it lie.

He turned back to Beth. 'I don't suppose you do haircuts too?'

'No.' She shook her head. 'That is a step too far. Just give it a wash and get the clippers out.'

'Clippers?'

'Yeah. You know. The things that . . .'

She saw his grin. 'Oh. You're joking.'

'Yes.' He nodded. 'Believe it or not, I do have a sense of humour.'

She glanced up. 'Really?'

He shifted his weight from foot to foot. 'Yeah.'

The silence between them grew. Beth found herself blushing.

'Hey.' Jake glared up at his dad. 'I'm the funny one, not you.'

'Are you, lad? Are you?' His dad started to tickle him under the armpits.

'No. Stop!'

'Stop what?'

Jake was cackling in seconds and soon Simon had lifted him right off the ground, turning him upside down so Jake was hanging, head down. Simon's eyes shone as he laughed with his son. Beth remembered how it had felt when her dad had looked at her like that. As comforting as sliding on a woolly glove on a cold day. The warmth spreading through her, the confidence of being loved.

She should leave them to it.

'I'm off running.'

Neither of them heard her.

'Bye.' She moved towards the door.

'Wait!' Jake called her back as Simon deposited him on the sofa. He wriggled up and went to the kitchen. 'I forgot the best bit!'

He picked up a bottle of something, ran to Simon, and sprayed it liberally all over his face.

'Arrrrrgggghhh.' Simon's face twisted in agony. A musky smell clouded the air, reminding Beth of teenage discos and desperation. Simon clapped his hands to his cheeks.

'What's wrong now?' Jake shifted from foot to foot.

Simon leapt around the room and Beth got a strong urge to giggle. 'I think you may have used a bit too much aftershave, Jake.' She discreetly opened the window.

Simon ran to the kitchen and stuck his head under the tap.

'Aaaaaahhhhhhh.' Water ran all over his face and head. 'That's better.'

Now Beth did giggle. Simon stood there, dripping, with his stained T shirt and plastered face. Her laughter swelled within her until she couldn't stop, and she was bent over, hands on her knees, body shaking.

'Sorry.' She flapped a hand in ineffectual apology. 'Sorry.'

Jake had started too. 'You do look pretty funny.'

Now Simon joined in.

And, just like that, he felt like a friend.

Beth pulled herself together first. 'Well, this has been . . .'

She was overcome by another wave of laughter. 'Good. But I'd better . . .'

Jake stopped her. 'Did you say you were going running? Just now?'

'Yep.'

Jake's smile was sly. 'Dad can show you a route, if you like. He knows the fells like the back of his hand.'

Simon gulped. 'I don't run any more. Sorry. Anyway, I've got you to look after, haven't I, Jake?'

'Well, you can go tomorrow evening, then? Jean asked me round. She wants me to show her how "the Facebook" works.' Jake's little chest puffed with pride.

'What do you know about Facebook? You're only seven.' Simon frowned.

'Oh come on, Dad. Everybody knows how it works.'

Simon's mouth opened and closed. He had clearly had enough shocks for one morning. He turned back to Beth. 'I don't know where my trainers are . . .'

'They're here.' Jake dived into the cupboard below the window. 'See?'

Simon's face was pure four-letter word. 'But . . .'

Beth gave him an out. 'If you don't want to that's fine. I can just go round the lake.'

Jake's smile was full of mischief. 'Go on, Dad.' He pulled a face. 'She might get lost if you're not there.'

Simon looked like a man facing the gallows. 'OK, then. See you tomorrow?'

'See you tomorrow.'

Simon started hunting through cereal packets. 'OK, Jake. Brekkie. What's your pleasure?'

As she headed down the back steps, Beth found herself smiling. She was still grinning as she drove to work an hour later, a piece of toast in her hand. She thought about Simon's face as he plunged it underneath the tap. About his dry humour. About the curves and planes of his face.

About how kind his smile was, now that she could see it.

10

Simon

Beth was very fast.

Simon's only hope when they had set off was that she would find the fells too steep, but that didn't seem to be the case. When he had seen her going in and out of her cottage in her nurse's uniform, always so careful as she checked her bag, she hadn't struck him as quick on her feet. Now he was rapidly learning how wrong he had been.

'This way?' She turned, jerking her thumb towards the winding path up through the woods. She was jogging on the spot, her white trainers beating a regular rhythm against the ground. He wished she would stop and take advantage of the bench to their left. He would throw himself down onto it weeping, if only his pride would let him.

'Yeah. That way.' He put his hands on his hips, leaning forward, his lungs feeling like they were about to burst. It took him a moment to realise they were at the very spot where he had proposed to Tamsin on Jake's first birthday. He still couldn't bear to remember the pain on her face as she had run away from him, Jake strapped to her chest, leaving Simon with his carefully prepared picnic – tiny cream cheese sandwiches, mini pork pies and strawberries from the farm at the head of the lake. Simon had no appetite once she had left, so he had carried everything back down to the cottage, the ring burning a hole in his pocket, only to find her back in the bed which had become her haven, curtains closed, her tears soaking the pillow. Jake was howling in the cot beside her, tiny fists pumping as he begged to be noticed.

Tamsin's voice had been so quiet. So flat. A world away from the girl who had sung in the Thai waves at sunrise. 'I was about to feed him. I just . . .'

'I'll do it.' Simon had lifted the tiny body onto his shoulder, breathing in the fresh baby smell that always quickened his heart.

Tamsin glanced over her shoulder. 'He's much happier with you, anyway. Aren't you, baby?' For a moment Simon wondered if she would take Jake, cuddle him into her, the way Simon always hoped she would.

Instead she turned her head away, drawing up her knees, succumbing to tears again.

A week later she disappeared.

It had taken him twelve months to sell the ring.

'Are you OK?' Beth was peering at him, her wide brown eyes alive with concern. 'You look – weird.'

'Do I?' He exhaled. It was just a hillside. Dry-stone walls, grass, ragged patches of heather. Rain and winds had long washed any trace of that day away. If only his memory could do the same.

Beth waited, her head on one side. Simon tried to smile. 'Well, maybe I look weird now you can actually see my face after Jake's makeover attempt.' He had gone to the village shop for milk this morning and the owner had barely recognised him. 'I get a shock every time I look in the mirror.'

'Well, I think you look great.' Her eyes met his, clear and honest.

'Thanks.' He was unused to compliments, keen to kick them away like a football from an opposing player.

'Let's go then, shall we?' She threw this back over her shoulder as she turned and ran onwards along the path. The gradient increased and stones rattled beneath his feet as he lumbered after her, telling his screaming muscles to keep going and knowing they would get their revenge later on. As his chest heaved he reflected that, if he did keel over, at least he was with someone who could take care of him.

The woods were at their best today. The sunlight dappled through the trees, the brook bubbled happily below them, and the path beneath his trainers was springy to his step. Jake loved it here, on the days he had enough energy to climb this high. Simon could see him here now, hand in hand with Emily, determinedly making their way to their Best Friend Kingdom – a group of wide flat stones arranged in a curving path across the water. They had claimed it as their own as soon as they were old enough to talk.

Above him Beth was opening up the distance between them. She only came up to his shoulder but her legs moved ten times as fast as his, and he suddenly realised that he had spent the last few seconds staring at her bum in its tight blue leggings. He looked hastily around, embarrassed, but their only companion was a pregnant ewe, who was far more interested in scratching her back on a tree trunk than in judging him.

Simon ran on. His legs ached, his heart was racing, but somehow he felt at peace, free from his daily worries about cashflow or Jake. Beth didn't ask anything of him. The movement of her arms as she maintained her steady pace was oddly soothing, and he found himself finding a rhythm that saw him making it up to the edge of the wood without collapsing for the first time in years.

Beth took a long drink from her bottle and then zipped it back in her pocket. She ran a hand through her short hair.

'Is this a . . .?' He was pleased to see that at last she was breaking a sweat. He was ninety percent dripping now.

'Kissing gate? Yeah.' They both stared at the weathered brown gate, surrounded by curved stone designed for a lover's embrace. He remembered Tamsin, laughing back at him, in those magical early days of her pregnancy, her red hair glinting as she waited for his lips to touch hers.

'Cute.' Beth pushed her way through the gate and ran on. Great. Now he had to follow.

She was already metres ahead. 'Do we just carry on up?'

'Yeah.' The slope was almost vertical. He might actually collapse. 'But – I mean – you can carry on without me. I've got a – a . . .' *Come on, brain.* 'I've got a stone in my shoe. You head on up.'

Please say yes, please say yes.

She jogged back to him. 'I don't think Jake would be very happy about that, do you?'

'Yeah, but . . .' He could pretend no longer. 'I . . .'

She saved him. 'I like walking too. And if I'm honest I'm knackered.'

'Thank God.' He let himself fall to the ground where he lay, limbs singing, staring up at the clouds billowing across the sky, casting rolling shadows onto the ground beneath. 'You were starting to seem like the bionic woman.'

He heard a low giggle and she flopped down beside him, stretching out like a starfish against the grass. She seemed younger, with the sun and a smile on her face. There was a mischief to her that he would never have imagined the morning they had met.

She looked at him, laughing. 'To be honest my legs were in trouble by the time we got to the end of the lane, but there was no way I was telling you that.'

'I wish you had. I won't be able to walk for a week.'

The breeze cooled him. He had got out of the habit of coming up here since Tamsin left. They had explored these hills together – he hadn't wanted to be up here without her.

Beth leant up on one elbow, absently plucking handfuls of grass.

'Jake's great, isn't he? So determined. With the makeover thing?'

'Hmmmm.' Simon grimaced.

She rolled on to her stomach, brow furrowed. 'You know he asked me if I was single?'

Simon groaned. 'Oh Christ, he didn't, did he?'

There was that smile again, warming her delicate features. 'Yeah, he did. Don't worry, though. I told him I wasn't interested.'

'Oh. Wow.' He looked back up at the sky. 'Don't hold back.'

'No, no, no!' She put her hand to her mouth. 'I mean, I'm not interested in *any* relationship. Not you. I mean, you're great. Really.'

The more she talked the worse it got.

'Oh God.' She was pressing her forehead with her hand now. 'I'm sorry.'

He decided it was time to let her off the hook. 'It's OK, Beth. I was winding you up. I know what you meant.'

'You did?' Her face cleared. 'Well, why didn't you bloody say something then?'

He raised an eyebrow. 'It was hard to get a word in.'

'Touché.' She grinned and stood up. 'Come on.'

'You're not making me run again, are you?'

'No chance.' She puffed out her cheeks. 'But a walk, maybe? To warm down? Go on. Show me the sights. I love being off the beaten track like this. It reminds me of my parents. My dad prided himself on his collection of Ordnance Survey maps.'

'A true fanatic.'

'Yeah.' She twisted her zip between her fingers. 'He loved it here.'

'Are they going to come and visit? Your parents?'

'No.' Beth dug into the ground with the tip of her

trainer. 'Dad died. And Mum said she'd never come back here now he's gone. Too painful.'

'I'm so sorry.' Simon saw the clench of grief across her face. 'It's the hardest thing, isn't it? Missing a parent like that.'

'You too?' Her eyes searched his.

'My mum died when I was fifteen.' He blinked, remembering the morning they had taken her body away. The rain. The long, dark car. His dad, stiff and silent. Her empty chair.

'I'm so sorry, Simon.' He felt a flicker of understanding pass between them. Her hand hovered in the air as if to console him, before falling back to her side.

She chewed her lip for a second. 'We're a right pair of miseries, aren't we?'

'Yeah. Jake was right – he really is the funny one.' Simon followed as she started walking again.

'So, have you always lived here, Simon?'

'Born and raised.' He fell into step beside her.

'Ever left?'

'Yeah. For a bit. Uni and stuff. Thailand, for a bit. But my heart's always been here.'

She came to an abrupt halt as they reached the crest of the hill. 'Wow. I can see why.'

Below them the fells dropped away into a wooded valley, rich with green and gold, the lake smooth as glass at the bottom.

'It's not bad, is it?' Simon stood next to her.

'It's amazing.' She nodded, clearly lost in her memories. 'Dad would have loved this view.'

He saw the way her mouth was tugging downwards and wanted to cheer her. 'How about you, Beth? Jake says you lived in New York?'

'Yeah.' Her voice was a dead end.

He took the hint. Subject change required.

'And did you always want to be a nurse?'

That was better. She brightened. 'Yeah. Since my dad died. The people who looked after him were incredible.' Her eyes traced the rolling lines of the hills. 'I wanted to be like them. For a while I thought I was.'

'I bet you're just as great as them.'

She didn't answer.

'And you love it? Your job?'

'Yes.' That darkness again. Whatever she was thinking about, it wasn't something she wanted to share.

Distraction. That might work. 'Want to see my old secret hideout?' He beckoned to her. 'It's just up here.'

'Yes please.' Her face was alive again. 'Lead the way.'

They were navigating steep scree now as he led the way over the top of the ridge towards the woodland beyond. Sheep stood either side of them, chewing on the grass, their balance as effortless as his was clumsy. He heard a squeal and whipped round to see Beth sliding halfway down the slope. She lay, arms flailing. 'Shit.'

He ran forwards and grabbed her by the hand. 'Are you OK?'

'Yeah.' She nodded, and he was relieved to see her push her way up. 'This place is wild.'

'I think you can handle it.'

'I might need to acclimatise.' Beth stood up tentatively.

'I'm used to subways and pavements. I feel kind of – exposed here. It's so quiet. Sometimes I love it, but sometimes . . .' That heaviness was back, a curtain pulled across a sunny window.

'Come on.' He started walking again, not wanting to intrude too much. She would tell him her story when and if she wanted to. 'We're close now.' He ducked past some windblown trees, trunks dry, their sparse leaves clinging to spindly branches, before dropping down into a grassy hollow below a dry-stone wall. The trees petered out below them, leaving an unfettered view of the lake and the hills beyond.

'If we tuck ourselves down – here – then . . .' He pulled her down next to him. 'We have the whole world at our feet.'

'It's beautiful.' She sat, hands hugging her knees, staring out at the hills rolling endlessly away, green, brown and grey. Above them a kestrel circled. Beneath them the land sloped into infinity. 'This is amazing.'

He felt a beat of pride. Pride in his land; pride in his home.

'Ouch. Cramp.' She put both hands round her ankle.

'Let me help.'

'Oh, no it's fine.'

'Please? I know what I'm doing.'

'OK.' Curiosity was stamped across her face as he shuffled round in front of her, taking her ankle in both hands and resting it on his knees. He massaged gently, finding out where the tension was coming from, pressing deep with his thumbs. Her skin was soft and smooth above her sock. 'How's that?'

'Hey.' She lay back on her elbows. 'You're really good at that.'

'Thanks. It's been a while.'

'I'd never know.'

A glow started deep in his chest. 'I used to be a physio.'

'Well, you must have been a good one!'

He manipulated the joint for a second or two longer. 'Stretch your ankle out now. Try rotating it?' He put it down on the grass.

She slowly did as she was told. She nodded, clearly impressed. 'Wow. You've got game.'

'Thanks.' He moved back to her side.

'So why did you stop working as a physio? To work with your dad? To help him out on the farm? That's good of you.'

No, it wasn't. He could feel himself shrivelling. He had liked the way she had looked at him just now, her eyes alight with admiration.

He scuffed his shoe against the ground. 'It wasn't exactly a choice.' He opened his mouth to explain but she got there first.

'Is it about Jake? Fitting work around his treatment?'

'Yeah.' He still felt a sting of shame, like he had given up too quickly on the career he had loved.

Beth nodded. 'It must be hard enough being a single dad anyway – much harder with a condition like Jake's in the mix. All that worry. It takes its toll.'

Simon plucked a handful of grass. 'I don't know life any other way.'

'Sure, but the pressure must be huge.'

He liked the way she said it. Calm. Factual. None of the dramatic sympathy he experienced from parents at school, with their wide eyes and soap opera gasps. *Oh my God, I don't know how you do it.*

'It's tough at times, yeah.' He rarely admitted this out loud. Five little words reaching across the space between them.

'Jake told me about his mum leaving.'

'He did?' Simon glanced at her, surprised. 'He normally makes up tall stories when people ask – says she's a war reporter or a princess.'

'I didn't ask.' Beth flicked a piece of grass off her leg. 'Jake just told me.'

'That makes sense. You're very easy to talk to.' Simon flushed, feeling he might have said too much.

'Thanks.' Their eyes met. 'You are too.'

Simon looked away first. 'I don't even know where she is. Tamsin, I mean.'

Beth rubbed her nose with the tips of her fingers. Everything about her was neat, from her perfectly arched brows to the way her hair tapered at the nape of her neck. 'You're not in touch, then?'

'Not since she left.'

She watched him, silent. He braced himself for further questions, but instead she pulled out a tube of Rolos from her pocket.

'Want some?'

'Yes please.' She tipped a couple into his palm and he chewed eagerly, caramel and chocolate rich on his tongue. Both of his had gone before she'd even finished her first.

He dug his nail into the flesh of his thumb, wanting to tell her more. 'Tamsin got very low, you see. Postnatal depression. She was on meds, but they didn't seem to help. All the hospital stuff with Jake – it was a lot.' He bit his lip. 'It's my fault. I should have done more. I should have worked it out.'

'Worked what out?'

'How to help.'

'Sometimes people don't want you to help.'

Beth spoke as if she knew. He remembered the tears on her face the evening she had moved in, the press of her palms against the glass.

She carried on. 'Do you miss her?'

'Yes.' He sighed.

'I'm sorry.'

'Me too.'

Beth folded her arms. 'Jake seems happy, anyway. He loves that toy duck she got him.'

'Yeah,' Simon shifted uneasily. 'I said Superchick was from her, but . . .'

'Ah. I see.' She smiled. 'Nothing wrong with a white lie or two.'

Simon felt a weight lift. 'I just want him to know how much she loves him, even though she's not here. You know?'

'Yeah.' Beth chewed slowly. 'He's lucky to have you, Simon.'

'I'm all he's got, poor little sod. And he's all I have too.'

'He adores you.'

Simon shrugged. 'He hasn't got much choice, has he?

I wish he had her around too – his mum. I know he's missing out. I keep thinking she'll come back one day but my mates think I'm daft to keep hoping.'

'Maybe she will, maybe she won't. But you and Jake seem happy. You have a lot of fun – I can hear you laughing through the wall.'

He thought of Jake refusing to put his school uniform on or loudly protesting his way to bed. 'And screaming, I'm guessing.'

'Only occasionally.' She raised her eyebrows. 'You're only human, right?'

'Yeah.' He nodded. 'But I'm sorry if we disturb you.'

'No. I love it. Makes me feel less . . .' She stopped. 'Anyway. Jake's a lucky kid.'

'If you ignore the life-limiting heart condition?'

'Yes.' She flushed. 'Sorry.'

'No. I'm happy you forgot. I like the way you see him as Jake the boy, not Jake the invalid. Not many people do.'

Beth put the Rolos back in her pocket. 'He'll always be Jake the boy to me.' She zipped it up. 'At least while he keeps coming in and stealing my biscuits while I'm in the shower.' Her laugh bubbled and as soon as it stopped he wanted to hear it again.

'The cheeky little beggar. I'll have words.' He got to his feet, stretching.

She shook her head. 'Please don't. Got to admire his initiative, no?' She held out her hand. 'Can you help me up?'

'Of course.' Her fingers were warm in his.

She put her weight on her ankle, face clearing. 'You fixed it. I owe you one.' She started to walk unsteadily along the ridge. 'So, have you dated anyone at all? Since Tamsin?'

He pulled a face. 'Like anyone would want me. No, I'm with Jake. And he's with me. And that's the way it is.'

'Well, if you ever need help with him, I'm right there, you know.'

'Really?'

'Sure.' She shrugged. 'It's not like I've got a social life yet and he makes me laugh. I'd be happy to watch him for you if you ever have plans.'

'That's really kind of you. I'm sure Jake would love that.'

'OK.' She looked at him sideways. 'And – can I just ask? Do you want to be a physio again? One day?'

He hadn't thought about what he wanted for so long that he didn't immediately know the answer. He gazed at the sky, at the trees, at the birds wheeling in and out of the clouds.

The answer came to him. Clear as a summer sky.

'Yes. I'd love to.' There was no feeling like it – the joy when a patient managed a few hesitant steps after months of pain; the puzzle of how to strengthen a knee or heal a wrist; the light on a patient's face as hope began to dawn.

'You could do it, you know. If you wanted to.'

He felt a pulse of frustration. First Lina, now Beth. Enough. 'No, it's too . . .'

'Just think about it.' Her hand was light on his arm. 'You're really good at it, Simon. My ankle says so.'

Somehow, he believed her. Somehow, he knew he could trust her.

She smiled. 'And thanks to your skills, we can run home now, can't we?'

Shit.

'But . . .'

She was already off.

Simon tried to propel his legs into action, fired, for once, by the feeling that he had someone on his side. Running behind his new friend down the fell that he loved, he felt the lock on his narrow life click open, and the sunlight begin to shine.

11

Beth

'Beth!' Jas beckoned her into the crowded bar at The Crown. They had opened the doors so they led straight into the back garden, which had a prime view of Haystacks looming majestically above them. A river made its way down the dark green slopes and rocks carved jagged silhouettes against the evening sky.

'Here you go.' Jas indicated the chair next to her. 'Welcome to the Florence Rightingales.' Beth nodded round at various familiar faces from her team as she sat down, stowing her bag at her feet, glad to see a glass of wine ready and waiting.

'Well done for coming.' Jas squeezed her arm. 'I wasn't sure you would.'

'Me neither.' Beth had called Jas that morning, after another sleepless night, when she realised that she wasn't going to get through her wedding anniversary without her friend's help. She had sobbed down the phone, using tissue after tissue as she relived the magical day three years ago when she had become Tyler's wife: her excitement as she slid on her ivory silk dress, the love on his face as he turned towards her, the intensity in his blue eyes as he made his vows. Then champagne on a hotel rooftop with family and friends, hot dogs and ice cream at dusk, their laughter still ringing out as the bright lights of Manhattan appeared below them. Tyler's hand had barely left hers, and she had never been more sure of herself, more confident, more loved.

It was all gone now. All that remained were two rings in a drawer and a stark white envelope containing a decree absolute and today Beth had cried until she had no tears left. Her eyes were sore and her mouth dry, and she knew that if she stayed at home all night she would go mad. So she had forced herself up, pulled a clean top on, smeared on lipstick and mascara and walked down the lane for Quiz Night.

Jas folded her into a hug. 'Are you OK?'

'No.' Beth drank half her wine in one go. She had already got through a bottle getting ready, but the more the merrier. She was a single woman now. She could do what she liked.

She downed the rest. 'But that helped.'

Jas chewed her lip. 'Do you need to talk?'

'Absolutely not. I've wasted far too much of your day already.' Beth filled her glass from the bottle in the cooler in the middle of the table. 'Now it's drinking time.'

'You mean quiz time?'

'Yes. That.' Beth took another gulp. 'Exactly.'

'OK then.' Jas tapped her pencil against the answer sheet. 'We're expecting great things from you. We have to beat that Smartypints lot this time, the smug bastards.' She raised a middle finger towards a thickset man on a nearby table. 'I can't deal with Sam crowing over me again.' He blew a kiss back, eyes disappearing as he smiled.

Beth found that she had already finished her glass. 'What round are we on?'

'Pictures.'

'Let's have a look.' Beth grabbed the sheet. 'Well, that's Olivia Wilde, that's Aretha Franklin and that's . . .'

'Sssssshhhhhh.' Jas clucked reprovingly as a woman on the table next to them scribbled the answers down. 'You do know this is a competition, don't you? You're not meant to give the next table the bloody answers.'

'Sorry.' Beth giggled, feeling the tension in her shoulders start to disappear.

'That guy over there craned his head right round.' Jas put her finger to her lips. 'He's obviously worked out you're our secret weapon.'

'Hardly.' Beth topped herself up again. The more she drank the less of a failure she felt. She pointed to one of the photos. 'That one's Mister Rogers.'

'Who?' Jas frowned. 'Is he on CBeebies?'

'No.' Beth shook her head. 'US TV star. Now deceased.'

'Nice.' Jas shook her head admiringly. 'We're going to beat those buggers this time.'

Taking a triumphant sip of her pint, Jas turned to watch a team in the far corner, whose members were clearly failing to agree about the answer to the latest question. 'Wow, Simon looks so much better without that beard.'

'He's here?' Beth's head whipped round before she could stop herself. He caught her eye and waved. She raised her hand in return.

Jas narrowed her eyes critically. 'Now, if he could just do something about his clothes he'd be a bit of alright.'

'Jas!' Beth appeared to have finished her latest glass of wine too. The world was starting to go muzzy at the edges, reducing to heat, to voices and to the pictures dancing on the paper in front of her. She closed her eyes and opened them again. It didn't help.

'Are you sure you're OK, Beth?' Jas was staring at her, head on one side.

'Totally fine. Yes. Yes.' She reached for more wine, but the bottle was empty.

She turned it upside down, just for good measure. Nothing.

'Concentrate.' Jas nudged her as the quizmaster coughed into the microphone. He had a quiff and a golden waistcoat, and spoke with all the gravity of a newsreader on election night.

'We are now onto the music round.' He adjusted his bright red bow tie. 'Question number one. Who released the following UK chart-topping albums? *Hounds of Love* for one point, *No Jacket Required* for one point and *Brothers in Arms* for – yes, you guessed it – another point.' He picked up his pint triumphantly, clearly congratulating himself on a job well done.

'I know the first one!' Jas wrote the first answer on the page. 'Take that, lover-boy.' She stuck her tongue out at Sam.

Beth was struggling to focus. She was increasingly convinced the pub had been mounted on some kind of spinning wheel.

'Hmmm. *No Jacket Required.*' She tapped her lip with her finger. 'What band was that again?'

Jas leant back in her chair. 'I was hoping you were going to answer that.'

Beth found herself staring over at Simon, who was hunched forwards in close consultation with his team. He had such lovely hair, thick and short.

Jas blinked. 'What? Hair?'

Beth blinked. 'Did I say that out loud?'

Jas rolled her eyes. 'You did.'

'Oh.' Beth jutted her lower lip out, puzzled. 'What was the question again?'

Jas shook her head. 'OK. You're officially off quiz duties.'

'Why?' Beth's head was whirling now. She checked the bottle in the cooler. 'There's no wine.'

'Yeah. You drank it all.'

'Did I?' Beth grimaced. 'My bad. I'll get more.' She started to get up.

Jas reached out and pulled her back down. 'I'm not sure that's a good idea.'

'It's a great idea.' Beth staggered to her feet. 'I'm good. All good. Yes.'

She made her way to the bar, leaning against it for support, enjoying the bustle as Betty and her team poured pints and uncorked bottles.

'Evening.'

Simon smiled down at her. Lovely Simon. Her friend. 'Hello.' Her elbow appeared to be sliding along the bar towards him.

'Are you OK?'

'Yes.' He stepped away to check the order with his team, and she narrowly avoided collapsing sideways onto the floor.

She propped herself up again as he reappeared, pointing at his cheek, where the razor had cut deepest. 'How's your face doing?'

'I'm healing.' His forearm nudged hers as more people piled towards the bar.

'Always knew you were a tough guy.'

'For that kind of cheek I'll make sure we thrash you in the quiz.'

'I'd like to see you try.' She glanced up, only to see there were two of him. Dots were appearing at the edge of her vision and nausea was rising.

He ran a hand over the smooth curve of his chin. 'How do you cope with all this air on your face the whole time? It's so cold.'

She could feel sweat prickling on her brow. 'Make-up. It gives me added protection.'

'Really?'

'No. Not really.' She laughed and her stomach turned over. Her mouth filled with bile. No. Not now. Please. Not here, in front of everyone and especially not today.

She stood still and stared at her feet. Inhale. Exhale.

'Beth, do you need to go outside?'

His voice was so kind. This was his night out, away from looking after Jake. Instead, he was looking after her.

'I'm fine.' She put her hand over her mouth and turned, stumbling over boots and trainers, her elbows jabbing through the crowd. Air. That was what she needed. Head down, she pushed through, thinking she was aiming at the door, only to find that she had arrived at the slot machines instead. She stood, bewildered, desperate to get out, desperate not to make today even worse.

'This way.' A strong hand took her elbow, steering her outside. She heard the squeak of a hinge and felt cool air on her face. Oh thank God. She was so happy she nearly cried. The hand was still with her, guiding her through the garden, past tables full of drinkers, through a metal gate and out round the back of the hotel that stood next to the pub, enjoying an uninterrupted view of Thistlethwaite lake.

'Take deep breaths.' Simon was next to her. 'I got you a glass of water, and Jas gave me your bag. She asked if she should come out and look after you?'

'No.' Beth sank down against the wall. 'No. I'm OK, thanks.'

'I'm not sure you are.' Simon sat down next to her, warm and solid in the dusk. She wanted to rest her head on his shoulder, then realised she already had.

She felt less sick out here. The sweet air revived her, and the sweat was cooling on her brow. She took greedy breaths, keeping her eyes open so the world didn't spin away.

'I'm sorry.' Her voice was so tiny it was drowned out by a hotel worker clanging bins around the corner.

'Don't be.' Simon shifted, bringing his arm around her shoulder as she nestled into him. 'We all do it.'

'Even you?'

'Yep. I didn't do well with Jake's diagnosis. I drank a lot back then.' He sighed. 'Too much.'

'I don't blame you.' His shoulder was so comfortable. She could stay here for ever. 'Anyone would.'

'Maybe.' He shifted against her. 'So, what's happened? Jake was feeling rough today – he did a bit of football at school yesterday so he was tired, you know? He heard you crying through the wall. We peeped through the window but you were on the phone. Jake's made you something. To cheer you up.'

'Ahhh. That's so sweet.'

'So what happened, Beth?'

There was no sugar-coating it. 'It's my wedding anniversary today. Three years. Only – obviously – I'm not married any more.' Her words ascended into a wail and hot tears spilled down her cheeks.

'Ahhhhh.' She could feel him nodding. 'That's tough.' He drew her even closer. 'Really tough.'

'Yeah.' She sniffed. 'But I'm being stupid, I know. It's just a day. I'm divorced every other day of the year too.'

'That doesn't matter,' Simon said simply. 'It's one of those moments. The landmarks. They're the worst. I always have mixed feelings on Jake's birthday, so I know what you mean. It sounds mad but I was hoping, right up to the minute he was born, that the doctors had got it wrong about Jake – that he didn't have HLHS. So now, on his birthday, I always feel happy, of course, that he's made it through another year, but I also remember that kick in the teeth when he came out and he was blue.'

'I bet you do.' Tears were rolling down her face now.

Tears for what she had lost; tears for what she had done; tears for her new friend and everything he had to deal with.

Gradually, she quietened. An owl hooted in the forest behind them and she could hear the lap of the water against the shore.

Simon's voice was gentle. 'So, do you want to talk about it?'

'Yes. No. I don't know.' She snuggled into him, her head lowered. 'Maybe. Why don't you ask me questions, and I'll answer if I can?'

'OK, then.' He rested his head back against the wall. 'Was your ex from New York?'

'Yes. Well, he was from Connecticut originally but he moved to New York when he was little. We met over here – at university. He was just starting his PHD over here, I was a first year nursing student, he was this glamorous older doctor, blah blah blah cliché cliché.'

'Did you fall in love in an operating theatre?'

'Ha. No.' Beth wiped her eyes. 'In a sticky student disco, actually. We were together for a few years, while we both studied, then it was time for him to go back to the States, and I decided to go too. Dad was gone, and my mum had moved away by then, so it was just me. No ties.'

'And what was it like living out there?'

'Amazing.' She smiled. 'Exactly as mad as you would imagine. Noisy. Energetic. Always so much happening, wherever you were. There's this – pulse – you know? Like everyone's got a technicolour story to tell, even the walls and the streets and the subway signs.' She sipped her water. 'I spent my first week there just wandering around with my mouth hanging open. Tyler used to tease me, saying I looked like a tourist.'

'Tyler? Is that his name, then? Your ex?'

'Yes. Tyler Langton. He's a surgeon. A pretty successful one – he's on the board of the hospital we both worked at.' Just the thought of the boardroom, with its floor-to-ceiling windows and long wooden table, made her pulse spiral. She could feel the weight of the door handle beneath her fingers, all those faces turning towards her. Ten years of service and not one of them had even tried to smile.

Not even Tyler.

Simon was now rubbing her back in small circular motions. 'And Tyler's still out there? In New York?'

'Yeah.' Her mouth was dry. 'He'd never leave.'

'And are you in touch?'

She was too drunk to talk about this. 'No. We . . . He . . .' She swallowed, edging round the truth. 'He found . . . someone else.'

She hugged her knees, leaning away from him now as humiliation started to burn. She didn't want Simon seeing her that way. Rejected. Weak.

'I'm so sorry.'

'Me too.' She knew she didn't deserve his pity. 'We drifted. We were both working all hours.' She took a breath. 'But I was trying to fix things – to be who he wanted me to be – and then I found him. In bed with Dana. My deputy.'

Simon stiffened beside her. 'What a bastard.'

'Yeah. Well.' The truth was that finding Tyler in bed with Dana wasn't the worst thing that had happened in the past year. Not by a long way.

Simon dug into his pocket. 'Tissue?'

'Yes please.' She blew her nose loudly. 'Thank you.' She held it out to him.

He laughed. 'It's OK. You can keep it.'

'Oh, yeah. Sorry.' She twisted it between her fingers, almost in a trance. 'There was this other thing too . . .'

'Yeah?'

She thought back to that night. The clock ticking on the wall. The lights bright around the nursing station. Her head throbbing as she checked the obs charts at the beginning of her fifth night shift in a row.

Her mind blocked.

The silence stretched and stretched until Simon broke it. 'No need to talk about it. Either way Tyler sounds like a total shit. One hundred percent arsehole.'

'Thanks, Simon.'

'Just saying it as I see it.'

The lights from the hotel cast glittery trails across the water. Beth could hear cries and applause from the pub, but all she wanted was Simon's shoulder to lean on, his arm around her shoulder. She closed her eyes. Maybe here, with him, she could sleep. Just for a second. One precious moment of feeling safe.

A couple of hours later she awoke, tucked up in her bed, warm and cosy. A picture from Jake was on her bedside table. He had stuck two A4 sheets together and drawn a tree house with eight floors, each one a map of excitements including a spa, a tennis court and a disco room with a spangly hang-out area. It was big and bright and full of cheerful stick figures having the time of their lives. He had written the title in capitals: BETH'S DREAM TREE HOUSE. I WILL BUILD IT FOR YOU. J xx.

Despite her sadness, despite the pain in her head, she smiled. Then she gave a sigh, drank the glass of water Simon had left for her, turned over and closed her eyes, hoping for sleep, hoping that she would dream of her friends next door.

12

Simon

He had packed a bag. He had handed over his keys. And his son was sitting on the floor, happily playing with Beth, whose hand was delving into a huge box of bricks as they planned how to recreate the Empire State Building. Jake was sketching out his vision and Beth nodded seriously as he showed her his sketches so far. It was time for Simon to get his stag on.

Since Quizgate, as Beth insisted on calling it, she had spent at least one evening a week here looking after Jake while Simon worked at the farm, and the cash in his pocket had made things considerably easier. She and Jake were firm friends – they played Minecraft together; kicked a football around out the back; or she made up stories for him on the days he needed to rest but didn't want to admit it. She would take great care of him while Simon was away – he knew that she would keep his boy safe.

Simon checked his phone. Barney wasn't here yet and they needed to leave. The stags were due to check into their hotel by four in order to be ready to climb the Blackpool Tower an hour later before beers, curry and a club. Ten men and one him trying to organise everybody. After years of barely going further than The Crown, his

143

head was giddy with it all. He hoped he had done enough to give Barney the good time that he deserved.

There was only one problem.

'Are you sure you want me to wear this, Jake?' He looked down at his black shirt, with a trail of bright yellow bumblebees buzzing across from his shoulder to his tummy.

Beth's lips twitched as she glanced up.

Oh God.

'Yes.' Jake pulled a face. 'Why? Don't you like it?'

'No, no. It's great.' Simon hoped he looked convincing. 'Really . . .' All the words in the world appeared to fly out of his head. 'It's really something.'

Beth giggled. Simon was about to glare at her when he heard a knock at the door.

He walked down the hall and opened it. 'Afternoon.'

Maybe the shirt wasn't as awful as he thought.

'Oh my God.' Barney recoiled backwards, hand shielding his eyes. 'Are we going to a children's birthday party? Is that my surprise?'

So it *was* that bad. Simon held his hand to his lips. 'Sssssshhhhh. Jake got it for me.'

Barney blinked. He spoke in an exaggerated whisper. 'He does know *I'm* the stag, doesn't he? I mean, tradition is that the stag wears the comedy costume, but I'm happy for you to take one for the team.'

'Ha ha.' Simon gave him an agonised look as they went down the hall. 'Just shut it, OK? He saved up all his pocket money to get it. It's part of his "get Dad a girlfriend" campaign.'

Barney grimaced. 'Oh. Well, he did you a favour with the beard and the hair, but I think your luck's run out on this one.'

'I said be quiet!'

'Alright. Sorry. Jake will have no idea that . . .'

'That what, Barney?' Jake was at their feet, beaming, arms raised for a hug.

Simon held his breath.

'That I am SO jealous of that new shirt you got him.' Barney swung him round, before putting him down and looking curiously at Beth. 'Afternoon. I'm Barney.'

'Hi.' She took his hand, tucking a strand of hair behind her ear. Her hair was getting longer now, reaching her cheekbones, framing her wide eyes. 'I've heard a lot about you.'

'Likewise. Simon's been singing your praises.'

Her eyes flicked to Simon and then away. 'Really?' She sounded genuinely surprised. That ex-husband really had done a number on her.

Barney shoved his hands in his pockets. 'You've been getting Simon out running. You deserve some kind of award.'

'I can't take the credit for that.' Beth glanced at Simon. 'All it took was a little blackmail from Jake.'

'Well, I've been trying to get him into a gym for years. Total failure.' Barney lifted Jake up, turning him upside down to squeals of laughter. Simon tensed despite himself as Jake's T-shirt hung down, exposing the scars on his chest, each one a reminder of fear and blood, of eyes trained on a beeping monitor, of sugary tea at dawn when another night had safely passed.

He relaxed when Barney placed Jake down again.

'Simon did well for a first-timer.' A smile played on Beth's lips. In her light green T-shirt and jeans she looked softer and more relaxed than she had been when she first moved in. He found himself wondering more and more about her story; what had happened in New York – what was so terrible she had been unable to say it out loud.

God, getting to know people was hard. So many layers. So much pain.

'Earth to Simon?' Barney looked at his watch. 'Time to go.'

'Yes. Of course.' He jangled his keys. He hadn't left Jake overnight for more than six years and suddenly he wasn't sure that he could. 'Now, you know where I'll be, Beth? When I'm coming back?'

'Yes. You've told me several times. And written it down.' Beth stood up, radiating a calm assurance that reminded him what a wonderful nurse she must be. 'Now off you go.' She looped her arm around Jake's shoulder. 'We've got this covered, haven't we, Jake?'

'Yeah.' His boy was clearly delighted at the prospect of more time with Beth. 'Go on, Dad. Get that shirt out on the town. The girls will love it.'

'Alright, lad.' Simon thought it far more likely that the girls would laugh at it.

He wanted to kneel down for one more hug. He wanted to give Jake a thousand reassurances. He wanted just one more kiss of that whirl of red hair.

But Beth's gaze was steady. And Barney was waiting.

He was going to show his friend the time of his life.

'OK. See you tomorrow then.'

'Bye, Dad.' Jake practically pushed Simon towards the door.

Barney nudged Simon. 'Better take the hint.'

'Yeah.' Simon waved to Jake, turned, and walked out of the house for a night away with his mates. Twenty-four hours away from home. He felt like Neil Armstrong stepping onto the moon.

'Let's get ready to rumble!' Barney chucked his bag onto the back seat of Simon's pickup and slammed the door.

'One minute in and you're already quoting PJ and Duncan.' Simon was grinning as he revved the engine. 'This is going to be messy.'

'You bet it is.' Barney looked like a kid eyeing his presents on Christmas morning. 'Me and the lads. Blackpool. Beer. What could go wrong?'

'Well . . .' Simon indicated the seat behind him. 'You might want to look at what you're wearing.'

'Oh no, I don't have to wear a shirt like yours, do I?' Barney's mouth fell open.

Simon checked the lane as he turned out. He felt lighter with every passing metre as they headed out of the village. Goodbye, white cottages. Farewell, sheep. 'Something even better than that, mate.'

Barney leant back, rootling around. He held up a spangly item of clothing.

'No.' He shook his head.

Simon laughed. 'You're to wear it all night, no matter what. Got it?'

Barney mouthed expletives as he examined the frilly

ballerina skirt and shiny leotard. 'You bastard. Just wait till you get married.'

This only made Simon laugh more. 'Well, that's not very likely, is it?'

'Jake seems keen on it. Giving you a makeover and that.'

'Aye. Well. He's seven. He's not got the nous to know what's right for me.'

Barney glanced at Simon. 'Beth seems to like you.'

Simon drove round a branch that had fallen on his side of the road. 'Beth's just got divorced.'

'That never stopped anyone.'

Simon thought about the tears on her face that night after the quiz, of her grief and her fragility. 'She's definitely not ready to move on.'

'Shame. She's a bit of alright.'

'You think?' Simon thought of her upturned nose, her full lips, the way she always glanced away before she smiled, as if checking whether or not she was allowed.

Barney preened in the mirror, holding the leotard up to his face. 'I'm going to look pretty tasty in this.'

'Watch out Blackpool.' Simon changed gear.

Barney tentatively inserted an arm into the leotard. 'Seriously though, you know Beth's nice. And I think she likes you.'

'No.' Simon shook his head. 'I mean, we're friends, but that's it. She isn't ready for anyone new. Jake's the one she's nuts about, not me. Besides, her ex was a surgeon. She's not exactly going to be after a farmhand like me, is she?'

'Don't do yourself down, mate.' Barney was now trying

to pull the leotard over his head. Sequins glinted in the sunlight. 'How the heck do people get into these things?'

'No idea.' Simon turned onto the main road where they instantly got stuck behind a tractor. He pressed play on the CD player and 'I Bet You Look Good on the Dancefloor' blasted through the pickup.

'TUNE.'

Simon opened the glovebox as he inched the pickup forwards.

'There's a tiara too.'

'Oh God.' Barney ran a hand through his hair, eyebrows rising.

'And . . .' Simon found what he was looking for. 'This is for you.'

He threw a bright pink wig onto his friend's lap.

'It goes underneath the tiara.'

Barney's blue eyes narrowed. 'You bastard.'

'You already said that. Put it on.' Simon hit the accelerator as the tractor turned off and the road opened up before them.

He was free.

It was going to be a great weekend.

13

Beth

Jake pushed his plate away. 'Dad wouldn't make me eat that.'

Beth groaned inwardly. The afternoon, which had started so well, was rapidly going south. After they had finished building the Empire State Building, now residing proudly on Jake's windowsill, he had wanted to make the Brooklyn Bridge too. The June sun was beating into the cottage, but all her attempts to get them both outside had been met with increasingly dismissive 'No's.

She had got hotter and hotter, craving the breeze of the fells on her face, but in the end she had been forced out onto the back step with a mug of tea, while he carried on inside. He was now listless and cranky, and her 'fun' status had been well and truly blown apart when she had served up veggie burgers for tea.

'What's this?' He prodded it with a finger. 'Is it food?'

'Of course it's food.' She took a bite and discovered it didn't taste quite as great as she had thought. She forced her face to remain enthusiastic.

He was now digging into the bun with his fingers, face wrinkled in disgust. 'Why is the burger green? Is that broccoli?' He made a spewing noise.

'Give it a try. It tastes great. Mmmmmm.' She rubbed her tummy in apparent delight. However, he was not two, so her brilliant tactic didn't work. She would be making aeroplane noises next and trying to fly it into his mouth on a spoon.

'Can I have crisps instead?' He was already halfway out of his chair and heading for the kitchen.

'No.' Her admiration for Simon was growing by the second.

'Why not?'

'Because I cooked *this* for us.'

Jake's lower lip was jutting out. 'But I don't like it.'

'You haven't tried it.'

'Yes I have.'

'No, you haven't.'

She could see the smile glinting in his eyes. 'Yes I have.' She started laughing.

So did he.

'Now, Jake . . .'

He mimicked her exactly, even down to the way she had leant forwards as she spoke. 'Now, Jake . . .'

A gauntlet was being thrown at her feet.

She took a breath. 'Can you stop repeating everything I say?'

He parroted back. 'Can you stop repeating everything I say?'

OK. She sat back. So did he.

She knew what to do. She stood up and launched into song.

'Heads, shoulders, knees and toes, knees and toes.'

She waited, to see if he would copy her. He was seven, and far too cool, so he didn't.

Phew.

Next she did the Macarena.

Now he was rolling his eyes.

'OK. Here's the deal, Jake. How about you actually try some of the burger which, despite the way you're looking at it, is not actually poison, and then we have some ice cream, and then we call your dad and say hello. Sound like a plan?'

He thought for a moment. 'S'pose so.' He took a bite of the burger. 'It's not too bad I suppose.'

Given his mood, this was the equivalent of a five-star review. She gave a mock bow. 'Why thank you, Lord Jacob.'

He frowned. 'Nobody calls me Jacob. Not even Grandad when he's cross.'

She picked up her burger and took a bite. 'Is he cross a lot, then?'

'Yeah.' Jake ate another mouthful. 'Him and Dad don't get on very well.'

'Why's that?'

'Grandad wants Dad to let me do more things. But Dad always says no.'

Beth crunched some lettuce. 'It must be hard for your dad, though?'

'It's hard for me too.' Jake's face darkened. 'And I just want to do what my friends do.'

'I know. But you're—'

'Don't say I'm different.' He was stabbing up his food now, chewing fast. 'I hate it when people say that. Just because my heart works differently doesn't mean I'm any different to my friends. I can do everything they can. You don't know everything.'

He toyed with his salad.

She backtracked. 'I'm sorry. You're right – I have no idea what it's like to be you and what you can do.' She sought words that might comfort him. 'But I'm not sure that anyone's really the same as anyone else. We're all different, aren't we? Different hair, different hobbies, different feelings.'

Jake chewed thoughtfully on a tomato. 'But it feels like there are lots of people who *are* the same. And they assume I'm different – that just because I can't run as fast as them that I don't want to play their games, or whatever. I hate it.'

Beth took a chance. 'I bet there are loads of things you can do that they can't.'

'Like what?'

'Like – making these!' She gestured to the Lego creations all around the room, mostly built from random bricks and imagination. 'Like knowing when people need amazing tree houses to cheer them up. Or when men need to shave off their beards. You – do things. You make things happen.'

This got a tiny smile. 'I suppose so.' Jake sighed. 'It hasn't worked though, has it?'

'What hasn't?'

'The makeover. Dad's still single.'

'What's the rush, Jake? There's lots of time.'

His eyes glinted. 'That's the problem. There isn't any

time. I . . .' He shook his head. 'Emily is the only one who understands.' He folded his arms, slumping down against his chair.

She looked back at him. 'Who's Emily?'

'My best friend. She was born with HLHS too. We're like twins, except she likes dancing and I like football. She's nearly as good at Nintendo as me.'

'Wow.'

Jake put his head on one side. 'And she might agree with you that everyone's different. Emily never wants to be like anyone else. She's happy to be her.'

'She sounds amazing. She must be really . . .'

'Don't say brave.' His face creased in disapproval. 'I hate it when people say that, too.'

Beth laid her hand gently over his. 'I was going to say strong.'

He visibly relaxed. 'Yeah. She's strong.'

'I can't wait to meet her.'

A cloud passed over his face and he dropped his fork with a clatter.

Beth waited.

'Have I eaten enough yet?' His frown was back.

'Sure.' She stood up. 'Time for ice cream, I think.'

'Can we call Dad first?'

'Of course.' She handed him her phone.

Jake dialled, face brightening. 'Maybe he's found a girl-friend by now.' He put the phone on speaker as it rang.

'Maybe.' She didn't want to tell him what really happened on stag weekends. The phone rang and rang but there was no answer.

Jake's face fell.

'Want to leave a voicemail?'

'Yeah.' Jake cheered up and shouted into the handset. 'LOVE YOU, DAD. TALK TO GIRLS. LOTS OF GIRLS. BYE.'

'Wow.' Beth put the phone down. 'That was loud.'

'He's probably in a pub. Pubs are noisy, so I thought I'd shout.'

He nestled down on the sofa, hugging Superchick as she brought him his ice cream.

'What are we watching?'

'Hercules! It's me and Emily's favourite.' He pressed play, and there was the eponymous hero, all out of place in his little village, due to his extraordinary strength. She could see why Jake and Emily loved this movie, as Hercules gradually found his hero's spirit and saved the world from the evil Hades, gaining acceptance as he did so. Jake leant forward as the story progressed, singing along to 'Go the Distance', whooping his hero along as he got closer to victory in the River Styx.

Jake leant into her as the credits rolled. 'You know, I'm not ashamed of my heart. I'm not embarrassed, like Hercules is at the beginning.' He pulled at a loose thread on his sock. 'That's not what I meant just now. I don't want you to think that.'

'I would never think that.'

'Maybe staying alive is my superpower.' He kneaded the cushion with nervous fingers. 'The doctors thought I might die when I was born. Did you know that?'

'Simon told me.'

Jake's shoulders were rigid. 'Sometimes I wonder if . . .'

She hugged him close. 'Yes?'

'Nothing.'

'OK.' She kissed his hair, pleased when he threw his arms around her and hugged her tight. 'Bedtime, champ?'

To her surprise, he didn't protest. He yawned his way up the stairs to his little room tucked away in the eaves, with its posters of football players and its bright red duvet. A picture of a girl with an elfin face was Blu-tacked next to his bed. She was in full dancing gear, a glittery headband holding back her long dark hair as she reached her hands up elegantly above her head. Passport booth snapshots were scattered around the walls, in which she and Jake seemed to be competing to pull the cheekiest face on earth.

Beth put Jake's tablets into his hand and passed him a glass of water. 'Is that Emily?'

'Yeah.' He put them on his tongue and swallowed them down.

'I can see why she's your best friend. She looks like a laugh.'

'Yeah.' He started putting his Minecraft pyjamas on.

Beth waited, staring at a pile of postcards covered in scrawl that lay in a heap on the duvet.

'What are these?'

'Nothing.' He grabbed them from her, stuffing them away in a drawer. She saw the name 'Emily' at the top of one of the cards. The two of them were clearly very close. How great for Jake to have a friend who was going through the same things as him – someone who really understood.

As she was saying goodnight, Jake stopped her. 'You can't go yet. We have to line up my toys first, so they can keep an eye on me at night. Dad always does that.'

'Oh, right. OK. What a great idea.' Beth was surprised Simon hadn't mentioned it. He had been pretty forensic about everything else, listing where the medicine was, what to do if Jake got sore legs, how to contact him in case of emergency, including numbers for his hotel and every single member of the stag party.

She picked a toy at random. 'Well, Tigger. How about you go here?' She gently placed him by Jake's head.

'No.' Jake picked him up again. 'He goes this side. Then Superchick next to him.' He moved the yellow duck across so he was next to the wall.

'OK.' Beth picked up a brown bunny. 'Bunny could go here? Next to the wall?'

'No. And he's called Rabbit.' Jake sighed. 'It's OK, I'll do it.'

'That might be best.' Beth was starting to crave the white wine that Simon had left in the fridge for her. She watched Jake as he arranged his team around him, lining his sergeants up until he felt safe.

'OK.' He snuggled down against his pillows. 'I'm going to read now.'

'Great.' Beth leant down and rested her hand gently on his head. 'Sleep soon. Sleep well. Night night.'

After closing his door, Beth headed downstairs and made straight for the fridge, pouring wine, moving over to the window to look at the view she had come to love so much. She sipped the cool liquid as the sunset cast a glow over the fells, gilding the trees with gold.

She wandered around the living room, looking at the books and photo albums piled up on the shelves in the corner. A tall green hardback had the words 'Year Book 2001' stamped on it in gold, and she put her glass down and pulled it out. She flicked through the pages, smiling. There was Simon with a wispy goatee alongside Barney, who was sporting some classic DiCaprio curtains. They were both squeezed into one black rugby jersey and a giant pair of tracksuit bottoms. Simon was voted 'Most likely to emigrate', while Barney was 'Most likely to accidentally become a dad'.

She giggled, remembering her own Year Book, complete with a picture of her in a cowskin jumpsuit attempting to hitch-hike to Dublin for charity. She could still remember being crammed into the back of a van with Jas, desperate to get the last ferry. They had scraped on board, only to realise on arrival that they would have to spend the night in the ferry terminal, while Tyler and his mates were holed up in some luxury hotel.

Tyler had always liked the finer things. At this distance she was starting to see that their relationship had looked better from the outside in. It was curated and careful – all granite countertops, spotless wine glasses and Insta poses. They had come a long way from their student selves. Him with his tousled hair and sleepy smile, her with her bright jumpsuits and stacked trainers. Now he was all suits and ties, shiny shoes and expensive cologne while she spent most of her free time in running gear. How he would sneer, if he could see her now. How he and Dana would laugh.

Beth was holding her glass so tightly her knuckles were white. She was walking back to the fridge, trying to slow her breathing, when she heard the scream.

Jake.

She ran, feet barely touching the stairs, arms pumping. Fear gave her wings. She wouldn't let anything happen. Not this time.

She pushed open the door and sprinted into his room.

Jake was writhing in his bed, arms and legs kicking out, running towards something he didn't want to see.

His duvet was half on, half off the bed and his forehead was sweaty beneath her fingers as she knelt down beside him. He was breathing fast. She wanted to comfort him, to turn all his worries to wishes. She tried to hold his hand, but he pulled it away. She was about to leave the room to get a cold flannel for him, but then he started to cry. High-pitched, heart-wrenching. It sent shivers down her spine.

So she snuggled down, cuddling into him, breathing in his smell of heat and sleep. She curled her arms around his body, thinking of Simon, wondering how many times he had done this, how many times he had been here, ready to comfort, ready to soothe. All the things Simon said about himself didn't tell anything like the best story; these were the moments that mattered – the unsung times, the private moments, a hand on a forehead, a kiss on a cheek in the middle of the night.

Jake twitched in his sleep, mumbling something about

Hades, but gradually his breathing evened out and he relaxed. His feet stopped paddling, his arms lay still. Beth found herself drifting off, his body warm beside her.

Beth was cosy. Comfortable. Needed.

Finally, after month upon month of jagged nights, reliving every mistake she had made, she slept.

14

Simon

S imon looked at the bouncer, drawing himself up to his full height. It was hard to feel persuasive while on a level with someone's chin.

'But they're great trainers.' He held up his foot and staggered backwards into the stags behind him. He took a deep breath, aware that he was slurring his words. The shots were starting to take their toll now and tequila was sharp on his breath.

Behind them a group of hens, in tiaras and bright pink catsuits, were trying to adopt Barney. They had surrounded him like ants around spilled sugar, and were lustily encouraging him to attempt a pirouette. His tutu flared upwards as his hairy legs did their best to oblige and he crashed into the wall, giving the lie to Simon's claim that their group was totally sober.

The bouncer folded his arms, just in case his muscles weren't obvious enough beneath his tight black T-shirt. A beefy inked angel ran down his left forearm until it met the intimidating bulge of his knuckles. 'Well, the shirt's not great either. We don't allow live animal prints. Club policy.'

'Why?' Simon felt his hackles rise. His son had given

him this shirt. No matter what anyone else thought, he was going to keep wearing it.

The bouncer leant closer and Simon could smell the gum he was chewing.

'Because I don't like them. You don't like it? You know where to go.' He jabbed a finger towards the bins at the far end of the alleyway.

Music banged out of the open door behind him. Simon hadn't heard bass thudding like that since Thailand but it all came back to him. The dark interior full of bodies pressing, dancing, jumping. Sweat dripping from the ceiling, arms raised in the air, plastic shot glasses in eager hands, a DJ dancing in a booth taking requests shouted from cupped hands. Once, he had loved this kind of place. Every Saturday at uni he'd been down Echoes in his jeans and shiny shirts, laughing with his mates, having just enough booze to tip him onto the dance floor where he might get lucky before someone realised he couldn't move for toffee.

Today, away with Barney and his mates, he had remembered the old him, the one who laughed and slept in till midday and who was only responsible for getting himself to lectures and having enough money to buy his packets of economy pasta and Cup-a-Soups every week. He hadn't needed a routine. He hadn't needed a cupboard full of medical supplies. Just him, his physio degree and a place to lay his head.

Jake had changed all that. At the thought of his son, he went to check his phone, only to discover that he was out of battery. Shit. He thought of Beth, her dark head next to Jake's as she put him to bed, and exhaled. His boy was in good hands. Then he realised that he had forgotten to tell her about lining up the toys. Another fuck-up to add to his amazingly long list today. He was lucky his best friend was the forgiving type. There he was now, arms aloft, attempting a twirl while the hens cackled around him.

'Nice legs!'

'Nice arse.' A girl who was certainly proud of her cleavage was pressing herself towards Barney, eyes glinting nearly as much as her tiara.

The queue was growing restive behind him. 'Look, do you need a hand here?' Lina's brother Casper had been busy proving all day that there was a reason Barney had tried to avoid inviting him on the stag. He was wearing a suit that definitely didn't come from M&S and had spent the afternoon looking at Blackpool's seafront and arcades with a barely veiled sneer. In return, the stags were all annoying him by calling him Ghost. He had downed so much booze that Simon kept hoping he would land head down in a gutter and they could be done with him.

No such luck.

'Look.' Here he was now, flashing his cash again. 'This guy . . .' He contemptuously flicked his hand towards the bouncer. 'He clearly wants money. Here you go.' He held out a wad of notes. 'Just let us in, won't you?'

Simon flushed. 'Actually, I don't think that's what this is about. He's wearing a Rolex. He's doing alright.'

'Go on. Take it.' Casper was practically giving the bouncer a facial with his tenners.

The bouncer's eyebrow flickered upwards. His shaved head gleamed as he stared at Casper's tie. A tie, for God's sake. On a stag do.

Then the bouncer moved, and Simon hoped for a wild second that he was going to unclip the rope that currently blocked their path inside. Instead he took a step forward, and any remaining flickers of optimism died their final death.

'Get out of it.' He jerked a thumb towards the bins across the street. 'Go on. Get out of it.'

'I can give you more.' Casper was now getting his leather wallet out of his pocket, and leafing through its contents. Who the hell carried that much cash? Did he think he was some kind of eighteenth-century gentleman with a pocketbook, rather than a guy who thought too much of himself because he happened to work in the Gherkin?

'Please.' Simon was begging now. 'Please let us in. This whole night has been a disaster. I need this.' He realised how tragic he must sound, desperate to get into a club full of bad music and people who were probably half his age. But then he was tragic, wasn't he? Working for his dad; barely able to cover his bills; already panicking about how his credit card was even going to begin to afford this night away. Barney should have chosen someone else to be his best man. Anyone else would have done a better job of things. That pissed bloke who was now vomiting into the bin would have looked stellar compared to Simon.

He took the bouncer's arm.

Big mistake.

'Let go.' The growling voice was straight off a Hollywood trailer.

Yes. Good idea.

Simon let go.

'Take a step back.'

Simon complied.

He had to try one more time. 'Please? You see, tonight is for my best mate.' He pointed at Barney, only to discover that he appeared to be drinking prosecco off a woman's arm. 'He's a great bloke. And I'm his best man, and today – well, frankly it's been—'

'It's been a total fuck-up.'

Thanks, Ghost.

'It hasn't gone well.' Simon repeated the litany of things that had gone wrong. First the hotel booking that had meant they were all sharing double beds tonight. The fact he'd booked the climbing on the Blackpool Tower at the wrong time, so they were all too pissed to be admitted entry. The curry house that had won jalfrezi of the year last year but had, on arrival, greeted them with a sign saying that it had been shut down due to hygiene regulations. And now this.

He had let his best friend down. Barney, who always kept an eye on Jake. Barney who had mopped Simon up when Tamsin left, and fed him and watered him until he was functioning again. His oldest and best friend, who had sat through a five-hour clinic back in spring, just so that Simon wouldn't be alone.

Simon's face burned with shame.

'Please?' He might as well kneel down, he sounded so bloody pathetic. 'Please let us in. I need a win here.'

The bouncer drummed his fingers on his forearms.

Maybe he was considering this. Maybe he was about to give Simon the break he so desperately needed.

He beckoned Simon close.

Simon admired his golden earring as he leant closer.

'Piss off.' The bouncer pulled back and unclipped the rope for the next group.

Simon sagged, all his optimism seeping away. There was a reason he never went on nights out any more. He was shit at them. He had spent hours organising this weekend, yet the more effort he put in, the more of a failure he felt when it all went wrong. Sometimes it felt like it would be better not to try. He would – one day – like to feel that he had got one precious thing right. Just one. Then he might be able to hold his head high again.

Casper was not happy. 'Well, this is a shit show, isn't it?'

'Thanks, Ghost.'

'Why are you still making that joke? It wasn't funny twenty years ago when the movie came out.' Casper dug his hands into his pockets. 'What's your plan now, then? Another game of *Fuzzy Ducks*?'

Simon weaved his way over to the wall on the opposite side of the alleyway. He slumped against it, as Barney did one last twirl for the girls who were now going into the club without them.

He wandered over to Simon, still waving. 'What happened?'

Simon got another beer out of the rucksack on his shoulder and held it out. 'I fucked up again. Sorry, mate. They won't let in people wearing trainers.' He looked at the group's footwear. 'Hang on. I'm the only one wearing them.' Inspiration struck. 'You could all go in without me!'

It took a second for his words to penetrate the beery fog. 'Yeah.' To the majority of the group this seemed like a depressingly good idea. Simon knew his chat wasn't up to much nowadays, but still. Ghost was already moving back towards the club. He turned to beckon the others. 'Let's go.'

Barney held up a hand. 'Hold on, hold on. Us stags stick together. No Simon, no club. Alright?' He slightly ruined the effect by stumbling over his own feet, but saved it by taking his tutu in both hands and performing a wobbly curtsey.

'That's not fair.' This from PE teacher Dev.

Oh God. Rebellion. They would all be at it soon. Simon dropped his head, so he couldn't see the contempt in their eyes. He thought little enough of himself already.

'Hey.' Barney held up a hand, adjusting his pink wig with what nearly amounted to dignity. 'We're all together. We're here. That's fun enough, isn't it?'

There was a resounding silence. Simon found himself thinking of the cottage, of that little red head resting against his. The comfort of those arms circling him as he read his boy to sleep. The year was slipping away with him. It was June already, and soon the hospital letters would arrive with details of pre-operative assessment clinics, Ronald McDonald accommodation and the date that the operation would take place.

He shook himself back into the present as Ghost decided to have a piss against the wall next to him. Some of it splashed up onto Simon's leg. He felt like he deserved it.

'I'm sorry, mate.' His words to Barney were lost in classic suggestions from the group as to where they could go. Strip clubs. Pubs. That bar that was back down that way with the sexy birds outside.

'Stop worrying.' Barney flung an arm around Simon. 'I'm having a great time.'

God, Simon loved him. Between them lay over thirty years of friendship. A friendship born on a climbing frame, one hand helping another to the top, and nurtured in pubs, over pints, through first kisses and first loves and the pain of learning that those loves could leave.

Barney took a swig from his can. 'Is Jake OK?'

'My phone died, but I reckon so.' Simon nodded. 'Beth'll have things sorted.' He felt a surge of warmth as he said it. It was such a luxury having someone right there who could help. Jean was great, but she was in her seventies and she did like to disappear on ballroom dancing trips. Beth was calm and kind and always ready to help.

'It's amazing, really, that you let Beth look after him at all. You've only known her a few months.' Barney hitched up his skirt.

'It feels longer.' It was true. She had somehow become part of his world. Part of their world. Some mornings he got up to find Jake round at hers having his breakfast, and she had already joined them in their weekly ritual of Sunday Toast in front of a movie.

'You don't normally trust new people with him.'

'Beth's a nurse. She's trained. Of course I trust her.'

'Being trained never made a difference before.' Barney reached up a hand to straighten his tiara. He now appeared quite proud of it. 'Do you remember that locum GP – you didn't believe she was right about Jake when he had chickenpox. You insisted he was on the wrong heart meds.'

'Oh.' Simon had forgotten that. 'Well—'

'And that dentist a couple of years ago? You gave him hell for screwing up Jake's filling, when really he had a load of mouth ulcers.' Barney swayed slightly as he patted Simon on the shoulder. 'I think it's safe to say you're a tough crowd.'

'Yeah, yeah.' Talking about mouth ulcers seemed like the final death knell of this stag do. The group were meandering now, split into twos and threes, their energy fading. Simon made one final effort to turn things around. 'Let's go to the pier. Play the slots. Who's in?'

This, at least, got a positive reception. Soon the herd was heading through streets ripe with mottled legs and eye-popping cleavage, past chip shops, ice cream parlours and pubs until they were on the promenade with bright lights sparkling overhead. In front of them, the North Pier glowed its welcome.

Simon could remember a date here with Tamsin just before Jake was born – he'd been trying to cheer her up, but she had spent the day hidden behind her grey scarf, unable to eat anything, let alone smile or laugh. He had held her freezing hand all day, trying to instil some life into it, trying to bring her back.

They reached the entrance to the promenade, and he blinked in the neon lights as the clack and ring of the slots reached his ears. Loud music reverberated around him and a pop-up bar by the entry archway was offering tequila at 50p a shot. The air smelt of meat and onions, and Simon's stomach growled. A man was holding out candyfloss to his date while a small child, who was evidently very much past his bedtime, was howling as his mum dragged him along by the hand.

'SHOTS.'

Ghost had got his second wind.

'YES.' Simon had to turn this around. He ran to get to the bar first.

Tequila. That was the answer.

'Are you all right for this, mate? I can get this, if you like.' Despite his wig, despite his tutu, Barney was still keeping an eye on Simon.

It was all wrong. 'No way. It's all good.' Simon handed over his card, lining up the glasses on the bar as the barman picked up the bottle.

'Are you sure?'

'Yeah.' Simon spoke with a conviction he didn't feel, but the tequila was flowing into the glasses and that had to be a good thing. He didn't bother with the lime, he didn't bother with waiting, he just took his shot and tipped his head back. The tequila lit a fire in his belly and he wanted more. He wanted a whole night of this.

'To Barney!'

He poured them all another, threw his head back and drank. He wanted oblivion. He needed to forget about tomorrow.

He needed to forget about what was to come.

15

Beth

'It's OK, Simon, I haven't broken him, promise. Though he nearly smashed my nose when we played football earlier. He's got a good right foot.' Beth watched with amusement as Simon folded Jake in his arms as enthusiastically as if he had been gone a year. Simon's voice was even lower than usual as he kissed Jake's whirl of hair. 'Hello. Did you miss me?'

'Not really.' Jake extricated himself. 'Look. We made the Sydney Harbour Bridge!'

'A multi-coloured version.' Beth finished washing the final plate from lunch before joining them on the carpet, looking at their creation with pride. The main body was in pink and purple, while the rest was in grey and yellow. It rested on a blue sea and tiny Lego figures were clambering on top, just like the real BridgeClimb.

'Wow. That's amazing.' Simon's face was a pale shade of green so she quietly got him a glass of water. He thanked her and gulped it gratefully before lying down on his side, head resting on his hand, to fully admire Jake's work.

'So . . .' Beth went over to Barney, who was sitting at

the table, checking messages on his phone, which he had plugged in on arrival. 'How was it?'

Barney glanced up. She could see the shadows beneath his blue eyes, but he looked positively human next to Simon. 'It was great.'

She slid into the chair opposite him. 'Is that why Simon is the same colour as the grass?'

Barney nodded, pulling one corner of his mouth downwards. 'Yeah. I think he needs some practice. It's been a while since he went on a major bender.'

'Any word on how the hen went?'

'Lina's already home in the bath with a face pack on, so I think it must have been a good one.'

'Great. I slept for two whole days after mine.' Beth's hen had been wild: dancing on tables; blasting out karaoke; pouring themselves into a packed club to salsa till dawn. Fries and shakes on the way back, heels slung from their fingers.

Barney looked uncomfortable.

'Oh God, sorry. I didn't mean that . . .' She stopped. 'I mean, I wasn't comparing my shitty marriage with your soon-to-be-amazing one.' She was getting hot now. 'I mean . . .'

Barney chuckled. 'You're alright, Beth. Don't panic.'

'Thanks.' She changed the subject. 'So tell me all. What happened?'

Barney scrolled through another message. 'You know. Shots. Curry. Being turned away from a club. The usual.'

'And how was climbing up the Tower?'

Barney shrugged, flicking some lint from his blue striped sweatshirt. 'That didn't quite work out.'

'That's a shame.' As she spoke, Beth noticed a flush was creeping up Simon's neck.

Barney checked his watch. 'But the pier was great. I won this beauty.' He pulled a purple teddy bear out of his bag. It had long pink eyelashes and a heart printed on its tummy. 'I'm sure Lina will be dead proud of me.'

'Of course she will.' Beth reached out to stroke its fur – recoiling slightly when she was hit with a blast of synthetic perfume. 'What's that? Strawberries?'

Barney grinned. 'Rank, isn't it? She'll be trying to lose this thing for the rest of our lives.'

'Well, you've got to have something to do once the honeymoon period wears off.' Beth panicked that she sounded bitter. 'Sorry. I . . .'

'Stop worrying, Beth.' Barney laced his hands behind his head, tipping the chair back. 'I know what you meant.'

She relaxed. 'Good. You must be so excited. Not long now, is it? The time will fly by, just you wait.'

Simon was on his feet now, leafing through the post that had come yesterday. His eyes widened as he ripped open a plain white envelope. He leant forward as he read, gradually looking even more in need of a bucket and a lie down. When he finished he was gripping the sink with both hands as he visibly inhaled.

'You OK, mate?'

Simon turned to Barney, distress stamped all over his exhausted face. 'Bit of news.'

'Yes?'

'Jake's operation date is through.' He walked over and put his arm around his son, already protecting him, already shielding him from what was to come. Beth had seen it in so many relatives on her ward at Mercy View – the way they held the pain inside them, absorbing it, never passing it on to the loved one lying on the bed.

'When is it?' Barney watched his friend and his boy, forehead creasing into a frown.

'It's in December.'

'Oh.' Barney nodded. 'Well, it's good to have it booked in.'

'Yes.' Simon didn't move. 'But it's two days after your wedding. So I . . .' He was visibly sweating now.

'What, mate?'

'It's just, that—'

'What?' Barney tapped his fingers against the table.

'I'll have to be in quarantine with Jake. On your wedding day.'

The words dropped into the room, bringing a loaded silence in their wake. A muscle flickered in Barney's cheek. Simon's gaze was glued to his friend, his eyes sharp with anguish.

'What?' Jake stood up, his breathing rapid beneath his T-shirt. 'But that's not fair.' His lower lip trembled. 'I can't miss the wedding – I'm the pageboy.' Mutiny glinted in his eye. 'I don't want to do stupid quarantine, anyway. I don't want the operation. I'm fine!'

Simon put a hand around Jake's shoulder, his eyes still fixed on his friend. 'I'm so sorry, mate. But I can't miss quarantine – I have to get him in there, healthy. If I get sick and pass it to him then the operation can't happen. And if it doesn't happen, then . . .'

He couldn't finish the sentence.

Neither could anyone else.

Beth was watching Jake. A tear made its way steadily down his cheek.

Barney remained uncharacteristically silent, head tilted towards the ground. Simon took a step towards him. 'Mate. I'm so sorry. Especially after screwing everything up this weekend. I feel awful.'

'It's not your doing.' Barney exhaled loudly, puffing out his cheeks. 'Can you move the date, maybe?'

'Not really. It's the NHS. You take what you get.'

Barney folded his arms. 'It's worth a try, isn't it?'

'Of course.' Simon chewed his thumbnail. 'I'll try. I promise. And I'm sorry about this, mate. I really am. You know how much I want to be there. I'll do my best to change it.'

'And if you can't?' Barney turned his palms upwards. 'Then what?'

'Then I'll do a video speech? I can record it?' Simon was scrabbling now. 'I'll think of something.'

Barney ran a hand through his hair, then tipped his chin up. His smile wavered, but he was trying. 'Maybe it's easier if we just say you'll miss it.'

'No. Not because of me.' Jake's face was defiant. The Dennis the Menace face on his T-shirt was almost mockingly cheerful and his thin knees stuck out of his shorts, as he stepped forwards, fists clenched.

'You can go to the wedding, Dad. I'll stay at home. I don't want you to miss it.'

Simon laid a hand on his head. 'It's OK, Jake. Barney, I'll sort it.' He was standing now, his voice rough and urgent. 'I will. I promise. I won't let you down.'

'I don't want to put pressure on you, mate.' Barney shook his head. 'I know you've got a lot going on.'

'I just . . .' Simon pressed his lips together. 'I have to be here for Jake.' His hands were twisting together and then away. 'He's my boy.'

Jake slowly covered his ears with his hands. Simon pulled him closer, stroking his hair. 'This isn't your doing, lad.'

Jake's voice was thick with tears. 'It is, though, it is!'

Simon's exhaustion was spotlit by the bare bulb hanging from the ceiling. 'I'm so sorry.'

Barney shrugged. 'I know.'

'You hated the weekend too, didn't you?' Simon was stroking Jake's hair so fast it was standing on end.

'No, mate.' Barney's voice rasped. 'I had a great time. But Jake needs all of you. I've always known that. I can ask someone else to be my best man.'

Simon looked stricken. 'What?'

'I can ask someone else to be my best man. To look after the rings and stuff.'

'But . . .'

'Look. Jake's much more important, OK?' A muscle flickered in Barney's cheek. 'It's OK, mate, really. I get it.' He looked away. 'Now, I'd best get back to Lina. She'll be wanting to check if I'm still in one piece.'

'I . . .' Beth could see Simon's knuckles white around Jake's shoulders.

'It's OK, mate.' Barney mustered a smile. 'Really. You've got far more important things to do than babysitting me on my big day.'

Jake didn't even raise his head when Barney walked across and gently knocked his fist against his. 'Fist bump.'

Nothing.

'Cabbage.' Barney closed his fingers around Jake's.

'Still nothing? Ouch.' Barney sighed. 'This is officially my worst exit ever.'

No one disagreed with him.

'Bye, Beth.' Barney picked up his teddy bear by the paw, put his phone in his pocket, and left the house.

Emptiness screamed in his wake. Beth wished she knew how to fill it.

'Cup of tea, Simon?'

He shook his head. 'No thanks.' He was still holding his boy and Beth knew it was time for her to go.

'See you both around.'

Simon looked up, eyes clouded. 'Thank you so much for looking after him, Beth.'

'I loved it.' It was true. A whole night of sleep followed by football and Lego. She felt lighter than she had in months. She turned at the top of the back step, looking back at the two of them, big arms around small shoulders, red hair against brown.

Then she walked up to her back door, unlocked it, and sat down in her living room, breathing in the quiet. Birds sang outside and the sun flooded in, but the shelves seemed too tidy, the floor too neat. Her cottage was a blank. Maybe she was too. She leant back against the cushions, hands folded on her knees, staring out at the sky, hoping that soon she would hear their laughter through the wall. The first sign of recovery – of Simon and Jake facing this next step. Sunday toast. A movie. One step, then the next.

She would help them in every way she could. And this time, she wouldn't be distracted; this time she would be everything they needed her to be.

This time, she wouldn't make a mistake.

16

Simon

'So there's no way you can change the date? You're sure?' Simon wedged the phone under his chin and pulled his pickup over on the verge. It had taken twenty minutes to get through to the hospital appointments team and there was no way he was hanging up now.

'No. I'm sorry. His consultant is away for the whole of January. We'd have to move Jake into February, and his notes advise against that.'

'Right.' Simon sighed. 'Thanks for your time, then. We'll stick with that date. Bye.'

He flung his head back against the headrest as he voiced a stream of four-letter words. He hated letting Barney down. He hadn't seen his best friend look that upset since he had thought Lina would dump him, when Barney had got so drunk he passed out on her front step one night. He had saved the day by declaring undying love for her and giving her a key to his flat. If only Simon could work out a similarly positive solution.

He pulled out again, cursing as the potholes removed yet more of his paintwork. He hoped that he would be having a day on his own in the combine harvester – time to work out what the hell he was going to do about this wedding mess. As the pickup bumped into the yard he remembered the day he had introduced Lina and Barney, at his birthday drinks. Barney, beer in hand, shiny birthday hat askew on his head, had clocked Lina within seconds of entering the pub. Beers had become a club, which had become chips and sauce at the kebab van in the small hours. And as Simon had fumbled with his key that night, he had seen Lina and Barney kiss.

Now they were getting married and he couldn't be there.

He hit the steering wheel with the heel of his hand, wishing that for once his life could be his own to live the way that he wanted to; wishing that Tamsin were there, not just because he still longed for her but because he wanted someone else on Team Jake. He would love someone else to share the responsibility – to give him flexibility where currently he had so very little. Another person to share his fears and to help him face them. Fleetingly, he thought of Beth, with her dark eyes, her empathy and the sadness that sometimes clouded her face like clouds in a spring sky. Occasionally, when they walked back down from their runs together, her hand brushed against his and he would think about clasping it tight. But then Tamsin would burst back into his head, her green eyes shining and her lips curving into that irresistible smile.

Over six years and counting. When would his heart give up on her?

He rolled his eyes at his own stupidity as he parked up and switched off the engine. Tamsin wasn't coming back. He might as well accept it. There was no happy ending round the corner for him – he was just a lonely man in a knackered pickup working for his dad.

'Morning.' William appeared next to his window, a cardboard box in his hands. His grey hair was brushed back, his eyes sharp. If his dad ever spent time feeling sorry for himself, Simon had never witnessed it.

'Alright, Dad? What's in the box?'

'It's for Jake. I thought he might like it.' William opened the passenger door and deposited it on the seat. The box smelt of history. Curious, Simon pulled open the flaps and looked inside.

'I didn't know you still had this!' He ran his hand wonderingly over the Lego service station set inside, which he could still remember getting on his fifth birthday. The word Shell was written in red on a white sign on the box, and petrol pumps gleamed, complete with hoses and black nozzles. A memory tugged at him, a light behind a fluttering blind: his dad, flat on the floor leaning on his elbows, carefully driving a car onto the forecourt. 'Come on, lad, let's get some service going here.' Simon could see his own hand now, eagerly unhooking a pump, proudly plugging it into the car his dad had manoeuvred into place.

William coughed, hawking spit into the mud of the yard. 'Enough gawping. Come on, I haven't got all day.'

Just like that, the blind snapped shut.

Simon bristled. 'Can't you be a bit more friendly, Dad? Or is that too much to ask?' His skin prickled. For weeks he had managed to suppress his temper, despite the way his dad ordered him about – making more effort with the casual labourers than with his own son. Since receiving the operation date, though, Simon's anger had been flaring higher, testing him, beating a constant tattoo in his brain.

He took his keys out of the ignition and shoved them in his pocket. It was a scorcher today – all over the Lake District people would be picnicking and climbing and swimming in clear cold water. He wanted to go to the foot of the lake and climb up through the waterfall to High Peak, the water cooling him, the air fresh and sweet. Instead here he was, in navy overalls, next to a man who despised him.

William's glance was fierce. 'What are you looking like a wet weekend for?'

'I'm not, Dad.' Simon grabbed his sandwiches and his flask of tea. 'What am I working on today? The combine again?'

'No. You're with me today.'

Wow. Life just kept on giving.

'Great.'

His dad sniffed. 'Sarcasm never suited you, lad.'

Simon managed to bite back an extremely sarcastic reply.

He took a breath. 'What are we doing, then?'

'Clipping the sheep.'

Simon groaned.

'It's all been set up. The shearers are here.' A crease bit deep between his dad's eyes. 'I know you don't like getting your hands too dirty, so you can see them into position with me.'

Simon wasn't having that. 'I was on silage all last week, Dad. I think we can safely say I'm not too fussy about a bit of muck.'

'Maybe.' His dad never conceded defeat. 'Come on, then.' Simon followed as William strode off, dogs at his feet, head high, back straight. He was whippet thin in his old checked shirt and cords, his wellies splattered with mud. Maybe it was a good thing he was so uncompromising – without that, the farm might have gone under long ago.

Simon was sweating already. He trundled behind as his father started to open the rusty gate into the lowest field. William winced as he resolutely pulled the frame towards him and then again as he let it go once Simon was through.

'Dad, is there something wrong with your shoulder?'

'No.' A shake of the head.

Simon felt resentment surge. 'Alright. I was only asking. I could have a look, you know.'

'No need.' His dad's voice dripped contempt. 'It always hurts more in the morning. It'll pass.'

Simon tried again. 'But I'm a trained physio, Dad. I could . . .'

'No thanks.' William gave a dismissive flick of the hand.

'Fine.' Simon stumped on. Brown bracken coloured the fells above them, and the cornflowers in the hedges were as blue as the sky. His boots crushed daisies and buttercups as he walked up towards the higher ground where the sheep grazed.

Simon had been helping with shearing since he was

young, and encouraging hundreds of unwilling woolly balls to run towards a pair of clippers had never been his idea of a dream day. His dad loved it though – just as he loved anything to do with his precious Herdwicks. He had never given up on them, not when he had to sell the cows when milk prices plummeted, not even when a developer offered to buy the house and the land and turn it into executive holiday homes. *William, the views would be worth a fortune*, the man had said, signet ring gleaming on his fat little finger. *It's Mr Withers to you*, Simon's dad had replied. *And I wouldn't sell this land if you offered me millions. It's Withers land, and always will be.*

Simon was so lost in thought that he didn't notice that his dad had come to a halt, and cannoned into his back.

William turned. 'There's something I've been meaning to ask you.' Up here, the sunlight revealed every vein and wrinkle on his face. His eyebrows were now pure white.

His dad was getting old. Simon was jolted into gentleness. 'What is it, Dad?'

William's red-veined eyes slid away. 'It's wonderful up here, isn't it?'

'Yes.' Simon turned to take in the patchwork of fields stretching away back down to the farmhouse and woods beyond. 'It is.'

'I've been thinking . . .' His dad hesitated, twisting his cap between his fingers as he spoke.

'Yes?'

'If I could ask again . . . Now you're working here anyway . . .' William pressed his lips together, raising his arm to straighten his flat cap.

'The farm . . .' He stopped. 'We need to talk.'

'Oh. Dad, I . . .' Simon didn't want to have this discussion again. It had been painful enough last time.

His dad leant down and picked some cow parsley, spinning it between finger and thumb. He peered off over Simon's shoulder.

'I thought that maybe you might have come round to looking after the farm. To taking it over, like.'

In his eyes was something Simon had never seen before: vulnerability.

'I don't know, Dad.' He looked around – at the drystone walls criss-crossing the fields, at the grass, at the mighty Haystacks looming in the distance. These views were part of his DNA, but he didn't know if he was the right person to shape their future.

'I thought maybe you'd changed your mind. Now you're not doing your physiotherapy any more.' The cow parsley was twirling faster now. Simon had never heard his dad speak so many sentences in a row. 'And with Jake so happy when he comes up here. I thought maybe you loved this place as much as I do.'

'I do love it, Dad. You know that. But there's more to it than that.'

'Not to me.' Again, the wince as he moved his shoulder.

'Dad, I love the farm. I do. But I love other things too.' Beth's face appeared in his mind, that day at his secret hideout, encouraging him. 'I might go back to – to physiotherapy. I'd like to. Once Jake's through this operation and doing a bit better.'

'But the farm's right here, lad. It's been ours for

generations.' His dad was trying to connect with him – to convince him. 'I always thought that you'd take it over from me.'

'I know that.' Simon shut his eyes. It was twenty years ago and they were having this conversation for the first time. Mum was gone and they had been circling that vast oak table for weeks, not talking about how much they missed her. Simon had just told William that he had set up work experience at the local general hospital over the summer holidays. His dad needed him on the farm.

Simon had refused to change his plans, partly because the thought of working alongside his silent, angry dad was unbearable, but also because he had always known that physiotherapy was what he wanted to do. He loved the science behind it, he loved looking after people, as his mum had done. It was what he was born to do.

And that was it. The argument had raged on and off for the next three years, until Simon got a place at Loughborough and worked two jobs to pay his way through. He didn't go home at weekends and holidays like his friends. He stayed away, feeling that was best for both of them. Birthday cards were exchanged. Christmas phone calls were made, and survived. But his dad didn't come and see him receive his first-class degree. And when Simon had landed his first job at a general hospital in Manchester, his dad hadn't said a word of congratulation.

He felt Simon had let him down. And Simon felt the same about him. End of story.

'I think you'd do right by the farm, lad.'

Simon glanced up, surprised. It was as close as his father had ever come to a compliment.

'And you seem happy up here.'

'I do?'

'Aye. You look better too – in the fresh air, and that.'

Simon was surprised. His dad had never seemed to notice anything that didn't have four legs and a woolly tail.

William nodded. 'And that son of yours too. It suits him up here.'

'It suits him being near your dogs.'

His dad gave a rare smile.

'Will you at least think about it, lad?'

'Yes. Alright.'

Simon followed William, his thoughts whirling, not understanding William's sudden urgency about this. Something must have changed. Fear jabbed him. 'Is there something wrong, Dad? You're not ill, are you?'

His dad turned, his hand on the gate at the top of the field. Simon noticed the way his hand shook as he opened it. 'No. Nothing like that.'

'Are you sure?'

William's face hardened. 'Of course I'm sure. I'm fit as I ever was. I'm just thinking ahead. Seeing you more – I just thought, that's all. It might work. I thought it might help.'

Simon's pride flared. 'I don't need help.'

'Then I'll stop offering.' William sucked air between his teeth. It set Simon's nerves jangling, reminding him of a lifetime of judgement.

'I'll go back to the hospital, Dad. Once Jake's through this operation. You'll see.'

His dad's look was full of a pessimism that Simon wished he didn't share. 'Will I, Simon?'

Simon spoke loudly, searching for certainty. 'Yes. You will. You *will* see. We're fine.'

'Alright, alright. Stop banging on, lad.' He remembered that bark from his childhood. Being sent to his room for failing to wash the parlour down properly. His dad's fist slamming on the kitchen table if Simon didn't turn up on the dot of seven for supper.

He mouthed nothings at William's departing back. 'I'm a good physio, you know. Ask anyone I've treated. Ask Jean.'

His dad strode steadily away and Simon's frustration felt so familiar it took him back to hearing the slam of the kitchen door as a child. Dad heading out, away from whatever triumph Simon was trying to tell him about. Mum stepping forward to try to fill the void. Her warm arms around him.

If only she were here.

His father turned. 'Are you coming or what?'

'Yes.'

Simon gritted his teeth as he trudged up to the pens. He was so tired of having to deal with this. He was tired of still being broke too, his earnings swallowed up in paying off credit card debt and food bills.

He just had to keep going until the Fontan, then he could regroup and work out how to restart his career. They were close to the pens of hot, panicking Herdwicks now and he braced himself for separating the writhing creatures so that they could be sheared one at a time. The smell was so sharp it kicked the back of his throat, and he was seven again, trying to shear a sheep and managing only to slice a huge chunk out of its shank. He could feel the flush of shame on his cheeks, his embarrassment as his dad told all his friends about it on auction day. All he had wanted back then was to be as strong as this tall, silent man. His dad, his idol.

Jake had showed him another way. A better way.

Simon entered the pen and was instantly buffeted by stressed, woolly bodies. He started the call, the 'Yep yep yep yep' as he pursued his first sheep for shearing. He cornered her, grabbing her by the scruff of her neck and pushing her through to the metal pen where the two shearers were waiting.

His dad was doing the same, a vein bulging in his neck as he reached down. Simon saw the clamp of his jaw and knew that he must be in serious pain. If only he would let Simon help; if only he would listen. Simon rolled up his sleeves, getting in amongst the sheep, and picking a black one at random to push through next. He would show his dad. He would prove him wrong.

He flung another one through.

His dad yelled above the manic bleats. 'Just show them who's boss, lad.'

'I am, Dad. I am.'

Simon bent to the task, relieved to be moving, pushing, using all the strength he had. He didn't know how to talk to his father. He didn't know what to do about the wedding. He didn't know how to stop holding a candle for a woman who had disappeared.

But he knew he had to keep going. He had to keep trying. He had to keep his boy safe and smiling. He had to be the dad that he wished his father had been.

Emily!!!

Phase 3 time! My makeover was great, and I got Dad an awesome new shirt too, but it made no difference. He STILL won't date anyone. So, I've signed him up to a dating site and wrote him this really great profile – I reckon he'll have a girlfriend by the end of the month for sure.

Love,

Jake xxx

17

Beth

The view was so beautiful it nearly distracted her. Nearly. She imagined leaping off this rocky outcrop and diving straight down to the deep blue water of the lake below, closing her eyes and swimming through the sticky August heat until she could no longer see the words that had arrived on her phone that morning.

Beth. We need to talk about the apartment, Tyler.

Even after all this time, it was nine words too many.

'Beth? Are you OK?'

She had forgotten that Jas was waiting patiently at the other end of the line. Her friend was worried. She had been calling non-stop all day, but only now, after a forty-minute run at twice her normal pace, had Beth calmed down enough to pick up.

'I don't know.' She put her hand to her head, suddenly dizzy. 'I just can't believe Tyler got in touch.'

'I know. I'm so sorry for just forwarding his message on like that. Saffy was up all night with a fever.' Beth heard the rush of air as Jas yawned. 'And I saw it on my Facebook wall at 3 a.m. and thought you'd want to know. I posted a picture of the quiz and half of your face was in the background. I guess Tyler knew we were mates, so he was keeping an eye on my feed. I'm so sorry.'

'It's OK.' Beth looked round to where Simon was lying behind her, exhausted from their run. She lowered her voice. 'I can't hide for ever.'

'You're not hiding, you're just living a different life.'

'I guess. I just thought – I don't know.' Beth plucked a handful of grass and let it fall through her fingers. Her stomach was swirling, acidic. 'I just thought he'd be happy I'm gone. And I thought the divorce was done. God knows I spent enough on my lawyer. I don't know why he'd need to talk to me. Unless . . .' She dug the tip of her trainer into the ground. 'Unless he's decided to break our agreement and keep hold of the apartment. Then he'd need to buy out my share.' A thought struck her. 'You haven't answered him, have you?'

'God, no.' Jas's voice was sharp. 'I'm not that stupid. I deleted the photo and blocked him. I should have done it ages ago. I'm really sorry, Beth.'

'It's OK.' Beth exhaled, tipping her face up towards the sun. 'Honestly. Stop worrying.' She was doing more than enough of that herself.

Beth glanced at Simon again. He was spreadeagled on the grass, hands folded over his stomach, his long legs tanned, face relaxed. 'Listen, I promise I'm OK, but I've got to go now.'

'OK. Well, call me anytime you need.'

'I will.'

Beth hung up and stared towards the horizon, her pulse rocketing. Peak upon peak reached for the sky as far as her eye could see, the green, brown and grey slopes fanning away into the distance. Today, though, the beauty didn't soothe her. Her mind was too busy. She felt scared. Angry. Hunted, like someone turning out their bedside light at night only to hear an unexpected sound down-stairs.

Simon spoke. 'Beth?'

'Yeah?' She walked across to him and reached for her water bottle, pleased she had tanned enough for the band of lighter skin on her ring finger to be invisible now. Here, she was just Beth: Beth who had got divorced in New York; Beth the nurse; Beth the neighbour; Beth the friend. No one knew her story. No one knew what she had done.

'Are you OK?' Simon raised his hand to shield his eyes from the sun as he looked up at her.

'Sure.' She tried to smile. 'That was a good run today. We really got some speed going.' Over the past few weeks, she and Simon had become regular running partners, and he was definitely starting to push himself harder.

'Yeah.' Simon reached out, his hand glancing against her bare leg as he stretched. She jumped, and he rapidly moved it away. 'Oh God. Sorry.'

'No problem.' She started pacing, full of energy, wanting to clear her head.

'Are you sure you're alright? You seem – wired today.'

'I'm fine.' She drummed her fingers against her thigh, trying to breathe. 'Sorry. Just a bit of a day. Ex-husband stuff.'

'Do you want me to punch him for you?'

It was a relief to laugh. 'No. It's OK. Thanks, though.'

She sat down next to him, kneading at the knots of tension in her neck. 'Is Jake feeling better yet? He looked so poorly the other day.'

'Not yet, but he's getting there.' Simon reached down to re-tie his lace. 'He must be feeling better because he ordered me out running.' His phone beeped and he took it out of his pocket.

'Oh, God. I'll kill him.'

'Why?'

Simon looked more annoyed than she had ever seen him. 'Jake put up a dating profile for me online with my actual phone number on it.'

'No.' She put her hand to her mouth.

'Yes.'

'Shit!'

'Yes.' Simon read the message on his screen. 'Here's a fairly typical reply. "*Hi Simon. I'm Gwendolyn and I'm very excited to hear about your amazing hugs. Could I have one? And maybe more?*"' He shuddered. 'There are pictures too.'

'No!'

'Yes! And believe me they're not ones you'd want to see. God, this is mortifying.' He switched the phone off, hurling it from him so it lay in the grass.

Beth stifled her laughter. 'Jake doesn't give up, does he?'

'I absolutely bawled him out.'

She nodded. 'I heard.'

'Oh God.' Simon put his hand over his face. 'I'm so sorry.'

'I just hear the sound. Not what you're saying.' Beth had actually retreated to her room and put headphones in to drown out the noise, but she wasn't going to tell him that.

'I just wish he'd stop, you know?' Simon ran his hands though his hair until it stood on end. 'I don't know why he's so obsessed with finding me a girlfriend.'

'Have you asked him?'

'Of course I have!' He looked at her with wounded eyes. 'But he just keeps saying I shouldn't be on my own. But I'm not, am I? I've got him.'

'You know that's not what he means.'

'Yeah, but still. I mean, who would want me anyway?'

'Well, Gwendolyn, apparently.'

'Ha ha.'

She looked at him. 'Oh come on, Simon. You're not being serious?'

'Of course I am!' He pointed at himself mockingly. 'What am I going to do, wow them with my muddy overalls?'

'There's more to you than muddy overalls.'

'Is there?' He gulped more water. 'I wonder sometimes. I've only been on a few dates since Tamsin left. Only one made it past the first drink.' He grimaced. 'And that ended in a fumble in a multi-storey that stopped when the car park attendant turned up. I've never parked there since.' His laugh was a low rumble.

'They just weren't right for you.'

'Or they were too good for me.'

'No way.' She felt a stab of conviction. 'You're great.'

His shoulders sagged. 'Not great enough.'

She couldn't believe he didn't see what she did. 'What do you mean?'

'Well, Tamsin left, didn't she?'

'Yeah. But that's one person. And from what you said she was seriously depressed. You can't judge yourself by decisions she made when she wasn't well.'

Simon's face softened. 'You're always so kind, Beth.'

'Takes one to know one.' She thought of the knocks on her back door, asking her to pop round for lunch on weekends. Of the notes he left in Jake's lunchbox, '*You superstar*' written on wrappers or cartons of juice. How, since Quizgate, Simon had made the time to bring Beth a mug of tea when he got home some evenings, as if he sensed that this was her worst time – the hour when she felt most alone.

Simon nudged her with his elbow. 'I think we got pretty lucky when you moved in next door.'

They stared at each other, and for a moment she imagined him leaning even closer, his arms closing around her, his warmth becoming hers.

She must get a grip. This was Simon, her friend. She hastily drank more water, tipping some over her head for good measure.

'Hey!' She had accidentally splashed Simon. He grabbed his bottle and squeezed it in her direction. 'Straight in the face! He shoots, he scores!' He raised his arms in triumph.

She saw her chance and fired the rest of hers at his chest.

'Arrrrgggghhhh.' He put both his palms to the spot and fell backwards, groaning dramatically. 'You got me. This might be the end. Tell Jake I love him.'

'Wow, I can see why you're not on the stage.'

'Hey!' He sat up, grinning. 'What happened to you being kind?'

'No one could be kind about acting like that.' She stood up. 'Shall we head back?'

Simon jumped to his feet, water dripping down his shirt.

'Yeah. Good idea. I left Jake terrorising Jean. I hope he'll be back to school next week as I don't know if she can take much more.'

'Jean can take care of herself.'

'True. Anyway, I suppose it's just how things are going to be until he has the Fontan. Up and down.'

He was so matter of fact. So lacking in self-pity. She felt admiration bloom. Tyler had complained about so many things – his rota, his salary, the way colleagues were promoted above him when he considered them to be his inferiors in every way. His hands would arc through the air, blue eyes glinting, as he listed all the reasons why his life was so hard, despite the Chief of Surgery plaque on his door.

Simon just faced things.

'How about we walk down through the Pass? The bluebells have gone now but it's still my favourite spot.'

'Lead the way.' They walked up a gentle incline, past a rocky cairn where a couple were sharing a Thermos of tea. Beth flicked a stray strand of hair from her face, her mind returning to Tyler's words. She couldn't be alone tonight, not with the message burning a hole in her brain. 'I can come round later? If you'd like? Make my famous burritos?'

Simon grinned. 'Great! Jake was hoping you might. And me, of course.' She felt a glow of acceptance. She liked the gleam in his eyes – liked knowing that it was there because of her. As she looked at him she noticed that the scar on his cheek was barely visible now. She remembered the feel of his skin under her fingers that morning, and blushed, digging her hands deep into her hoodie. Out of the way. Safe.

He had come to a halt.

'It's straight down there.' He pointed at the vertical drop to their left.

'You what?' She assumed he was joking. There was no way any human could get down that. All she could see was incline. 'Do you have a rope? Some crampons? A distress flare?'

'No.' Simon set off at his normal speed. 'You just walk.'

Oh.

'Wait for me!'

He stopped and turned. Now he was watching her. That was even worse.

She swallowed her fear and took one step. Then another. This was fine. She could totally do . . . She missed her footing and fell, scraping her knee across a rock as she slid downwards. She scrabbled to get a hold on something. Anything. Another rock scraped her arm and she gave a small scream.

Oh God, she would be at the bottom soon with two broken legs.

'You're alright, Beth. You're alright.' Steady arms were helping her up. She let herself be held, leaning into Simon, absorbing his strength.

'What are you, part mountain goat?' She had to joke to mask her trembling. She looked up at him, staring at the lips that were now so close to hers.

That thought again. Of drawing him close. Of putting her mouth to his.

She forced it away, looking down at her feet, and then wishing she hadn't. She appeared to be standing on the edge of the world.

'Look up, OK?' Simon's hand was gentle under her chin, tipping it upwards. 'Look at the horizon. Your feet will look after themselves, I promise.'

Her mouth was sandpaper, her breaths too short and too fast. She felt like sitting down until a helicopter could airlift her home. 'Are you sure?'

'Yes.' He held her by her upper arms, his mouth curving upwards. 'Just keep hold of my hand. I'll walk just ahead of you, and I won't let go, OK?'

'OK.'

'Just follow me. We'll be fine. I promise.'

'OK.' She sounded like she was being squeezed in a mangle. She tried to get her breathing under control. His palm was rough against hers, so different to Tyler's cool, smooth grip. Simon's fingers were warm and sure, leading her calmly downwards, despite her trembling legs and unsure feet.

He turned to check on her, so close she could see the tiny freckle on his chin. Again, something was telling her to stroke his cheek. To press herself against him.

She really must be in shock. That bloody message and all the questions it brought with it. The fears and the guilt. She staggered on, trying to keep her balance, until Simon came to a halt in front of a rocky stream. He pointed behind them and she turned to see quite how far they had come. The outcrop where they had started was way above them, so high she could barely see it now.

He grinned. 'See? You did it. We're nearly through the worst of it now. Let me lift you over.' He planted his feet either side of the bubbling water.

She baulked. 'No, thanks. I'm perfectly capable of—'

His hands were already around her waist and she was in the air. She felt a beat of regret as he put her down on the other side.

'Thanks.' She couldn't look him in the eye.

'No problem. Now, just a few more steps down this way until we reach the edge . . .'

'OK.'

'And look.' He was next to her now.

She gasped. They were at the top of a gravel path that meandered through a rich, verdant valley. The slopes were decorated with banks of purple heather, daisies bloomed and the trees gleamed in the afternoon sun. The stream they had crossed chattered beside them, matching the blue of the sky.

'Wow.'

'Thought you'd like it.' Simon walked on. 'It's one of

the best kept secrets in the Lakes. In April and May it's full of bluebells, everywhere you look. I'll bring you.'

She felt tears prickling her eyes. He was so kind.

She didn't deserve it.

'It's incredible. Thank you.' His hand swung next to hers, so close she could reach out and take it.

She stepped to her left, opening up a wider gap between them.

'Maybe Jake's right.' Simon sipped water as they passed a yew tree, a bird perched on one of its spindly branches.

'About what?'

'Maybe I should go on a date with one of Jake's lonely heart picks.' The corner of his mouth tugged upwards. 'It'd get him off my back, for starters.'

She was surprised by a sharp pang of jealousy. 'Yeah. Maybe.' She kept her voice light, belying her confusion. 'Great idea.'

'Is it?' He stopped and turned and he was so close she could see the map of lines across his face. Goodness shone from every pore of him as his eyes searched hers. 'I don't know any more.'

'Simon . . .' Her voice was low and hesitant. 'I . . .'

'Yes?' Those eyes, that mouth.

She found herself taking his hand. She didn't want to think about Tyler – to think about contacting him and feeling small and incompetent and in every way worse about the woman she was. She wanted to feel Simon's lips on hers. She wanted to lose herself.

Before she knew what she was doing she raised her mouth and kissed him.

Their lips met, pressing, exploring. His kiss was soft, warm as the sun on her back. She wanted more, pulling him closer, hungry, fierce.

Then he pulled away.

'Beth. I . . .' He put his hand to his mouth, frowning, as if he wanted to wipe the kiss away, to erase it.

Her heart plunged. 'I'm so sorry.' She leapt away from him, embarrassment flooding her, reaching for her water. 'The sun must have gone to my head. I don't know what I was thinking.'

'It's just . . .' He folded his arms and took another step away. 'It was a surprise. And I . . .'

She didn't want to hear his reasons. She just wanted to run.

But she couldn't. This was Simon. Her friend.

'I'm really sorry, Simon.' Beth wanted to turn back time. In another life she and Simon walked on together, talking, easy. She couldn't lose this friendship. 'Please forget about it? We're just – two mates, out on a walk. The sun made me go a little nuts. No big deal.' She was babbling like a teenager addressing her first crush.

'OK.' His laugh was too big and too hearty. 'The heat. Yes.'

'I'm sorry.' Beth opened her mouth to say more, but Simon was moving away from her so fast that he wouldn't have heard. She kicked herself for being so stupid. She was in no position to want Simon. She trudged along the path, shame seeping through her, head down, hoping against hope it wasn't too much further back to the village. She could dive into her cottage, close all the curtains and regroup.

'How much further?'

'Not far.'

Good. This silence was mortifying.

Simon walked slightly ahead of her, arms swinging, clearly wishing he was anywhere but here. And Beth had become clumsy, her trainers heavy on the rocky path, so full of embarrassment that she barely noticed the beautiful white farmhouse that appeared through the trees as they rounded the bend towards the lake.

Her mind remained a blank nearly all the way home.

'Still up for burritos?' She needed to re-establish normality – to get their friendship back on track.

'Sure.' He didn't look her in the eye.

'I'll come round in a bit, then?' Beth looked up at him. They were just by the turn in the lane. In a moment they would be home. And life would go on.

'Yes.' He nodded, eyes not meeting hers. 'I mean, no.'

She turned away, humiliated. 'Oh, OK.'

'No, Beth.' He grabbed her arm. 'That's not what I mean. I . . .'

'It's OK. I get it.' Wow, he really had hated their kiss. Tears stung her eyes, but she blinked them away. Not now. Not yet.

But Simon was still holding her. 'It's just – I want to explain. It's not . . .'

She saw Jake appear round the corner. Thank God. Escape. She didn't need to see any more pity in Simon's eyes – she could see exactly how the land lay.

She waved. 'Jake!'

'DAD.'

Simon jerked away from her, letting her arm fall.

'DAD?' Jake's voice was high. Sharp.

'What are you doing, Jake?' Simon was running towards him now. 'You need to rest.'

'Dad! You need to come. Now.'

Simon took Jake's hand and ran towards whatever had caused his excitement.

Beth followed, coming to a halt when she saw the woman standing on the gravel in front of the cottages. That red hair. The pale face. The pink Mini with its door still open.

Jake pointed at her; a woman who had his eyes and his smile. His face was stamped with wonder as he pointed at her. 'Look, Dad!'

Jake's mum was here. Tamsin was home.

Beth couldn't bear to look at Simon – to see the joy erupting on his face at the return of the woman he had waited over six long years for. Beth wasn't part of this scene. She was just the nurse next door, the woman still making mistakes, a coward too afraid to answer a message from the life she had lived before.

She walked quietly to her front door, opened it and went inside. The hall closed in on her – lonely and cold. Sliding down to the floor, her head buried in her arms, Beth began to cry.

18

Simon

After all his years of waiting, there she was. Tamsin.
He heard Beth crunching away across the gravel,
but he couldn't move or speak. He just wanted to drink
Tamsin in.

Her hair still glowed red-gold in the sunlight; her ivory
skin was flawless and that faint blush still swept across
her perfect cheekbones. Her full mouth curved up at the
corners as she turned to him. She was so beautiful it
stopped his breath.

Simon tried to speak. He failed.

He tried again. 'Hello.'

'Hello, Simon.'

Her smile was different; smaller, colder, her full lips
hidden behind a harsh slash of red lipstick. Her hair,
which once hung carelessly down to the middle of her
back, was now cut into a severe bob, the ends coming to
a blunt point at her shoulders. She wore a green jumper
flecked with glitter, her jeans were tight and her black
boots spiked into heels. She was no longer a girl, every
emotion visible on her tremulous face. She had a sheen
to her now, a clarity – like a pencil sketch filled in with
a thick black marker.

But her eyes were still the same. A deep green, wide, endless. Here she was right in front of him – everything Simon had missed. Everything Jake needed. The woman who could make their family whole again.

He thought, fleetingly, of Beth. Of the sweet confusion of her kiss.

But Tamsin was back, vivid and real. He stepped forward, leaning down, aiming to kiss her hello, but only achieving a painful clash of cheekbones when she turned her head. He caught an acrid whiff of perfume, and then she was down on her haunches, smiling at Jake, leaving Simon on his own.

He stood, twisting his water bottle between clumsy fingers. Then he looked down and remembered what he was wearing. His knees looked particularly knobbly in these shorts and his shirt was damp with sweat. In his fantasies he had always been in her Koh Tao sweatshirt and clean jeans, smelling of aftershave, cool and relaxed; the man she had fallen for.

Instead he really needed a shower.

Jake was back beside him now, hand creeping into Simon's, looking up at him for reassurance. Tamsin got to her feet and closed the door of her car. The three of them stood there on the gravel as the silence grew.

Jake tugged on Simon's hand. 'Do you think she's tired, Dad?'

'What?' Simon's brain was stuck on hello.

'You said she left because she got so tired.'

Tamsin's eyes met Simon's, then jerked away.

Simon coughed. 'So I did.'

Jake frowned. 'Maybe we should invite her in, Dad? To put her feet up?'

'Good idea.' Simon swallowed. 'Would you like a cup of tea, Tamsin?'

Tamsin's nod was brief. 'That would be lovely.'

'Can I carry anything for you?' Jake walked towards her, uncertainty in every step. He and Tamsin looked so similar and yet Jake had no knowledge of who his mum really was. Simon realised that he had precious little too.

When he had last seen Tamsin, she had been defeated, a young girl in a strange place, consumed with guilt and shattered by the medical crises which came hand in hand with HLHS. He had seen the spirit seeping out of her with every broken night and every 999 call; he had known that she had left them because she genuinely believed that Jake would be better off without her.

He had carried that version of her in his heart for all these years. But now, as she stood here, glamorous and real, it was increasingly obvious that Tamsin was now a woman. A woman who was doing well. He noted the registration plate as she closed her car door – it was only a year old. And even Simon knew what the intertwining 'C's on her handbag meant – Chanel.

Tamsin smiled shyly at her son. 'No thanks.' Her teeth tore at her bottom lip. 'I'm staying at a hotel in Keswick.'

'Oh.' Jake's mouth curved upwards, and it was Tamsin's smile. 'Can I show you round?'

'I'd love that, baby.'

Simon knew perfectly well that their son hated being called baby, but Jake said nothing. Tamsin walked up the step she had last descended six years ago. Her shoulders were taut. So were Simon's. He was clenching his jaw so hard his teeth ached.

She was over the threshold now, her heels clattering in the hallway. She looked around, blinking in the gloom, and Simon found he was seeing the cottage through her eyes. He didn't like what he found: the twisted coats hanging off the pegs; the muddy shoes piled haphazardly by the door; the flaking wallpaper above the stairs. If it had changed at all since the day she left, it was for the worse.

Jake led her through to the living room.

'This is . . . ow!' Tamsin's ankle turned over on a pile of Lego that Simon would have tidied away if he had known she was coming. His skin prickled as she inspected the room which was the heart of his and Jake's world. The window behind her was smeared with fingertip 'J's, drawn in condensation on one of Jake's more bloody-minded days, and the sofa was doing its level best to look as if it belonged on a bonfire. Simon wanted to take the grey underpants hanging on the radiator and bury them where they could never be seen again.

'How are you, then, Tamsin?'

Inspirational stuff. Wordsworth would have been proud.

'I'm well.' She sat down cautiously on the edge of the sofa.

'I'll get you that cup of tea.'

'Actually, no thanks. I'm good.' She leant back, flinching when she encountered Jake's hairbrush in one of its many hiding places. She laid it on the coffee table, next to the pile of clean washing Simon hadn't got around to putting away.

'Let's do Lego!' Jake emptied a bucket of pieces at her feet, and started raking through them. At last, he looked comfortable. 'Dad says you love Lego. He says that's why I'm so good at it – because you are too.'

Simon held his breath, hoping Tamsin would go along with another one of his white lies.

'Yeah. Sure. Lego's great.' She puffed her cheeks out, exhaling. 'Are there instructions?'

'No.' Jake didn't look up from the bricks. 'We just build. How about we make the Blackpool Tower?'

'Um.' Her laugh was a coiled spring, tight and cold, not the low bubble Simon remembered. 'I'm not sure I know what that looks like.'

'It's OK. I'll help you.'

Simon couldn't help but smile at Jake's patronising tone. His eyes tangled with Tamsin's and he saw to his relief that she was amused too.

Emboldened, he asked the obvious question. 'So why are you here? What made you come back? Now, I mean?'

She stayed focused on Jake, her hands cupped to hold the pile of black pieces he was passing to her. Her knee jiggled and one of her thumbnails was bitten to the quick.

'I wanted to see Jake.'

'Why this year?' Simon sounded more snarky than he had intended.

She flushed. 'Fair question. I just – couldn't stay away any more. I mean . . . He's going to be eight years old soon. I can't believe it.'

Jake's eyes were saucers. 'Are you going to be here for my birthday?'

Tamsin took a breath. At last, there was the gentleness Simon remembered – there was the vulnerability softening that lovely face. 'I'd love to, if you'll have me.'

'OK.' Jake chose a black base and started building. 'You'd better get me a present though.'

'Ja-ake.' Simon rolled his eyes. 'Sorry, Tamsin.'

'That's OK.' She grinned. 'And of course I've got you a present.' She ruffled Jake's hair in a way that had irritated the living daylights out of him since he turned three.

Again, Jake made no comment.

Simon wished he could breathe. He dropped into the armchair, only for a cloud of dust to rise up into the air. It caught in his throat and in only a moment he was bending over, coughing, tears streaming down his cheeks.

Cool, Simon, cool.

He felt a small hand connecting with his back. One thump. Two. Then footsteps, running to the sink. Jake reappeared, holding up a glass of water. Simon gulped it down, gasping for breath.

'Chill out, Dad.' Jake shook his head despairingly at Tamsin. 'I have to look after *him*, most of the time.'

Her mouth twitched. 'I can see that.'

Simon's cheeks burned.

Tamsin put the Lego down beside her. 'Jake. Have you got any pictures or anything to show me? Anything you've done at school? It's been a long time – I'd love to see what you've been up to.'

Simon guessed that she wanted Jake out of the room

so that she could tell Simon whatever she had come to say. His pulse quickened and he drank the last of the water, hoping that he would at least be able to trust his voice to answer her.

Jake was on his feet in seconds. 'I've got loads of things upstairs. Albums. The mug with my face on it that Dad uses for his toothbrush. I'll get you everything!'

He ran to the door and off down the hall, his cough the only sign of the last few days of illness.

As Jake's footsteps clumped overhead, Simon thought of the time he had first seen Tamsin – walking along the white sand in Koh Tao – long hair damp, laughing with that friend of hers. Carly, maybe – he couldn't remember. The one with the wild curls who had got so cross with Tamsin for being glued to Simon that she had stropped off on a motorboat with an Australian biker.

It had been easy back then; easy to know how to make Tamsin laugh; easy to know how to draw her into him, his hands sliding around her waist, her scent heady as her mouth pressed eagerly against his. Feeling the heat of her, the pulse of her, each moment more sweet until it was him and her and the sea, and everything he had ever wanted in the world was his.

Now they were two metres apart, and he had no idea how to even start a conversation.

'So how are you, Simon?' Tamsin sat up straight on the sofa, her legs neatly crossed. He couldn't stop staring at her high heels. When he had last seen her she had worn flip-flops and long dresses, silver bracelets jangling at her wrists.

She was waiting for his answer.

'I'm well. Apart from the choking, that is.'

She didn't smile. He could feel sweat pooling underneath his T-shirt.

Tamsin looked out of the window. 'It's still beautiful, isn't it? The view?'

'It is, isn't it? They wanted to build a mobile phone mast up there but Jean and the locals got up one of their campaigns – like the one against the car park, do you remember? When Jake was little?'

Her frown was back. 'No. Not really.'

'Oh.' Phone masts and car parks. She'd be heading straight back home if he kept this kind of chat going.

'So . . .' She recrossed her legs, the left now on top. 'I'm back.'

'Yes.'

Silence fell again as he waited for Tamsin to continue. She didn't.

He rubbed his hands together, he had no idea why. He had spent years planning what he would say if she reappeared, but every single word evaporated now that she was here.

'So . . . Was I right? Do you like Lego?'

Tamsin glanced at the door, speaking in a whisper. 'No.'

'Oh.' Silence fell again.

Come on, brain. This was Tamsin. The love of his life. He spread his hands wide. 'I'm sorry. I didn't know what to tell him when he asked about you. It was . . .'

'Oh no, please don't say you're sorry.' She shook her

head. 'I totally get that things must have been hard. It's nice that you told him things about me, even if they weren't really true.' Her voice was clipped, as if she was giving a boardroom update. She was becoming more of a puzzle by the second. The image of the two of them embracing, reunited, which he had held close all these years was shifting, dissolving.

Simon shook the thought away. Tamsin had only just returned – they both needed time to adjust. He moved across to the sofa, trying to create some kind of intimacy between them. All he wanted to do was touch her. Her hand lay next to his, her nails so polished he could almost see his own reflection, a chunky gold ring on the slender second finger of her left hand. Somewhere, underneath the scent and the accessories, was the girl with the haunted eyes whose baby had been born blue. The thought of her scream still pierced him – the way her arms had reached for Jake, finding only air, as the doctors rushed him away the minute she had borne him. Now she was all closed up, a flower before sunrise. But the real Tamsin was under there, somewhere. He just had to find a way through.

'What have you been up to, Simon?' Her eyes darted around the room, resting on the books piled up in the corner, then on the cracked iPad on the floor. Her fingers twisted in her lap.

'We've just been here, really. Same old, same old. I worked in an office for a while – can you believe that?'

That got a grin. 'You? In an office? Really?'

He remembered the two of them, legs dangling out of a kayak, pretending they were fishing, when really they were just kissing and staring at the sky. The sea was cornflower blue; the sky endless. He had bet her a million pounds that he would never take an office job. He wondered if she'd remember.

Her eyebrow rose and there it was – the glint that had set him on fire. It was all he could do not to kiss her as he felt the old complicity, the old mischief. 'You owe me a million quid, then. That'll sort my mortgage out.'

That brought him up short. 'You've got a mortgage?'

'Yeah.' She nodded. 'I bought a flat in south London a year or two back. Home, sweet home.'

He swallowed, digesting this. 'What are you doing for work?'

'I started a degree about a year after . . .' She shrugged. 'You know. And then, after graduating, I started out in marketing. I landed a few great clients, got promoted, got lucky I guess. I'm an account executive now for a branding agency.'

'You're an account executive?'

'Yeah. For the past year or so.' She shrugged, as if this were nothing.

'Sounds like you're doing alright.' Again, the words were sharper than he had intended.

She put a hand on his arm and hope sparked.

'Look, I am here to see Jake, Simon, like I said but I'm also here to say sorry. To you. And to him. I just wish it hadn't taken me so long. There's no excuse.' He opened his mouth but she galloped on. 'Those first few months after leaving I just went to ground. Every week I meant to come back, but then one month passed, then another, then it was a year, and then I started studying and I sorted myself out and I got scared of how much you must hate me.'

'I could never hate you.'

'You're so kind, Simon.' She patted his hand. 'I guess, deep down, I knew Jake was better off with you, anyway. You always were so close, you two.' She sounded almost wistful. 'You're such a great dad.'

She had always said this, right from that very first night when he had held their son's tiny hand in paediatric ICU. Jake had cried when she had touched him, seeming to sense the intensity of her distress. In the end she had gone to the "milking parlour" – a windowless room just off the unit where mums pumped breast milk into bottles to feed their babies – while Simon had stayed with their son.

'I just do my best, Tamsin.'

She put her head in her hands and he heard the slow swoosh of her exhale. 'God, this is hard.'

'Is it?'

'Yes!' There it was – the pain he remembered. 'There wasn't a day that I didn't think of Jake. Not a day I didn't miss him.'

Simon got the impression she had said this before. It was as if she was reciting from a script set in a therapist's room. He wondered who she had talked to and what they had said – if their words had led her back here at last.

She turned her face to his. 'I couldn't handle it like you could, Simon. Any of it. You were so calm. It was you he wanted in the night, you he reached for in the hospital.' She took a shuddering breath. 'It broke me.'

'I know.'

'And I knew you'd look after him.'

'We get by.'

'I can see that.' Her voice quivered.

Despite her silence, despite her absence, he still wanted to comfort her. 'The thing is, that first year was the worst. You were there for the hardest bit, Tamsin. I tried to find you – to tell you that Jake was doing better and to get you to come back. But I didn't know where you were.'

He thought of Jake's childhood. Of the dens they had built in the woods, of the storytelling under the tent of his duvet at bedtime, of the notes Simon would find in his pockets in that loopy scrawl, addressed to Daddy Cool or Mr Incredible. As Simon looked back, these were the moments that mattered, the memories that he would treasure. Everything else just faded away. The clinics, the sickness, the nights Jake had wept with pain and Simon had held him and dried his tears. They were just the darkness before the light; the pause before the next gleam of stars.

He was glad to have been here.

'Simon?' Tamsin's hands shook as she hooked a strand of hair behind her ear. He got a whiff of that unnerving scent again. It belonged behind an executive desk. 'Is it OK if I stay for a bit? If I try to get to know Jake? I've got a few weeks off, and then I thought I could come up at weekends when I can – but only if it's OK with you.'

He pictured the boy who was currently rooting through

boxes upstairs, trying to share the past six years with the woman who had given birth to him. He thought of the photos without her face next to Jake's; the questions at school about where she was; the drawings Jake had done with a blank where his mum should have been.

Protecting Jake – that was his only priority.

So he had to ask. 'Who for?'

'What do you mean?'

'Do you want to get to know him for you, or for Jake? Because I hope it's for both of you, and if it is then you need to stick around. For good. You can't come and then just disappear again. It's not fair on him.'

She nodded, absorbing this. 'I know that.' She tipped her head to one side in a gesture he remembered. Then she nodded decisively. 'And I'm here for both of us. For me and for Jake.' She tried to smile. 'I want a relationship with him. For ever.' Her eyes darted towards his. 'And maybe, with you?'

He held her gaze, hope rekindling. Then he took her hand. 'OK, then.'

Her eyes were bright with unwept tears. 'Thank you, Simon. Thank you.'

A tap ran next door. Beth would be making dinner now. Burritos, bursting with cheese and fried onions. On another day they would have been sharing them, laughing with Jake over Saturday night TV. That kiss had come from nowhere – women like Beth dated surgeons, not single dads who could barely afford their rent. The way Beth had hastened to get away from him afterwards proved that.

Anyway, Tamsin was here now. His dream come true.

He spoke in a rush. 'Tamsin. I've waited so long to say this. I'm so—'

'Here you go!' Jake burst back into the room, bearing a precarious pile of photo albums, exercise books and, riding high on top, his favourite yellow duck. Tamsin let go of Simon's hand.

'I've still got him!' Jake waved Superchick in Tamsin's face. 'Look!'

Simon started praying. *Go along with it, Tamsin.*

There was a flicker of camaraderie on Tamsin's face. 'Hello again. You're looking good, duckie!'

Jake frowned. 'He's called Superchick.'

You couldn't fault her acting skills. 'Of course he is. I was just testing.' She picked up a particularly battered exercise book. 'Now, tell me everything.'

As she sat cross-legged on the floor next to Jake, Simon walked to the kitchen and opened a beer. He watched the two of them, seeing Jake gradually coming into his own, as he talked of football and sports day or the head teacher's award he had got for his HLHS story at the start of Year 3. His eye fell on the picture of Emily sticking out of the top of the box, dancing onstage at Theatre by the Lake in Keswick last year, and his pulse quickened, fearing what Jake might feel. What he might say.

But Jake chattered on, telling Tamsin all about his friend. And Tamsin leant forwards, resting her chin on her hands, and she listened, giving him all the time he needed.

When Simon had dreamed of Tamsin, it had only ever

involved falling into her arms. But this Tamsin was so different to the girl he had fallen for all those years ago. She was practically a stranger.

He would have to get to know her again. Simon watched the two of them together, his heart swelling. Tamsin was back in the cottage. That was all that mattered.

All Simon had to do now was make her stay.

19

Beth

Beth put the last chair back in its place and surveyed the classroom. Five minutes ago it had been full of Year 3s making healthy diet posters, thinking about protein, starch and sugar. She was glad the school holidays were over now – the children gave her something to think about – something that wasn't Simon or Tyler or the feeling that the problems she thought she had left in New York were inexorably heading her way.

She hadn't answered Tyler – choosing instead to communicate via the lawyer she had consulted so often she would almost call her a friend. But her mind whirred on nonetheless, keeping her up night after night, casting shadows and fears, to the point where Beth frequently didn't even bother going to bed. Instead she lay on the sofa staring blankly at the TV, before giving up at daybreak and going for yet another run.

'That was great, Beth. The kids loved it. Thank you.' Barney bounced across from the whiteboard as if he had springs in his heels. 'Even I want to eat my five a day now, and Lina's always on at me about eating more healthily.'

Beth laughed. 'Really? You told me the day we met that you're a regular at the gym.'

'Yeah.' Barney picked up a stray piece of paper from underneath one of the small wooden desks. 'But only to work off my Cadbury habit. And my beer habit.' He ticked the list off on his fingers. 'And then there's my pie habit.'

'Don't tell anyone.' Beth pretended to check for listeners. 'But I have a pie habit too.'

'Never. Well, don't worry. Your secret's safe with me.' He patted his midriff. 'I've got to stay in shape for the wedding though. I've hired my morning suit now and it's a tight fit.'

'Of course!' Beth leant against the windowsill, remembering Simon's face after the stag when he had discovered the clash of dates. 'Did you . . .?' She stopped.

'Find a new best man?' Barney gave a wry smile. 'Yeah. It's not the same, but – I don't want Simon to feel bad, so . . .' He shrugged. 'It is what it is.'

His kindness touched her and she was about to say so when a familiar face appeared at the classroom door.

'Beth!'

'Jake!' She leant down and hugged him. 'It's so good to see you!'

He stepped back, pulling a white envelope from his pocket. She felt a pang of concern as she saw the shadows beneath his eyes, the pallor of his skin. She wondered how it felt having your mum walking back into your life after such a long time away.

She stood up again, seeing children out in the playground, chattering and giggling as they made their way out of the school gates towards home. She saw Simon going against the flow, making his way towards the main entrance, and resisted an urge to hide.

She turned back to the boy in front of her. 'How are you doing?' The truth was that over the past two weeks she had missed seeing Jake's face at the window more than she could say, missed his chatter about new Minecraft updates or the contents of his Lego magazine.

'Good.' Jake twisted the envelope between his fingers, opening his mouth as if to share something more. Then he held it out. 'I wanted to give you this. I knew you were here today, so . . .'

'Thank you!' Beth took it and started ripping it open.

'It's an invitation to my birthday party.'

'Oh. Wow. Thank you.' She could hear Simon's voice outside. Her mind ran yet another replay of the way he had pulled away from her, the pity in his eyes.

She stared at the invitation, edged in footballs and gold. 'There's a mistake on here, surely?'

'What? No!' Jake peered over her shoulder.

'It says you'll be eight.'

'Yes.'

'But you're twelve, surely?'

She knew it was a lame joke, but she had to keep talking. Anything to avoid looking at the man who was about to walk through the door.

Jake clapped a hand to his forehead, eyes rolling in despair. 'No.'

'Oh. Silly me. And yes, I'd love to come.'

'The party's two weeks on Saturday. You need to wear a swimming costume.'

'Great.' She took in this information. 'What?'

'You'll see.' Jake gave an impish grin as Simon walked in. Despite all her stern words to herself her stomach cartwheeled at the sight of him. Tall, smiling, strong.

Time to leave. Beth bumped into a desk as she rushed to pick up her bag. She had to get out of here.

'Hi, Beth.' At least Simon was clearly as embarrassed as she was. He raised his hand and dropped it. 'How are you?'

'Fine.' She stared at the floor, her cheeks hot. 'Just leaving, actually.'

'Oh. OK.'

'Dad, can we go now? I said I'd be on Minecraft at 4. Loads of my friends will be on. We're going to build a prison!' Jake's expression told Beth that there could be no greater thrill in the world.

'Just a second, kiddo. I need to chat to Barney for a minute.'

'Da-ad.' Jake's head dropped in disappointment. Suppressing her desire to escape, Beth stepped towards him. 'Simon won't be long. How about you tell me more about this party of yours?' She took him off towards the window, away from the two men.

'It's a kayaking party.'

'Oh, wow.'

'Yeah. It's at my favourite place by the lake. Dad and I go there for picnics sometimes.'

'That sounds amazing.'

'Yeah, and you'll be there, and Tamsin, and Dad, and Barney and Lina. It's going to be awesome.'

Behind Jake, Beth could see that Barney was leaning towards Simon, his expression serious. Simon's arms were folded, eyes dark, as he listened.

'And will your friends from school be there?'

'No.' Jake fiddled with the zip on his coat. 'They're coming round for tea and Minecraft on my actual birthday.'

'Great. Emily too?'

A beat of silence. 'No.' Two red spots appeared on Jake's cheeks. 'She can't come.'

'Oh, that's such a shame. You'll miss her, I'm sure.'

Jake was running the zip up and down its track now. Again and again. She heard the word Tamsin from Barney, and caught a glint of mutiny in Simon's face.

She looked away, feeling as if she was intruding. 'So will you be celebrating another time then? With Emily?'

'Emily?' Simon turned and was halfway across the classroom before Beth could answer. 'What are you talking about Emily for?'

Beth blinked. 'I was just asking Jake if she was coming to his party.'

Simon put his arm protectively around his son, his eyes flashing. 'What? Are you joking?'

'Why would I be joking? She's his best friend.'

'But she . . .' Simon's mouth worked, and his eyes told Beth that she had said something very, very wrong. She stood, uncomprehending, staring at the cheery yellow sunflowers on the walls, made from pipe cleaners and tissue paper. Jake was quiet. Too quiet.

Beth looked at Barney, but even he was grim.

Her voice faltered. 'What is it? Emily's his friend. He

told me all about her. He said he'd be seeing her soon. Didn't you, Jake?'

A tear rolled slowly down Jake's cheek.

Simon put his fingertip beneath his son's chin, raising it gently. 'Jake? Did you say that?'

'Yes.' Jake's eyes were full of anguish.

'Oh, Jake.'

'I didn't want to tell Beth that Emily died.' Jake's voice was rising now. 'I wanted Emily – to still be here. She's the only one who understood me. I write to her sometimes. I talk to her too. It makes things – better.' His face cracked, and the only sound in the colourful classroom was the raw sound of his sobs.

Beth's hand flew to her mouth. Emily with her dark hair and bright eyes. The dancer. The Nintendo queen. The little girl with arms aloft on Jake's wall. Jake's best friend, the only person who understood what it was like to have HLHS.

Emily was gone.

Simon's face was heavy with sadness as he knelt down and hugged his boy, trying to take away a pain that would never be forgotten.

'I'm sorry, Dad.'

'No, lad.' Simon's voice shook. 'Don't say sorry.'

'But I told a lie.' Jake buried his head deep in his dad's shoulder.

'That's OK. You wish she was still here.' Simon kissed his son, his own eyes misting with tears. 'I wish she was too.' Beth could see him biting down hard on his lip, fighting with everything he had to be strong for his boy.

'I'm sorry.' Jake's shoulders shook.

In that moment, she knew that she hadn't been wrong in that moment in the valley, when she had reached for Simon. She cared about this man. She believed in him. He was kind. He was courageous.

She would be his friend, if that was all she could be, however much it hurt.

Simon's eyes were closed now. 'Don't be sorry, son. Please, don't be sorry.'

Beth knelt down and put her arms around Jake too. Barney did the same for Simon, and the four of them held each other as Jake's sobs quietened and then – eventually – stopped.

Beth was about to speak, but Barney got there first.

'I think I've got a Twirl in my desk. Anyone want to share it?'

'Me.' Jake shot his hand in the air. 'But I don't want to share it.'

The relief in Simon's shaky laugh made Beth's heart contract. He dabbed the tears from his son's face, his fingers gentle as he wiped his raw, puffy eyes. Then Jake walked over to Barney, taking the Twirl triumphantly and biting into it as he made his way out of the door, Barney's arm around his shoulders.

Simon dropped onto a small wooden chair, clearly shattered.

Beth hovered, feeling useless. She wanted to hug him, but he might think she was about to jump on him again. In the end she rested a hand on his shoulder, squeezing, trying to give what comfort she could.

Simon sat quietly, regaining his composure. Then he raised his head.

'Want to talk about it?' She sat down opposite him, itching to take his hand. Instead, she folded her hands in her lap and leant backwards, away from him. 'Don't worry, I won't try to kiss you again. Promise.' She managed a grin and was pleased to receive one in return.

'It was one of the worst things I ever had to do, telling Jake that Emily had gone.' Simon exhaled. 'He met her on the ward when they had their first HLHS operation. She was a few months older, but they were peas in a pod.' He glanced at Beth and the pain cut deep on his face. 'She was so much fun. She liked Spider-Man, and wore a cape and danced whenever she could. She loved the Grinch so much she wore a different T-shirt every day of the week, all of them with his face on it. She and Jake were thick as thieves.' He rubbed his forehead with the heels of his hands, pressing deep.

'It came out of nowhere. One minute she had been for her Fontan, and it had gone well and she was back home. Then she died, in her sleep, just like that.'

'Oh God. The Fontan.'

'I know.' Simon nodded, his mouth set. 'The same operation Jake's having in December. Like I said, it went well, but then she had a cardiac arrest at home, a few days after being discharged. She was gone before the ambulance arrived.'

Beth stared at him. 'I had no idea. Jake talked like she was still here. Like she was alive.'

'Well, he wants her to be, doesn't he?' Simon shrugged. 'God knows, we all do.'

Beth thought of the photos of Emily on Jake's bedroom wall – of the life in every fibre of the little girl's body and face.

Simon picked up a pencil from the pot on the desk in between them. 'She died just before her birthday, so her mum went ahead and had a party anyway. There were great piles of iced buns – Emily loved them. She would have had them for breakfast, lunch and dinner if she could.' He rolled the pencil between his fingers. 'Grinch balloons, that dance game on YouTube on the telly. Emily adored all that. All of us were there laughing and celebrating her little life – her short life . . .' Beth could see him fighting back tears and winning. 'Laughing and chatting as the kids played, when all of us could see her parents were breaking in two. And we all knew it could be us at any moment.'

'Oh, Simon.' Her heart swelled for him; for Jake; for their grief, for his loss, for the knowledge that his little boy had to have the same operation in a few weeks' time. 'I'm so sorry.'

He stared resolutely at the floor. 'It's how it is. We all know we're walking a tightrope every day. Kids with HLHS can go at any moment. Tomorrow, it could be Jake . . .' He put his head in his hands and it took everything Beth had not to reach out and hold him.

But he was strong, as she had always known him to be. There were no tears, no self-pity. Instead he raised his head again a minute later and looked her straight in the eye.

'I'm just glad Tamsin's back, before . . .'

'Before the Fontan?'

'Yes.' His eyes drifted away again, staring out of the window. 'Because who knows . . .' He stopped.

'Simon.' Beth leant forward. 'Jake isn't Emily. You know that, don't you?'

'I . . .' His face was clouded with doubt. She wanted to rub it away.

'Jake's living his story. Emily lived hers. You need to remember that.'

He moved so his elbows were resting on the desk, his face inches from hers. 'Yeah. You're right.' He exhaled. 'You always know the right thing to say, don't you?'

'If only that were true.' She was staring at his lips again. She forced herself to stand up and move away. 'How are things? With Tamsin?'

'Good.' Simon glanced at his watch. 'I'd better get back actually.'

'That's nice.' Beth needed to get out before he mentioned the kiss.

'Beth.'

Too late.

'Yes?' She picked up her bag.

'I'm sorry I haven't been round. To chat about what happened . . .'

'It's fine.' She hastened to cut him off, moving towards the door.

Simon moved with her. 'It's just – well, Tamsin's been here, and . . .'

'Oh God, of course.' She gave a dismissive wave of

her hand. 'Like I said, a moment of madness. It won't happen again.'

Even as she said it she wanted to reach out and hold him.

'If you're sure.' He looked relieved. 'We don't need to – talk?'

'I'm sure.'

'OK, then. So, are you heading back home?'

'Yes.' Beth swallowed. 'I mean, no. I forgot I need to do – something.' She was babbling now, desperate for him to leave. She couldn't face the small talk on the way back to the cottages, the awkward silences, his hand so close yet so untouchable.

Beth put her bag down. 'So you go ahead. I'll see you at the party.'

'OK.' He lingered for one more moment. 'I'll see you there, then.'

'Yes. Bye.'

She kept her smile on until he had left the classroom. Then she sat down and rested her head against the grooves of the tiny desk, closing her eyes, letting the heaviness settle, as she accepted the fact that she was definitely falling for the man who lived next door.

Autumn

20

Simon

'Are you sure about this, Jake?' Tamsin surveyed the landscape as the wind whipped her hair around her face. She had never looked more beautiful, yet even after nearly three weeks of seeing her every day, Simon still had no idea what was going on inside her head. As Barney hadn't hesitated to point out at school last week, her being here didn't make sense. However much Simon tried to ignore his friend's words, he couldn't help thinking they were correct.

'Camping's great, Tamsin. You'll see.' Jake tried again to light the sticks piled up in the fire pit, but his match went out before they could catch.

Jake was fast becoming a mystery too. After years of knowing what his son was thinking almost before Jake did, Simon was feeling out of his depth. The Emily conversation had shocked him to his core. He had missed the signs, he had missed his son's pain. He couldn't let it happen again.

'Tamsin will get the hang of it.' Simon walked across, pulling the hood of Jake's coat up over his son's head as a light rain inevitably started to fall.

Tamsin cast him a grateful glance, drawing her coat

closer around her. 'Of course I will. I'm just a little rusty.' She was trying so hard to find a way through to Jake, as if to compensate for all the time she had missed. Expensive gifts were produced at random, new hoodies or games or a scooter with orange flames on its base. Jake liked the presents but he was still wary of this woman who had left him behind.

Simon sighed. Far from simplifying things, Tamsin's return had so far provided complication and confusion. Simon just wanted to take her in his arms, but something about her held him back. He caught her sometimes, standing in the cottage, staring at a crack in the wall or a pile of washing-up, a look of distaste on her face. Simon had seen pictures of her smart Tooting flat, with its stainless steel fittings and its immaculate leather sofa, and could understand why.

Simon felt smaller around her, just as he had felt smaller when Beth had made it very clear last week quite how much she regretted kissing him. 'A moment of madness' she had called it and a part of him had minded. A part of him had minded very much indeed.

And so the cycle continued relentlessly, day after day. He was exhausted from trying so hard and doubting so much. Suddenly overcome by his own powerlessness, Simon grabbed the matches, striking one against the box, holding it to the pile of sticks. At least he could still light a fire.

The match fizzled out. He struck another.

Nothing happened.

Simon bit back a swear word. It was official. He couldn't get anything right.

'So what do we do now?' Tamsin gazed longingly at the path which they had climbed only minutes before, Jake on Simon's shoulders so he wouldn't get too tired.

'Well, we put the tent up for starters.'

'OK.' Tamsin blinked at the large green bag that contained their shelter for the night. 'How?' She pushed a lock of damp hair behind her ear.

'It doesn't take long.' Simon unzipped the tent bag, seeing the familiar black poles, the big roll of green material and the silver pegs. He winced as he saw that there was still a mouldering clementine in there from their trip to the Dales last summer. He saw Tamsin spot it, the slight wrinkle of her nose as he put it to one side.

The quicker he got this tent standing, the quicker they could all crawl inside and start trying to have a good time. He dragged the heavy canvas out and tried to lay it on the ground, but rapidly discovered that the wind was working against him. As soon as he got one corner down and moved on to the next, the first corner had already risen up into the air.

The far left one was going now. 'STOP.' He flung himself down on top of it. He had to get this right, if only to prove that he was good for something. Jake ran over to grab the opposite corner. Tamsin did the same with a third.

A team. That was what they were. Simon got the first peg into the ground, hammering for his life, rain starting to lash his face.

'Go Dad!' Jake's enthusiasm was back. The tent was flapping hard but Jake clung on to the rebellious canvas as Simon drove the peg home. He moved to Tamsin's corner, seeing that her knuckles were white. She was shivering. He held the mallet high and gave the peg an almighty thwack. It sensibly disappeared into the grass.

'You can go inside soon.'

'I know.' Her teeth were chattering.

Simon bashed in the final peg, as the rain turned to hail.

'Poles!' Simon picked one out of the bag, clicking the sections into shape.

'On it.' Jake took one too, then Tamsin, and they worked together, feeding them through, until the tent arched into shape.

The hail increased in strength.

'Wow.' Tamsin blinked the water out of her eyes. 'We've got to get inside!' She heaved her rucksack through the entrance.

Jake didn't need telling twice. Tamsin went in after him, and finally it was Simon's turn. He zipped the door shut behind him.

Tamsin squeezed water from her hair. 'What a day.'

Simon landed beside her. He felt around in his pack and pulled out some hand warmers. 'I brought some of these, just in case.' He dug further. 'And a Thermos of hot tea.'

Tamsin smiled. 'God, you're brilliant, Simon, you really are.' She reached out and squeezed his hand.

Simon stared at her, full of sudden hope. Their eyes tangled, and his breath quickened. Years of longing rose in him, and – at last – he could see she was feeling it too.

Then she looked away.

'Do you want one?' She passed a hand warmer to Jake, watching attentively as he ripped it open and pressed it between his fingers.

'Aaaahhhh. That's better.' Jake pressed it happily between his palms.

Tamsin nudged him. 'Hey. It's your idea that we're up here, you crazy kid.'

'Wait. There's more.' Simon delved in his bag again. 'Hot water bottles, anyone?'

'You legend, Dad.' Jake grabbed one and held it close.

'Don't get it all wet. Get your coat off first.' Simon lifted the thick parka from his son's shoulders and hung it on the hook in the entrance. He took his own coat off, revealing the battered Koh Tao sweatshirt Tamsin had given him all those years ago. He watched her eagerly, waiting for her gasp of surprise.

It didn't come. She glanced at him, then back to Jake. 'Have you got any food?'

Simon silently handed them both a bar of chocolate. 'Yes!' She took it eagerly. 'A Crunchie. My favourite.'

The chocolate definitely meant more to her than what he was wearing. 79p from Aldi versus six years of loving expectation.

He took a moment to absorb this.

'See? This is fun, isn't it, Tamsin?' Jake chomped down on his Twix.

'Yeah.' Tamsin took another bite of her chocolate. 'I like it in here. All cosy. The wind howling outside. The three of us together.'

Again, hope surged, but she was looking only at Jake. Her hand inched towards their son, as if she wanted to hug him, but then she withdrew it again. She was a child with her nose pressed to a shop window, no money in her pocket, a toy in her sights.

Simon watched her regroup. 'Shall we play a game?'

'Great idea.' Simon got out the travel compendium he and Jake took on every camping trip. 'Tamsin? What do you like? Draughts?' They had played it again and again over breakfast in Thailand, while drinking pineapple juice and coffee and planning what to do with their day. 'Do you want to play Jake first?'

'Sounds good.' Her phone buzzed. She pulled it out, scrolling through messages, not seeing the disappointment on Jake's face. 'Sorry. Why don't you two play? I've got to make a call.' She started crawling towards the entrance, her face pale.

Simon felt a prickle of worry. 'Is everything OK?'

'Yes.' She unzipped the door. 'It's just . . .' Her eyes didn't meet his, and her middle finger tore into the skin around her thumb. 'I'm pitching for a big client on Monday. A drinks company? One of my friends used to work there, and this is the only time we can talk.'

'But it's mad weather out there. You can talk in here. Don't mind us.'

'No.' She shook her head. 'Sorry. I'll be back soon.'

When she had gone the tent suddenly felt very empty. The sides juddered and shook. Jake finished his chocolate. Simon did the same.

'I hope she's OK, Dad.' Jake pushed the draughts board

away, lying back and staring through the tiny window at the top of the tent. The sky was dark, the clouds jagged.

'Penny for them?' Simon joined him, lacing his fingers underneath his head.

'I'm just thinking.' Jake looked very pale in the half-light.

Simon reached out a hand and took his son's fingers. 'What about?'

'You.' Jake turned his head, his eyes searching Simon's face.

Simon squeezed his hand. 'Why?'

'Because I think it all makes sense now.'

'What does?'

'Why my plans didn't work.'

'What plans?'

Jake hugged his hot water bottle, turning on his side. 'All these years you've been in love with Tamsin. Haven't you?'

'I . . .' Simon's mind went blank.

'That's what Grandad says, anyway. That you love her.'

Irritation flared. 'Well, Dad doesn't . . .'

'And I've been trying to help you. Meet someone, I mean.'

Simon grinned. 'I've noticed.'

'And you haven't been on a single date yet.' Jake's earnestness tugged at Simon's heart. 'And I didn't get why. I mean, there are so many women out there. There must have been one to fall in love with.'

Simon shifted uneasily at the thought of all the messages he had deleted. Jake had tried so hard. 'I'm sorry, Jake. I've let you down.'

'No, no. That's not what I mean. I mean that I see now. That you've loved Tamsin all along. But . . .' Jake frowned. 'Why haven't you told her?'

'It's complicated.'

'Why?'

Such a simple question. Simon reached for the words to explain. 'You can't just say things like that. She's only just come back. And she might not want anything to happen between us, Jake.'

'But you love her?' Jake was watching him intently.

'I . . .' The truth was Simon didn't know. Tamsin was his first love, his white sands and adventure love. 'I don't know. Maybe.' He was unnerved by the intensity on his son's face. 'But you don't need to help with this, Jake. You just need to live your life. OK? Don't worry about me.'

Jake was sitting up now, legs jiggling. 'I do have to help, Dad.' His voice was a harsh staccato. 'I don't want to leave you alone, OK?'

'Leave me alone?' Simon stared at his boy.

'Yes. I can't do that. I won't, Dad.'

Slowly, the pieces fell into place. The call from Emily's parents. Jake in the corner at the party, next to the iced buns, clinging to Simon's hand so hard his fingers had ached. Jake leaning down to talk to the girl in the lift on clinic day.

'Jake, you don't think that the same thing will happen, do you? That you'll . . .' He had to steel himself to say it. 'That you'll . . .'

Jake spoke softly. 'Die.'

Simon swallowed. 'Yes. That you'll die? Like Emily?'

No answer. Outside the wind howled but inside Jake's silence screamed even louder. 'Jake? Most people do fine after the Fontan. Most people do great. It changes their lives.'

'Not Emily's.'

'Emily was Emily. You're Jake.' Simon kept his voice gentle, thinking of Beth in the classroom, her face alive with kindness. 'You're not the same as her. She lived her story – you're living yours. You're not going anywhere. I won't let you.' As he spoke he felt that powerlessness again – if only he had control over Jake's operation, if only he had control over any damn thing at all.

'You don't know that.' Jake's voice rose, shrill and chilling. He grabbed his knees, rocking backwards and forwards, head lowered.

Simon grabbed him and held him, hugging his boy close.

'Jake, I . . .'

'I don't want to talk about me, I want to talk about you.' Jake's eyes were feverish as he raised his head. 'Do you love her?'

'I . . .'

'Do you love her, Dad?'

Simon knew that Jake needed this – he needed something to aim for, something to believe in. He needed to believe that Simon would not be left alone and that he, Jake, had the power to make that happen. He wanted Simon to be with the love of his life. And Simon wanted to see hope on his son's face. So he swallowed his doubts and blocked the voice telling him that maybe he and Tamsin weren't destined to be together. He ignored her silences, her sudden exits, the sense that she was hugging a secret close. He ignored the memory of Beth's lips against his.

Maybe he did love her. Maybe this wasn't a lie.

He took a breath. 'Yes, Jake. I love her. I love Tamsin.'

At last Jake relaxed. 'OK. Game on, then.'

'But Jake. You don't have to do anything . . .'

'Made it!' Tamsin was back, grappling with the zip, head bent against the gale. Simon got up to help her and she slithered inside, shivering, her cheeks slick with rainwater and what might have been tears. She was upset, eyes red-rimmed. Whatever had happened on the phone call, it had clearly not been good.

Conscious of Jake's eyes upon him, Simon took Tamsin's freezing hands in his and started rubbing them warm. She was so close he could smell the rain in her hair.

'That's better. Thank you.' She rested her head against his, as their son looked on. The world howled around them but the two of them were still. Slowly, he pulled her cold hands towards him, tucking them away inside his hoodie, bringing her even closer.

'I'm sorry you have to head back tomorrow, Tamsin. We'll miss you.'

'Well, actually . . .' She tipped her head up. 'I think I'm going to stay a little longer.'

'You are?'

'I am.'

'What about work? The pitch?'

Her face darkened, then her smile was back. Her words rushed out. 'It's been rearranged. It's not for a couple of weeks now.'

Simon heard the catch in her voice and wondered if this was true.

'That's great,' he said cautiously.

'Yeah.' She smiled and he felt bad for doubting her. 'So that means I get to spend more time up here with you. Doesn't it, Jake?'

'Yeah.' Jake stared meaningfully at Simon. 'It does.' And he walked over on his knees and put his arms around Tamsin's waist. Tentatively, carefully, but it was more than he had ever done before. She pulled away from Simon and curled around their boy. The joy on her face lit up the tent, firing a spark in Simon – a spark of something like hope.

The tent quivered and shuddered around the three of them, keeping them safe. He circled his arms around Tamsin while hers were looped around Jake.

She was the mother of his child. And that child was a wonder.

That was surely enough to overcome everything. Enough to build the happy family that Simon had dreamt of for so long.

21

Beth

She hadn't seen the wetsuit coming.

Beth stared at it as it lay on the pebbly beach between two twisting tree roots, bright red and at least one size too small. At this rate she would be spending the whole of Jake's birthday party trying to get inside it.

'Erm. Thanks, Jake. And happy birthday.' The boy threw his arms around her and the warmth and the fizz of him made the world seem a little brighter.

'Thanks.' He let her go. 'This is my favourite place in the whole world. And you're one of my favourite people. This is going to be the best birthday party ever.'

'Of course it is.'

Beth looked down again. The wetsuit didn't look any better the second time. 'But I think I might – you know – sit the kayaking out. I'm not sure the wetsuit will fit.'

Jake pouted, cosy in his full-length black wetsuit underneath what looked like several sweatshirts. He was twice his normal width with all his extra layers. 'But you've got to. I've always wanted to kayak and Dad managed to borrow some just for today. We thought you didn't have a wetsuit, so we borrowed this from Jean.'

'Jean?' Beth blinked. 'Landlady Jean?'

'Yeah. She uses it when she goes paddle boarding.'

'Wow.' There was no end to her landlady's skills, it seemed. Beth eyed the suit again. 'It's very kind of her, but maybe I won't need it? The water can't be *that* cold. It's quite warm today, isn't it?' To prove her point she nonchalantly walked to the water's edge, removing a sandal and dipping her toe in.

'Oh man!' She hastily removed it.

'See?' Jake grinned. 'You do need it. In case you fall out.'

'Ye of little faith.' Beth sounded more certain than she felt. 'And what about you, Jake? How are you going to stay warm?'

Jake beamed. 'My friend Darren lent me loads of stuff – extra shorts and tops, boots, a cap. I'm super-warm in here.'

'Good.' He certainly looked it.

'You need this too.' Jake held out a hat. Small. Silver. Shaped like a cone on a medieval princess's head. 'A party hat.'

Beth took it, twisting the elastic nervously in her fingers. She had last worn one of these during that nightshift on the ward in New York. Her last, as it turned out. It had been a junior nurse's birthday and Beth had organised a party, complete with chocolate cake and lemonade in paper cups.

Beth looked out across the lake, caught in the memory of what had happened later that night. Every moment a regret, every decision wrong. Her mind burned as she watched the pine trees trying to reach the sky with their spindly branches. Memory after memory assaulted her, despite the blaze of autumn colour on the wooded hills around the lake, despite the sight of the pretty white house in the hills where smoke was puffing upwards as an autumn fire was lit. She drew her jacket closer around her but nothing could make her feel warm.

A small hand squeezed hers. 'No need to look so sad. It's only a hat.' Jake was watching her, his head on one side. 'You don't have to wear it.'

'Of course I will.' Beth put it on her head, turning to left and right. 'How do I look?'

'Silly.' He giggled.

Footsteps crunched across the pebbles behind her. She turned.

'Hi. You must be Beth?'

It was Tamsin.

Beth instantly felt inadequate. It wasn't Tamsin's fault – she was just one of *those* women: one who could carry off a wetsuit, who could twist her hair on top of her head so that it looked like a magazine headshot rather than a mess. Knowing she would be here, Beth had dressed up specially this morning. She had felt a beat of pride as she got into her car in her favourite purple silk blouse and soft leather jacket from Chelsea Market. As she looked at Tamsin she realised how pointless all her efforts had been. She might as well have enjoyed twenty minutes on the sofa and worn the battered compost sack that she kept by the back step.

'Great to meet you.' Beth went in for a kiss as Tamsin went for a handshake. They hadn't even said hello properly yet and already Beth was sweating. She looked around for Simon but he was up by his pickup, bringing the final kayak off the trailer. Just the sight of his broad shoulders was enough to make her heart beat faster.

She took a deep breath. Simon was her friend. She was his friend. End of story.

She turned to Tamsin. 'So, are you enjoying being up here?'

'Yes.' Tamsin's smile revealed perfect white teeth. 'It's wonderful. Getting to know Jake again.' She rested her hand affectionately on Jake's head. 'And Simon, of course.'

Jake looked up at his mum. 'He's the best, isn't he?'

'He certainly is.' Tamsin smiled across at Simon, receiving a wave in return. Beth's heart sank. They were clearly an item. Of course they were.

She must try to be happy for him.

'How about you, Beth? I hear you're a new arrival too. How are you enjoying it here?'

'I . . .' Beth stopped as Tamsin's phone buzzed. She pulled it out of her bag, turning several shades paler. 'Excuse me.' She wandered a few steps away, tapping furiously.

Jake turned back to Beth. 'I've missed you, Beth. Where have you been?'

'Where have *you* been, you mean?' Beth nudged him with a smile. She bent down, head against his. 'I left your present at home – come and get it sometime?'

His smile warmed her. 'Yes please.'

Tamsin stabbed the screen furiously with her fingertip. 'There.' She nodded. 'Now I'm all yours, baby.' She put an arm around Jake's shoulder and he leant back against her, as if he had been doing it his whole life long.

'Are you going to put that on, then, Beth?' Tamsin pointed to the wetsuit.

'Sure.' Beth steeled herself. This wasn't going to be pretty.

'Beth! Jake!' She turned to see Barney crunching his way over the beach, accompanied by a smiling woman who must be his fiancée, Lina. 'Happy birthday, mate.' He whipped Jake up in his arms, turning him round faster and faster in what was clearly a well-practised routine.

'Hi Beth.' Lina's grip was steady. 'Great to meet you at last.'

'You too.' Beth liked the look of her – bright, kind, a grin tugging at the corner of her mouth.

Barney put Jake down, turning towards Tamsin. 'Hello, again.' Now his smile was insincere. The temperature dropped several degrees. 'Nice of you to come this year.'

Beth winced. Lina, standing just behind Tamsin, cast her fiancé a furious look, making a chopping motion across her neck and mouthing, 'Stop it.'

Tamsin bit her lip, vulnerable as a deer facing a gun. 'Hello, Barney.' They greeted each other with a kiss that was more air than skin.

Barney clearly felt his niceties were complete. He turned to Beth, 'Good to see you.' He squeezed her shoulder and pulled her in for a hug that she hadn't been expecting.

'You too.' Once released, Beth scurried away, holding her wetsuit nemesis, aiming for the pickup. Simon had disappeared, and she hoped that she would be able to get the wetsuit on behind it, out of sight of everybody.

She put it down, eyeing the red neoprene, hoping it would prove to be the one wetsuit in the world that actually suited her.

'Hello, Beth.' Simon appeared from the back of the pickup, where he had been crouching down so low she hadn't seen him. 'Just checking the tyre pressure. It was a bit dodgy all the way here.' He didn't meet her eye, instead glancing down at the beach, his eyes sliding over Tamsin and on to his boy.

'Tyre pressure?' A stubborn part of her glowed at being this close to him.

'Yeah.' He flushed. 'Well, no. Not really.'

She folded her arms. 'So what were you actually doing?'

'I just needed a moment.' He exhaled. 'Tamsin got him tickets to Legoland. The queue-jumping ones that cost well over a hundred quid. Meanwhile I got him a Lego lunchbox for fifteen pounds, and even that was a stretch.' He bit his lip. 'I'm so embarrassed. Thirty-five years old and nothing to show for it. I'm so broke.'

Beth refrained from pointing out that one of the reasons he was broke was because he had been a single dad for the past six years.

'Don't worry, Simon. Honestly. Jake doesn't know what things cost.' Her voice sounded too jolly, too perky – as irritatingly upbeat as a Christmas jingle. She toned it down. 'He doesn't care who gives him what. He just cares about us all being here with him.'

'Do you think so?' He put his head on one side, doubt stamped across his face.

'I don't think. I know.' Her brain whirred, seeking

evidence to bolster her case – to take his anxieties away. 'He hasn't said a thing about his presents. So that proves it!'

'I suppose it does.' Simon brightened. 'Thanks. And don't tell anyone, will you? I'd hate word to get out, but the truth is I'm struggling to pay my rent this month. Jake needed new shoes – that kind of thing. I just can't seem to get ahead.'

Beth wanted to make him feel better. 'Well, I wouldn't have guessed, so no one else will.' She took a step away from him. Best to keep her distance. 'Nice day for it, isn't it?'

'It is.' Simon grinned, but Beth saw the way his gaze was fixed on Tamsin. He tore his eyes away. 'It's not my choice of party though. Too cold. But Jake went crazy when I suggested we did something else. He was just so – determined. Like with the football team thing. You know he's been training every day, to get his strength up?' Worry darkened his face. 'And I just figured – with what he said about Emily and the operation coming up – it was time for some fun. Seize the day, you know?'

Beth wanted to reach out, but kept her arms fixed at her sides. 'Sounds good.'

'Do you think I'm doing the right thing, though?'

She looked him dead in the eyes. 'I think you know what you're doing. Look at Jake.' Beth pointed to the beach, where Jake was being held upside down by Barney. 'He's happy. Now why don't you try to enjoy yourself too?'

A muscle flickered in his cheek. 'Thanks. I will. I'm

sorry to offload. Things have been different since Tamsin arrived, and . . .'

She cut in, diverting him. She didn't want to know anything about him and Tamsin.

'I need to get changed now, Simon. I'll see you down there?'

'Oh. OK.' His face fell. 'See you there.' He turned away and loped off.

'It's just you and me now,' Beth muttered at the wetsuit. She took off her clothes quickly until she was just in her swimming costume, hoping that would minimise the shock, but the wind sliced through her in seconds. She inserted a foot and began pulling up the leg, swearing in disbelief when – five minutes and a whole lot of gymnastics later – she found the crotch was only up to the middle of her thigh. By the time she was zipped up she looked like someone in her twilight years with a serious postural condition.

She picked up her clothes, shoving them into her bag and peering round the end of the pickup. Simon had Jake on his shoulders and the two of them were singing the Lego movie theme tune at the tops of their voices. Barney and Lina were whooping them on, but once again Tamsin was glued to her phone, a tiny scowl playing across her brow.

The material clung to Beth in all the wrong places and the pressure on her legs was so great she could barely walk, but this was Jake's birthday so down to the beach she went.

'Who's coming with me, then?' She grabbed a bright

yellow double kayak and started to push it into the water. The quicker this party got going, the quicker it would end and she could go home and switch the telly on loud and pretend she wasn't interested in the man next door.

'Do you know what you're doing?' Simon splashed to her side.

'Yeah. I've done this before.'

She had last kayaked when she was eleven, but Simon didn't need to know that. She needed to move, to burn off her anxiety, to submerge her attraction to Simon in ice cold water.

The kayak was floating now. A duck watched her curiously from the edge of the beach, before lifting its tail and diving.

Beth took hold of the kayak and tried to jump in, only for the seat to escape her so that she fell sideways and landed in the water.

'Oh my God.' She inhaled half the lake as she struggled to her feet again. 'Sorry.' She turned to Jake, only to see everyone on the beach was giggling. Beth took a bow, laughing at herself. The water was so cold it was bringing her to life.

She tried again, this time deliberately overshooting the seat and landing with a splash.

Jake was running towards her now. 'I'll come with you!'

'Well, you get in first, then.' She stopped her antics and held the kayak steady as he climbed in. She fixed the spray deck around him to keep him dry, and then clambered in herself. She paddled carefully. Precious cargo.

'You go with Tamsin, Dad!' Jake was directing operations, his voice high against the wind. 'Then Barney and
Lina together. We can do races!'

Beth turned towards Jake. 'Are you going to paddle
then?'

'In a bit.' He was watching his parents, face intent.
'Once everything's sorted.'

Simon was holding the canoe for Tamsin to get in. She
screamed as her feet encountered the chill of the water
and leapt in from a distance, only for her legs to end up
trailing outside. Simon grabbed them, pushing, until
Tamsin was somehow squeezed into the seat, laughing
and pushing her hair out of her eyes. Then Simon was
in, fast and neat, flicking water at Barney and Lina. Barney
dug his paddle into the water and sprayed some back,
while Lina set to and got their kayak moving.

'This is the start line, just beneath the trees.' Jake pointed
to the water just outside the cove. Beth dipped her paddle
in one side, then the other, leaning into the water. They
inched forwards, gaining speed.

Barney laughed exuberantly as he splashed Simon some
more.

'Hey!' Simon responded in kind.

'Aaaarrrggghhh.' Tamsin got a paddle-worth of freezing
water in her face.

'Barney! Be careful.' Simon looked severe.

'You can handle it, can't you, Tamsin?' Barney didn't
look even remotely sorry.

Beth saw Tamsin grabbing a paddle. Next thing Barney
knew, he was covered in water.

'Got you!' She raised her arms in the air, before giving Simon a high five. Tamsin started laughing, throwing her head back and then her whole body, so she was lying draped over the back of the canoe, her red hair a soggy halo. She sat up straight again. 'Your face, Barney. Seriously. I wish I'd got a picture.'

'Right.' Barney shook his fist. 'Time for revenge!' He and Lina aimed their kayak straight towards Tamsin and started to paddle. Beth turned to see what Jake wanted to do, but he was transfixed. He was watching his parents as they leant close to each other, clearly talking tactics. Simon was half-turned towards her, and Tamsin's hand was lying over his.

Jake watched them as avidly as if they were starring in a movie that he never wanted to end.

The hurt took Beth's breath away. She quietly sat in the kayak, muscles gradually chilling, letting the boy be. However cold she got, it would never freeze her as much as seeing Simon so close to another woman – a woman who had clearly stolen his heart.

Emily!!!

*Tamsin's back. My mum. It was a bit weird at
first, but it's good now. And the best thing is Dad
loves her, so now I just have to help him tell her and
then they'll be together for ever. It's awesome.*

*The operation is pretty soon now. I wish you could
tell me what it's like. You always make me feel better.*

Love

Jake x

22

Simon

'**D**ad?'

'Oh.' William looked up, Lego tree in hand. 'Hello, lad.'

For a second Simon wondered if he was in the right place. Dishes in the sink – check. Toys all over the floor – check. Laundry drying on every available surface – check.

Yes. He was home.

'Look what me and Grandad made.' Jake was on his knees, tiny spire in hand. He placed it carefully on top of what had to be the Thistlethwaite village church, resplendent in yellow brick on top of a hill made out of green Duplo.

Simon blinked. 'What are you doing here?'

His dad set the tree down. 'Jake called me.'

'You did?'

'Yeah.' Jake nodded. 'Jean has a cold so I thought she should rest. And I like hanging out with Grandad.'

'Oh.' Simon nodded, trying to disguise his surprise.

'And don't worry – I've made him a mug of tea and everything.' Jake sat back, radiating satisfaction. 'We've had a great time. Come and look.'

Bricks were scattered all over the carpet. The village

shop stood in its place at the crossroads, complete with its green and white awning and tiny hanging baskets. There was the playground and the school with a Lego football player outside it, arms raised. Jake. Then, up on a hill, there were two white cottages with grey roofs. A couple sat in front of them, plastic hands clasped.

Simon and Tamsin.

Simon felt the pressure mounting. Jake's need for him and Tamsin to get together was like a steel weight on his shoulders. Somehow every time he was about to talk to her, or try to move things forward, she eluded him. He leant towards her, he put his hand on her arm, he made her laugh whenever he could and yet in the quiet moments where a kiss might begin she would stand up or rattle mugs in the sink or take a call on that blasted phone.

He wished he could talk to Beth about it all. He missed her kindness, her insight, her laugh. He missed seeing himself through her eyes. He missed his friend.

His dad was watching him from the floor, eyes unusually soft. 'Are you alright?'

Simon bent down and started taking off his trainers. 'Yeah, Dad. I'm fine.' His left foot got stuck and he wrestled fruitlessly with the laces for a minute, before kicking the whole thing impatiently across the room.

'Grandad's amazing at this, Dad.' Jake sat back on his haunches, gazing proudly at the village laid across the carpet.

William chuckled. 'I had a good Lego teacher, lad. Simon was mad about it when he was your age.'

Simon gazed at him suspiciously, waiting for the inevitable put-down.

'Do you remember what we used to make, Simon?' His dad started clipping bricks together, his brown cords flapping around his ankles as he leant forwards to gather what he needed. 'You used to tell me off if I used the wrong pieces.' He nodded at Jake. 'That's where you get it from, lad. Peas in a pod, you two.'

Jake laughed. 'Are we?'

William nodded. 'Aye. No doubt about it. Me and your dad, we used to make all sorts.' His bricks were becoming a dry-stone wall made out of black and grey bricks. 'We even made Simon's mum, once. For Mothering Sunday. Not life size, but pretty big.'

Again, Simon had that feeling of a torch being shone into a dusty cupboard, the glint of unexpected treasure.

'You made Gran?' Jake's eyes were bright. He loved hearing about his gran.

'We did.' The smile lines deepened around William's eyes. 'We made her out of Lego and she looked like – what did she call it? A roly . . .'

'. . . poly with a pinhead on top.' Simon grinned as he and his dad finished in unison.

He flicked the kettle on. 'She wasn't happy with us, was she?'

'No. No apple pies for a month.'

It was the first time William had mentioned Simon's mum in years. Simon savoured it, knowing he might never do it again. His dad's love for his Mary was rolled up and stored away inside him where no one else could ever see it.

Simon got out the teabags. 'Her apple pies were the best, Jake. Cinnamon, the softest pastry – amazing.' He could almost taste the sweet fruit in his mouth, hear the puff of the pastry as his spoon dug in. 'Tea, Dad?'

'Aye. If you're making it.' His dad leant forwards to get more bricks and winced.

Simon kept quiet. He had offered help. His dad had to want to take it.

He busied himself with the tea.

Jake put a hand on William's arm. 'Come on, Grandad.'

'What, lad?'

Jake turned to Simon. 'Dad, Grandad has something he wants to ask you.'

Simon poured hot water into mugs. 'Is it the rota? Because I'm OK to do fencing next week, if that's easier. I—'

'Dad.' Jake's voice was sharp. 'Will you just listen? You two never listen to each other.'

Simon did as he was told.

His dad swallowed. 'My shoulder. It's – it's not great. So I was wondering if . . .'

Simon waited, hardly believing what he was hearing.

'If you might have a look at it?' His dad's mouth worked. 'I mean, it's probably nothing, but . . .'

'Yes!' Simon leapt across the room. 'I've been itching to get my hands on you for weeks.'

His dad shook his head ruefully. 'I thought it would go away.'

'Dad.' Simon unzipped his hoodie. 'That didn't work when you had a hernia and it doesn't work now.' He flexed his fingers and stretched his arms above his head, readying himself.

'OK, Dad. Take your jumper off and stand by the window.'

His dad complied with unusual obedience. Things must be bad.

Simon stood behind him, his fingers working their way through his dad's shirt to the bone and skin beneath. He could feel stiffness in the muscles, a tension that spoke of months of pain.

'Can you raise your arm?'

His dad swore quietly as he tried to do so.

'OK, OK.' Simon was gentle. He felt alive, certain. He could feel pain, and he knew that he could fix it. God, he had missed this. 'If you lie on the sofa I'm going to start working on the joint, OK? I think you've probably got a shoulder impingement, but I just need to make sure. We'll try to improve your flexion – your movement – over the next few weeks.'

'Alright.' His dad lay on the sofa, and Simon began gently manipulating the joint. The muscles were cold and heavy, but his hands knew what to do: part instinct, part training. Even after his long break from physiotherapy, his fingers dug and explored, beginning to reawaken long-forgotten fibres.

'You look really happy, Dad.' Jake was watching him with beady eyes.

'Do I?' Simon grinned. 'Sore shoulders are my thing.'

William made a sound like a rusty gate closing, and it took a moment for Simon to realise he was chuckling. 'Mary always said you'd surprise us.'

Simon stopped, his breath catching. 'Did she?'

'Aye.' His dad turned his head. 'She bought you a science book when you were knee-high, and you dragged that thing around for years. You couldn't read it, but you sat in the yard and you pointed at the pictures all the livelong day.'

Another memory emerged from its dusty corner. 'Oh my God, I remember that. "Science Year", wasn't it?'

'That was it. Mary used to call it your blanky, because you took it to bed with you too. Cuddled it at night and everything.'

Jake giggled. 'You're such a geek, Dad.'

'And proud of it.' Simon massaged a particularly sticky muscle with his thumbs.

His dad groaned and Simon released the pressure.

William frowned. 'No, no. Carry on.'

Simon did so. His dad sighed. 'I found it the other day. The book.'

'You did?'

'Aye. And reading it – I could imagine you there. Sitting there in your stripy trousers, the dogs all round you. And Mary, going and sitting with you, so you could show her all your favourite pictures.'

Simon trawled his memory and felt a jolt of sadness. 'I don't remember that.'

'You know, that's why I thought you might be happy taking over the farm.' William shifted in his seat. 'Because it was Mary's place too. Always will be. And I know how much you cared for her.'

Simon had such a big lump in his throat he could barely speak.

'Thanks, Dad. I'm still thinking about it, you know.'

Jake came and stood beside them. 'You see, Grandad? Dad's good, isn't he?'

Simon saw the affection on William's face as he turned towards Jake. 'Yes, lad. I think he is.'

Simon felt a glow in his chest.

'I told you.' Jake took the old man's hand in his. 'Everyone needs help sometimes. Even you.'

Simon smiled down at his boy. 'Jake's the pro at all this. He's had a lot of practice.'

'No I'm not. I'm not a pro.' Jake turned away, face shuttered. Simon could have kicked himself – he didn't want to remind his son about the operation, not if he didn't want to think about it.

Jake dropped to his knees again. 'I need to make the football pitch now.' He started hunting through the bases stacked up by the wall. 'I need a green base. Where are they all?' His voice was rising, his breath quickening. 'I can't find one!'

Simon left his dad for a moment, crouching down and gently pulling a green base from the bottom of the pile. 'Here you are.'

'You hid them all.' Jake hung his head, lip jutting forwards.

Simon put an arm around his shoulders, only for it to be thrown off. Jake bent over the pieces, cupping his hands under his chin, for all the world as if he had built a wall around himself and was hunkering down behind it.

'Jake?' Simon leant towards his boy. 'What's up?'

'Nothing.' Jake's brows lowered in a frown.

Simon didn't move.

Jake flicked an angry hand. 'Stop staring at me. I said nothing's wrong.'

Simon reached for him again, only for someone else to get there first.

'Hey. Lad. You can't make a football field like that. You need these.' His dad held out a cluster of plastic bushes. 'For the hedgerows?'

Jake's hand reached out and his grandad placed the pieces in his hand. He looked at Simon over Jake's head and nodded.

Simon let out a breath he had been holding in for years. Because in that nod was warmth; in that nod was understanding. In that one small gesture was a thaw that Simon had been wanting for years.

23

Beth

The bell of Thistlethwaite Stores jangled behind Beth as the green door swung shut. She unwrapped her chocolate bar and sat on the low wall outside, the sweat drying beneath her T-shirt and her leggings caked in mud from her five-mile run up rain-soaked pathways and along the ridge above the village. Since Tyler's message, she increasingly found that the past was whispering all around her, snapping at her in the small hours, nipping her as night became day. Only the sharp cold air of the fells and her feet thudding against the ground gave her any chance of keeping it at bay.

She took her first bite, almost groaning with pleasure as the sweetness hit her tongue.

'Hi Beth.'

Oh God no.

'Hi, Tamsin.' Beth spoke through gooey caramel, fighting to swallow. She knew she must be turning the colour of the post box standing to her left. Finally, she managed to gulp the mouthful down.

Tamsin slid a hand into the pocket of her coat and pulled out a pair of sparkly silver gloves. 'I parked up at the cottage but the boys aren't there yet. Thought I'd take a stroll. Take in the scene. You know?'

There was a fever to her today, an energy that Beth hadn't seen before.

'Well, it's a great day for it.' Beth gestured to the bluebell sky. 'Enjoy . . .'

Tamsin cut in. 'But they'll be back soon, I guess. Maybe we could walk back up the lane together?'

'Great.' Beth groaned inwardly, shoving the rest of the chocolate reluctantly into her pocket. She would have to enjoy it later.

Tamsin pulled the second glove on. Her eyes were bright and there were spots of colour in her cheeks. 'How have you been? I haven't seen you since the party.' She tapped her fingers incessantly against her leg as they walked down the steps and onto the lane. A cluster of starlings flew above them and a magpie rattled in the trees.

'I'm good. Busy.' It was true. Beth had been taking on extra shifts in different schools, anything to stop her mind from replaying its endless slideshow of the past, which now included the humiliation of the failed kiss. 'You? Have you been back to work yet?'

Tamsin shook her head. 'No.'

'That must be nice. Having all that holiday.' Beth sped up. She wanted home. A shower. The end of this conversation. She didn't dislike Tamsin, but being around her reminded her too vividly of what she had lost.

'Beth?'

'Yes?'

A huge coach came groaning down the narrow lane and they pressed themselves into the hedgerow to avoid it. Beth got a mouthful of fumes as it swept past.

Tamsin spoke again. 'I've got something to ask you.'

'What?' Beth started walking again as the bus rumbled on.

'It's about – Simon. And Jake.' Tamsin's teeth were tearing at her lower lip.

'What do you want to know?' Beth felt a beat of irritation. Tamsin must know just as much about them as Beth did – more, probably.

'Well . . .' Tamsin was trotting to keep up with her. Her heels scuttered over the slippery road and she nearly fell. Beth reached out and caught her, feeling a tingle of shame. Tamsin was young. Her boy was having major surgery soon. Beth needed to be kind.

She slowed down. 'What do you want to ask?'

Tamsin pushed a stray lock of hair behind her ear. 'It's . . .' She stopped. 'You know, I never thought it would be like this. I never thought Simon would be so kind to me. So welcoming.'

'Well, you are Jake's mum.'

'I know, but – I just thought Simon hated me. For so long I convinced myself Jake was better off without me. Every year I had this really sad party. For Jake's birthday?'

Beth felt a rush of sympathy, imagining this girl alone, remembering her son. 'What did you do?'

'I got a cake, and candles, and a present for Jake – I'd spend hours in the toyshop choosing it. And then I'd take the day off and just – think about him. You know? And I'd let it all wash over me. Memories of Jake, and Simon, and the operations, and the days when I just couldn't get out of bed. That first year – it was so hard.' Her voice was thick with uncried tears.

Beth stepped into a gateway, turning towards her. 'It must have been hell.'

Tamsin's head hung down. 'I was just so – crap at it all. I thought I'd be a natural – all breastfeeding and cuddles and lullabies like those mums you see on TV – and instead I was mean and shouty and a total and utter bitch to Simon. I used to shout at Jake, too. When he was tiny. When he couldn't even argue back. I still hate myself for it.' A tear trickled down her cheek.

Beth stayed silent, tentatively stroking the quivering back.

Tamsin wiped a tear from her cheek. 'God, I'm so sorry, Beth. I don't know where all that came from. Simon's right – you really are easy to talk to.'

Beth pulled a tissue from her pocket. 'Here you go.'

'Thanks.' Tamsin even looked good when she blew her nose. She wiped her eyes and put the tissue in her pocket.

Beth drank from her water bottle. 'Ready to walk again?'

'Yes.' Tamsin nodded.

They passed the turn in the lane just before the cottages. A robin hopped from branch to branch in the hedgerow, his red tummy swelling proudly, regarding them with his head on one side. They were nearly home.

She turned to Tamsin. 'So, what was it you wanted to ask me?'

'It was just about Simon, really.'

Beth shrugged. 'Well, you must know him as well as I do. I . . .'

Tamsin ignored her. 'Is he happy, Beth? Working on the farm?'

'What do you think?' The words were out of Beth's mouth before she could stop them.

Tamsin shrugged. 'I don't know. He never talks about it.'

'Well, you knew him before. When he was a physio. What was he like then?'

'That's exactly it!' Tamsin's face lit up. 'When I met him he was so passionate about his job. I mean – like – *so* passionate. It was all he talked about. He'd come home and tell me about knee pain or rheumatic joints and he got so excited about it, you know? I mean, you're medical. You get it, right?'

'Yeah.' Beth nodded. 'I get it.'

'Yeah. And . . .' Tamsin was reaching for words. 'The other day I was in town. In the supermarket. And I saw him – he didn't know I was there – I saw Simon going through all the stuff in the bargain bins. Like, properly hunting. And I figured that he must be really broke, the way he kept looking through, trying to find something cheaper. It was heartbreaking. And I thought maybe I could help.'

Beth's patience was fraying. This was between Simon and Tamsin – it had nothing to do with her.

'Well, I think you two need to talk, don't you?'

Tamsin touched Beth's arm insistently. 'But has he ever talked to you about it?'

Beth thought of Jake's party – the despair on Simon's face as he had told her how little money he had, the way he had implored her to keep it a secret.

Her phone started to ring and she pulled it out of her pocket. It was a withheld number, hopefully her solicitor getting back to her about Tyler and the apartment and what needed to be done.

Beth turned to Tamsin. 'I've got to go.'

'But you haven't answered my question.'

Beth hurried to her door, distracted and hot, Tyler's face looming in her mind. She couldn't believe he still had the power to make her feel this small, even from thousands of miles away. He was the one breaking their divorce agreement, not her. He was the one in the wrong yet still her hands were shaking and her pulse was spiralling upwards.

'Tamsin, I've got to go.'

'Please?' Tamsin's lips were quivering. 'I just want to help him. Help both of them.'

Beth stared at her. Maybe being honest with Tamsin would help, despite Simon's plea for secrecy. Maybe if Beth and Tyler had been more honest with each other, they wouldn't have ended up still needing solicitors even after their marriage was over. Maybe the truth would make Tamsin understand what Simon had sacrificed for their son and help them to build a better future for Jake.

She dug into her pocket for her keys. 'Look, Tamsin, I think you should talk to Simon about this, but yes, he misses his old job and yes, he needs more money. He's broke. He could barely afford Jake's birthday present, and he's struggling to make his rent, too. And if you want to help him, move up here. See Jake more. Help Simon out. That's what he needs from you.'

She put her key in the lock.

'That's what Jake needs too, Tamsin. If you want my honest opinion. Now, I've got to go. See you later.'

'Thanks, Beth.'

'Sure.' Beth opened the door and raised her hand in farewell.

She closed it behind her, answering the call just as her solicitor rang off. She felt a beat of frustration as she took her trainers off and hung up her hoodie. She just wanted things resolved with Tyler. She needed this to end.

She envied Tamsin, waiting for the warmth and chatter of Jake and Simon. Beth's cottage was silent, and loneliness chilled her like frost across a window pane. She turned the shower on and got her chocolate bar out of her pocket. Then she put the whole thing in her mouth, slid out of her running gear, and stepped under the hot water.

24

Simon

Barney put two pints down onto the small round table. 'So how many fences did you destroy today, then?' He removed a packet of crisps from either pocket and sat down. Simon ripped them open.

'Fences? Oh, just the one. How many children's futures did *you* destroy?' Simon sipped his pint, enjoying the feeling of the cool liquid gliding down his throat.

Barney grinned, pulling his jumper over his head leaving his hair standing on end. 'Just the two.' He cracked his knuckles dramatically. 'They had it coming.' He grabbed a handful of crisps. 'And I missed lunch – bloody staff meeting overran.'

Simon pushed the other packet towards him too. 'Eat. Please. The last time you missed a meal you drove into the back of my pickup.'

'Low blood sugar.' Barney crunched another handful.

Simon laughed. 'Yeah. Something like that.' He braced himself to raise the elephant in the room. 'How's all the wedding stuff going?'

'Great, yeah.' Barney didn't quite meet his eye and Simon felt an unaccustomed awkwardness between them. He just couldn't see a way around it. If only the wedding

wasn't just before the operation. If only it wasn't so important for Simon to stay fit and healthy and to keep Jake
safe so the Fontan could go ahead.

Barney attacked his pint. 'Lina and I keep looking at
our honeymoon resort too. The place really is incredible.'

'It'll be the best.' Simon reached over and chinked his
pint against Barney's. 'I'm so happy for you both. I hope
you know that.'

'I'm just sorry you can't be there.' Barney put his elbows
on the table and leant forwards. 'And honestly mate, no
hard feelings. It's just how it is. And at least Ghost's
speech will be so bad it'll give us something to laugh
about for the next seventy years, if me and Lina ever run
out of chat.'

'I guess so.' Simon grimaced. 'Get it on camera. Please?
I could do with a laugh.'

'Consider it done, mate.' Barney crunched a crisp.
'Now. Your turn. How are things with you and Tamsin?'

'OK.' All Simon wanted was a relaxing night at the
pub. He was tired of thinking about Tamsin, tired of
feeling as if he was constantly failing Jake.

Barney tapped his fingers against his glass. 'You're not
really thinking about getting back with her, are you?'

Simon stared at his friend. 'Mate. I know you don't
like her, but . . .'

'Because it's a really bad idea.'

Simon looked away from his friend's stare, watching a
farmer covertly feeding his cheese sandwich to the dog
under the table. Simon's head was aching, his eyes were
gritty, and this was the last thing he needed.

Barney leant forwards. 'Tamsin left you, remember?'

'Barney . . .' Anger began to prickle. He was under enough pressure already. He didn't need this. 'What's with the inquisition?'

Barney sat back, narrowing his eyes. 'You are thinking about it, aren't you? Getting back with her? You're still in love with her after all these years? Really?'

He made it sound so ridiculous that Simon's temper began to rise. Barney didn't know what Tamsin had gone through. Barney didn't know what Jake had asked.

Simon stared into his pint, seething.

Barney was still going. 'Also, she comes up here in her brand new car, and she's got a great job, and yet she's given you nothing for Jake?'

Simon's pride prickled. 'I've got it covered.'

Barney rolled his eyes. 'There's no need to growl at me. But she should be supporting Jake financially too.'

'It's not like that.'

'Of course it is! She's got a nice job! She's been staying in that posh hotel for God's sake. She's got cash.'

'And I haven't?' Simon felt pride surge. He looked at the pub carpet, following the red swirls with his eyes, seeking a calm that wasn't there.

'Well . . .'

Simon's head snapped up. 'What?'

Barney's voice lowered. 'Well, you could do with a bit of help here and there, couldn't you, mate?' He shifted uneasily in his seat, clearly aware that he might have gone too far.

Simon clenched his fists, not trusting himself to speak.

Barney gripped his pint. 'I'm sorry. That came out wrong. I just think she should offer. To help support Jake. That's all.'

'I'm doing fine.' Simon flicked a shred of crisp from his T-shirt.

'Right.'

'This isn't helping, Barney. I really care about her. And Jake wants us to be together. So . . .'

'So? You're going to go along with it?' The incredulity in Barney's voice was infuriating.

'Yes. No. I don't know.' Simon's voice was louder than he had intended. 'I just have to keep Jake well. Happy. Until the operation. It's pretty much the only thing I need to do right now. And it's harder now he's older – now he knows what's coming and he's scared. I mean, his best friend died, Barney! And Tamsin – she's a part of that.' He took a long breath to steady himself.

Barney looked contrite. 'I'm sorry. I've been a prick.'

Simon needed him to understand. If he could explain this to Barney then maybe he would understand it himself. 'This me and Tamsin thing – it goes way back. We've been through a lot together.'

'But what about you, mate? Is it really what you want?'

Simon couldn't answer.

Tamsin was here, and Jake wanted the two of them together. And Simon would try for his son, as he always did. He would do all he could to make it work.

Barney's blue eyes bored into him. 'And what about Beth?'

Simon shrugged, helpless. He thought of those wise

eyes, the tilt of her head as she laughed, of the press of her lips against his own, of her bubbling laugh. He thought of her kindness, of her understanding, of the way she always saw him in the best possible light.

'You like her, don't you?' Barney's face was unusually serious.

Simon opened his mouth to agree. But Beth wasn't an option. Beth had kissed him and instantly regretted it. He was her moment of madness, not her future.

So instead Simon did the only thing he could. 'No, mate. She's my friend. That's all. Just a friend.'

And he sipped his pint again, changing the subject, hoping that Barney would believe him, hoping that his thoughts of Beth would disappear so that he could make Jake's dream come true.

25

Beth

'Come on, Beth. At least think about it.' Jas flipped her sunglasses on top of her head as Saffy dragged her determinedly across the playground.

Beth shook her head. 'I told you, Jas. I'm not ready.'

'But this job is made for you. It's exactly what you were doing in New York – the job you raved about, remember? Ward manager in critical care? Tick. At a specialist centre? Tick. The only bummer is it's in Manchester, so you might have to move.'

'But I'm happy here!' Just the thought of that level of responsibility made Beth want to run. The damage she could do to someone who was seriously ill . . . She wasn't ready for that. 'And I've only been in this job six months. Surely you don't want me jumping ship already?'

'Of course I don't.' Jas lifted Saffy onto a bright green roundabout, a turtle's head smiling merrily at its centre. 'But you've got to get back out there. You can't let what happened hold you back.'

'I'm fine here.' It was the truth, she thought, crossing her legs defiantly, ignoring the nagging voice in her head reminding her of the intensity and the adrenaline of the critical care ward. How she had loved her job:

the difference you could make over the course of a shift – corners turning, eyes opening, lives restarting.

Jas pushed the roundabout and Saffy started to spin. 'Oh come on, Beth, you'd have leapt at a chance like this once. Don't just give up.'

'I'm not giving up. I'm keeping people safe.' The words snapped out before Beth could stop them.

Jas gave a low whistle. 'You don't really think that, do you?'

'I know it.'

Frustration pulsed in Jas's voice. 'You know, we all make mistakes, Beth.'

'*You* don't.'

'Yes I do.' Jas sighed. 'I just don't flay myself about them for ever.'

'I'm not doing that! I did something terrible, Jas.' As ever, when Beth thought about that night, her pulse started to spiral. This was precisely why she didn't want to go back into critical care – she knew that, as soon as she did, she would feel this panic, this fear, every single second of every single working day.

Jas was spinning the roundabout so fast Saffy's plaits were a blur. Her mouth was set. 'I think you're being too hard on yourself.'

'You weren't there, Jas! I know you're trying to make me feel better, but I was the one who did it, and I was the one who was escorted out and fired, OK?' Beth's words rang out, jagged, stark, out of place next to the smiling turtle and the bright red baby swings.

She put her hands to her aching head and sank onto

the bench, her emotions overwhelming her. She was chained to her old life as tightly as if she was still living it. She had been naive to think that moving here would make things any different.

'Time to get off, Saffy.' Jas stopped the roundabout and Saffy staggered off, a pale shade of green. Jas walked over to Beth and rested her arm around her shoulders.

'I'm worried about you.'

Beth stared at the ground. 'I'm fine.'

Jas shook her head. 'You are such a bad liar. Are you sleeping?'

'A little. But I keep dreaming about the night it happened – a kind of mad, Tarantino version of it, anyway. I'm putting up the IV, and then I hear the alarms and then I try to help, but then everyone at Mercy View starts chasing me and punching me and there's this loud banging music and . . .' Beth tailed off. 'No. I'm not sleeping.'

Jas's brow knitted into a frown. 'God, they treated you so badly. Tyler and the rest of the board should be shot. They just hung you out to dry. It makes me sick.'

Beth's mouth tasted bitter. 'I was the one who made the mistake, though. The one who . . .'

'It wasn't that simple, Beth. I wish you could see that. There was a reason you were in such a state. And Tyler of all people should have had your back. He owed you that much.'

'But it was my fault.' Beth stared at Saffy in the sandpit, merrily driving a truck into a hole. How wonderful to be so unaware of the past or the future – to be so free.

'No, it wasn't!' Jas exhaled loudly. 'They just made you feel like that. They scapegoated you, even though you'd given them ten years of your life. I bet you'd never even had a complaint before.'

'That's true.' In fact many of her patients had swung by when they had fully recovered, dropping off chocolates and cards, a constant stream of thanks for the care she had given them.

Beth had forgotten that.

Jas was on a roll. 'One mistake in ten years.' Jas held up her forefinger to emphasise the point. '*One.*'

Beth felt nausea rise.

'One too many.'

Jas drummed her fingers against the bench. 'You always were too hard on yourself, Beth.' She sighed. 'And think about the people who are still there. What if management do that again? I bet they're still overworking every poor bugger on your ward. Someone needs to make a stand.'

Beth had never thought of that. She had never thought of anything except running away. She felt a prickle of shame.

Jas stood up. 'Anyway. The job applications close in a week. I'm emailing you the details tonight. So there.'

Beth couldn't help smiling. 'You never give up, do you?'

Her friend took a bow. 'Thank you. It's a gift.' She dug into her bag, bringing out a flapjack bar and a bright orange cup of juice and giving them to Saffy. The girl grabbed them eagerly, before running across to the purple pirate ship on the edge of the playground.

'Come up here, Mum.' She drank the juice and then started to climb the lowest ladder, flapjack dangling from her teeth.

Jas got up and walked towards the pirate ship. 'Not too high, Saffy.'

'Up, up, up.' The little girl stepped onto the deck, moving towards the next ladder.

Jas called over to Beth. 'If I die you can have my Take That collection.'

'Don't say that or I might accidentally push you off.'

'That's my girl.' Jas followed her daughter and placed her foot on the lowest rung. 'Here goes.' She began her ascent, Saffy cackling above her.

Beth stayed on the bench. A family had just filed through the gate, and a toddler was running towards the sandpit, green dinosaur cap askew on his white-blond hair. A girl hung upside down on the climbing frame, plaits dangling, arms nearly grazing the floor. Their dad sat on the wall, sunglasses on his head, long legs stretched out, enjoying a precious moment of peace.

Beth folded her arms against the cold. Across the fields behind the playground she could see purple heather blazing across the hilltops and bright yellow crab apples in the hedgerows. She inhaled the sharp, fresh air, trying to calm herself, trying to find her way back to whoever she was born to be.

She had been so sure of herself once, always ready to step up. She had volunteered to treat a woman with a seizure in the middle of a Broadway musical. She had raised her hand on a plane when the pilot had asked if there were any medics on board. She ran her finger along the grain of the bench, as if trying to find that conviction again.

She lifted her head, sighing.

Maybe she just needed more time.

A vehicle turned the corner, heading towards her, and she raised a hand as she recognised Simon's battered pickup, its bumper almost entirely covered in mud.

They were right on time.

She stood up and waved, seeing Simon at the wheel with Tamsin beside him. Her smile became too tight, her heartbeat too fast. The pickup slowed to a halt and Jake got out.

He walked slowly towards her. 'Hi Beth.'

The sight of him instantly made her feel better. 'Jake.' She hugged him, happy that they were going to spend the whole evening together. She had barely seen him since his party and she had missed the way that he made her forget anything but the snap of one brick to another, anything but the present.

Simon leant out of the driver's window. He was wearing a black jumper and his eyes shone. Date night eyes. Inwardly, Beth sagged, but she forced a smile.

'Are you sure about this, Beth? I didn't know Jake had asked you to look after him until an hour ago.' He glanced affectionately at his son.

'It's called a surprise, Dad.' Beth saw deep shadows beneath Jake's eyes. 'Of course I sprung it on you.' He took her hand. 'I wanted them to have a romantic night out, Beth.'

'Great idea.' She realised she was gripping his hand like a vice and hastily relaxed her fingers.

Simon raised his hand. 'Thanks, Beth. I owe you one.'

'Yeah, thanks, Beth.' Tamsin grinned, leaning over to change the music on the radio. Her hair was pulled back in a twist, and tendrils fell artfully around her face in a way that Beth had never managed to achieve, even when she had long hair. 'Kiss please, Jake.' She leant out of the window.

Jake walked up to her and kissed her. 'Bye . . .' He hesitated a moment. 'Bye, Mum.'

Simon's head whipped round. 'Did you say . . .?'

Tamsin grabbed Jake's hand. She pulled him back, opening her door and getting out, pulling him close. Then she turned to Simon. Her smile could have set the world on fire. 'He called me Mum.'

Simon nodded. 'I heard.'

Jake sighed loudly, but Beth could see the pleasure in his eyes. 'It's only a word, Mum.'

Tamsin shook her head. 'No, Jake. It's not just a word. It's the best word in the whole world.'

'Apart from dad.' Simon laughed.

Jake huffed. 'Will you two stop chatting and get driving, please?' He put his hands on his hips. 'You'll be late if you don't hurry up.'

'That told us.' Tamsin got back into the pickup. 'Let's go, shall we?'

'Yes.'

'Have a good time.' Jake waved as the pickup moved off. Beth raised her hand too, but Simon didn't look back.

She kicked a stone with unnecessary venom. It scuttered into the ditch.

'Save me!' Jas called down from the top deck of the pirate ship, where she was now clinging to a rail.

'Sorry. Got to go.' Beth indicated Jake. Saffy's giggle followed them as they left the playground.

Jake stopped halfway up the lane, his breathing laboured.

'Jake?' Beth put her arm around him. 'Are you OK?'

'My head's achey.' Jake kept walking. 'I didn't want Dad to know.'

'Well, you succeeded.' Beth resolved to keep a close eye on him. 'They looked like they were going to have a great night.'

'I booked the restaurant for them and everything.' There was no mistaking the pride on his face. 'It's a fancy Italian place. Great ice cream.'

'Lucky them.' What Beth meant was lucky Tamsin, but Jake didn't have to know that.

She extracted her untouched water bottle from her pocket and gave some to Jake. He swallowed it eagerly.

'If I'd known you weren't feeling good I'd have come up to the cottage and met you there.'

'I'm fine, Beth.' There was a note of irritation in his voice. He clearly didn't want to talk about it. 'We did football today. At school? It's my first match in a couple of weeks.'

'That's so exciting!'

'Yeah.' Jake looked almost well again, enthusiasm lighting up his face. 'Can you come and watch?'

'I hope so. I'll check the rota at work. But I'm sure Jas will let me – I wouldn't miss it for the world.'

'It's going to be the best game ever.' They were nearly home now.

'Just be careful, OK?'

'Yeah, yeah, I know.' He rolled his eyes as he opened the gate. 'Dad's been going on and on about it. I'm going to wear a million layers so I don't get cold and I'm going to follow the golden rule and stop if I get too breathless to talk. Because then Dad will be happy.'

Beth laughed. 'OK.'

'But I won't get breathless. I'll score millions of goals!'

'Gazillions, I reckon.'

'Or bazillions!'

Beth put her key in the door and ushered Jake inside. 'I'll get us some tea.'

'Thank you.' He lay down on the sofa, flicking through channels. Beth opened her cupboards, assembling the ingredients for a basic pasta sauce. She rattled the spaghetti into the pan and sprinkled salt into boiling water.

She set the gas to simmer. 'Do you want some milk, Jake?'

Silence.

'Jake?'

She turned and peered over the kitchen counter to see that he was sound asleep. His work was done for the day – he had sent his parents off on a date, he had made their dreams come true. She sat on the arm of the sofa, gazing at him. Jake might only have half a heart but the way he lived was unafraid, bold, courageous. He made her shuffling half-life, hiding from memories, dodging the past, seem unbelievably small.

Jake tried to shape his world; Beth tried to hide from hers.

Staring at the steady rise and fall of his chest, she found there was a glimmer of the old Beth inside her. She would never escape what had happened, she knew that now. But her mistake didn't have to be an ending – just as Jake's heart condition didn't mean he had to live his life on mute. Maybe it was time Beth started showing a little bravery too.

Fired by sudden certainty, she got up and placed a blanket gently over the sleeping boy and walked through to the bedroom, delving beneath her bed until she found the file of official papers that she had placed there on her first afternoon in the cottage. There it was, Mercy View written in black marker across the front.

She blew off the dust and carried it back to the living room, settling onto the end of the sofa, so she could keep an eye on Jake as she read. She ignored the churn of her emotions as she opened it, and ran her fingers over the papers, over typed letters, formal letters, rotas, printed emails and handwritten notes from patients she had cared for in New York. As she read, she realised that she had been good enough to do that job – to help patients in their most critical hour. And, more to the point, she had tried. She had worked herself into the ground. And all she had got in return was a termination letter and a hearing. She had just accepted it, taken her punishment, run away. But what if she tried to be like Jake? What if she tried to fight?

An idea started to form in her mind. An idea that made her heart race. A plan.

It was a plan the old her would have approved of. As she thought it through she felt a lift, a return of something like self-confidence. She grabbed a pad from the coffee table and started reading in detail, making notes as she went. She was finally doing something – taking action at last.

When two pages were full, Beth sat back, resting her hand on Jake's head, thanking him for showing her the way. Thanking this little boy she had only just realised she loved.

26

Simon

'I can't believe he called me Mum.' Tamsin toyed with her tiramisu, before putting her spoon down. 'Did you know he was going to?'

'No.' Simon had been just as surprised as she had.

'I've waited so long to hear him say that.' Tamsin twisted her glass round in her fingers. She was restless tonight, knee jiggling under the table, eyes darting around the restaurant, resting on the shiny gold pans on the walls or on the bunches of herbs hanging from the ceiling beams. Maybe she was as nervous as he was. And for the same reason.

'I just feel so – happy, you know?' She laid a hand across her chest. The fact that Jake's words meant this much to her made Simon's heart swell. He just wanted her to love Jake as much as he did. 'I never thought Jake would accept me again. I didn't think he'd ever forgive me.'

She moved the roses in the centre of their table one inch to the right, then back again.

'It's changed everything.'

'Has it?'

'Yeah.' She put her elbows on the table, leaning forwards towards him. 'Everything.'

Simon swallowed, garnering his courage. She was only inches away. The candlelight flickered on her face, softening the red lipstick, glinting against the gold locket at her throat. She was breathtaking. And she was here. He thought of the two of them giggling in the kayak at Jake's party; of them both singing along to Adele's 'Someone Like You' on the journey here; of the little boy who was half him and half her and who wanted their family to be complete.

It was time.

'Tamsin. I . . .'

'Simon. I . . .'

They both stopped. Hesitated. Laughed.

Tamsin picked up her wine and put it down again without tasting it. 'You first, Simon?'

'OK.' He reached out and took her hand.

'Tamsin, it's been amazing having you back here. Watching Jake with you, the three of us together – it's everything I've dreamt of.' He took a sip of Coke but his mouth was still dry. 'I always held a candle for you, you know? No one else even came close.' He blinked the image of Beth away, forcing himself to keep talking. 'And now . . .' Tamsin was still, too still, the light on her face gradually dwindling.

Simon kept going, knowing that if he stopped then the doubts that were swirling through his mind might overcome him. The speech he had prepared came back to him now – written in those long years of missing her, the time before she actually reappeared a new Tamsin, a different Tamsin.

Her fingers stiffened under his, but Simon talked on. He had no choice. He couldn't live his life on pause any more.

'I think – no, I know . . .' Her face was panicked now. Fearful, even. Nothing about this felt right but he had to push on. For Jake. 'I know that we can be great together.' He had to keep talking, a rush of words to break down whatever barrier she was building in there. He could practically see her mind squirming, wriggling, a fish caught on the end of a line.

'It's a lot, I know.' He leant forward, only to see her leaning back. 'But Jake would be so happy. I mean, he would be overjoyed. It's all he wants – you and me, back together.'

'Simon . . .'

'We can be together again.' With every word, the feeling of wrongness grew. 'We . . .'

'Simon . . .'

Jake. Do it for Jake. 'You could move in with us, until we can find somewhere bigger. After the operation, maybe?' There was Beth again, but he pushed her away. 'I still have feelings for you, Tamsin.' It wasn't totally untrue. 'And Jake wants us together – that's pretty obvious, isn't it?'

She still hadn't spoken.

'So let's give it a try, eh?' She had that look in her eyes – the one he had first seen when Jake was born and she looked as if she was trying to hide from life, from the world, from everything, from him. Evasion. And guilt.

He ignored it. He pushed forwards, angling his face until it was close to hers. 'All I want to do is kiss you.'

As he said it, he knew that it was a lie.

But it was a good lie. A white lie, told for his son's sake.

Tamsin held his eyes for one second. Two.

Then she started to cry.

Oh God.

He dropped her hands and sat back in his seat.

'I'm sorry, Tamsin. I didn't mean to upset you. I just thought . . .'

'It's not you, Simon.' She rested her face in her palms, shoulders shaking.

He begged she wouldn't say it.

'It's me.'

There it was.

'I'm a mess.'

'No you're not, Tamsin.'

'You don't understand!' Her eyes were bright with tears.

'So tell me, Tamsin. Tell me what's wrong.'

A long silence.

'Please? Tamsin?'

She raised her eyes. 'I'm pregnant.'

Simon blinked.

'What?'

'I'm about sixteen weeks along now.' Tamsin sipped her water, tears glistening on her cheeks. 'I've been wearing loose tops and stuff so you couldn't see.'

'You've been deliberately hiding it?'

'No. Yes. I don't know.' Her sobs increased again. 'I just . . .' She took a shuddering breath. 'I didn't know what to do, you know?'

He picked up the spoon and drew the tiramisu towards him. Eating it gave him something to do, somewhere to look. Flames of anger were building within him, licking at the edges of his self-control. All those weeks of trying to connect with her. All those hopes.

'Who's the father?'

'Don't be like that, Simon.'

He took a mouthful of tiramisu, barely tasting it. 'It's a fair question. Who is he?'

She was pleating a napkin with her fingers. 'His name's Kris. I met him at work. He's a banker.'

Of course he was.

'And you didn't think to mention any of this to me?' His mind was a blur of anger and hurt. All that rebuilding. All that expectation. All that wasting time thinking that the three of them might have a future.

He thought of Jake's hopeful face and was shot through with pain.

'I didn't know how to tell you, Simon. It's been so hard.' He couldn't believe Tamsin was asking for sympathy when she was the one in the wrong. 'And Jake was so great, so the days just went on and on, and somehow I still hadn't said anything.'

'Like all those days when you meant to come back, and you didn't?'

She recoiled, eyes huge.

Simon didn't care. He finished the tiramisu and pushed the plate away.

'So why did you come here, Tamsin? Seriously?' Heads turned at the surrounding tables as his voice rose, but he didn't care. 'Because you said it was for you and for Jake. And maybe for me, if I remember rightly. But you've lied to him – you've let him hope for something that can never happen. And you've lied to me too.' His voice shook with rage. 'So explain to me why you really came. Because right now, I have absolutely no idea.'

'Simon, stop. Please?'

He sat back and folded his arms, waiting. He wasn't going to make anything easy for her. Not any more.

'OK then.' She was fiddling with her signet ring now, fingers worrying at the heavy gold. Simon wondered if it was from Kris. 'I'll try and explain.'

Her voice was so soft he had to lean forward to hear her.

'It started when I did the test. Insomnia. Then panic attacks.' He heard the catch of fear in her voice. 'Like I was – when I left here. I started reliving everything. The anomaly scan. Do you remember?'

'I remember.' That small room, the tremble in the sonographer's voice as she asked them to wait and went to get a colleague. The half hour of Tamsin getting into position after position as they pressed the probe to her belly. Blurry pictures on a screen. Then the starkness of the words, when they finally came. 'We think there may be a problem with your baby's heart.'

'I'm so scared it's all going to happen again, Simon. I'm so scared this baby will have half a heart too. Because . . .'

Despite his anger, Simon nearly reached for her, knowing what she was about to say. 'Because I'm its mum, you know? And look what happened last time.' She was lost in a hell of her own. 'Kris didn't get what was wrong with me – I hadn't told him about Jake, you see?'

For some reason this hurt Simon more than anything she had said until now. Not to even acknowledge their son – Simon couldn't understand it. He couldn't forgive it.

'So I spiralled, and I panicked, and I started fucking up at work. Presentations up in flames, losing clients – you know.' She was gulping for breath now. 'And Kris just kept being logical, telling me that so few babies are born with heart problems that I shouldn't worry so much. I felt like I was going mad. So I . . .' She swallowed. 'I ran away.'

'No.' Simon put his hand to his head and leant his face against his palms. 'Tamsin. Not again.'

'I know. History repeating itself, right?' She wasn't even trying to mop up her tears now. 'I took time off from work – they were happy to give it to me, given how much I was screwing things up. And I told Kris about Jake and everything and I said I needed some time. He's been calling and texting – you've probably noticed that. He's a good guy. And I came here. Because . . .' She chewed her lip. 'Because I thought that if I could get here and make things right, then maybe everything would be OK. With . . .' She dropped her hands to her belly, eyes distant. 'With this little one.'

'And what about Jake?'

She started, having clearly forgotten where she was. 'What?'

'Did you think about him? About what he might want,

once you came back? He is desperate for us to be together – it's all he wants. Did you think about that?'

'You're not being fair.'

'Aren't I?' He gripped the edges of the chair so tight his hands hurt.

What a mug he was. Soft. His dad had been right all along.

Well, not any more.

'You should have talked to me, Tamsin. You should have been honest – we could have made a plan. Instead, you've burst back into Jake's life, made yourself a part of him, with no real plan as to how long you're going to stay. And you've lied and you've lied and you've lied to us both.'

'I never lied. Not directly.'

'Seriously?' He was shaking now. 'Well, you certainly didn't tell the truth.'

'I know.' Her sudden acquiescence surprised him. 'I know I've got things wrong. But I want to help.'

Now, he laughed. A horrible, mirthless sound that went on and on.

'You want to help. Go on, then. How?'

Her pale face was set. 'Financially.'

His pride flared. 'I don't need your money.'

'I didn't mean it like that.' She was so earnest. He didn't understand how she had any right to be so earnest. 'But you could do with some space – some time for you. I could take Jake, maybe? To London? He'd love it down there. Gigs. Theatre. Great schools.' Her eyes gleamed with manic zeal.

Simon's stomach dropped. 'What? You want to take him to London now?'

'Yes!' She was alight. 'It's a great idea. You could go back to being a physio then. You used to love that job.'

'I don't need you to take Jake to London to go back to being a physio, Tamsin. What I need is someone here who can help me to look after him. Someone else to pick him up from school sometimes, or to look after him at weekends if I'm doing a shift. Someone close by. Not someone in bloody London.' He couldn't believe they were even talking about this. 'The village is his home, Tamsin. Don't even talk about taking him away.'

'I'm just trying to help.'

He shook his head, exhausted, and gestured to the waiter for the bill. This evening was well and truly over.

She leant towards him. 'You don't really want to be working for your dad, do you?'

He breathed in, taking the full weight of her words; seeing himself through her eyes. Gone were the days when he helped people to walk again. Instead, he was a man with a big overdraft, a man with a dead-end job, a man to be pitied.

But he couldn't regret a second, because he had Jake. His boy's laugh. His scribbly pictures. His way of saying the right thing at the wrong time. Their walks. Their bike rides. His brave smile from the sofa on the bad days. His thin scream as yet another cannula was inserted into a vein through bruised skin. His arms in the air as he crossed the finishing line at sports day. His boy. Their boy.

How was Simon going to tell him?

His anger returned, hard and unbending.

'I don't want any money. And I don't want your help. And I certainly am not going to let Jake go to London with you.' The waiter delivered the bill and scurried away. Sensible. 'You need to tell Jake about Kris, and about the baby, and you need to do it soon. He deserves that, at least.'

'I will.' He saw the way her hand trembled as she reached for her purse.

'I'll get this.' His voice was a hiss. 'I can afford to buy my own food, thank you.'

She swallowed. 'Thank you. And I didn't mean . . .'

'Stop. Stop now.' Simon couldn't bear to hear another word. 'Just tell him. Please?' It would be him picking up the pieces, him trying to mend Jake's brave little heart. And right now, he had no idea how.

'I'm so sorry, Simon.'

Simon didn't answer. All he wanted was to be at home, with his boy. Maybe money was tight, maybe Simon couldn't provide big toys or big holidays, but he could provide love. He always had. And he always would.

No matter what Tamsin threw at them, no matter how much damage she caused, he would carry on doing what he had been born to do – looking after his son. Tamsin wasn't going to take Jake away. Not now. Not ever.

Simon wasn't sure of much, but he was sure as hell about that.

Winter

27

Beth

Beth closed the front door behind them, and pulled Jake's bobble hat down over his ears.

'So, are you sure you want to go to school today?'

'Yes!' Jake galloped across the gravel to prove his point.

Beth feigned confusion. 'I can't think why. There's nothing special happening today, is there?'

'Yes there is!' Jake ran back and whacked her on the arm.

'Is there?' Beth scrunched up her face. 'And what's that, exactly?'

'My first football match!' He raised his arms above his head, his feet skipping right and left in the brand new football boots that Tamsin had bought him.

'And what position are you playing in?'

'I'm the winger. I won't be on for long, but I'm going to score loads of goals.'

'I bet you are.'

'I've been practising so much.'

'I know. I've heard you.'

He was zigzagging down the lane now.

'Hey. How about you take it slow? You don't want to run out of energy before we get there.'

'I'm fine. Stop worrying, Beth!'

'Hi Jake!'

Beth turned. 'Jake. Baby.' Tamsin was walking towards them, wearing a long turquoise coat, jeans and boots. As usual, her phone was glued to her hand. An ancient Range Rover rattled past, mud glued to its wheels and sides, and Tamsin sprang back, narrowly avoiding landing in the ditch. 'Hi Beth.'

Beth raised a hand.

'Mum!' Jake reached for Tamsin's hand, clinging to it, vibrating with joy.

'Are you excited, baby?' Tamsin looked even lovelier than usual this morning, but her eyes darted around as if expecting sniper fire and Beth noticed that her thumbnails were bitten to the quick.

Beth moved away as Tamsin's arm encircled Jake's shoulder. It was one of those crisp winter days when the sun was low in the blue sky and the trees were gilded with russet and gold. In a garden on the hillside a bonfire was in full progress and Beth could smell the bitter smoke and taste it at the back of her throat.

Jake pulled on his mum's hand as they approached the school. 'I'm playing left wing, Mum.'

'You said, baby.' Tamsin kissed the top of her son's head, checking her phone for the fifth time since she had met them. She started tapping out a message as they reached the school. Jake turned and took Beth's hand, and they made their way up the stone steps together towards the sports field at the back of the school. A football pitch had been chalked on to uneven grass and at one end leaves had fallen onto the pitch. A man who Beth recognised from the village shop was trying to rake up the piles, but was too busy chatting to one of the teachers to really make much progress.

'Good luck, baby.' Tamsin crouched down in front of her son, who looked about half the size of the team that was just getting off a battered green minibus in the car park. One of the boys could have been twelve, with huge arms and a moonlike face. Beth looked at Jake and felt a jangle of nerves. He threw his arms around his mum, arcing his body into hers. Red hair against red. He pulled away, and Beth could see the joy on his face as he headed over to his team. She was about to call to him, when he turned and came back. 'High five!' He held up his hand. Beth did the same. 'Too late!' He pulled his away just in time.

'Got me.' She held out her arms, palms raised.

'Every time.' He walked away, chin up.

Tamsin was again engrossed in her phone, so Beth walked over to Jean, who had turned out to watch her nearly grandson play his first match.

'Hello, pet.' Jean dug her hands deep into the pockets of her thick green coat. She had electric-blue glasses on today and tiny gold hoops in her ears. 'I'm so excited. Jake has been waiting for this ever since he could walk. I can't believe his big day is finally here.'

'Me neither.' Beth kept her eyes on his tiny figure, currently touching his toes with the rest of the team.

'I hope they trounce that mob from Kendal.' Jean nodded, her hair remaining steadfast in the breeze. 'They fouled us something awful last year. Jake was meant to play then too but the poor lad got a chest infection and had to sit it out. I've never seen tears like it.' She inhaled. 'Simon took a week off work in the end, trying to cheer him up.'

'I bet he did.' Beth saw Jake looking at his mum, a ball precariously balanced on his head. Tamsin didn't look up from her phone. She was tapping furiously, brows lowered.

'Nice one, Jake!' Beth knew she was overcompensating, but she gave him a thumbs-up for good measure. She was becoming more and more tempted to chuck Tamsin's phone over the hedge at the edge of the playing field.

The boys were running now, warming up for the big match. Beth saw Jake among them, his thin legs pumping, head high, and felt a stab of pride.

'Hello, hello.' Simon appeared, walking across the field, his father beside him. The two men were the same height, walking in rhythm, faces expectant.

Jean walked over to them. 'Glad you made the effort to come this time, William Withers.'

Simon's dad smiled. 'Well, my grandson wouldn't have spoken to me again if I hadn't.'

Simon waved a hello to Beth, and despite herself her heart lifted at the sight of him. His navy overalls had a white stain on the shoulder and his wellies were covered in mud. As he got closer she could smell a mix of rain and earth. It was now one of her favourite scents – the Lake District and him.

Tamsin approached, clearly trying to smile.

'Hello.' Simon's expression was muted, mouth down, shoulders low.

'Hello.'

The temperature dropped.

'How are you?' Simon's eyes were dark, with none of their usual kindness.

'Fine.'

'Nice of you to come.'

Tamsin couldn't keep still, tapping her phone against her leg. 'I said I would.'

Beth watched them, wondering what had happened that night at the restaurant. When she had last seen them they had been glowing, laughing. Now they could barely look each other in the eye.

Jean caught Beth's eye, and grimaced as Tamsin returned to her phone.

'How are you, Beth?' Simon came and stood next to her.

'Good.' Her smile felt tight. She felt on tenterhooks around him, no matter how hard she tried to pretend otherwise. 'I can't wait to see Jake in action.'

'Me neither. He was so excited last night he was flying.'

'He still is.'

Simon shuffled from foot to foot. 'Thanks for bringing him up here. I wanted to get a couple of hours in at the farm.'

'It's no problem at all.'

Simon dug the tip of his boot into the ground. 'His first football match. I can't believe it. One of those moments, you know?'

'Yeah.' Beth smiled. 'It must be.' Jake looked over and saw his dad, and Simon raised his fingers above his head, shaped into a heart. The little boy made the same gesture in return, also throwing in an extravagant star jump for his grandad.

Simon grinned. 'I'm so proud of him.'

'Me too.' Tamsin stepped forward, at last slipping her phone into her pocket.

Barney waved at Simon, as he shepherded the kids towards the centre of the pitch for the match to begin. The two captains competed to see who could jiggle around most as the coin was tossed into the air, and then the Thistlethwaite captain raised his hands in triumph and Jake started trotting towards the wing.

'Go on, my son.' Simon could barely keep still. Beth smiled to herself. At last Simon got to be the dad on the touchline – the dad he must have imagined he would be all those years ago before Jake was born. Even Tamsin was focused, watching, as the game began.

After five minutes they had all sagged as the Thistlethwaite captain, Jimmy, hogged the ball again and again, tearing down the pitch while the rest of the team jumped around eagerly, unable to get anywhere near it. He was two goals in when Barney held up a hand and gave him a brief lesson in the art of passing.

One minor meltdown later, things got interesting. Now the teams were much more evenly balanced, and at last Jake got nearer the action. He was running so fast his legs were a blur, before he tripped and an opposing player stole the ball, haring down towards the Thistlethwaite goal.

'Keep on them, Jake!' Simon was leaping up and down.

The Thistlethwaite goalie cleared the ball away, and it travelled past the halfway line and miraculously landed at Jake's feet.

'He's got the ball again.' Simon was leaning forwards, practically on the pitch himself, cheering as his son dribbled up the wing. Jake's head was down, his arms pumping through the air, and he made it half way down the pitch before crossing it towards his friend Darren, who got to the ball and poked it into the back of the net.

'Yes!' Simon's arms were up in triumph as he grabbed Beth and danced her round. Jake meanwhile, was whooping round the pitch, his face alight. Tamsin had her phone out taking pictures, and soon Simon followed suit.

'YES!' Simon was practically dancing. He turned round to share his excitement with his dad, Jean and Beth.

Beth was jumping up and down with joy, just turning to hug Simon when she saw it.

She saw Jake fall.

She froze. The little figure with the red hair wasn't celebrating. He wasn't jumping with delight and excitement like the rest of his team. Instead he was falling, as if he had been felled by a stone. A moment later he was lying flat out on the grass, arms to his side, his legs pulled up beneath him.

No.

Beth stared, willing him to get up, willing him to move.

Nothing.

She turned to Simon, and her fear must have been

painted across her face because he whipped round to see what she had already spotted. She put her hand on his arm, once, briefly, and then she was moving. Beth heard a scream from Jean, a gasp from someone who might have been Tamsin, but she was already running. Her blood was racing, her mind was screaming, but she ran sure as an arrow towards the boy who lived next door.

This was what she had been dreading ever since that night shift. This was the emergency she wasn't ready for, and now it was here and at its heart was a little boy she loved. The world receded around her – Barney, the whistle in his mouth, sprinting towards the inert figure on the ground; the parents' cheers turning to silence as they stared at the figure lying immobile on the pitch ten minutes into his very first match.

Jake should have moved by now. He should have got up, shaking his head, laughing at them all for being fooled by the joke he had played.

But he hadn't.

'Move.' Beth screamed at a boy staring transfixed at his teammate. 'MOVE.' She dodged round him, until she was next to Jake. Speed was everything. Every second counted. She dropped to her knees, eyes assessing, hands reaching for his wrist.

For a moment she remembered the last time. Another body lying still. Another face, white and bloodless. Then she blocked the memory. This was about Jake, and only him. He needed her and she knew what she had to do. She wasn't going to hide any more. She was ready.

She felt on his wrist for a pulse.

Nothing.

She checked his neck.

His heart had stopped.

Now Simon and Tamsin were beside her. She glanced up. Tamsin was keening, a terrible, primitive sound. Simon was on his knees, keen to help, face ashen.

Beth spoke fast. 'Call an ambulance.'

'OK.' He had his phone out already and made the call, staying by Jake as he talked.

Beth's training kicked in. 'We need to turn him over.'

Simon wedged the phone under his ear, and helped her. Tamsin's hair flew around her face as her boy lolled against Simon, head down, arms limp.

'Help.' Her voice was tiny. 'Please help him.'

'I'll try.' Beth wiped her mind. This was no longer Jake from next door. No longer Lego Jake. No longer Simon's Jake.

This was CPR. Beth just had to follow the steps, as if it was another child – any child – one she didn't know. She had to save him. She went into autopilot, laying him out flat on his back, willing the eyes to open, his chest to move. She placed her right hand on his forehead, tilting his head back while gently lifting his chin with her left. His airway was now open but his chest remained still.

She pinched the soft part of his nose closed, allowing his mouth to fall open, took a breath, and put her mouth over his. His lips were so cold. She had to remind herself to breathe gently and steadily, waiting for his chest to rise and then fall. She repeated this five times, and then began compressions. She only thought of the rhythm, pushing down on Jake's chest, feeling the stillness, feeling the bone beneath her fingers. *Come on, Jake.* When she had finished she sat back. Then she gave two further breaths.

Jake. Don't leave us.

She was starting to shake now but she kept going. She kept up the compressions, knowing that the longer he was out the more hypoxic he would become; knowing that his brain might become damaged; knowing that it might be her fault, that she might be missing something as she had before. She was counting the minutes. His lips were turning blue. Inside his brain, areas would be starting to shut down. No more of that grin. No more of that laughter.

Focus, Beth. Focus.

Tamsin was clawing at Beth's arm, eyes wild. 'Can you save him? Please save him.'

Beth couldn't answer her – couldn't comfort her. She started compressions again, keeping her rhythm despite aching wrists and hands.

And there it was, a cough. Jake's eyes opened, full of terror, and he tried to rise up against her, his arms hitting her away.

'Oh, thank God.' For a moment she lowered her head and rested it on her knees. Now he was back, she could feel the ache in her neck, the rapid beat of her pulse, the scream of her wrists.

She leant over him. 'Jake.'

He was trying to sit up, but she put a hand gently on his chest to keep him down. 'Jake. It's Beth. You need to stay still, my lovely, OK? The paramedics are on their way.'

'Yeah, mate.' Simon was holding Jake's hand. 'You gave us a bit of a scare there.'

Tamsin was clinging onto the other, tears rolling down her cheeks.

Jake shook his head. 'No. Hospital.'

Tamsin shook her head. 'I know you don't want to go, baby. But they need to run some tests, OK? You need to go to hospital.' Her voice was unsteady. 'I can come with you.'

Beth saw Simon's face fall. 'I normally go with him.'

'Please?' Tamsin was about to fall apart. 'I . . .' She dropped her hands to her belly. 'I need to be with him.'

Simon spoke only to Jake. 'I'll be right behind you. Promise.'

'I'll drive you.' Beth wanted to help – wanted to do everything she could.

He nodded thanks, eyes turning back to Jake.

His son's eyes were closed.

Beth could hear sirens. Thank God. The gaggle of supporters watched, as the paramedics drove across the field and then jumped down, bags in hand, uniforms strangely comforting, running across to kneel at Jake's side.

'Hello.'

Beth recognised Jas's boyfriend. 'Sam.'

'Beth.' He was calm. Professional. 'What's happened here today then?'

Beth told him, sharing every detail – how long Jake

was unconscious, what she had done, how many compressions she had given. It was a language – a precision – that she thought she had lost, but it was still in there: the terminology, the accuracy, the clinical information that was needed in an emergency like this.

Simon spoke, his voice a rasp. 'He's got HLHS. Can you get him to the cardiac centre in Manchester? He needs specialist intervention, and it stops them having to transfer him later. Please?'

Sam nodded. 'We'll radio them and check.' He never took his eyes from Jake, his fingers taking his pulse, while his colleague took out the pulse oximeter to measure the oxygen level in Jake's blood. Jake remained still, his eyes closed. Beth hoped he was fighting in there – hoped he was saving his energy to keep his heart pumping, to keep the blood moving around his beautiful, precious body.

Five minutes later the paramedics lifted Jake onto a yellow stretcher and into the ambulance. Tamsin jumped in and they slammed the ambulance doors, before bumping off across the field. Beth watched, shivering as the shock set in, reaching for Simon's hand as the vehicle gained speed and drove off towards whatever Jake's future held.

28

Simon

'I'll drive. You're in no fit state, Simon. Keys, please.'
Beth's words weren't a question. She held her hand out, as the ambulance sirened its way out of the tiny car park in front of them.

Simon's hand shook as he handed them over. Beth wrapped her fingers around his for a second. 'He'll be OK.'

He couldn't meet her eyes. This woman who had saved his son. He was trying to breathe but the panic was rising. He was trying to think, but all he could see was Jake's body lying there on the ground, cold and still.

'Simon.' There was a sharp note this time. 'Look at me.'

'He just wanted to play in one game.' Simon tasted blood where he had bitten his cheek to stop the tears. 'One bloody game. I . . .'

'Simon? Look at me.'

At last he did. He saw calm and courage – someone he could believe in.

Beth squeezed his fingers. 'This wasn't anybody's fault. These things happen with HLHS. It's awful, but it's just how it is. Nobody's responsible.'

'Thank God you were there.' He closed his eyes, not caring that he was crying, not caring about anything except Jake.

'He'll be OK.' Beth's arms were around him now, and he leant into her, smelling the coconut of her shampoo. He needed her warmth and her strength. God, he had missed her.

Beth spoke fast. 'He wasn't out for long. And Simon?' He pulled away. Her brown eyes shone with sympathy. 'We've got to get going. Now. Jake needs you.'

'Yes. OK.' Simon nodded. 'Let's go.'

Beth walked around to the driver's seat and opened the door. Simon was aware of a clutch of friends, staring, waving, crying. His dad appeared, eyes red-rimmed, squeezing Simon's shoulder. Barney ran over and gave him a hug. Then Beth put the key in the ignition and revved the engine and Simon got in, his brain reeling. One minute Jake had been flying, the next he was gone.

Simon kicked himself as the pickup jolted its way onto the lane. He should have learnt by now never to let himself relax. He had let his guard down and in return he was reliving the shock of his son's mortality. Not one day, not one minute of Jake's life could be taken for granted. There was no 'when he grows up', there was no taking one's time.

Stupid, Simon. Stupid.

His head jerked forward and he heard the scream of the accelerator as Beth put her foot down. A sheep leapt into the hedge ahead of them.

'Come on.' Her jaw was set as the ambulance came

into sight at a junction ahead of them. She hit the steering wheel with her hand. 'Why are they going so slowly?'

'Its sirens are on.' Simon watched the hedgerows flashing by as they caught up. 'And they're already going at seventy on a country lane.'

'Yeah, but it's Jake in there.' Beth frowned, drumming her fingers on the wheel. 'They should be using a helicopter.'

It hit him full in the heart. Beth loved his son. It was there in everything she did; in the way she had run to Jake on the football field; in the way she was hunched over the wheel, urging the pickup on; in the way she came and looked after Jake again and again, never asking for anything in return.

And now she had saved Jake's life.

He turned to her, voice shaking. 'Thanks, Beth. For this. And for – what you did back there.'

'No need to thank me.' She spoke through gritted teeth as they finally left the winding lanes and got out onto the main road. 'I'm just glad I was there.'

'Me too.' Simon wondered what was happening in the ambulance ahead. He dialled Tamsin, but there was no answer. He remembered previous ambulance journeys – Simon squeezed against the side while paramedics ripped open plastic coverings, inserted needles, monitored every breath. Simon had never taken his eyes off Jake. He had answered questions about medication or allergies, leant backwards or forwards as the paramedics required, but he never ever stopped watching his boy. Thinking of his son on that stretcher, and not being by his side, was driving him crazy.

Beth glanced at him as she turned left, seeming to read his mind. 'OK, so I reckon that in the ambulance they'll be doing an ECG to see what's going on. They'll probably be giving him fluids as well, and just checking his heart rate is stabilising. I've met the lads before. One of them – Sam – is going out with my mate Jas.'

'Yeah.' Simon's mouth was dry.

Beth's mouth twisted into a wry smile. 'Anyway, Jas swears there's no better paramedic than Sam, and she's probably right. She's a tough crowd.' Beth overtook a dawdling Citroën and pressed the accelerator to the floor. The pickup shot forward, squeezing through a narrow gap in front of a Sainsbury's lorry. Simon glanced at her in admiration.

'If you ever give up nursing, you could always try being a getaway driver.'

'I'm just trying to get you there. They're the worst, aren't they? These journeys.' Beth chewed her lip. 'You must be desperate to be with him. To know, for sure, what you're dealing with.' She glanced at him. 'Sorry – I'm talking too much. I can be quiet if you'd like?'

'No.' Jake's lifeless face was stuck in his mind, white and cold. All that laughter, all that joy, wiped clean like a blackboard at the end of class. 'Keep talking. Please.'

'OK.' Beth grabbed some chewing gum from her pocket and popped it into her mouth. 'Want a piece?' She nipped past a tractor, brow furrowed. Thank God she was driving. His shakes were starting to build at the thought of the hospital. The yellow walls of Beach Ward. The machines and tubes.

'No thanks.'

'OK. Can you just take this for a second?' She threw the pack towards him as she braked and he caught it, twisting it between restless fingers. She skilfully got back into the left hand lane, nipping in right behind the ambulance in time to turn off towards the motorway.

'OK. I'll keep talking. Just stop me if it gets too much.' She kept her eyes on her mirror as they merged onto the motorway. 'When I was doing my specialist training in the States I did patient liaison for a while. I used to sit with parents while their children were in surgery or being examined. They all said the waiting was the worst bit. The what-ifs were worse than the reality, when they eventually got to hear it.'

'Yeah. They were right.' Simon stared out of the window. 'Though reality bit pretty hard back there.' He saw three lorries in a row and remembered the days when Jake would count them in the back seat. One lorry, two lorries. Christ. A sob choked him and he leant forward, resting his head on his hands.

'I don't know if I can be strong enough for him, Beth. I don't know if I can do it.'

After a moment her hand landed on his shoulder, and he reached up and grabbed it, like a lifeline. Thank God Beth was here. Thank God she had moved in next door.

'You can, Simon. You already are.'

He clung to her fingers, not letting go, lowering their hands, until their palms rested together, comfortable and comforting. She let go as she changed gear but then her hand met his again and it steadied him as they ate up the miles in pursuit of his sick boy.

'How do you know? That I'm strong enough?' Simon had never felt weaker. He had never felt more like giving up.

'Because you do it every day. You're strong for him every day.'

He wiped his eyes fiercely with his sleeve. Jake mustn't see him like this. 'Am I?'

'Yes.' She had so much faith in him, as if she saw him through a golden filter. 'You do, Simon. Look at how you are with him. How you put him first. How you make him feel safe. Safe enough to run on a football pitch on a freezing day. Safe enough to kayak on a lake in October, when he only has half a heart.'

'But look what happened today. He nearly died.'

'But he didn't, Simon.' Beth glanced in the wing mirror, overtaking an Audi that had just pulled out between her and the ambulance. 'He's still here. And, like I said, this is HLHS, isn't it? You never know what's going to happen. And Jake will always have that memory, of the cheers and the glory and playing with his friends. What a wonderful gift to give him.'

Simon stared at the ambulance doors, wishing he could see through them.

'It should be me in there with him.'

'I know.' Her knuckles were white against the steering wheel. 'You and Jake – you belong together.'

'Yeah.' Simon saw Jake's white mask of a face again. The image would never leave him, he knew that already.

Beth shook her head. 'If I hadn't met you two . . .' She stopped, tongue protruding from her teeth as she navigated the thickening traffic as they approached the city. 'You know, when I came here I didn't really know why. I had some childhood memories, Jas, a job that was right there for the taking – but I had no plan. I was escaping. Running away. But you two?' Her voice thickened. 'You and Jake . . . You were the reason I stayed. Because I fell in love with the pair of you.'

Simon opened his mouth and closed it.

Beth put her hand to her mouth. 'Oh my God I'm so sorry. I don't know why I said that. Today of all days. After what just . . .' She shook her head. 'I'm such an idiot.'

'It's OK, Beth.' Simon's head was reeling.

'I'm sorry. I know you and Tamsin are . . .'

'Me and Tamsin are nothing.'

'Oh?'

'She's with someone else.' He shook his head. 'And pregnant.'

'What?' Beth's mouth fell open.

'And she even said she wanted to take Jake to London.'

'No.'

'Yeah. It was a bit of a surprise for me, too.' He didn't want to think about this. Not today. 'But listen, Beth. Don't be sorry. For what you said. I'm just surprised. And I . . .' He pressed the heels of his hands to his eyes, trying to push out all the fears, all the what-ifs, all the memories. He didn't have room for them now – he needed all his energy for Jake.

'I get it.' Beth's voice was soft. 'We're nearly there now.'

Simon's world was just a pair of ambulance doors and the boy behind them. Everything else receded as they turned off the road, following the ambulance up the ramp that led to the sliding glass doors of A&E. Here he was again, about to enter the hospital he and Jake had visited more times than any hotel, more times than any beach or any theme park.

'Here we are.' Beth's face was white. 'I'll go and park.' She glanced at the crowded multi-storey. 'It might take me the rest of the day. You get in there. To Jake. Where you belong. OK?'

She squeezed his fingers and he didn't want her to let go. She seemed so strong. As if she had all the strength he lacked.

'Come and find us, won't you?' He clambered out of the pickup, legs wobbly, heart racing. The ambulance doors were being opened. He had to get to his boy.

'I'll be there as soon as I can.'

He turned, hand on the door handle. 'Thank you, Beth. Thank you.'

He pushed the door shut and she drove off, leaving him to run towards his son. Jake was on a trolley, inert, being wheeled at speed into the bright lights of the hospital. Tamsin was with him, hair back in a ponytail now, eyes bright with tears.

Simon put his hand on Jake's, falling into step with the paramedics pushing him along. 'How is he?'

Tamsin spoke in gasps. 'I don't know. They're going to get him up to the catheter lab and see what they can do to stabilise him.'

'Hello, lad.' Simon put a hand to Jake's alabaster cheek. 'How are you doing?'

Jake's eyes remained closed.

'Hang on in there.' He stroked the thick red hair back from his son's forehead as he had a thousand times before. Tamsin was isolated in her pain – retreating, turning away from Simon. They had never been a team, not really. He could see that now. He had forgotten how lonely that first year had been, even with her right there beside him. He realised, as they raced along the hospital corridor, that maybe he had never been in love with her at all. Maybe he had been in love with sun and sand and freedom and then with the little baby covered in wires lying between them. The little baby who had been forced to fight harder for one precious day than most people fight in a lifetime.

That Simon was long gone now. He had dissolved the minute Simon had circled Jake's tiny finger with his own and seen that perfect mouth curving into a smile.

'Simon?' There was Jake's consultant, Miss Maya, moving towards them.

'How is he?'

'We need to do more tests, but his heart rate is unpredictable and we need to get things under control. We'll take him up to the cath lab and get him set up. I'll see you there in about ten minutes.'

'OK.' Simon nodded. He put his mouth to Jake's ear, wishing the head would turn, wishing the eyes would open.

'You can do it, Jake.' He kissed his son's cheek. Tamsin

said nothing, clinging to Jake's hand until he was wheeled away.

And then it was just the two of them. Tamsin turned away, sliding down the wall until she was crouching near the floor. An old man shuffled past in a dressing gown, wheeling a drip behind him.

Tamsin's voice cracked. 'Oh God, this is all my fault.'

Whatever their differences, Simon had to comfort her. 'It's nobody's fault.' He found himself repeating Beth's words. 'This is HLHS, isn't it? You never know what's going to happen.'

Her sobs redoubled and she bent down, head towards her knees, her entire body wrenched with sobs. 'I'd forgotten how tough this is.'

'Yes.' Simon's vision blurred as he remembered the stillness on the pitch – the split second of silence before Beth had started to run to their boy.

'We need tea.' His voice was shaky.

'I couldn't drink a thing.' Tamsin's voice was a whisper.

'Well, I need it. Why don't we get one in the cafe and then we'll head up to the lab? The sugar will help. Honestly.'

'I suppose.' She gave a sniff that was more of a moan, and he got out a tissue and passed it to her.

They walked along a wide busy corridor to the cafe, and took their places in the inevitable queue. In front of them a woman told whoever was at the other end of the mobile line that she wouldn't be home tonight as they had a major trauma coming in. Her grey hair was scraped back in a bun and her clogs were stained yellow. She rubbed a hand to the back of her neck and he could see the cluster of moles emerging just above her scrubs. Ahead of her a small child pointed carefully at a donut in the display cabinet. When the girl turned her face towards him he saw that her left cheek was swathed in bandages.

He looked at Tamsin. She was shaking and pale. He put his arm around her and drew her close and she let him. It was what they both needed. They were two parents whose child was in danger. Two people pulling together.

'How have you done this?' She was trembling. 'How have you done it alone?'

'For Jake.' He pulled her closer, smoothing her hair with his hand. 'I had to.'

'He looks so small.'

'He does. But remember how tough he is. That first surgery. Do you remember how long it took?'

'Yes.'

'Hours longer than they thought it would – and no one told us anything. I think I ate about twenty-five Mars Bars in that waiting room.'

'The one with no windows and the broken coffee machine?'

'Exactly.' They reached the front of the queue and Simon ordered two teas and two muffins. Tamsin had shaken her head when he asked her if she wanted anything to eat. She had always been the same. Later, he would offer her some and she would devour the entire thing in seconds.

'Right. Let's get up there.'

They started to walk back past the entrance towards

the lifts when Beth appeared, Simon's car key dangling from her fingers. She fell into step beside them. 'Where is he?'

'Cath lab. We're just heading up there.'

She was breathing fast. She must have run in here from the car park. 'Is it OK if I come too?'

'Yes.' He tried to smile. 'Always.'

Her eyes held his and something gleamed between them; something exciting, something new. She gave him strength. She gave him hope.

When they reached the fifth floor Jake was on a trolley just outside the lift, surgical gown on, head turned towards them, eyes searching. He saw them and attempted something like a smile. Simon's heart cracked.

'Dad.' Jake reached out, his eyes fixed on Simon, fingers reaching only for him. 'Don't leave me alone again.' The smile dissolved into tears, and Simon felt a stab of guilt so sharp it stopped his breath.

'How are you doing, lad?' He came to Jake's side and leant over him. His son was here and he was still alive. His boy was fighting.

Simon took his hand. He was here. He was ready.

He was going to fight too.

29

Beth

Beth felt a smattering of snow on her face as she got out of her car. The bare trees were dancing in the wind, and she shivered in her thin raincoat, so pre-occupied about Jake that she had taken the wrong one from the peg that morning. It was only when she had got to her first primary school of the day, ready for flu immunisations, or Nostril Day as Jas called it, that Beth had realised she had forgotten to bring the kits she needed too.

Jas had tutted down the phone and muttered about focus, but she had given Beth an extra big hug when she had arrived with spare kits, and had also passed her an extra chocolate Digestive when they had their tea break. 'Sam said you were amazing, getting Jake back like that.' Jas had nudged Beth, eyes sharp. 'Now, how about that job in Manchester? They've extended the application deadline, you know.'

But Beth couldn't think about the job. Her head was full of Simon and his little boy. It had been two days since the football match; forty-eight hours since she had told Simon that she loved him. Feeling Jake's body beneath her hands, being with Simon driving along the motorway, both had unleashed her. She was alive again, awakened at last.

She might see Simon at any moment. Her step quickened as the snow started to swirl, and she leant her head back and opened her mouth, dodging around until a flake landed on her tongue. She landed another, then another, until she was running around like a child at Christmas, tongue protruding, cheeks aglow.

Wheels crunched onto the gravel. She turned and there he was. Simon.

'Don't eat them all.'

He was leaning out of his window, breath clouding in the freezing air. Her nerves fizzed as she walked awkwardly towards him, her pulse rising, her world in his hands.

'How's Jake?'

'He's doing really well. His blood pressure's good and he's eating again. Tamsin's in the Ronald McDonald room at the hospital tonight. I'll head back in the morning.'

'I'm so glad he's OK.'

'Aye. Me too.' Simon got out, flinging his head back and stretching. 'It's so good to be out of there,' he said as flakes landed on his upturned face. 'Fresh air. I know it's only been a couple of days, but God I missed it here.'

'I bet.' She wanted to reach out and touch him. She wanted to kiss him, make him hers. But she had no idea what he had made of her telling him she loved him – no idea whether her feelings were reciprocated.

He rubbed his wet face with his hand, eyes shadowed with exhaustion.

She looked up at him. 'Can I make you a cuppa? Some food, maybe?'

'I thought you'd never ask.' He smiled. 'My place, though? I just want to be home.'

'Sure.' They walked up the steps to his cottage. She stood back while he pushed the door open, her eyes lowered, her heart racing. It took every particle of her strength not to touch him.

'Come in.' Simon gestured her inside. She leant against the wall in the hall, seeking the strength of the stone behind her back. He shut the front door and beckoned her down to the living room.

She followed him, as she had so many times before, but today everything felt different, every movement charged.

'I'll do that.' She put her hand on his arm as he started filling the kettle, pointing him towards the sofa. He sank onto it, his hands twitching nervously, like a student waiting outside a head teacher's office.

She put teabags into mugs and added steaming water. 'Sugar?'

'Two, please.'

He ran a hand over his face, leaning back against the cushions. She glanced back at him, thinking how she loved him, this quiet man, this good man, this man who tried to overcome whatever was thrown at him. This everyday hero in overalls and wellies, who had appeared at her car window and stolen her heart.

She picked up the mugs and carried them over, sitting down next to him on the sofa.

'So, Beth.'

'Yes?' She put the mugs down on the coffee table. His eyes glanced around the room, landing on the bookcase, on the windowsill – anywhere but her. 'We should probably – talk?' A flush was rising up his cheeks. 'After what you said, and all.'

She shook her head. 'I think we can leave it. You've had a big couple of days. I don't want to be a problem.'

'You'd never be a problem, Beth.'

She swallowed, thinking about everything she hadn't yet told him. 'I don't know about that.'

She should tell him. Now.

'I do. I know it.' Simon raised his hand and gently, hesitantly, stroked her cheek. It took her breath away.

'Tyler thinks differently.'

'Tyler is a prick.'

Beth laughed.

'I missed that laugh.' Simon's hand was on hers. 'And I missed you.'

'Me too.' She chewed her lip. 'I thought you were with Tamsin. All these weeks, I've been convinced you were together.'

His face fell. 'I'm sorry. Things got confused. And after we kissed – you saying it was a moment of madness – it just made me think that you didn't see me that way. And Tamsin was here, and then . . .'

She put a finger to his lips. 'It's OK. It doesn't matter now.'

'Well, can we just be honest, from now on? Please?'

She steeled herself. 'Yes.' She had to tell him everything,

before this went too far. The Beth he saw wasn't all of her. His Beth was rose-tinted. He needed to see the rest – whole and flawed and messy. He needed to choose the real Beth. She wasn't going to hide any more.

He deserved the truth.

'Look, Simon . . .'

'What?' His eyes were so kind. Eyes to dive into. Eyes to trust. He was leaning towards her now, his fingers stroking her cheek, so gentle her body was screaming for more. She forced herself to arch away.

'Back in New York – things happened. Things you need to know about if we're – if we're going to get anywhere together.'

'OK.'

She took a deep breath. 'You know about me and Tyler, and him leaving me for Dana, my deputy, so I won't go over that again.' Her pulse was quickening. She knew what was coming next. She stood up, walking across to the other side of the room, giving him the space he might need.

'Anyway, it was a tough time but I kept going. I loved my job, you see. Or rather I would have done, if there had been enough staff. Tyler was on the board of the hospital, and I was noticing that recruitment had stopped – people left and they weren't replaced and sometimes there were barely enough staff to run a shift. Our staff-patient ratios were shot, and it got harder and harder to give the quality of care we all aimed for.

'I was lobbying the board, hard, for extra staff, saying it was only a matter of time before an incident happened, but nothing got done – just talk and thanks and the odd agency nurse being sent in and then disappearing again. So I kept covering more and more shifts – we all did – and I got more and more exhausted. There was building work in the apartment above mine so I could never sleep in the day.' She could still hear the whine of those bloody drills. 'And I was so sad about Tyler. Seeing him with Dana all the time.' She bit her lip to stop the tears. 'I was a wreck, but I couldn't stop working, I couldn't take a break. I was too busy trying to keep the show on the road.'

She was getting to the hardest part now. She leant against the wall, folding her arms, bracing herself. 'Anyway, this one night I'd barely slept when I went on shift. It was my fifth night in a row, and I had the rest of the week off. I had plans, a weekend in Napa with some friends. I was excited, for the first time in ages.

'I was doing the evening meds, going round with the trolley, and I came to this elderly woman. Caroline Garcia. Eighty-two, cardiac issues. Lovely lady, always lots of family around her.' The shakes were starting to take hold. 'And I was talking to Dana, who was busy telling me what Tyler and her were doing that weekend.' She could still see the smug smile on those cherry-red lips. 'And I was fuming inside, that she had the gall to stand there and tell me all this, and I was calculating what dose to give Mrs Garcia and I drew it up and hung up the IV and moved onto the next patient.'

Simon was still, listening hard.

'The next thing I knew she was in cardiac arrest.' Beth

could still hear the alarms beeping, hear the running footsteps of her colleagues, the voices questioning her. 'I'd got the dose wrong. I'd got the decimal point in the wrong place.' Her voice was a moan. 'It didn't take long.' She remembered watching, trying to think, trying to fix things. 'It didn't take long for her to die.' She covered her face with her hands. 'Because of me.'

Simon was beside her, arms around her, head leaning against hers. She didn't deserve such kindness.

'It was a mistake.'

'Yeah. But . . .'

'And you were exhausted.'

'But she was my responsibility, Simon. I got it wrong.'

'You were under stress.'

'That didn't matter to her husband, did it?'

Simon said nothing, holding her tight.

'It was the worst thing – telling him. Knowing it was my fault. Knowing he would be going home to an empty apartment, knowing she would never be there again. I ruined his life.'

'You made a mistake. And she was elderly with a cardiac condition, so . . .'

'I killed someone.' Beth sobbed into his chest.

Simon reached out and she heard the rustle of tissues. He pressed some into her hand and she held them to her eyes.

'Beth, you do one of the hardest jobs in the world. You care for the sick, you give them the medicine they need, you hold their hands, you watch over them. You are the angel at their bedside.'

'Some bloody angel.' More tears fell.

'You know, I can still name every single critical care nurse who has looked after Jake. And believe me there have been a lot.' Simon took her hand and led her back to the sofa, where she sat down and buried her face in her hands. 'And you know why?'

'Why?'

'Because they all made such a difference. Because they all stood out. Because they all made his life better, and mine too.'

'But . . .'

'And that's what you did, Beth, for so many patients, and that's what you will do again. You will be an even better nurse because of what happened.'

'No, I . . .'

'You will, Beth. This is one mistake. A terrible one. But don't let it stop you.' He took her hand, pulling it down from her face. 'Nursing is what you were born to do.'

She gazed at him, tears staining her cheeks, and she saw faith in his eyes. Despite what she had done, despite her mistakes, he still believed in her.

His thumb traced a pattern across the back of her hand. 'You tried, Beth. You'd flagged the problem to your bosses. You'd asked for help again and again. It was them who chose not to give it.' His words were steady and sure. 'This isn't all on you.'

'But . . .'

'What was it you said to me? In the car the other day? That these things happen sometimes with HLHS? That I shouldn't blame myself?'

'Yeah, but that's different. I . . .'

'It's not different. You were part of a team – the whole team responsible for Mrs Garcia. And the hospital board didn't play its part – they put you in an impossible position.' The certainty in his eyes moved her. 'Look at who you are, Beth. Look at how you saved Jake. Don't let one mistake define your life.'

'They fired me. There was this whole inquiry.' She shuddered at the memory of entering that board room, and facing them all. Her voice was choked with tears. 'I was worried I'd lose my licence, but my lawyer said there was no case for that, because of my record, Mrs Garcia's health, the fact I reported it as soon as it happened and followed protocol. She said they shouldn't have fired me, that I should stay and fight. My colleagues did too, but I knew. I knew it was my fault.'

'You didn't.'

'I did, Simon. There's no point hiding from that. And God knows, the board agreed.'

'They wanted someone to blame, Beth.'

'Well, they were right! I was the one who did it.'

'By mistake, yes. And what a price you paid for it. Your job. Your confidence.'

He was so close. So comforting.

Beth thought of Caroline Garcia lying cold on the bed, her husband crying beside her.

Happiness was so precious. So rare.

'Beth?' Simon put his fingertip under her chin, tipping it upwards. 'You're an amazing nurse. Look what you did for Jake. He owes you everything. I owe you everything.'

And before she could think any more, he pressed his lips to hers.

His mouth was soft. He leant into her, his arms closing round her just as she had dreamt it, his hands stroking her back. His breathing was ragged and so was hers. But he was saying something. Trying to say something, anyway.

'Toooslknaskn.'

'What?' All she wanted to do was kiss him more.

He pulled away, his breathing ragged. 'Too many clothes on. We've got too many clothes on.'

'Oh.' She nodded. 'Yes.'

His chest rose and fell. 'We should do something about that.'

'We should. Now.'

'OK then.' He leant forward and grabbed her heavy polo neck, pulling it up and over her head. He gave a low whistle, smiling that slow sweet smile.

Then his lips nuzzled her neck, and then moved gently downwards. By the time he was unbuttoning her shirt she could barely speak at all. It had been so long since she had done this – so many months of sleeping alone, getting up alone, eating alone. She had missed hands on her body, breath against her cheek, that urgent, ferocious dizzying pull towards someone else.

She had missed this intimacy. She had missed being wanted and wanting in return. Her breath left her body as Simon reached her underwear and gently ran a finger underneath the cotton. She shivered and then she was reaching for him, her fingers teasing, her lips tasting. His

334

gasp filled her with such pleasure that she found herself climbing on top of him, pulling off his shirt, not caring about his stubble or his heavy belt buckle cutting into her thighs – not caring about anything but him and her together at last.

Afterwards, they lay on the sofa, her head against his chest, his arm warm as it circled her.

'Wow.'

'Yeah.' She shifted against him, not wanting to break the spell. 'Wow.'

She could feel him grinning. 'I can't believe it took us so long.'

'Well, I had seen you in your running gear.' She giggled. 'It took me a while to get past that.' She kissed his bare skin, never wanting to let him go.

'Well, I'd seen you in your nurse's outfit.' He gave a low whistle. 'It's amazing I held off for so long.' His lips grazed the top of her head.

She leant up on one elbow. 'It's my watch, isn't it? My fob watch. That's what really turns you on.'

'It's your lanyard, actually.' She loved the lines that deepened round his eyes as he smiled. 'I can't resist a lanyard.'

Beth smiled. This was so easy. It was so long since anything had felt easy. She wanted to talk about what had brought them here and where they might go. She wanted to feel his heat around her, inside her, and to make this moment last for ever.

She put her hand on his thigh, feeling the bones and the flesh of him, still not quite believing that he was here. He wasn't in love with Tamsin. Somehow he was hers.

'You need to forgive yourself, Beth.' He pulled her even closer.

For the first time she wondered if perhaps she could. If perhaps the plan she had sketched out, the documents in her Mercy View folder, might work – if it might help the other staff she had left behind in New York. If it might help the patients.

Simon continued. 'Because what you did – with Jake – that was incredible. You are incredible. So incredible I have no idea why you're here with a guy like me.'

And then all her words disappeared as she pulled him to her, loving him and holding him, until she couldn't remember the past or the future – her only truth was him and his touch and his heart beating against hers.

30

Simon

Simon knew he shouldn't be smiling this much while driving his son back from the hospital, but he couldn't help himself. Jake was snug in the back underneath the battered old patchwork blanket that had covered Simon's own bed as he grew up, the one knitted by his mum on the long needles that had clackety-clacked their way through every television show of his youth. Jake was weak, but getting stronger, and Miss Maya had said he would be quite safe at home until the operation.

He thought of Beth. Again. Of the gleam in her brown eyes last night and the way she had arched herself towards him as her hands traced his body. He hadn't felt self-conscious as her thumbs had traced the soft folds of his stomach or her lips had pressed against his thighs. Everything had flowed, everything had fitted. With her he felt taller, stronger, better. Seeing himself through her eyes, he knew that he could be any version of himself he wanted to be. He could get his registration back and become a physio again. He could fight to keep Jake here. He could do anything. With her, he could fly.

And he could help Beth too. Help her to believe in herself again. He had seen her pain when she talked about the past – the flush of shame on her cheeks, the guilt in every movement she made. She had seemed so fragile, and yet she was made of the kind of steel that brought dead people back to life.

'What are you so happy about?' Tamsin's voice brought him back to the present. Her face was pinched and tired, her skin pale.

'Nothing.' Beside them Crummock Water was smooth, its surface glossy, rippling in the winter sun. One day he could take Beth kayaking there. They could bring fishing rods and drop lines off the boat into the water, pretending they were going to catch fish, before giving up and getting fish and chips and eating it on the back step with Jake.

Tamsin fiddled with the radio, seeking a signal, before sighing and switching it off. 'You're grinning again, Simon.'

He flicked on the indicator. 'I'm just happy Jake's back with us.' Over the past couple of days the two of them had entered an uneasy peace, united in their aim of getting their son well enough to go home. Now they were on their way, the rest of their lives were about to start again and there were things they needed to discuss.

He glanced towards her. 'When are you going to tell Jake about Kris and the baby?'

'I want to have the scan first.'

'But . . .'

'I just – need to know that everything's OK before I tell him. I . . .' Tamsin stared at the road. 'I'm not ready.'

Simon took a breath and tried again. 'Look, I understand you're scared. About the scan, I mean. But Jake . . .'

'I can't, Simon.' Tamsin angled herself away from him, leaning her face against the window. 'Please.'

'But you will? After the scan?'

'Yes.' She sipped from her water bottle, eyes glinting. 'And what about you?'

'What do you mean, what about me?'

'Have you been thinking about London?'

Not this again. 'No.'

'Why not?' He heard a snap in her voice.

He checked the mirror again. Jake was still asleep, head lolling to one side.

'Because this is Jake's home, Tamsin. This is where he belongs.'

'Why won't you even think about it?' Her voice was rising, shrill with unhappiness. She looked exhausted. A memory stirred, of her lying on the bed, curtains closed.

Simon took a breath. 'Tamsin, Jake needs to be with me. It's what he knows.'

'He knows *me* now.'

'Yes. And that's wonderful. But . . .'

'And Beth said you're broke.'

He stiffened. 'She said what?'

'She said that you're broke and you hate your job.' Her voice was cold, searching for his weak spots and spiking home. 'She said that you couldn't even afford Jake's birthday present.'

No. Beth wouldn't have. He had told her to keep it a secret.

Tamsin continued. 'She said you're behind on rent too. So you need my help. Don't you? To look after him?

To keep our boy well and safe and give him what he needs?'

Simon turned off onto the bumpy road that led over the fells down to the village, his mind whirling. Beth had shared his secrets with Tamsin and now they were being used against him. Tamsin was threatening to take Jake away, and Beth had given her the weapons she needed.

The image of her last night, warm and smiling in his arms, was already starting to taint. That Beth wouldn't have shared his private confidences. That Beth would have respected his wishes, would have had his interests at heart.

He would never have believed it of her. He had trusted her with his hopes and dreams. He had been more open with her than with anyone, but now he was exposed. If he couldn't trust Beth, then there was nothing between them. If he couldn't be open with her then she was just another Tamsin, lying and pretending and making him believe in things that weren't true.

Damn it. There were tears in his eyes.

'Dad?' A reedy voice came from the back seat. Simon furiously wiped his tears away and smiled at his boy in the rear-view mirror.

'How are you doing, Jake?'

Jake stretched, his hair sticking straight up.

'I'm OK.' He rubbed his eyes. 'Your driving's a lot better now, Dad. Less jerky than it used to be.'

Simon relaxed. 'Cheeky.'

'You love it when I'm cheeky.'

'I do.'

Tamsin had turned, her hand on Jake's knee. 'Are you OK, baby?'

'Yeah.' Jake yawned, settling his head back against the window. 'Wouldn't mind a drink though.'

'Here you go.' Tamsin passed over his bottle, only to see that Jake had already fallen asleep again. He was always like this after hospital stays – sleeping suddenly and long, waking, talking, only to fall asleep again.

They were nearly home now.

Half an hour ago Simon had been desperate to get back – back to the woman next door who had changed his life; the woman with the dark hair and the kind eyes and the optimism that he lacked. She had been his Beth, his future.

'Just so you know, you're aiming straight at a tree.'

'Shit.' He swerved.

'Listen.' Tamsin looked at him. 'Let's talk about all this after my scan, OK? But I want to have a relationship with Jake, and if that means him coming to London then that's what needs to happen. We can work something out.'

'He's staying here.' A dry-stone wall ran along the road to their right, and he wanted to smash his fist into it until every last bit of it fell.

'I know it's hard, Simon.' That hand on his arm again. 'I see how close you are.'

He bit his lip. He would not cry.

'Simon?' Her mouth was trembling. 'I've missed Jake so much. If you knew . . .'

Simon changed gear. No more listening. No more

sympathising. 'No, Tamsin. He's not leaving. I don't care what you say.'

'Well, we'll see about that.'

'Yes we will, Tamsin. Yes we will.' He turned onto the gravel drive and his heart clenched as he saw Beth's cottage. The little red door, the smoke coming out of the chimney. She would be home by now, like she always was on a Friday, cooking herself some lunch before settling down to watch one of the old movies she loved so much.

He had learnt so much about her, without even trying.

He put the handbrake on and stopped the engine.

'Let's get Jake inside.'

He got out of the pickup, opened the back door, unclipped his son and carried him up the steps into the cottage. Beth's door opened just as he reached his own.

'Hey there.' Her eyes were liquid with love. If only it was yesterday. If only he had never found out that she had betrayed him.

He clutched Jake close, treasuring his warmth.

'Hi.' He couldn't waste energy on talking to her. He couldn't even look at her. His head was buzzing and his anger was building – soon every cell of his body would be on fire. He hated her for letting him down. He hated that yet another thing he believed in had come crashing down around him.

She stepped forward. 'Simon? Is everything OK?'

'I can't talk. Got to get him to bed.' He pushed his way inside the cottage without looking at her.

He heard an intake of breath and knew it must be hers.

'Simon?' He could imagine the pain on her face. He could imagine her confusion. He handed Jake to a sullen Tamsin and she carried him inside, still sleeping.

Simon walked back out and looked at Beth. The red mist was on him. Years of anger, at last finding a target. He couldn't stop it any more.

'Did you tell Tamsin about how broke I am?'

'I . . .' She put her hand to her mouth and he knew in that moment that it was true.

'Even though I specifically asked you not to?'

'Oh God.' She had turned white. 'Yes. I did. I'm so sorry. I was on a call, and . . .'

'You broke my trust?'

'I'm sorry.'

His voice was thick with rage. 'She's trying to take Jake away, Beth. She says that because I'm broke she should take him to London and give him what he needs – give him a better life.'

He heard a moan and knew it was hers.

He stepped away from her. 'Beth, I trusted you. You were the one person I thought was true. I thought you were on my team.' He wasn't sure if he was seeing Beth or Tamsin in front of him but it didn't matter. He was tired of taking the hits, he was tired of being so passive, of being trodden on and lied to and made to feel a fool.

'It's too much – I've had to deal with too much. It's just me and my boy and that's all I have the energy for right now. I can't – take on any more unknowns. I can't live like that. If things can't be easy between us – if we can't trust each other – then there's no point. I have to get Jake through surgery and that's safer on my own. I'm happier on my own.'

Even as he said it he knew that he would miss Beth, and he knew how much.

'But Simon . . .'

'No.' He turned and pushed his door open, anxious to get back to Jake. Anxious to get away.

'Simon, please!'

Her face. It slayed him.

But he didn't care. He didn't.

He had to get Jake through the Fontan. He had to hunker down.

He had to forget about Beth, however much it hurt.

31

Beth

Jas put down her glass, exhaling in disgust. 'I never had Simon down as a dickhead, but it seems I was wrong. I'm so sorry, Beth.'

'He's not a dickhead. He's angry.' Beth left her drink untouched. She had stayed up for hours, waiting for his knock on the door, or his feet climbing the back step. But nothing. Fuelled by all the wine in her fridge she had even found herself standing outside his front door at midnight, hand raised, only to lose confidence and turn away.

Simon had been angry with her before, back in the spring, but this was different. Then, she had been a stranger. Now, she was so much more.

Or she had believed she was.

'You can never bloody tell, can you?' Jas shook her head in despair.

'It's not his fault.' Beth picked up a crisp but felt too sick to eat it. 'I did tell Tamsin about how short of money he is, when he'd specifically asked me not to.'

Jas's eyes flashed. 'You were trying to help!'

'Maybe. But Simon doesn't see it that way. And it's Tamsin who's the real problem. I can't believe she wants to take Jake away.' She drummed her fingers on her glass. 'No wonder Simon went ballistic.'

'Yeah, but with the wrong person.' Jas's curls bounced out of her ponytail as she put her glass down on the table. 'Bloody men.'

Beth frowned. 'It's just – it felt so real when we were together. So right.' She slumped downwards, so her face rested on her right hand. 'Then, when he was angry last night he looked like he wanted to kill me, but he looked so lonely too.'

'All the more reason not to be a dick to someone who's on your side.'

Beth sighed. 'I just feel so dumb. I thought he really liked me. Enough to listen to me, anyway – to let me explain.'

She shivered as she remembered the fury on Simon's face. The way his whole body was reaching away from her, as if touching her might pollute him.

'He does like you. That's the weird thing.' Jas crunched a handful of crisps. 'So, what are you going to do?'

Beth shrugged. Jake's operation was only days away now. She had imagined she would be part of his team – at his bedside, bringing food to keep Simon and Tamsin fuelled as they sat next to him in recovery. But now all that was over.

'Well, I can't stay living there, can I?'

'Hey.' Jas hit the table with her hand. Some walkers on the next table looked round nervously from their maps.

'You can't just give in like that. You don't have to leave because of Simon.' She was in full indignant mode now.

Soon she'd be whipping out a notebook and making lists in fierce red biro. Bullet points: *Find Simon, Kill Simon*, etc, etc.

'Maybe I need to leave for me.' Beth measured her words carefully. 'I was looking at that job link you sent me last night and I put in an application. With Jake, on that football pitch – I remembered I can do it. I can look after people when they need it most. And – I love doing it. Maybe it's time to get back in the ring.'

'Now this I love.' Jas reached out and squeezed Beth's shoulder. 'Well done.'

'I think it's time.' Beth put her head on one side. 'Maybe that's the one good thing to come out of all this. My private life is a bloody mess, but at least I can stand to look at my own CV now. After what happened with Jake . . .' Her throat thickened. 'I know I can do it.'

'Great.' Jas noisily slurped the last of her cocktail. 'Now I just need to go and see Simon.'

'No.'

'Please? Or I can set Saffy on him for you?'

'No, Jas, honestly, please, please don't. I don't want any fuss. He's got so much going on. You can't beg a man to love you.' Beth's head ached, and she yawned. She just wanted to go to bed and actually sleep, rather than lying there and listening for every creak and rustle from his room beyond the wall. Everywhere she was in the cottage she heard footsteps, the click of the kettle, the clatter of cutlery against the table, the scrape of chairs against the floor.

It wasn't just Simon she missed. She was desperate to see Jake too.

Jas's mouth softened in sympathy. 'So you love him, then?'

Beth nodded miserably. 'Yeah.'

'Oh holy shit. More wine.'

Beth didn't want more wine. She suddenly wanted to be at home, to cry all the tears in her heart; to pull the covers up over her head and let everything else fall away.

'I'm sorry, Jas, I've got to go.' She stood up. She was worried that her face was about to crack – that once she had started weeping she might never stop. She would cry for Simon – for him not being the man she had believed him to be. She would cry for Jake and his uncertain future and the pain that he still had to face. She would cry for herself, separated from them, wishing she could be part of their lives again.

She had come all the way here for a fresh start, only to be broken-hearted again.

Jas stood up and hugged her. 'I'm sorry I can't make you feel better.' She swayed slightly and clung onto Beth's arm. 'But I just want to say that I think you're amazing. And you should go for that job. You're a great nurse, Beth, and you always will be.'

She reached for Beth's hand. 'You have to forgive yourself.'

Beth remembered the same words in Simon's mouth. The press of his hand against hers. His kindness. His belief. Beth straightened up and started putting her coat on.

'Love you.' Jas reached out and hugged Beth again, holding her close.

'Love you too.' Beth nearly dissolved, right there, but somehow she got out, coat on, bag on her shoulder, and trudged her way up the lane.

The light was on in Simon's house but no one waved from the window. She took longer than usual putting her key in her front door, creaking it open slowly, lingering on the step, but no one came out to talk to her. As she took her coat off in the hall, hanging it up on its peg, she felt despair seeping through her. She walked through to the living room, hearing cooking sounds from the other side. Simon was frying something. There was a clang as a pan landed on the hob and a sizzle as meat met oil. Once, Simon would have made some for her. Once, he would have knocked on the wall to summon her through.

Beth put her bag down, resolve strengthening within her. Jas was right. She was going to go next door. She was going to talk to Simon, to make him see he was wrong. This time, she was going to fight. She turned and headed for the door, but just as she reached it she heard a knock. It was Simon. It must be. She wrenched it open. Maybe he had changed his mind. Maybe he was going to tell her he loved her and take her in his arms and . . .

'Hello.'

It was Jake. Small. Freezing. Fragile.

'Hello, you.' She dropped down so her face was level with his. 'Do you want to come in?'

'I can't.' He glanced nervously at his front door. 'Dad will kill me if he knows I'm here.'

'OK.' She absorbed this. 'How can I help?'

'You need to leave.' Jake's mouth was set, his eyes miserable.

'What?' She had expected it from Simon, but not from Jake. 'Why?'

'Because you're in the way. Of Mum and Dad.'

'I . . .' Beth opened her mouth to defend herself, to list all the reasons why he was wrong, to tell him what was really happening between his parents. 'But your dad's not even talking to me.'

'It doesn't matter. His face is so sad, whenever he looks at your door. He doesn't even look at Mum any more. They don't speak, really.' His voice cracked.

She opened her arms and he stepped into them. 'I'm sorry.' She stroked his back. 'I'm so sorry, Jake.' Whoever was wrong, and whoever was right, Jake didn't deserve to feel like this. Not now, so close to his operation. Not ever.

She loved this little boy and she could never ever knowingly make him unhappy.

He pulled away. She saw the shadows under his eyes and the powdery whiteness of his skin. She remembered the feeling of his ribs beneath her fingers – the shallowness of his breath when she had revived him. This was a boy who needed hope. This was a boy who needed to believe his dream could come true.

Beth had to play her part.

So she didn't explain herself. She didn't protest. She looked at Jake's set, sad face and decided to go. She could leave the village and stay in a B&B for a bit. She could get the hell out of here and deal with the heartache later. She could do it, for Jake.

'Is this really what you want?'

'Yes.' He bit his lip. 'And no.' Then he raised his hands to his chest, making a heart shape with his fingers and thumbs, and stood on his tiptoes to kiss her. 'Thanks, Beth. And – I'm really sorry. I love you.'

And he turned and ran, leaving only an open door and a freezing wind behind him.

In a whirlwind, Beth went round the cottage, picking up clothes and throwing them into her bag. She washed up plates and cutlery and placed them carefully back in the cupboards. She hoovered and cleaned and straightened, leaving rent money on the table alongside a Good Luck sign she had made for Jake out of Lego. Blue pieces and white. His favourites.

With one last glance from the window towards the fells, she left, closing the front door behind her and posting the key back through the door. And then she drove away from the cottage, away from the people she loved, towards an unknown future.

Later, in a cosy room in a B&B in Keswick, she lay on the bright yellow bedspread, staring up at the oak beams beneath the sloping ceiling. She thought about Simon, with his anger and his courage. And she thought about Jake, so sick, still trying even now to make his plan a reality – trying to make his dad fall in love.

She pulled the Mercy View folder out of her bag. She knew what she had to do and at last she knew who she was: a nurse, an expert, someone who cared. Yes, she had made a mistake, and she would carry that weight for ever. But if she didn't go back now, if she didn't take her evidence there herself, then Mercy View hospital might make more mistakes. Beth would not give up. She would be as brave as Jake – as brave as Simon.

She released a breath that had been months coming. And then she was on her phone, researching, checking, planning. If she had learnt one thing in the past year it was to do things now; not to wait, not to overthink or second-guess.

Half an hour later her flight was booked.

She was going back to Mercy View hospital. She was going back to face her past.

She was going back to New York.

Hi Emily

I saw you. The other week – at the football match?
I heard you calling me. I was nearly there, next to
you, and then I was – back. Flat on the ground.
Staring at the clouds.

Dad and Mum still aren't together. I've failed,
Emily. I wish you were here to help me.

My Fontan is really soon. Please be there with me.
Love,
J xx

32

Simon

Jake leant forwards, his chin on his elbow, drinking in the view. 'Thanks for driving me here, Dad. I wanted to see it one more time, before—'

'Before what?' Simon looked out over the rippling lake, towards the tall fir trees that covered the hillside beyond like a dark green carpet. A brave duck bobbed on the surface, her beak dipping tentatively into the water. Moorhens clustered by the bank and grey rocks rose up at the edge of the beach just in front of the pickup, reigning supreme over the wintery landscape. Outside, the wind whistled. It seemed years ago that they had all been here for Jake's birthday rather than only a few weeks. Jake now was so different to Jake then. Jake now was tired, slow, sleepy – Jake then had been laughing, splashing, alive.

Simon's stomach skewered. They would get Jake back. The operation would save him. Simon had to believe that. He rested his aching head against the headrest, struggling to stay still. His breaths were too tight, his mind fixating on the operation next week.

'Nothing, Dad.' Jake shifted in the seat next to Simon. The patchwork blanket Simon had tucked around him came loose. 'Are there any good stones for skimming?'

Simon peered over the dashboard. 'Yeah. I reckon there are. Want to try?'

'No thanks. I just wondered.' Jake snuggled further down beneath his blanket. He hadn't properly got out of bed since the football match. Instead, he lay on the sofa in T-shirts and tracksuit bottoms. He had his Nintendo at his side, but he hadn't even got up the energy to turn it on. No matter what food Simon gave him he barely ate it, instead lying back and ingesting comfort telly as if he could live on that alone. Tamsin was down in London, Barney was in the eye of his wedding preparations and Beth – Beth was gone.

Simon sighed. His anger with her was fading. If she hadn't left so suddenly, he would have talked to her by now, found out why she had told Tamsin his secret, tried to understand. But now her phone was off and she had disappeared.

'Dad?'

Jake sounded high and feverish and Simon turned and put a hand to his forehead, alert to any sign of illness or infection.

Simon forced a smile. 'Yes?'

His son attempted to reciprocate. It was so feeble it hurt to see it. 'Where's Mum?' He rubbed his eyes with his fists, mouth splitting into a yawn.

'She's in London for the weekend. She's got a presentation she can't miss, but she'll be back on Monday.'

'I miss her.'

'It's not for long, lad.' Simon put a gentle hand on his shoulder. 'You'll see her soon.'

'But . . .' Jake was muttering now, tears forming in his eyes. 'You two. You have to—'

'What do we have to do?'

'You have to . . .' Jake's eyes drifted off, fixing on a tree branch that seemed to be tapping out a rhythm in the sky.

'What, lad?'

'You have to get together, Dad. You're meant to be together.'

Simon's whole body sagged. Tamsin still hadn't told Jake about her pregnancy, and time was running out. Simon didn't want to pretend to have feelings that weren't real. He didn't want to lie to his son.

Beth. She was the woman he had wanted. He had talked to Barney about what she had said to Tamsin, only for his friend to call him a stupid arse and to come round to tell him why in immense detail. Barney had knocked on Beth's door, calling through the letter box that Simon had always had a temper and he was alright once you got used to it. There was no answer. She had already gone.

Jake was speaking again.

'You and Mum love each other, Dad. Just like they do in the movies.' Jake's eyes were full of a desperate conviction. 'I've watched loads of films, so I know what I'm talking about.' His son's face was now so pale that his freckles stood out like muddy footprints on a white carpet. Jake took a breath. 'She's the love of your life, Dad. I know she is.' His fingers were busy, zipping and unzipping his hoodie. 'I don't want you to be on your own, Dad.'

'Oh my boy.' Simon put his arms around Jake and held him. 'I know. But I won't be. Because you're going to get through this.'

'I'm scared, Dad.' Jake's breathing was becoming jagged again.

'I know you are.' Simon moved his hand in slow circles on Jake's back. 'I am too. But I promise – this operation's going to do wonderful things for you.'

'You don't know that, Dad.'

'You're right, I don't know it. But I believe it. The other operations were amazing, so this one will be too.' Simon lifted Jake's chin. 'Do you believe me?'

'Yeah.'

Christ, it was hard not to cry. If only Beth were here. She would know what to say. She always knew.

Jake spoke again. 'This operation feels so hard, Dad. I'm so tired now. All I want to do is sleep.'

Simon folded his son into him, resting his head against Jake's. 'Then rest. Your heart is doing its best and you're nearly there. It's OK to be tired. We have Netflix. You're all sorted.'

He thought he heard a ghost of a laugh.

Jake spoke into Simon's chest. 'Sometimes I feel like it might have been better . . .' Jake dashed away a tear.

'What?'

'It might have been better if I had never been born.'

Simon flinched. 'You don't really think that?'

Jake was really crying now. 'Look at how much trouble I am. I'm always ill. You have to miss work – you had to give up the job at the hospital and you really loved that.

And I know you're meant to be working for Grandad this week but here you are again having to spend all your time with me.'

'No.' Simon shook his head. 'That's not how it is. I . . .'

Jake's voice was rising. 'And then you and Mum splitting up. That was my fault too. If I hadn't been ill you'd still be together.'

'That's not true.'

'Yes it is. Everything bad in your life is because of me.' Jake was buried so deep in Simon's jumper that his voice was increasingly difficult to hear. 'I make everything harder.'

Simon kissed the top of his head. 'Will you let me speak now?'

''Spose.'

'OK then.' Simon inhaled, fixing his eyes on the sky. He needed to get this right. No words had mattered more. He spoke into his son's hair. 'Jake, I can't imagine anything worse than you not being here – so many days and moments and laughs and meals would have been grey without you. Please never ever feel that it would have been better if you weren't here.'

No answer.

'My world is brighter with you in it, Jake. It's better with you in it. You are the best thing in my life every day and in every way.'

Jake tipped his face upwards. It was streaked with tears. 'What about Mum?'

Simon reached for the right words to tell him. Of

course, it was falling to him rather than Tamsin. Maybe he had always known that it would.

Maybe it was for the best. 'I was very happy with your mum for a while, but I don't know what the future holds for us.'

'Don't you love her?' The shock on Jake's face was very hard to see. 'Did I get it wrong?'

'*You* didn't get it wrong. I did.' Simon gently tipped Jake's chin up again. 'And I do love her, in a way. I love her because she's your mum. I love her because she gave me one half of you. I will always love her for that, no matter what.'

'So can't you marry her?'

'It's not that simple, Jake. I'm sorry. I wish it was.'

Jake's tears began again. 'But what about you? You'll be all alone if—'

'Can we stop talking about what-ifs, Jake?' As Simon spoke, he felt his conviction growing stronger. He was right, he knew he was. And as he spoke, things clicked into place. 'Because you can't live like that. *We* can't live like that. We have to think positive – we have to make the most of what we've got.'

He thought he heard a grunt of assent.

'Good. So, here's what's going to happen. You're going to have an operation and you're going to survive it, just like you survived the others. You had your moment on that football pitch – maybe that was your Emily moment, I don't know. I'll never know.

'But maybe this is your time to get lucky. Maybe you're going to be a nine-year-old and a ten-year-old and then a teenager, and then we might have to stop speaking to each other for a bit, because you'll find me very, very embarrassing, and then we'll carry on together, OK? And one day you'll be taller than me and you'll pat me on the head and tell me I've got no hair left, but we'll still go to see Sunderland lose, because that's our thing. We can't live for what might or might not happen tomorrow – we have to make the most of today. Alright?'

'Maybe.' Jake's frown bit deep. 'But you need someone to love you. A love of your life.'

'Don't you get it, Jake?' Simon's voice broke. 'Tamsin's not the love of my life. She never was. All these years I've had someone else. Someone better.'

Jake's forehead creased in puzzlement. 'Who's that?'

'*You.*' Simon pressed his hands to his son's face – to his beautiful, miraculous, wonder of a face. He could kiss every freckle a thousand times over and it would never be enough. 'You. You're the love of my life. Can't you see that?'

'Me?'

'Yes. You.' He squeezed Jake in his arms. 'Alright? You are brave and funny and you amaze me every day. If I could change one thing in my life I would have HLHS for you. I would take this pain away, if only I could.'

'I wouldn't let you.'

'Well, I wouldn't give you a choice. I'm your dad.' Simon wagged a finger. 'You have to do what I tell you.'

A pause.

'I love you too, Dad.' Jake leant into him. 'Are you sure about Mum, though?' His voice was lighter, with some of its old cheek.

'Yes I'm sure.' Simon kept hugging him close, treasuring him while he could. When Tamsin came back up on Monday, they were going to talk to Jake about the future. They would do it together – try to find a way through. Simon had texted her good luck for her scan that morning. Despite all that had happened between them, he needed her to know that he was thinking of her – that he cared.

'How about Beth?' Jake was peering up at him. 'Do you love her?'

'Why do you ask?'

'I just wondered.'

Beth's smile shimmered in Simon's mind, the angle of her chin as she turned to him, the warmth of her arms around him.

'Beth's gone.'

'Because of me.' Jake's distress was spiralling again. 'I told her to leave, Dad.'

'What?'

'The other day. I went round and told her to go. Because I wanted you and Mum together.'

Simon's mouth dropped open.

'Beth was in the way, wasn't she?' Jake's logic was so clear, Simon couldn't be angry. 'I wanted to help.'

'And she went? Just like that?'

'Yes.' Jake bit his lip. 'She looked really sad, though. Did I do the wrong thing? I did, didn't I?'

Simon couldn't let himself reply.

'I'm sorry, Dad. I was just trying to help.'

'I know.'

Jake snuggled into him. 'Are you angry with me?'

'No, Jake. Not with you.'

'Are you sure?'

'Yes.' Simon tried to smile. 'I'm not angry at you. But I'm pretty mad at me. I didn't give her a chance, you see. I didn't let her explain. I called her out on one mistake.' He shook his head. 'Which is exactly the opposite of what I should have done.'

'You could call her? Talk to her, Dad?'

'No.' Simon shook his head. 'She deserves better than me.'

Jake leant his head back against the seat. 'I'm sorry, Dad.'

Simon started the engine, seeing Jake's head starting to roll sideways as he slipped into sleep. Nothing to do but to get home. Nothing to do but to keep going. He pulled out onto the road and started to drive back to the home that now felt so much emptier without the woman next door.

33

Beth

'Well, you nailed it by the sound of it.' Jas pushed a coffee across to Beth. 'Well done.'

Beth added milk to her coffee, her hands still shaking. That hospital meeting room had been huge, the interview panel so big she didn't know where to look. Her PowerPoint presentation had suffered a glitch in the middle, leaving her talking endlessly over an image of a heart, and she had sweated so much she wanted to burn her suit. Apart from that her interview had been a breeze.

Jas pointed at the blueberry muffin dominating the plate in the middle of the table. 'Sure you don't want some?'

'No thanks. I'm about to sit still for ten hours, I think I'd better keep my sugar levels in check.'

She glanced at the departure screen behind them again. Her flight was still on time. Just seeing those letters, JFK, filled her with a mix of excitement and dread: surprising Tyler; going to the hospital with the sheaf of papers she had been putting together over the last few days; seeing the ward she had last left with a security escort and the boardroom where her ex-husband had joined with the rest of the executives to condemn her.

She sipped her coffee and burnt her lips. 'Ouch.' She pressed them together, flapping her hand in front of her mouth. It made absolutely no difference. It never did.

Saffy ran up from the cafe counter, where she had been eyeing up the various treats on offer. 'I think I want the cinnamon bun.'

Jas turned her head towards her daughter. 'Are you sure?'

'Yes.'

Jas smiled. 'Totally sure?'

'Yes.' Saffy smiled and Beth saw that another one of her front teeth had come out.

'OK, then.' Jas stood up, getting her long pink wallet out of her bag. 'Let's go get it.'

In their absence Beth tried to force her breathing to slow down. She wasn't even there yet, and already her pulse was racing. When she had left she had assumed she would never go back to New York – she had felt that chapter of her story ending, a stone rolled over the entrance to a cave. But now here she was, choosing to go back, choosing to tell her story.

'Look at my doughnut, Beth.' Saffy was attempting to clamber up onto a high metal stool.

Beth gave her a squeeze. 'Changed your mind again, then?'

Saffy pouted. 'I liked the sprinkles.' She opened her mouth wide and devoured half of it in onc bite.

'Easy tiger.' Jas rolled her eyes. 'Try to enjoy it. Linger. You know?'

'Yes, Mum.' Saffy's cheeks were puffed wide as she pushed more doughnut into her mouth.

'Did you get a chance to look at any flats?' Jas leant forward on her elbows. 'For when you get the job?'

'Ha ha.'

'You did, didn't you?' Jas started splitting the remains of the doughnut into smaller chunks. 'Go on. Spill.'

Beth arched an eyebrow. 'I found a nice one, just down by Media City.'

'Knew it!'

'Pretty near the hospital, and looking out over the water. It's just small, but it's got everything I need.' Beth shrugged. 'But I probably haven't got the job. I gave a pretty ropey answer to the clinical governance question.'

Jas shook her head. 'I'm sure you did brilliantly.' She sipped her hot chocolate. 'I have total faith.'

'Thanks, Jas.' Beth wished she had her friend's confidence.

'All part of the service.' Jas smiled.

Beth drank her coffee, thinking of the wrench of leaving Thistlethwaite for good. Already she missed her view, the lane, the jangle of the bell in the village shop.

And Jake and Simon. She missed them most of all.

'So.' Jas's eyes gleamed. 'No regrets?'

'No point in regrets, is there?' Beth put her coffee down. 'Time to move on.'

'Then my work here is done.' Jas clapped her hands in satisfaction. 'And you have a plane to catch.'

'I do.' Beth's stomach plunged. 'Oh God. I'm really nervous.'

'All the more reason to get on that plane.' Jas nodded her head emphatically. 'You bloody go and give them what for.'

'OK, then.' Beth checked that she had everything she needed: passport, ticket, boarding pass, a magazine that she wouldn't ever read.

She was ready.

'Bye.' Beth tried to smile, only to find her lips were trembling.

Jas stood up too and hugged her. 'I'm going to miss you.'

'You too.' Beth held on tight. 'Thank you for everything you've done, Jas. I couldn't have got through all this without you.'

'I know.' Jas pulled back and Beth could see tears in her eyes. 'I am amazing it's true. Now go back there and get some of that closure I hear so much about.'

'OK.' Beth took a deep breath. 'Here I go.'

Jas held her by the shoulders, as she had months ago outside the Health Centre when Beth's Lake District journey had begun. 'You're a great nurse. You saved a boy's life last month. But until you go back to the States you'll never really believe in yourself. Do you see?'

'But what if it's all awful? What if . . .?'

'No more what-ifs, Beth.' Jas was practically pleading now. 'Go, now, and sod bloody Simon and sod bloody Tyler because this is about you and your heart and your job. And I love you, but please can you go now because they're calling your flight, and I think Saffy's just about to launch into the doughnut stratosphere and I need full eyes on her.'

'OK, OK.' Beth hovered, giving herself one second more. Her friend was right. She had to go. She turned away and pushed her way through the crowds towards the security gates.

Next stop: New York.

34

Simon

'Jake?' Tamsin's face glowed as she walked into the hall. Simon could smell the winter air on her coat, see the flush on her cheeks. 'Baby? Can you come here? I've brought someone to meet you. The guy I told you about on the phone?'

'Sssshhhh.' Simon raised his finger to his lips as he took her coat. 'Jake's asleep.'

'Really?' Tamsin checked the clock on the wall. 'But it's 11 in the morning.'

'He's tired.' Simon still didn't know how to talk to her. The anger was there, no matter where he put himself, no matter what he did. He couldn't forget it or smooth it over. It was a wall of resentment between them.

He heard a heavy tread on the step and a large hand appeared in the doorway, attached to a tall man with a skiing tan and an American accent.

'Hi. I'm Kris.' It was the kind of hand that wouldn't take no for an answer.

'Hi.' Simon shook it, briefly, then turned away. 'Come in.'

He had tidied the cottage last night, knowing they were coming, wanting to present himself in the best possible light, wanting to make his case to keep Jake here. However, now the winter sun shone through the windows, ruthlessly exposing the dirty panes of glass and the dust on the corner of the table that he had wiped but not well enough, he felt a beat of shame.

Maybe Jake shouldn't be here. Maybe what Simon provided for him wasn't good enough. Maybe he should set his boy free.

'Tea?' He started filling up the kettle before they answered. It was something to do. Something to fill the time until they raised the issue that Simon didn't want to address.

'I love your place.' Kris had sunglasses pushed up over his dark hair and the kind of energy that Simon could only envy. His deep blue V-neck was rolled up at the sleeves, his jeans were spotless and his white trainers had clearly not spent any time tramping over muddy fields like Simon's had.

Despite all this, Simon warmed to him. Kris had a voice that rang with humour and his brown eyes were kind. 'What a view. Wow, Tamsin. It's even better than you said.'

'I know.' Tamsin seemed different too. She was more relaxed. No tension in her smile. No aggression in her eyes. 'Could I just have a glass of water, please, Simon?' She sat on the sofa and crossed her legs.

Simon filled one at the tap and handed it over. Her hand was over her belly – protective. Proud.

He sat down next to her.

'The scan. What happened?'

Her smile told him all he needed to know.

'She's looking great.'

'She?'

'Yeah.' Tamsin glanced at Kris and the temperature in the room rose several degrees. 'It's a girl. And they can't see anything to worry about.' Tears glistened in her eyes.

'Oh. Wow.' Simon took her hand. 'I'm so happy for you.'

She squeezed his fingers. 'I know you are, Simon. And thank you.'

Simon was happy for Tamsin – he knew how scared she must have been. But at the same time he couldn't help feeling sad for himself. She was glowing, loved. He had thrown his chance away, let his temper get the better of him. He had thought again and again about calling Beth or messaging her, but then he would remember the pain on her face and stop himself. He had made enough of a mess – he didn't want to cause any more damage.

He felt a hand on his shoulder and looked up to see Tamsin leaning towards him. 'Simon. Are you OK?'

He shook his head. 'Not really. I know what you're here for. I know what you want to talk about. London. Jake going there. And I know I need to listen. Properly listen.' He was starting to feel sick. Right now he had about two pounds in his bank account. If Tamsin wanted to fight him for Jake, he had no idea how he could fight back.

But he knew Jake should be here in Thistlethwaite, with him: chatting over tea about football or what Jake had played at lunchtime; walking to the woods after school and eating cheese and pickle sandwiches amongst the bluebells; even lying in bed watching telly and feeling terrible. This was Jake's home.

Tamsin spoke softly. 'Simon. I do want to talk to you, but not how you think. Kris and I have been talking. And we think we've come up with a plan that will work for all of us – for us and Jake too.' She put her hand on Simon's arm. 'And you too, I hope?'

'OK.' Simon clasped his hands together, fear knifing his stomach.

'It's only an idea.' She talked quickly, fiddling with the gold ring on her finger. 'But it would keep Jake in my life. And yours. And that's what we all want, isn't it?'

'Yes.' Simon swallowed. It was too early to hope. He needed to hear more.

'So . . .' Kris went and sat next to her on the arm of the sofa, gently rubbing her back. Kindness radiated from him like heat from a fire. Simon could see how Tamsin leant into him, how she trusted him, how he would protect her.

'So?' Simon's voice was dry.

'So . . .' Her voice was crystal clear. 'I'd like to start by apologising, Simon. For pushing so hard about Jake and London. I was so scared about the scan, it's like I was trying to take control of the one thing I could. I felt like everything was spiralling out of my grip, and I got really fixated on Jake being with me. I knew it hurt you, but I did it anyway, and I'm really sorry. You didn't deserve that.'

Simon couldn't speak.

'I just need to come out and say it.' She raised her head, eyes blazing in her pale face.

'Say what?'

'I need to say thank you, Simon.'

Simon blinked. 'Why?'

'For being with Jake. For not hating me. For letting me back into his life.' Her words were rushing now, gathering speed, a river racing towards a waterfall.

'No need to thank me. You're his mum. And what are you saying, Tamsin?'

She gave a shuddering sigh. 'I'm saying I don't want to take him to London.'

'Then . . . what . . .?'

She hesitated, wiping a tear from her cheek as Kris smiled encouragingly.

Simon's fear rose again. 'You can't abandon him now, Tamsin. I told you that. You're in, or you're out. There's nothing in between.'

'I know.' She smiled. 'I know. Don't worry.'

'So?'

'So we're relocating.' A glance at Kris. 'To Manchester.'

Simon's jaw dropped. 'You are?'

'Yes.'

'Oh, wow.'

'I know.' She smiled. 'It was Beth's idea, really. She said that's what Jake needed, at the same time as she told me how things were so difficult for you.'

Beth. Of course. And he'd bawled her out for one mistake while at the same time she had planted the seed of something wonderful. He was such a fool.

Simon leant back against the cushions. 'Jake will be so happy.'

'Do you think?' There was that vulnerability again.

'I know he will.' Simon reached out and hugged her. 'Thank you.'

Tamsin shook her head.

'No. Thank you, Simon. Thank you.'

He drew a shaky breath and got to his feet. 'Right. Tea.'

As he poured steaming water into mugs he saw the way Tamsin leant her head on Kris's shoulder; the way his arm circled around her; the way he kissed her cheek and stroked her hand.

How he wished Beth could be there beside him.

How he wished he hadn't messed up his happy ending.

35

Beth

The air was fresh as Beth stepped out of her hotel. She did up the final button on her coat, before swinging her blue scarf around her neck. The snow had been cleared along the sidewalk, but still she stepped carefully, trying to slow herself down as the big moment approached. Her stomach clutched with nerves as she joined the crowds heading for the subway and started to walk down the steps. She hesitated, her hand on the rail, as a teenager pushed past her impatiently. Then she turned back, bumping into a sighing commuter. She needed to be above ground. She needed the air and the light that she had got so used to in the Lakes.

Even after such a short time away she missed Thistlethwaite. She missed the sounds from the cottage next door; missed sitting curled up on the sofa with her morning coffee steaming in her hand; missed stepping out of her front door and hearing nothing but birds singing or the whisper of the breeze. She missed Simon and Jake. But here, surrounded by the energy and colour of New York, amidst the honking traffic, the pushing pedestrians, the towering skyscrapers – here she felt a renewed sense of determination; a need to finally have her say.

She saw a cab and raised her hand. It was time. She was finally going back to the place that had loomed so large in her mind for so long. She was going to face up to what she had done.

Beth leant forward to give the driver the address and turned her phone off. She needed to be disconnected today – free to focus on everything that was to come and what she needed to say. The bustling streets, with their shops and restaurants, sped past the window. She glimpsed a branch of Birch and remembered sipping fragrant hot chocolates with friends from her team one sunny September day, talking about what movie they would see that night and how rude the new surgeon was. They passed a big fancy-dress store, where Beth had chosen a Grinch costume for a Hallowe'en party, that had subsequently proved too small to put on.

As the cab idled by a traffic light, Beth realised that this city, which Tyler had introduced to her, had become hers. Since Tyler had left, Beth had forged her own path here. Until those final, frantic few months as the team dwindled, she had spent Sundays with friends, feet up, reading papers, cooking the kind of breakfasts that last all day. Pancakes, syrup, bacon, waffles, all washed down with gallons of orange juice and coffee. She had strolled in Central Park. She had taken the ferry to Staten Island, to see the Statue of Liberty at sunset.

New York was full of those happier memories too. And as the cab got closer to Mercy View, Beth realised that her pain had blurred. She could remember the good chapters of her life here, not just the miserable ending.

She stared out through the window as she let herself remember, let herself relive. She knew now that trying to fight these memories was to fight part of herself. The best thing she could do was to let them flood in.

The cab was drawing up at the hospital, next to those grey steps that she had last seen all those months before. She paid the driver, took a deep breath and stepped out.

The air still smelt the same – of cinnamon rolls from the stall on the street corner and of fumes from the cars on the street. There were flecks of ice in the air. She looked at the doors, revolving endlessly round to welcome the sick and the healers, and she hesitated for one more moment.

Then she squared her shoulders. No more hiding.

She marched up to the door and stepped inside. Ten seconds later she was in the atrium, surrounded by lush green plants and the sound of running water. She thought back to her little NHS clinics in Cumberland, taking place in tiny huts or school classrooms. It didn't matter where she was – making people better was what counted. She glanced towards the long stainless-steel reception desk, noting with wry amusement that there was a new statue of the founder of the hospital behind it. He certainly didn't have that much hair in real life.

The receptionist was new and didn't recognise her name when Beth signed in. Beth headed towards the lift, her visitor pass around her neck, and pressed the button for the fifteenth floor.

She was going to surprise Tyler before the meeting that really mattered.

Her heels sank into the plush carpet as she reached

the executive offices, so rarefied they were graced with a floor of their own. She and Tyler had laughed at their sleek coffee machines and manicured secretaries, until Tyler had been voted onto the board and gained an office of his own.

She walked down the corridor towards him, finding the courage to smile at everyone she saw. She looked so different with her short hair that it took people a while to recognise her. Brows furrowed, eyes followed, but she knew that they would make the connection – that in a second her arrival would be all over the building. *Beth's back. Beth's here to see the Chief.* Nudges, pointing, gasps.

Let them gossip. She didn't care. She gulped down her nerves and held her head high. Jake's face flashed into her head. She could be as brave as him. Or at least she could try.

She reached the oak door with its pompous brass plaque. *Mr Tyler Langton, Chief of Surgery.* She raised her fist to knock, and then thought better of it. It would be much more fun to surprise him.

She opened the door and walked straight in. She half-expected to see Dana straddling him on the desk, but fortunately the office was empty except for her ex-husband himself. He looked up from his screen, new half-moon glasses halfway down that long aquiline nose.

'Beth.' He stood rapidly, banging his chair into the floor-to-ceiling window behind him.

'Tyler. Hi.' She held out her hand as she strode towards him. 'Good to see you.' She kept her voice light and airy, for all the world as if she had just popped in from a trip to the shops, not trekked halfway across the world without a word of warning.

'It's good to see you.' His hand was cool around hers, so different to Simon's warm clasp.

'Is it? That's nice.'

She sat down on the chair in front of his desk and surveyed him properly, this man who had left her and hurt her, who had failed to say one good word for her and then only got in touch when he wanted to break their divorce agreement and needed her blessing. She wondered how she had ever loved him – she wondered how she had been fooled into thinking so little of herself.

His white-blond hair was still shaved close to his head, and she would recognise the musk of his aftershave anywhere. His navy suit was freshly pressed and she could guarantee that his shoes under the desk had been polished to within an inch of their lives.

She smiled sweetly. 'How's Dana?'

'Oh.' He picked up some papers. 'We . . .' He put them down again. 'We're not together any more.'

'No?' She felt a beat of vindication. 'What a shame.'

'Yes. Well.' He tapped an irregular beat on the desk. Then he stood up and started to pace, jangling the change in his pockets. It was just as annoying as it had always been. As he moved she realised she had popped up to see him in here so many times, but now – for the first time – she felt like his equal.

He came to a halt, turning, and giving her what she knew to be his most charming smile.

'Thanks for coming, Beth. It's so good of you.'

'It is, isn't it?'

His Adam's apple bobbed as he absorbed this, his eyebrows raised.

'I take it this is about the apartment?'

'Well.' She crossed her legs. 'No.'

'Oh.' Another swallow. 'Then why . . .?'

'I'm here because I want to be, Tyler. Because I don't have to be at your beck and call any more. We both signed a divorce agreement – you're the one trying to change it, not me. So really it should be you coming to see me, shouldn't it?' She folded her arms decisively.

A vein stood out in his neck. He was annoyed now. 'So why are you here?'

She kept her voice light. 'To give you this. Before I give it to the CEO in about ten minutes' time.' She pulled a neat plastic binder from her bag and held it out.

Nerves flickered across his face. 'What is it?'

'Read it and you'll see.'

He bent his head and started flicking through.

Beth knew every page by heart. That night, with Jake sleeping beside her, she had pulled the file out from underneath her bed and started to put everything together to tell her story. The file contained it all: her degree certificate (hons); every commendation she had ever received; every glowing piece of patient feedback; every fulsome appraisal. Thank you notes from colleagues, gifts from relatives, a piece in the local paper about how she had gone the extra mile for a patient with no family at Christmas time.

Tyler's forehead knitted as he read. She knew he had

no idea why he was reading it, but he was too proud to ask why.

The second part would show him. In that section she had inserted the emails she had sent him requesting better staffing on the ward; the risk assessments she and her colleagues had carried out, flagging that lack of staff was likely to cause a clinical incident; the conversations she had undertaken with him and other board members highlighting the dangers if things continued as they were. And finally copies of her shift patterns that final month. Night after night after night on duty. Too many hours, too little sleep, too much risk, no one in management giving a damn.

The file told a story of a nurse who had done her best, of a nurse who cared so much about her patients that she pushed herself too hard to care for them. A nurse who had been left alone to face a problem that she hadn't created.

Nothing could ever erase her mistake and nothing would ever release her from her guilt. But Beth could see now that the hospital had let her down even before it fired her, even before it sent her packing with only two weeks' pay. Beth had given the wrong dose to Caroline Garcia, but her state of mind had been created by an organisation that hadn't listened to the ward sister on critical care who kept on asking for help.

Beth watched Tyler as he read to the end.

He looked up. 'What have you done this for? Do you want money?'

Beth let the silence grow.

Once she had loved this man. Thank God she had learnt to see through him.

'No, Tyler.' Beth stood up. 'I don't want money.'

'Your job back, then?'

'No.' She lifted her bag to her shoulder. 'I've got a great job, thank you very much. And I wouldn't come back here if you paid me five times what you paid me before. I'm here because I want to make sure that no other clinician is ever treated the way I was by Mercy View, that no other patient is put in danger. I gave this hospital so many years of my life – so much of me – and you all turned your backs on me the moment I needed you. All I want is to make sure it never happens again. So I'm taking a copy of this to the new CEO and to every ward sister in this place. Because they need to know what happened to me – what really happened, so that no other patients have to suffer, and no other nurses are scapegoated like I was.'

She walked towards the door, heart racing, mind flying. She had done it. She had faced him and made her case.

It felt fantastic.

She turned back to him. The folder hung from his hand, and he was pinching his forehead between his fingers in a gesture she remembered only too well.

'Oh. And Tyler?'

'Yes?'

'About the apartment?'

'Yes?'

'Never message me or my friends again. My solicitor is ready for you. We're done here.'

And with that, smiling, she walked away.

36

Simon

'It feels so much better, lad.' William patted his shoulder in satisfaction.

'Good.' Simon stood back, arms folded. 'Lift your arm up? Higher?'

His father did so, lips set in a line, clearly anticipating pain.

'That feels alright.' A smile slowly spread across his face. 'That feels bloody great.'

'Good.' Simon grinned.

'You're good at this, aren't you?'

'I'm glad you think so.' Simon moved across to the kitchen, accidentally pulling out the mug that Beth always used to use, white with 'I love New York' written on it in red. He stared at it for a moment, remembering her eyes dancing above the rim. He missed her like hell. Jean had shown some other tenants around today and Simon had wanted to kill them. The cottage was hers, and always would be.

He put the mug at the back of the cupboard, behind the black Cluedo one with a revolver on it that he never used. Out of sight, out of mind.

If only.

He turned back. 'If you keep on doing the exercises, Dad, you should be pain-free in a week or two.'

'Well, thanks, son.' His dad pulled his blue jumper back over his head. It was cold in the cottage tonight, despite the heating.

His dad's head appeared again above his V-neck. 'When are you going back, then?'

'Back where?'

'To the hospital. To work.' His dad's nostrils flared as he stared straight into Simon's eyes.

'I . . .' Simon puffed his cheeks out. 'How did you know?'

He had called Lina the day before, asking for shifts from January, when Tamsin would be up in Manchester. She was going to take a few months off to settle in and get to know the place, and had offered to come and see Jake whenever Simon needed to work. It gave him the flexibility he needed and, in the pain of losing Beth, at least he had something to look forward to at last.

His dad's eyes glinted. 'Word gets around.'

'I'm sorry, Dad. I was going to tell you myself.'

'No bother.' His dad smiled. 'I've taken on an apprentice. Jean's grandson.'

'Oh yes?'

'Gary. He's strong, and he'll learn. And the sheep like him, and that's a good start.'

'Oh.' Simon realised he had accidentally added about half a bottle of milk to his tea. He put the bottle down, and tried to find a clean spoon for the sugar. 'But . . . Why, Dad? I know you were dead set on me taking over.'

'Aye. Well, believe it or not I can be a daft old beggar and I'm not right all the time.' William smiled. 'And in this case I know I was wrong. My shoulder feels brand new, and it's all thanks to you. You should help more people like me, not be fixing fences or chasing sheep.'

Simon felt tears threaten. It seemed to be an everyday thing at the moment. 'I don't know what to say.'

'Then don't say anything.' His dad's eyes gleamed. 'And stop adding sugar to my tea.'

'Oh. Sorry.' Simon flushed. 'I wasn't concentrating.'

'Well, that's pretty bloody obvious.' William took a sip and nearly choked. 'My poor teeth. There's enough sugar in there to make jam.'

'Sorry.' Simon rubbed his eyes, grainy from lack of sleep; from nights spent thinking of Beth and dreaming about scalpels meeting his son's skin.

His dad's eyes narrowed. 'So, are you missing her then?'

'Who?'

'That nurse. Beth.'

Simon looked out of the window, wondering if his real dad was about to walk in. His real dad didn't talk about emotions.

'Jake said she'd gone.' His dad coughed.

'Yes.'

His dad sat down on the sofa and stared at the carpet for a moment or two, as if seeking inspiration. His knee clicked as he crossed one leg over the other and Simon saw that he was wearing the bright red Santa socks that Jake had given him last Christmas.

Simon walked over and sat next to him.

'It's a right mess, Dad.' He was too tired not to be honest. 'I really miss her.'

'She had a lovely smile.'

'She was lovely through and through. Too good for me.'

'What a load of rubbish.' He was surprised by the intensity in his dad's voice.

Silence yawned between them, broken only by his dad's slurps of tea.

Simon opened his mouth. 'I'm sorry that Jake is asleep, Dad. So you can't see him, I mean.'

William shook his head. 'Not to worry.' His brown eyes held Simon's, reminding him of a childhood in which his dad had held out open arms, had taken him fishing or den-building or boating out on the gentle surface of the lake.

He had forgotten it all, but over the past weeks of treating his dad, of really talking to him about things that weren't just the farm or the rota, the memories had returned.

His dad coughed awkwardly. 'I wanted to say something, Simon.'

'What?'

'I've been a stupid old bugger and I'm sorry.'

Simon put his own mug down.

'What for?'

'For pushing you about Jake – trying to get him to do more. You were just looking after him, I know that now. I found it easier to pretend it wasn't happening. To think that he was probably alright, that those doctors were just making a fuss.'

Simon shook his head. 'That didn't work so well with Mum, did it?'

'No.' His dad stared at his lap. 'No. God rest her.' Then he raised his head. 'Do you know I still talk to her? When I'm having my dinner sometimes. And she answers me – or I think she does, anyway.' Lines bit deep around his mouth. 'And last night she told me I'd been a right old sod, and I needed to apologise.' He sipped his tea. 'So here I am. I'm sorry about the lad. I'm sorry for everything he's got to face. But I know you're there with him. And I know there's no one better for the job.'

Simon's emotions swirled. He didn't feel up to any of it. Not without Beth.

'Thanks, Dad.'

His dad coughed. 'You know, I was always scared of hospitals. I don't know how you do what you do. I just can't stand the smell.'

'Is that why you never came to see Jake?'

'Yes. And I'm sorry for it.'

'Well, you'll get your chance soon.'

His dad swallowed. 'I'll be there. And there's another thing.'

'What?'

'I want you to go to Barney's wedding.'

Simon sighed. 'No. I have to be with Jake. We're in quarantine, remember?'

His dad frowned, eyes flashing. 'You should be there. You boys love each other like brothers. You need to be there for him on his big day.'

'I know, but Jake . . .'

'Leave him with me. Go for an hour. Stand outside the marquee. Wear a mask – I don't care. But you have to go.'

'Why?'

'Because he's only getting married once and you'll always regret it if you don't go. And so will he.' William sipped the last of his tea. 'I'll keep that boy entertained, I promise you. And I've been very careful all week to make sure I'm healthy as can be.'

Everything in Simon resisted. This wasn't what he did. Jake first – that was his rule. 'No, Dad. Jake needs me. And I can't give him any germs, or . . .'

'So keep your distance. Get a microphone. Whatever it takes, lad. But you must go.' His dad put a hand on his arm. 'It's about living, isn't it? That's what Jake showed us all on that football pitch, running and running until he fell. He was living. It's time for you to live too. You can't protect him every second of every day. You can let us help. Even me, your grumpy old git of a dad. Yes, Jake's having an operation. Yes, it's hard. But your friend has a big day on Saturday, and there's only one person he wants to be there as his best man. So go.'

Simon gaped. 'Dad. I don't think I've ever heard you say so many words in a row.'

'Well, don't count on it happening again.' His dad put his mug down. 'Now, are you going to go to that wedding or do I have to kidnap you and drive you there myself?'

For a moment, Simon allowed himself to believe he might.

'Are you sure?'

'Of course I'm sure.'

'Then . . .'

'YES.' Jake was standing by the door. 'Take lots of pictures, Dad. I want to see everything.'

Simon went over and took his boy in his arms. 'You're happy about this?'

'Yes.' Jake grinned. 'You were getting boring anyway.' Mischief lit up his face. 'It's time for a change.' He pulled something from behind his back. 'Here you go, Dad. Your phone. You must have left it in the loo again.'

'Thanks.' Simon put it in his pocket. 'You're absolutely sure it's OK?'

'Yes.' Jake folded his arms. 'And it's my choice. My operation. So you have to do what I say.'

Simon felt excitement firing inside him. 'Well, alright, then. I'll go. I can't fight you and Dad. I'm not strong enough.'

'Yes!' Jake raised his hands in the air. 'High five, Grandad!'

William raised his hand and their palms slapped together.

And Simon stared at this man and this boy. His father and his son. And he felt the understanding between them growing, giving Simon the gleam of a brighter future.

37

Beth

Beth stared at the long wooden bar, admiring the ornate tea cups hanging at angles in front of the wide array of polished glasses and optics. The green leather of the bar stools and discreet lighting from golden lamps could not have been further from The Crown, with its red carpets and Betty cracking filthy jokes behind the bar. Here, every booth had a neat reserved sign, quietly awaiting their glamorous clientele. Even dressed up in her smart dress and heels, Beth wasn't sure she was one of them.

But she didn't care. She had a mojito. And she had done what she came to New York to do. She didn't know if Mercy View would change anything as a result of what she had told the CEO, just as she didn't know whether Tyler would ever feel guilty for not standing up for her. All she knew was that she had tried. She had put her case and she knew that now she could lay down some of the burden of the past year and start to move on. She had made a terrible mistake and the guilt would never leave her, but Beth was a nurse and it was time to get back on the ward and to doing the job she loved.

She watched the waiter in his black waistcoat and white

shirt, proudly placing glasses onto a small black tray. She thought of the fizz and pop of the streets outside, of her afternoon in Brooklyn, getting coffee from her old cart and a meatball sub from the bodega on the corner. Being here made her feel that anything was possible, that she could start again.

But New York wasn't home any more.

Home was where Simon was.

She leant her chin on her hand and took a sip through her metal straw. The cocktail was cool and tangy on her tongue. She forced her thoughts away from her old neighbours and on towards the future.

She had got the job in Manchester. They had called her earlier that afternoon, talking salaries and references and start dates. She was heading back to the NHS, away from the glossy gleam of Mercy View towards concrete NHS sprawl. Tasteful lights versus brutal neon. From pink scrubs to navy blue. But the exterior wasn't what mattered – it was the heart of things that counted. And on that ward in Manchester, with patients needing care and thought and love, Beth knew that she would be happy. She would look after her team; she would always take that extra moment before making a decision; she would be the best nurse that she could be.

Beth sat back, looking at a couple who had just come in through the heavy swing doors, the man's hand on the woman's back, her gaze locked on his. Had she and Tyler ever looked like that? She couldn't remember. All she knew was that next to Simon, Tyler disappeared. Tyler was constantly starring in his own TV show – to him, the world was his for the taking. Simon lived a different life – one where he was never in control and yet smiled and fought his way through, for the sake of the little boy at his side.

Beth's eyes glazed with tears. She missed them so much.

She felt her phone buzz, and wearily pulled it out, expecting a change to her flight back or a message from one of her referees.

She stared at the words, hope dawning, before picking up her glass and downing the entire mojito in one. The words she saw meant everything. The message she read was clear.

She raised her hand to the waiter, indicating that she wanted the check.

Then she sat back, smiling at the screen, as a new life opened up before her.

38

Simon

Simon stood at the bottom of the hotel driveway. Barney and Lina were getting married, and he was actually going to be here to see it. His shoes were shined, his suit was immaculate, and he had even dug out some aftershave and put it on.

'Oh God.' A tractor rumbled past and Simon had to leap over the cattle grid by the hotel gate to avoid his entire body becoming covered in muck. Ahead of him the driveway curved round towards the broad grey sweep of the hotel. The wrought ironwork of its facade shone and the branches of the trees to either side of the entrance were lit with hundreds of fairy lights which flickered in blues and reds and golds.

At the back, on the lawns that led down to the water, was his best friend, marrying the love of his life. Barney's voice when Simon had called to tell him he was coming to the wedding after all – if Simon could have bottled that joy, he would have done, for it would have seen him through Jake's operation and beyond.

Simon had come this far – he and his shiny shoes were going to finish this. Two hours, that's what he had agreed with Barney – a balance between his son's safety and his friend's big day. No mingling at the beginning as the guests were ushered inside, just straight to the ceremony. Simon's head was up and he knew that his dad had been right – this was where he needed to be today. For Barney, and for himself.

He walked quickly along the gravelled driveway, past cars parked in every available space and past the wedding car itself, grey and long and luxurious, the driver still straightening the cushions inside.

Simon's breaths were quickening as he arrived in the lobby. Winter roses in dark pinks and white were clustered in huge bouquets on every available surface, and pink ribbons were draped up the double staircase that led up to the rooms upstairs. He and Barney had been waiters here in their teens – sharing fags and beers when their shifts ended before staggering home together to sleep it off.

He pushed his hair back from his forehead as his eyes landed on a huge board to his right with the words 'Chambers Wedding' printed in flowing font at the top, next to an arrow. He followed it through an ornate hall where Barney had once tried unsuccessfully to snog the then-manager, and out into the gardens.

Ahead of him, at the centre of the smooth green lawn, he saw the marquee. Silver stars wound their way up the poles of the tent, and rows of padded white chairs were draped in silver ribbons. He saw guests in hats and fascinators, and eyes being wiped even before Lina made her entrance. Barney was at the front, chatting to his dad in the front row. He saw Simon approaching and his smile alone made the day complete.

The music was starting. Simon ran around to the side of the marquee, away from the other guests but with a perfect view of Lina as she walked down the aisle to Tracy Chapman's 'The Promise'. She was tall, she was beautiful, she was so sure of every step she took. Her long white dress had tiny silver stars scattered over the sleeves and her hair was long and shining around her shoulders.

Barney held out his hand and she took it. Simon's breath caught as he saw his friends, Barney and Lina, holding hands as if they had been born to do only that. As if this was who they had always been destined to be.

The celebrant tucked her blonde hair behind her ear and began to speak. Simon turned to the rows of family and friends, his thoughts inevitably turning to Beth. He wished she was here. He wished he had her hand to hold. All Jake's efforts, all his searching, and the woman Simon needed had been right there in the cottage next door.

'If anyone here knows of any lawful reason why this couple should not be married, please can they say so now.'

Barney turned and looked mock-threateningly at the silent rows of family and friends. Then he turned back to his bride – his beautiful, smiling bride, and they made their vows. And the sun burst through the cloud, and the Test Match Special theme tune played over the speakers and his best friend was married and Simon hadn't missed a thing.

Barney leant towards Simon, before he and Lina proceeded out of the marquee to whooping and cheers.

'Thanks for being here, mate. I know I'm not allowed to hug you, but it meant the world.'

'It meant the world to me too.' Simon found tears in his eyes. 'Now get out there and enjoy yourself, you sappy git.'

It was strange, being at the wedding but keeping himself apart. Simon stayed on the fringes, relishing the whirl from a distance, enjoying being here for his own sake alone. He took pictures for Jake – of Lina and Barney posing for photos, her laughing up at him like a sunflower finding the light; of the glasses and the food; of the wedding cake that he knew Jake was eagerly waiting to try.

Jake. The operation. Simon's stomach swooped. It was so close – he knew he wouldn't sleep now until it was over. But being here helped – there was such life at the wedding. Such love. He saw champagne being pressed into eager hands, stories being told, old faces recognising each other, and at the heart of it all were Lina and Barney. Two of his closest friends – together for ever.

One of the staff had clearly been told to keep Simon supplied with many of the copious canapes that were appearing from the kitchen. Potato blinis with chives and cream cheese, smoked salmon and dill on tiny pancakes. In two days he would be living off hospital sandwiches, so Simon took full advantage and tucked in.

Lina came towards him, stopping a metre away. She sipped her drink. 'Thanks for being here.'

'My pleasure. I wouldn't be anywhere else.'

Lina's face was serious. 'Are you OK? About Monday?'

He was touched by her thoughtfulness, especially on this, her biggest of days.

'Yeah. I'm OK. We're ready.' He wanted to move on – this wasn't the time to think about this. 'That is if he survives today – my dad wants to teach him chess. I fear for them both.'

She laughed, the line of her throat long and lovely.

'All set for tomorrow, Lina?'

Her eyes glinted. 'Actually . . .'

'Your honeymoon?'

'Well. I . . .' Lina's words were cut off as her father banged the gong. Several minutes later, with his ears still ringing, Simon led the applause as Barney and his new wife were clapped into their wedding reception. Simon looked around from his position just outside the marquee. Every detail was perfect: white napkins shaped into swans, white plates with a silver rim, shining silver cutlery and each table with a Barney and Lina quiz card to fill out as a tribute to Barney's weekly trips to The Crown.

Today was everything Simon could have wanted for his friends and more. Here was love in the laughing faces and loud voices. Here was love in raised wine glasses and reminiscences. Barney and Lina were lit up with it; as bright and translucent as the lights on the trees dotted around the garden.

Barney tapped his spoon against his glass.

Game time.

'As you know we're doing speeches first today, due to the awkward bugger over there who's not even coming inside.' Barney sighed melodramatically, pointing at

Simon, but his smile gave him away. 'Anyway, here he is, complete with his own microphone – a man who knows me far too well . . .' Barney smiled across at Simon. 'A man who nearly couldn't make it today but who came through for me at the eleventh hour, as he always does.'

Loud cheers greeted these words.

'So here he is . . .' Barney held out his hand. 'The one, the only, SIMON WITHERS.'

The room erupted as Simon stepped just inside the tent so he was visible but not too close, pulling out his notes, but suddenly knowing that he wouldn't use them.

He took a breath. These words mattered.

He looked at his friend. He thought of the past year and of Beth and Tamsin and his little boy. Words began to arrive in his head. One, then two, then sentences. Maybe it wouldn't be the funniest speech, maybe it wouldn't have them rolling in the aisles but it would come straight from his heart.

'Ladies and gentlemen.' His voice sounded dry and breathy. He stared at the faces in front of him, focusing on slowing down. 'I'm not one for making speeches, but when I think of Barney I have far too much to say.' He grinned, as he heard a smattering of laughter. 'Some good . . .' This was met with a general groan. '. . . And some very, very bad indeed.'

A bigger wave of laughter boosted him. 'I know I'm meant to tell you about how he and I once got lost in Amsterdam and ended up sleeping on a bench with some tramps and a bottle of whisky. Or how smelly his trainers are. Or how he would live on Findus Crispy Pancakes for the rest of his life if he could.' Simon paused. 'But obviously I'm not going to mention any of that.'

He felt more certain of himself now. 'Because today I just want to say that this man, this newly married man, is one of the best people I know. He is one of the bravest people I know – he must be as he took on Lina . . .' Simon waited, as the screams and shouts died away. 'He doesn't like hospitals but he came to the clinic with me and my son because he knew I needed him. He wanted me here today but he accepted that I couldn't be, again because he understands me and loves me for exactly who I am. Barney listens and he cares and he raises those he loves up high, and for that reason, Lina, you are one of the luckiest women I know.' The room was quiet now, everyone listening intently for Simon's next words. 'Barney and Lina – I salute you. I love you. I wish you a long and happy marriage. I am so very, very happy for you both.' The room erupted in cheers.

Simon held up his finger. 'Now, anyone want to hear the story about Barney, the bull and the chainsaw?'

'YES.'

Simon shook his head. 'Uh-uh. No way. I'm taking that one to my grave.' He raised his glass. 'Now will you all please be upstanding – to Barney and Lina!'

'To Barney and Lina!'

The bride and groom led the applause and Simon felt a kick of pride. He had done it. He had stood up there and opened his heart. He might have lost Beth, but he had not lost his best friends. He led the toast, draining his glass dry, thinking that this was living: being with people you loved, celebrating with them, holding them through the lows and cheering them through the highs. Moment by moment. That was the only way to live.

Ten minutes later he was back in the car, heading towards his boy. His dad loomed at the front door.

'Is Jake OK?'

'Aye, lad.' His dad smiled. 'I'm not sure about the chess set though. Jake wasn't a fan.'

Simon untucked his shirt, comfortable at last. 'I did warn you.'

'He reminded me of you. He has quite a temper.'

Simon smiled. Adrenaline was rushing out of him now, and fear was replacing it. One more day. Then, the hospital.

'Right.' His dad smiled. 'You're going to check on him, I suppose? To see if I've finished him off?'

'I am.'

Simon went upstairs and stood looking at his sleeping child, curled up like a comma in his bed, toys lined up, face at peace. Simon had lived his life today, and Jake was OK. He wasn't broken just because Simon had left him for a few hours. He could go back and be a physio – his boy would still be there when he got home, there with his mum who loved him or his grandad who would keep trying to teach him chess until the end of time.

It wasn't Beth, but it was wonderful.

Simon kissed Jake's forehead, tucking him in more tightly, dimly registering a noise downstairs.

'Simon?' His dad was at the bedroom door.

'Yes, Dad?'

'There's someone here to see you.'

'Is there?'

'Yes. Come down, son.'

'Who is it?' Simon shut the door behind him and started to walk down the stairs.

'Hello?'

It was a voice that he loved. A voice he had missed. A voice that brought calm and courage and hope.

'Hello, Simon.'

It was Beth. And he knew in that moment what joy felt like, what it was to be a firework spinning across the night sky. Beth was back where she belonged – Beth was back by his side.

39

Beth

Simon's eyes. The way they didn't leave her as he walked towards her, the way they held hers as he came closer. She was finally home.

'Beth. You came back.' She had spent the past four thousand miles thinking of that face, that hair, those eyes. He reached for her, but she stepped back.

'I know you're in quarantine till the Fontan, and I'm fresh off a flight. But I couldn't wait. I got your message. And I thought it was best to give my answer in person.'

Confusion clouded his face. 'I'm sorry?'

'Your message.'

'What message?'

All her certainty started to drain away. 'The message you sent. Saying you were sorry.' She delved into her bag, starting to dig for her phone, knowing she was turning red. 'Saying you were in love . . .' She looked up at his blank face, her heart racing. '. . . with me? Is that true?'

Simon's pause seemed to last a lifetime.

'It is, Beth.' His voice was thick. 'Of course it is.'

Relief overwhelmed her. All she wanted to do was to touch him, but they had forever for that.

Simon put his head on one side. 'But I think perhaps Jake has been busy again.'

'Really?' She held out her phone, showing Simon the message that had brought her back.

Beth. I love you. I never told you that and I don't know why. Please come back. Please make my heart whole again. S x

Simon stared at the screen, clearly struggling to speak.

Finally, he smiled. 'Well, mission accomplished, Jake. He never gave up, did he?'

'No.' She put the phone away. 'Thank God he didn't.'

'And when you read it – did you . . .' Simon chewed his lip. 'Did you think you could forgive me? For getting so angry? For not letting you explain?'

She gazed up at him, taking her time. 'I forgave you that same day, Simon. But I didn't know if you loved me. And then, when Jake asked me to leave, I . . .' She hesitated. 'I had no choice. I'd do anything for him.'

'I know.' He stood there, smiling, everything she wanted, everything she needed. 'I love you, Beth Carlyle.'

'And I love you, Simon Withers.'

'I am desperate to kiss you.'

'Me too.' She giggled. 'This is actually hell. I should have waited till Monday.'

'No, you shouldn't.' Simon's voice caught. 'And I'm sorry.' She drank him in, this kind man, this strong man. 'I'm sorry for getting so angry with you.'

'It's OK. Everybody makes mistakes, I of all people understand that.' Beth gazed at him, soaking in his strength and heart and honesty. 'And I need to say thank you.'

'What on earth for?'

'For letting me into your lives. For forgiving me for my terrible driving that day.'

'I didn't say I had.'

She checked his face and saw a gleam of amusement. 'Jake is amazing, Simon. So determined. So kind.'

Simon nodded. 'He is.'

'And he's lucky too. To have you. He's funny because you are. He's kind because that's what he sees in you. He is caring because of you. And he only knows how to be brave because *you* showed him how.'

'I think we showed each other.'

Somehow, they had inched closer to each other. Too close. She could feel the heat of him, smell the aftershave he so rarely wore. She took a step back. 'You're looking a bit smart.'

Simon grinned. 'Barney's wedding.'

'You went?' She blinked. 'That's amazing. How was it?'

'Incredible. I thought – well, Jake thought – that it would be OK.'

'And was it?'

'Very much so.'

She heard a creak on the stairs.

'Beth?' She could see a tufty figure in pyjamas on the bottom step. 'Is that you, Beth?'

'It is, Jake.' She crouched down on her knees. 'I can't come in – quarantine – but I'm here. I'm home. Thank you. For sending the message.'

'I knew I was right.' Jake yawned. 'See, Dad? I was right. You did need someone. You needed Beth.'

Simon smiled. 'Is that so?'

'Yeah.' Jake yawned again. 'I just had the wrong someone. It was Beth. It's always been Beth.' He blew her a kiss. 'Thanks so much for coming back.'

'Thanks for asking me.' Her eyes met Simon's, thinking of the operation on Monday. 'I wouldn't be anywhere else.'

'I'd better take Jake back up to bed.' Simon hesitated, watching her. 'Will you have me, Beth? Is Jake right?'

'Of course I'm right, Dad.' Jake shook his head despairingly.

Beth looked at Simon's face for a long moment.

And then, distanced as she was, she curled her fingers into a heart, and Simon and Jake did the same. And in that moment was forgiveness and love and the promise of all the happiness she had never believed she would deserve to feel again.

40

Simon

'Where's Superchick, Dad?'

'Right there on the pillow.' Simon tied his son's bright green hospital gown around his neck. The yellow duck smiled as happily as if he was about to attend a party rather than a five-hour heart operation. Jake grabbed him, burying his face in the white fuzz of the toy's hair.

'Don't forget the bottom one, Dad.'

'I won't.' Simon carefully tied a bow next to Jake's waist. 'There. Your pants are under cover now.'

'Thanks. And Tigger? Where's Tigger?'

Tamsin picked up the stripy tiger. 'Here you go, baby.'

'Thanks.' Jake cradled the toys close. 'I need them both in theatre. They're both having operations, just like me.'

The lump in Simon's throat was so huge that he struggled to speak. 'Well, you three are a team, aren't you? You have been, right from the start.'

Tamsin reached out and lightly touched Tigger's head. 'We got this guy from the hospital shop, didn't we? As soon as you were born. The girl behind the till told us he'd just arrived that morning too.' Her eyes were glazed with tears, but she kept her chin high and her smile strong. Behind her, Kris reached out and clasped her shoulder.

The more he saw of him, the more Simon liked him. Kris was calm. Kind. He steadied her.

Simon looked back at his son. This final wait was so hard: seeing the hospital name bands around Jake's slender wrists, the looming machines waiting for his return from theatre, the drip standing by for the pain-killers and fluids Jake would need. In a few hours Jake would be silent, sedated, only speaking to express pain. This boy with all the talk and bubble in the world. His boy. His Jake.

A hand curled around his. A soft kiss landed on his cheek.

He turned, remembering that today was different. Today was better because of who was beside him.

'Coffees.' Beth was there, calm and considerate. She handed a paper cup to Tamsin, then another to him.

'Thank you.' Simon drew her close, wondering yet again how he had got so lucky. This woman had chosen him. And with Beth beside him, he knew he could get through this. With her the bad memories receded, leaving hope for the future in their wake. Jake needed this oper-ation. And they needed him. So, Simon would just have to pray that on this day, in this hospital, the Fontan procedure would bring his boy more football, more Lego, many more years of being Jake Withers.

Jake pulled the hospital TV screen towards him.

'Dad. It's not working.'

Simon turned his attention to the screen. It was some-thing to do. Something to concentrate on. By focusing on the screen, he could ignore the swirl of doctors and nurses whispering just outside the stripy curtains of Jake's cubicle; he could suppress the adrenaline that was pulsing through him at the thought of what lay ahead.

'Hello!'

Simon looked up, surprised.

'Barney!' His mouth fell open. 'What are you doing here?' Damn it. This might break him. 'You're meant to be in Mauritius!'

His friend reached down and gave Jake a hug that nearly smothered him.

'This little guy was more important.'

'But it was your honeymoon!'

Barney gently lowered Jake back to the bed. 'Lina convinced them to push our flights back forty-eight hours. She's a very persuasive lady, my wife.'

And then Lina was there too, face alive with love, bearing bags of snacks and sandwiches that she put on the floor before shrugging off her long gold Puffa. She came over and hugged Simon and it took all he had to hold back his sobs.

He wasn't alone any more. And his boy wasn't alone. Their friends were with them, lifting them up, raising them high.

Jake was sitting quietly on the bed, hugging his knees, eyes wide as he gazed at the grown-ups around him. He looked so small – the wrong person to be at the centre of everything that was going to happen today. Maybe he was thinking of Emily, wondering how she had been feeling while she was waiting for her Fontan, knowing that soon afterwards she was dead.

The thought sent a shiver down Simon's spine. He was only metres from his son, but it wasn't close enough.

He pushed the TV away. 'Lina, are you any good with these things?'

Lina nodded. 'I am a telly ninja. I'm on it, my friend.' She gave a small salute. 'By the way, I've got your first shifts lined up. Three days a week, just like you asked, supervised, at first, until you get your registration back. Once Jake's recovered, of course. We can't wait to have you back.'

'Thanks.' He nodded. Later. He could think about all that later. For now he needed his son right next to him. He sat down on the bed, curling his arms around him and hugging him close.

'You're really hot, Dad.' Jake's voice was muffled.

Tamsin's arms joined Simon's, and the two of them buried their heads in his hair.

'Ugh. I'm going to die of hot!' Jake shook them off just as Miss Maya appeared at the end of the bed. Her dark hair was pulled back, and she was already in a set of navy scrubs. Her hands were still at her side – the hands that had already worked such miracles for his boy. Maybe today would be the next.

She looked only at Jake, her dark eyes gleaming. 'Ready?'

'Yeah.' Jake's voice was steady.

Simon wasn't ready. He wanted more time, more hugs, more moments with this boy who had changed everything.

'Wheelchair or walk?'

'Walk, please.' Jake took Superchick and Tigger and held them close.

'OK.' Miss Maya turned. 'I'll go and get ready. I'll see you down there.'

There was a pause while Jake lowered himself to the floor. He looked up at them all, eyes glinting. 'What are you all looking so serious for? You're freaking me out.'

'Sorry, lad.' Barney ruffled his hair. 'See you later, kiddo. I'll be the one who's eaten all your grapes.' Lina hugged Jake and then turned away before he could see her tears.

Beth got down so her eyes were level with Jake's. She put her hand to his cheek, and then reached into her pocket. 'Here's something I made for my dad once. I brought it back with me from New York.' And she handed over a small Lego heart. 'Take it in with you. It's extra lucky.'

'Superchick can hold it for me.' Jake tucked it into the duck's stripy blue pyjamas. Then he reached up on tiptoes to hug her.

'Come on, then.' Simon reached out his hand, and Tamsin held out hers and the three of them were off on the walk that haunted Simon's nightmares. Past the nurses' station, with doctors speaking urgently into phones and nurses conferring quietly while the cleaner mopped around their feet; past the dialysis ward with its huge grey machines attached to tiny figures lying still; past the playroom where a little girl was systematically pulling all the tiny Sylvanians off their shelves. They reached the lifts, where a smiling staff nurse pressed the button for the basement.

They stepped inside and the doors rumbled shut.

The staff nurse glanced down at her watch. 'Nice day out there.'

'Yes.' Simon stared at his shoes until the lift juddered to a halt. He held onto Jake's hand like a vice as they walked out into the corridor, turning left, his legs feeling heavier as they reached the door of the anaesthetic room.

It was just the same. He could never forget this place. Cream walls, heat, the clatter of instruments being prepared. People – so many people – in masks and scrubs, all so big and all there to try to make his son's life better and longer.

He saw the small table at the centre of the room, the table that marked the boundary between this chapter of their story and the next. Beyond it might lie an ending, or the beginning of a bigger life – an even more beautiful life.

A nurse held out her hand.

'Are you ready, Jake?'

Jake turned to him and Simon hugged him close. The tears were starting now, as they always did, but he had to hold on. He forced himself to let go so Tamsin could have her turn. Then the nurse led his son to the table, and Jake climbed up, gazing trustingly at the team gathering around him. He looked at Simon and curved his fingers and thumbs into a heart. Simon did the same. Their eyes met for one beat. Two. And then Jake turned to stare at the ceiling.

In the corner of the room, Tamsin was dissolving. Simon stood, hearing cheery chat from the anaesthetist about which TV programmes Jake liked, as skilful hands ripped instruments out of plastic packaging, and a needle was attached to the cannula in Jake's hand. Jake counted down until his voice faded and he was still, a yellow duck and a Tigger in his arms.

There was nothing to do but leave.

He turned in the doorway, glancing back.

Come on, Jake. Come on.

Simon walked out into the corridor, bending over as his soul snapped and the pain ripped through him. Soon his son would be swathed in surgical drapes, his chest open, his heart held in Miss Maya's hands. Simon wanted to be there alongside him, but all he could do was walk away, wait, worry about what might happen next.

All he could do was hope.

His son was determined. His son was loved.

That would have to be enough.

Simon took Tamsin's hand and walked, wordless, back up to the ward.

And there, waiting by his son's bed, was the woman he loved.

'Simon?' Beth held out her arms, and he ran to her, and she folded herself around him, supporting him, loving him. And there – finally – Simon let himself cry.

41

Jake

'**C**an you count down from ten please, Jake?'
    'Ten.'
Emily?
'Nine.'
Are you there? I did it. Dad's happy. So I'm happy too.
'Eight.'
Emily? Can you hold my hand?
'Seven.'
Please? I won't be scared if I'm with you.
Six.
There you are. I love you.
Fiiiii
                iiiii
                    iiiiii
                        iiiiiiiiiiii
                            iiiiiiiiiiiiiiii . . .

Spring

42

Beth

Beth stood staring down at the grave. It was so new, the stone at its head a stark white compared to its older, moss-covered companions. A shard of sunlight lit the words 'In Loving Memory' as she leant down and gently placed her daffodils alongside the other flowers that people had brought today. The grave was a blaze of colour: there were irises and early roses, cowslips and tulips; flowers to mark a life lost; blossoms to mark a brave fight; blooms to celebrate a light extinguished too early.

A cool breeze rippled across her face and she shivered, digging her hands deeper into the pockets of her coat. She was learning now not to trust a Lake District spring. The warmth burst out of nowhere, teased her into short sleeves, and then disappeared just as quickly, leaving Beth wearing the wrong boots or not enough layers. The longer she lived in Thistlethwaite, the more a part of her the Lakes became: the rhythm of the seasons as familiar to her as the New York subway map had been.

Her working week was in Manchester, but her weekends were spent here in the village. No matter how busy she was, or how much paperwork she had to do, she always made it back in time for at least part of the Thursday night pub quiz at The Crown, while the Sunday church bells for the evening service drew her weekend to a close.

She had found her forever, and she knew how precious that was.

She heard footsteps behind her.

'Are you alright, love?'

Arms folded around her, so familiar now that it was as if they had always been a part of her. Simon leant forward, kissing her neck, his hands resting on the growing curve of her belly. 'Do you need to sit down?'

'No. I'm fine.' She rested her cheek against his.

'You're not too tired?'

'No.' Ever since the blue line had appeared on the pregnancy test, Simon had been on alert. It would be this way until their baby arrived, Beth knew that.

He squeezed her even closer. 'Are you sure?'

'Yes, I'm sure.' She leant her head back, letting him take her weight, as she looked up at the clouds dappling the sky, their edges lit with gold as the sun pushed its way through.

'I'm just thinking about what might have been. If . . .'

'Me too.' Simon sighed. 'Me too.'

There was a jolt from behind them.

'Hey.' Simon laughed down at the boy at his elbow. The boy with red hair and freckles splattered across his face. 'Jake! Be careful!'

'Sorry.' Jake weaved in and out of their legs, his ankles sticking out of his green Grinch onesie. 'But Emily wouldn't like all these sad faces. We're here for her – we should be having fun!'

Simon kissed Beth on the lips before bending down to his boy. 'What do you have in mind?'

'Tag. And you're it!' Jake wheeled around and dodged away, rejoicing in his newfound energy, heading down the path that led out of the graveyard and across the quiet road to the village hall beyond, where Emily's family and friends were waiting for them. They had decided to hold an event every year on Emily's birthday, to raise money for the bereavement charity that had supported them since her death. This year it was a scavenger hunt, starting in the village hall, and Jake was desperate for them to win.

'Last one there's a doozie!' Jake turned, his hand on the gate, putting his thumb to his nose and waggling his fingers at Simon.

Simon leant towards Beth. 'I have no idea what a doozie is.'

'Me neither.'

'But I probably don't want to be one, do I?'

She shook her head. 'You'd better do something about it then, hadn't you?'

'Good idea.' Simon turned and ran after his boy, down the path and across the road, leaving her alone with the hills and the church, its stone buttery yellow in the gleam of the morning.

A year ago Beth had come to the Lakes having lost everything – now she couldn't believe how much she had found. She stared at the stained-glass window, at its reds and blues, at the arms of Mary curved protectively around her saviour son, her smile infinite, her halo bright.

Forgiveness, that was what Beth had found here. Forgiveness and hope. She wondered how she had ever believed that one mistake could halt a life in its tracks. Her heart was strong; it had cracks and bruises, dents and doubts, but it still believed in life and love, and that belief was her guiding light.

Here, in a tiny village nestling in the hills, she had found kindness where she had expected judgement. She had found joy where she had expected only despair. She had found her boys and her version of happiness.

She turned to see Simon whirling Jake around at the entrance to the hall. Jake's legs were flying out, his face alight. She was a part of them now, and they of her. And Jake was still here. For now. For this breath. This day. This moment.

She mustn't waste a second.

Beth tipped her face towards the sun and hurried to meet her future.

Acknowledgements

First of all, huge thanks to you, the reader, for choosing this book and for reading it all the way to the end. If you liked it, please tell all your friends and family about it (and colleagues too, why not?!) and please review it if you can – your words and stars can make all the difference.

A big thank you goes to my Book Crew: Daniel Masterson, Keira Lippiett, Rowan McKinnell, Zac Tyler and Charlotte Torrance, for the huge injection of honesty and fun they have given this story. Corinne McKinnell, Jo Tyler and Frances Torrance – thank you for fielding all my questions. I am very grateful to Kaisha Holloway and Kirsten Blissett for their wisdom, and to Mum, Dad, Liz Clark and Ally Sneesby for being my Lake District guides. To Isabelle Broom, Ali Lippiett and Sarah Masterson – love and thanks for everything and more. I am very lucky to have you.

I am extremely grateful to Carole Reid, Sarah Furniss, Gemma Moore, Lucy Grothier, Liz Wilkinson, Caz Bullen, Bev Ball and Dr Owen Miller for their medical input to this book. Caryl Evans, you are officially a gem. All inaccuracies are entirely my own work.

Thank you to Sam Jones at the charity Little Hearts Matter for putting me in touch with families affected by Hypoplastic Left Heart Syndrome. Huge thanks to everyone I spoke to – your honesty and courage were truly inspiring. Particular thanks go to Jade-Marie Archer, Dawn-Louise Archer, the Barker family, Cheryl Wilding, Micah Wilding, Pam Price, Matt Price, Kay Offord, Rhiannen Offord, Catherine Hinchliffe, Amelia Hinchliffe, Claire Tulloh, Teddy Tulloh, Emma Canetti and Arabella Canetti.

I am endlessly indebted to the many wonderful book bloggers who do so much to celebrate all things literary, and to my cheerleading author friends and Word Racers, without whom I would never ever get to The End. Huge thanks go to Alex Michaelides – you know what for.

I am so lucky to have my amazing agent Hannah Ferguson in my corner – my champion and my cheerleader. You really have gone above and beyond this time. Thank you to the wonder that is Kimberley Atkins for finding so many tactful ways to say 'not quite there yet' and for working so tirelessly to make this book as good as it can be. Thanks to Sadie Robinson for your eagle-eyed copy editing and to Emma Knight, Maddy Marshall and Amy Batley for bringing so much energy, expertise and enthusiasm to everything that you do.

And finally, to my trio: Max, Aidan and Evie. This book wouldn't be here without you. Thank you for the laughter, the encouraging notes and pictures, for the dancing and the well-timed sandwiches. I love you all more than I can ever say.

Reading Group Questions

1. Love appears in many forms throughout the novel – from friendship, to romance, and parental love. Can you think of any others? What do these different presentations of love tell us about the characters and their motivations?

2. Simon is a warm and caring single father, and he has sacrificed a lot to look after Jake. What do you think the book has to say about the sacrifices parents, and fathers in particular, make for their children? How does Simon's relationship with his own father fit into this?

3. Beth moves to the Lake District for a fresh start, and struggles with feelings of guilt after an incident that took place at the hospital in New York where she previously worked. To what extent do you think her feelings of responsibility are fair? How would you act in her position?

4. Jake's mother Tamsin copes with her son's illness in a very different way to Simon. To what extent can

you relate to her feelings, and her choices? Do you think Simon should forgive her? Should Jake?

5. The book is told from two different perspectives, Simon's and Beth's. Why do you think the author chose to write it in this way? How did it help you to understand the two characters and their experiences?

6. *Unbreak Your Heart* is set in the picturesque Lake District. What effect do you think the setting has on the book? Would the story work as well if it was set elsewhere?

7. The book opens with a quotation about hope, which is a major theme in *Unbreak Your Heart*. Can you think of some of the main ways this is shown? Are there any moments where hope seems to be lost?

8. At the end of the book, Beth's life looks very different to how it did at the beginning. Do you think her ending is a fitting one? What are your hopes for each of the characters in *Unbreak Your Heart*?

Bookends

When one book ends, another begins...

Bookends is a vibrant new reading community to help you ensure you're never without a good book.

You'll find exclusive previews of the brilliant new books from your favourite authors as well as exciting debuts and past classics. Read our blog, check out our recommendations for your reading group, enter great competitions and much more!

Visit our website to see which great books we're recommending this month.

Join the Bookends community:
www.welcometobookends.co.uk